SURRENDER

"I can hear each beat of your heart, Sophie," Alpin said against her temple, his voice deep and seductive. "I can hear the blood rushing in your veins. I can smell your desire," he whispered and lightly nipped her earlobe. I can taste it upon your lips." He teased her lips with fleeting kisses.

"And I can feel your desire, Alpin." She nipped at his bottom lip and smiled faintly when he growled low in his throat. "It feeds my own." The way his narrowed eyes glowed, his nostrils flared, and his features tightened into a predatory expression should have frightened her, but Sophie only felt her passion soar. She suspected she might look nearly as feral as he did as she ran her tongue between his lips and said, "So taste it, Alpin. Drink deep . . ."

**Books by
Hannah Howell**

The Murrays

HIGHLAND DESTINY
HIGHLAND HONOR
HIGHLAND PROMISE
HIGHLAND VOW
HIGHLAND KNIGHT
HIGHLAND BRIDE
HIGHLAND ANGEL
HIGHLAND GROOM
HIGHLAND WARRIOR
HIGHLAND
CONQUEROR
HIGHLAND
CHAMPION
HIGHLAND LOVER
HIGHLAND
BARBARIAN
HIGHLAND SAVAGE
HIGHLAND WOLF
HIGHLAND SINNER
HIGHLAND
PROTECTOR
HIGHLAND AVENGER
HIGHLAND MASTER
HIGHLAND GUARD
HIGHLAND CHIEFTAIN
HIGHLAND DEVIL

The Wherlockes

IF HE'S WICKED
IF HE'S SINFUL

IF HE'S WILD
IF HE'S DANGEROUS
IF HE'S TEMPTED
IF HE'S DARING
IF HE'S NOBLE

*Seven Brides for Seven
Scotsmen*

THE SCOTSMAN WHO
SAVED ME
WHEN YOU LOVE A
SCOTSMAN
THE SCOTSMAN WHO
SWEPT ME AWAY

Stand-Alone Novels

ONLY FOR YOU
MY VALIANT KNIGHT
UNCONQUERED
WILD ROSES
A TASTE OF FIRE
A STOCKINGFUL OF
JOY
HIGHLAND HEARTS
RECKLESS
CONQUEROR'S KISS
BEAUTY AND THE
BEAST
HIGHLAND WEDDING
SILVER FLAME
HIGHLAND FIRE
HIGHLAND CAPTIVE
MY LADY CAPTOR
WILD CONQUEST

LYNSAY SANDS

RICHELLE MEAD

HANNAH HOWELL

SARANNA DEWYLDE

ETERNAL LOVER

ZEBRA BOOKS
KENSINGTON PUBLISHING CORP.
www.kensingtonbooks.com

ZEBRA BOOKS are published by

Kensington Publishing Corp.
119 West 40th Street
New York, NY 10018

All Kensington titles, imprints, and distributed lines are available at special quantity discounts for bulk purchases for sales promotion, premiums, fund-raising, educational, or institutional use.

Special book excerpts or customized printings can also be created to fit specific needs. For details, write or phone the office of the Kensington Sales Manager: Attn.: Sales Department. Kensington Publishing Corp., 119 West 40th Street, New York, NY 10018. Phone: 1-800-221-2647.

Zebra and the Z logo Reg. U.S. Pat. & TM Off.

First Kensington Books Trade Paperback Printing: April 2008
First Kensington Books Mass-Market Paperback Printing: April 2009
First Zebra Books Mass-Market Paperback Printing: March 2022
ISBN-13: 978-1-4201-5372-9
ISBN-13: 978-1-4201-5373-6 (eBook)

10 9 8 7 6 5 4

Printed in the United States of America

CONTENTS

BITTEN   1
by Lynsay Sands

HEART OF THE MUMMY   99
by Saranna DeWylde

THE YEARNING   201
by Hannah Howell

CITY OF DEMONS   307
by Richelle Mead

Bitten

Lynsay Sands

Prologue

The room was nearly pitch black. The weak glow of moonlight coming through the only window gave little illumination, but that didn't matter. Darkness was their friend for this trap.

Keeran crouched behind the chest that had been positioned to block him from the view of anyone entering the room. Hand clenched around his sword, muscles tensed, he stared with fixed attention at the crack of light coming in under the bedchamber door.

A rustle reached his ears as his father shifted in his own hiding place on the other side of the chamber. Keeran turned his eyes in that direction, but while he could see the dark shape of the bed between them, he could see no sign of his father in the gloomy corner beyond it. Keeran knew he was equally invisible to the older man.

Another rustle. It was the barest of sounds, but he recognized it for a sign that the older warrior was restless. They hadn't been hiding there long, but Keeran was restless as well, eager to claim vengeance for the deaths of his mother and sister.

His gaze returned to the dark corner and Keeran silently cursed his father for refusing to remain at his side as he had wished. After losing both his mother and sister in quick succession, he'd wanted to keep his sire close as they awaited the beast they were sure would strike again this night.

His mother and sister. Keeran felt grief try to claim and weaken him, but staved it off. He needed anger now to strengthen him, so deliberately reflected on the events that had led up to this night.

Keeran had returned from more than a year fighting the king's battles to find Castle MacKay in an uproar and his mother dead. It was his father who had told him the tale of what had come to pass. Some weeks past, young village girls and boys had begun to die, found pale and bloodless, two marks on their throat as if bitten. Panic had been quick to set in among the MacKay clan. Since the attacks had all taken place at night, parents began locking their children away the moment the sun went down, but this did little to slow the deaths. Two more young girls turned up dead in their beds, both only feet away from their sleeping parents.

As clan chief, Keeran's father was expected to both stop these deaths and to avenge them. He immediately set up a night watch to patrol the village, then gathered a group of men to hunt the source of the attacks. It was the third night of the hunt that Keeran's father came across what appeared to be a man feasting on the neck of one of the warriors assigned to patrol the village.

Geordan MacKay had told Keeran that for a brief moment, he had been so overwhelmed by the horrible realization that the ancient myths of night-walking beasts who fed on the blood of men were true that he had been unable to move. Vampires existed. But he had soon shaken off his temporary paralysis and attacked, taking the creature by surprise and hacking off his head before the vampire could straighten from his last victim.

News of the kill had spread quickly, and the clan had gathered to greet him as Keeran's father had made his triumphant ride into the bailey, the headless vampire across his horse before him. They had all cheered when he held up the head, jaws open, deadly teeth exposed. A huge bonfire had been started and the body and head unceremoniously dumped on it to be sure the creature could not return to life. Then they had celebrated his death and the return of safety to the MacKays well into the morning.

Keeran's father had thought his troubles over then. He had killed the vampire plaguing his people. They were safe now. And they had been. At least the people in the village. But the very next night, his wife had fallen victim to the bloodless death. Geordan MacKay had awakened in the morning to find her lying pale and still beside him. Obviously, there was a second vampire, and this one had possessed the gall to kill Lady MacKay while she lay sleeping beside her husband. The horror was not over.

Keeran had arrived home the afternoon of his mother's death and joined the hunt for this new beast that night. That hunt proved fruitless, as did the next night's hunt, and the next. In the dawn after the third night, the men had returned to the news that Keeran's sister was dead. This new vampire had got past the patrols and guards that had been set everywhere and had killed her in her sleep, as had happened with their mother.

It had been obvious at that point that this second creature knew that Geordan MacKay had personally killed the first vampire and was now seeking vengeance. That being the case, Keeran had been the next logical victim. Father and son, both furious and grief-stricken, had redoubled their efforts to hunt down this new threat, but after nearly a week of searching, the laird of the MacKay clan had decided they should change their approach. They would lay a trap.

His plan had been simple. They would stuff straw under Keeran's bedclothes, hoping the creature would think him asleep there. Then each would take position on either side of the bed so that no matter which side he approached from, one or the other would be positioned to come up from behind and tackle him.

His father's plan had seemed a good one at first, but that was before they had doused the fire in the hearth, snuffed out the candles, and been plunged into stygian darkness. Suddenly blind, Keeran had feared they wouldn't be able to see the vampire to attack him when he came. But his father had insisted they would see him enter by the torchlight in the hall spilling into the room when he eased the door open.

With no better plan to take this one's place, Keeran had acquiesced and backed into his assigned corner. It was a relief to find that his eyes did adjust to the darkness and that, aided by the weak moonlight coming in through the window on the opposite wall, he could make out the dark shape of his bed.

Realizing all at once that this was no longer true and that the room seemed even darker than before, Keeran turned his gaze toward the window. It appeared that a cloud had been passing over the moon. Even as he looked, it moved away, allowing the faintest light back in. Keeran was just relaxing when another sound reached his ears.

Stiffening, he shot his gaze to the corner where his father stood invisible in darkness. Had that been a moan? He held his breath, straining to hear until his head ached with the effort. Keeran heard no other sound, but icy cold was creeping over him and he had the sudden uncomfortable sense of being the hunted rather than the hunter.

"Father?" he called in a bare whisper of sound.

Silence so thick it seemed to have a life of its own was his only answer. Keeran felt the hair on the back of his neck prickle. Had the beast got in? Nay. Light would have spilled into the room from the door had anyone entered. Still, his senses were on alert and his instincts were shrieking that there was trouble.

"Father?" he said, louder, to combat the sudden eerie sensation of being alone and exposed.

When there was no answer this time, Keeran eased up from his crouching position and moved carefully around the chest toward the door. They had removed all the rushes from the floor except for a foot-wide space around the bed. This had been to ensure they would be betrayed by no footfall as they crept up on the vampire when he appeared. Keeran was grateful for this forethought as he made his silent way to the door.

Relief coursed through him when he felt the wood of the door beneath his seeking fingers. Pausing just to the side of it, he listened for a moment, then pulled it open and thrust it wide.

Light immediately spilled into the room. Blinking as his eyes tried to adjust, Keeran turned to the corner his father had taken, prepared to apologize for the skittishness that had made him open the door, only to freeze as the man's crumpled figure came into view. For a moment, Keeran was bewildered as to what the older man was doing lying there slumped against the chest he should have been crouched behind, but then he saw the blood dribbling from two small puncture wounds on his neck. He also noted that—while pale as death—Geordan MacKay was breathing, taking in short, gasping breaths.

Instinct sent Keeran hurrying across the room toward his father. He had just reached the foot of the bed when movement out of the corner of his eye made him stop his forward motion and turn. In his concern, he had forgotten the monster they had been lying in wait for. It was a fatal mistake.

Keeran's sword was raised by the time he completed the turn, but the sight of the woman who stepped calmly out of the shadows so stunned him that he froze to gape.

She was slender, pale, and petite. She was also one of the loveliest women Keeran had ever seen. Her face was a pale oval, with perfect features framed by midnight hair that cascaded over her shoulders and out of sight down her back. His gaze stopped briefly on her large, lovely eyes, then dipped down to her sweet, blood red lips and stayed there. Keeran might have stared at her all night had a sound not drawn his attention to his father again.

" 'Tis her. She is *Vampyre*. Kill her!"

Keeran felt as if he had been punched in the stomach at these words. He turned back to the woman, expecting a denial. Surely this beautiful creature could not be the monster they sought? But he found her smiling an unholy smile. A shudder ran through him as she licked her lips and he realized the crimson color had been his father's blood. This *was* the beast who had killed his mother and sister and had now felled his father.

Red-hot rage immediately coursed through Keeran. He started to bring his sword down, but found she suddenly held the razor-sharp blade in a grip as hard as the steel she grasped. Keeran could neither raise nor lower it. Without hesitation, he drew the sword toward her as if her hand were a sheath. She didn't even flinch as it sliced into her flesh. Neither did she bleed, he realized. Only the dead didn't bleed.

Before he could attempt to hack at her again, the woman's open hand shot out at him. He barely had time to note the move, let alone block it. Her cold palm slammed into his throat with incredible force, then her fingers closed with a strength no human could possibly muster. She followed that with a lightning-swift blow to his chest that sent him to his knees as the air was punched out of him. The woman then stepped forward, dragging him around by the throat at the same time so that she stood behind him and they both faced his father.

The sword had dropped from his hand when she had punched him. Now weaponless, Keeran could only grab at her hand, trying desperately to tear it away. His shock at his inability to do so had his eyes bulging as he attempted to suck air down the throat her viselike grip seemed to have sealed closed. He was a warrior: strong, hard, and twice her size, and yet she was stronger.

"Hellbound creature!" Geordan MacKay gasped, and the woman holding Keeran as easily as if he were a rag doll laughed. It was a tinkle of amusement, more suited to a ballroom than this tense moment.

"Undoubtedly." She sounded amused, but her voice turned cold as she added, "But you shall go to your Maker knowing that I am taking your son and heir there with me. 'Tis a fitting punishment for your killing my mate, would you not say?"

Keeran saw his father try to rise from his slumped position at this claim, even as he himself attempted to break the grip on his throat. Neither of them succeeded. His father fell back with a weak moan of despair even as Keeran felt the sting of the beast's death kiss on his neck. That first nip was all the pain there was to his death. Then ecstasy exploded where the sting had been, spreading from that spot through his whole body. Much to his shame, Keeran felt his body respond as if to a lover. Then cold began to creep over him and his vision began to narrow. His last sight before the encroaching darkness claimed him was of the tears leaking from his father's regret-filled eyes and rolling down his pale cheeks.

When awareness returned to him, Keeran found himself lying abed and not knowing how he'd gotten there. He rolled weakly onto his side, then stilled at the sight of his father lying dead in the corner, a stake through his heart.

"He is dead. It is done."

Keeran's eyes shot to the window where the woman stood, shrouded in the gray light of predawn. She had awaited his regaining awareness before making her next move, and he suspected it would be to stake him, too.

"Nay. I'll not put you to rest," she announced, apparently able to read his mind. "Your father shall suffer more in his heaven knowing that you walk the earth, taking life to sustain your own as I do."

"Never!" Keeran spat, repulsed by the very idea.

"We shall see." Her smile was cold and cruel. "You will find you will do much to end the pain of hunger when it strikes."

Realizing now that she did not have the mercy to kill him, Keeran turned his gaze aside, wishing she would just go away. He wished to be left to his misery and mourning. But while he could avoid looking on her monstrous beauty, he couldn't shut out her voice.

"The dawn comes. You should seek shelter ere it arrives and sends you to hell in a blazing glory. A most unpleasant experience, I am sure."

Keeran jerked his gaze back to her, prepared to spit out that he would rather die than live this walking death as she did, but he was just in time to see her slip through the window and out of sight. Now he understood how she had entered without alerting them, and realized that they hadn't had a chance. Neither of them had even considered she might enter through the window. Keeran's room was in the tower, too high for any mortal being to reach. They had underestimated the creature.

At least now she was gone.

Keeran relaxed on the bed with every intention of staying right where he was and allowing the sun to show him the mercy she would not, but when the first rays of light began to creep through the window and touched his feet, it felt as if someone had set a torch to his boots. It affected him even through his clothing. Jerking his foot out of that finger of light, he tried to sit up but found he was yet too weak.

Cursing himself for not staying where he was even as he did it, Keeran managed to roll off the bed, hitting the floor with a body-jolting thump. This gave him some respite from the sun's rays, but he knew it would not be for long. Unshuttered, the window would soon allow the light in to fill the room. Yet he was too weak to gain his feet, let alone walk somewhere that the light could not reach him, and he refused to call out for help. He would not have his people see him this way. As far as they were concerned, their clan chief, Geordan MacKay, and his son and only remaining heir, Keeran MacKay, had died this night. He would have it so. He would not remain among them to sully them with his presence.

His gaze slid to the side and landed on the chest he had hidden behind. Mustering the little strength he had left, Keeran managed to crawl inside it. Relief flowed through him when the lid dropped closed, enshrouding him in a cocoon of darkness. It was quickly followed by shame that he had not had the courage to stay where he had been and allow the sun to destroy the monster he had become.

Chapter One

Emily spat the invading water from her mouth and coughed deeply, wrenching against the ropes around her torso as her body tried to expel the liquid that had made its way into her lungs. When the fit was over, she sagged weakly where she stood, forcing herself to keep her eyes and mouth closed. Both instinctively wanted to open.

Despite being ceaselessly pounded and buffeted by the wind, Emily felt starved for air; she longed to open her mouth and gasp in oxygen. She also yearned to open her eyes, but there was little to see. She was trapped in cold, wet darkness, alternately suffocated by the hard slap of the wind and pounded by the battering waves. Were it not for the solid surface of the mast at her back and the ropes digging into her body, she would have thought she'd fallen overboard and was drowning.

Emily almost wished she *were* drowning; at least then there would have been a foreseeable end to this torture. As it was, she was being beaten by waves that crashed over her, first slamming her back against the mast as they hit, then pulling at her, trying to rip her away from where she was lashed as they washed away. She was in agony, every inch of her flesh screaming at the abuse of the icy water and tearing ropes. No doubt by now the bindings had more than rubbed her raw. She imagined she was bleeding through the cloth of her gown, the ruby red drops washed away by each succeeding wave. And it seemed to her that this had been going on for an eternity, long enough that she began to fear she had been drowned by the brutal waves and was now in some form of purgatory. A punishment, no doubt, for her lack of proper concern when her uncle had been washed overboard. Was lack of grief at the death of a family member enough to see you in hell? she wondered. Despite knowing she shouldn't, Emily blinked her eyes open and lifted her face to the sky. She was immediately blinded by another wave.

The storm had come on quickly. One moment it had been a bright and sunny morning, just coming on noon, in the next the sky had turned an ominous green that had gone darker and darker until all signs of daylight had disappeared. Emily had known from the sailors' reactions that this was to be no normal storm. The mood among them had quickly become as heavy as the clouds overhead as they hurried to batten down everything onboard. She'd understood why when the ship had begun pitching wildly about. Then the rain had started, followed by the lightning that had briefly and intermittently lit the sky enough for her to see the great walls of water that the ship struggled through. Even the brief glimpses she'd had of those mountainous waves had left her gaping in horror. She had begun to pray.

Had this been a passenger ship, Emily would have ridden out the storm in her own cabin. No doubt she would have been lashed to a cot to keep from flying about and been blissfully ignorant of the true violence of the battle they faced. But this was one of her uncle's cargo ships. There were no cabins. She'd spent the first part of the storm clinging to the side of the ship beneath a small wooden shelter, but as the storm had intensified in fury and she'd found it increasingly difficult to keep her footing, the captain had insisted on lashing her and her uncle to the mast. Her father's brother had insisted Emily be taken first, and she had been touched by this very first sign of familial caring from the man. Then he had ruined it by shouting that if they managed to get her safely to the mast, he would risk the journey.

It had taken seemingly forever for the captain and the first mate to get Emily to the mast. The wind had kept grabbing at the long skirts of her gown and trying to whisk her away. By the time they had lashed her to it and gone back to collect her uncle, the wind had been a living thing, grasping and greedy. Worse yet, on their return the ship had been cresting one of the enormous waves that had been assaulting them for hours. The men had not been able to reach the mast before they were picked up by a rogue wave that crashed over the ship. Her uncle and the first mate had been swept overboard like so much flotsam. The captain had been smashed into the side of the ship with a violence that had left him injured, but alive and still onboard. Emily had known at that point that— barring a miracle—they were all lost. Her opinion had not changed in the eternity that had passed since then as she had first watched the seamen struggle to fight the storm, then watched them being overwhelmed by it until it had grown too dark to see at all.

The time since then had been interminable, filled with the crash of waves, the sting of rain, and the never-ending, howling wind. At first, there had also been the occasional screams of sailors being washed overboard, but Emily had not heard any for the last little while. She was beginning to think that she was the only soul left alive onboard, and didn't know how long that would last. While the ship was still afloat, she was in dire danger of drowning where she slumped against the ropes binding her.

A sudden low crack and groan pierced the howling in Emily's ears. It was accompanied by a shudder that ran through the boards under her feet and the mast at her back. Emily lifted her head and tried to penetrate the black, her heart thundering somewhere in the vicinity of her throat as she struggled to understand what this meant. It sounded as if the ship had hit something. This couldn't be good.

Another wave battered her body and Emily moaned as her head cracked violently against the wooden mast. For a moment, the gloom was illuminated by stars dancing behind her eyelids and she was wretched with pain. It was then that the wind and water were abruptly cut off. She could still hear the wind, but it no longer beat at her as it had. Emily didn't open her eyes until a hard form pressed itself against her.

Blinking her eyes open then, she was surprised to find that there was some light where until now there had been only darkness. The storm was apparently easing and some small moonlight was struggling through the clouds, enough that she could make out the ruffled front of a white shirt before her nose. Then that cloth and the body beneath it were pressed against her face and she felt arms close around her. Before she could quite understand what was happening, the ropes that had held her in place for so long slipped away. Stiff and weak from hours spent in the punishing wind, Emily felt herself crumpling downward, then was caught under the arms and lifted up.

"Hold on to me." The words came to her clearly, though she almost thought she had imagined them, for surely even spoken into her ears she should not have heard them so clearly in this wind? Nevertheless, Emily did her best to obey the instruction, but her limp arms were incapable of following direction. She lifted helpless, apologetic eyes to the face looming above hers and was briefly caught in its dark beauty. Sad, gray eyes that seemed to reflect the moonlight peered out at her from a pale, chiseled face that was both handsome and somehow tragic. Emily knew instinctively that this man had suffered untold sorrow.

Her thoughts died an abrupt death as another fierce wave crashed over the boat, slamming both her and her would-be rescuer back against the mast. Her head cracked against the wood once more, this time a violent slam that made the night explode in a blinding light that faded as quickly as it had appeared, taking consciousness with it.

Emily blinked her eyes open and stared into obscurity. For a moment, she feared she was still on the ship and that the storm had merely passed, but then she realized this couldn't be. She was dry, lying down on a relatively soft surface, and covered by what felt to be a mountain of blankets. She was saved! That glad thought was followed by the question of *how?* and a brief picture of a pale, handsome face beneath wind-tossed hair flashed in her mind.

Emily sat up abruptly and winced at the tenderness in her stomach, a reminder of her ordeal through the storm. She suspected she'd be tender for some time to come.

"And should be grateful to have escaped so lightly," she reprimanded herself, then gave a start at the rusty sound of her own voice. Her throat was raw and sore, though whether from the seawater she had swallowed or from her own shouts she just didn't know. Whatever the case, she determined to be grateful for this little reminder of her experience as well. No doubt, the men who had been washed overboard would have welcomed the opportunity to complain of so little.

Emily peered around the dim room as she shifted to the edge of the bed. There was little enough to see: unidentifiable shapes barely visible through the gloom. It appeared to be night still, or again. She wasn't at all sure how long she'd suffered the brutal storm. For that matter, Emily had no idea how long she may have slept afterward.

Her gaze settled on a large black rectangle that might be a door, and she slid off the bed to move cautiously toward it, inching forward with care lest there be something in her path. But when Emily reached what she'd hoped was a door and stretched out her hand, her fingers encountered only heavy cloth. Drapes.

Gripping the material with both hands, she yanked them open. Midday sunlight exploded into the room, searing her eyes and sending her staggering back. Blinking rapidly, Emily turned away from the blinding light and got her first glimpse of the room she occupied. The sunlight lit it admirably. Too well. She almost wanted to slam the curtains closed again. The room she occupied was a gloomy prospect. No amount of sunlight could brighten the decor of gray and blood red with its coating of dust and detritus.

Grimacing, she rubbed her arms and shifted to place one foot on top of the other on the cold stone floor, then glanced at the loose cloth covering her arms. Her dress was gone. She wore a long, flowing white nightgown in its place. Embarrassment tried to claim her at the thought of someone—the sad-eyed man?—undressing and dressing her, but she shrugged it away. Surely it had been a maid and not her rescuer who had changed her? Emily hoped so, but another glance at the room was hardly reassuring. It did not reflect the efforts of a maid.

Her ruminations on the matter were interrupted when a click drew her gaze to the door she had been seeking. The large wooden panel swung inward and a head sporting gray hair in a neat bun poked in, swiveling until two bright eyes found her.

"Oh! Yer up."

"Yes. I—" Emily paused. The head had slipped back out of sight through the door. In the next moment, the wooden panel burst wide open and the head reappeared, this time atop the rather large, comforting body of an older woman carrying a tray.

"Well! I was beginning to think ye'd be sleeping the day away." The woman sailed cheerfully across the room to set the tray on a small table next to Emily. "Not that I'd be blaming ye if ye did. But I've been ever so curious since the master brought ye home." She fussed over the tray briefly, then pulled out a chair and smiled at Emily.

"Here ye are, then. I've brought you some good, nourishing food to restore ye after yer trials. Have a seat, lass, and—och!"

Emily had moved automatically toward the chair, but paused abruptly at that alarmed sound. The woman sounded like a chicken about to lay an egg and looked about as ruffled, her matronly body bristling and jerking back as if to flap wings that didn't exist.

"Ye can't be standin' about barefoot on the castle's cold floors, lass. Ye'll be catching yer death, ye will. And ye've naught but the lady's gown on." Pausing, she slammed her palm into her forehead. "Oh, saints alive! I didn't think to leave ye any slippers or a robe. I'll fetch ye one right quick, ne'er fear. Ye just get off the stone floor and settle yerself at the table. I'll return directly."

The woman fled as quickly as she'd entered, leaving Emily feeling quite lost. She hadn't had the opportunity to ask a single question, and there were quite a few she would have liked answers to. After a moment, the scent wafting off the food drew her to the table. Emily's stomach growled as she surveyed the offering. There was quite an assortment: bread so fresh it was still warm, a steaming bowl of oatmeal, eggs, bacon, fresh fruit, cheese, and pastries that looked divine.

Overcome with hunger, Emily briefly forgot herself and fell on the food like a ravenous wolf. She had made great headway into the meal when a loud dragging sound, as if some huge piece of furniture were being tugged across a floor, reached her ears and made her pause and glance to the open door where the sound was emanating from. When her benefactor's ample behind came into view, Emily stood and moved curiously to the door. Huff-ing and puffing and bent almost double, the older woman dragged what turned out to be a chest to the doorway.

"Oh! Let me help." Emily rushed forward, concerned by the older woman's flushed face.

The woman waved her away. "Ye'll just be getting in the way. Back to the table, lass. I've got this."

Ignoring that order, Emily took up position on the far end of the chest to help maneuver it the rest of the way into the room and to the foot of the bed. She wasn't surprised to find the older woman out of breath when they both straightened, but the fact that she was as well was a tad alarming. Emily was usually much more stalwart than this and could only think that the storm had really taken her strength out of her.

"There now." The woman popped open the lid of the chest and began to rifle through the neatly folded clothes inside. "These were the master's mother's things. Or sister's. I think," she added with a small frown as she lifted out an old-fashioned gown and took in its almost medieval look. "Well, they were some relative's."

An ancient relative, Emily thought with amusement as she peered over the gown the woman was refolding and returning to the chest.

"Anyway, this is where he had me get the nightgown ye're wearing, and he said ye could make use of whatever ye needed." She grunted with satisfaction as she came up with a slipper, handed it over, then bent to hunt its partner.

Emily examined the soft cloth, then slipped the shoe onto one foot, happy to find it fit snugly and was comfortable. She donned the other slipper when it was found, then a robe as well.

"There we be." Beaming with satisfaction, the older woman steered her back toward the table. Her eyebrows rose in surprise when she saw the dent Emily had already put in the provided fare. "Well now, I like a lass with a healthy appetite."

Emily flushed at that approving comment. She had gobbled down a good portion of the food in the short time the woman had been gone. She'd felt near to starving the moment she'd spotted the food, which reminded her of her first question. While they'd breakfasted before setting out for the docks, the storm had hit before they could manage lunch aboard ship. Emily had no idea how long it had been since she'd eaten. It felt like days. "How long have I slept?"

"Well, now." Her hostess settled comfortably in a chair across from her and paused to reach for one of the pastries before answering her question. "It was near dawn yesterday when ye were brought here. A drowned rat ye were, I can tell ye. Barely alive, I think. I changed yer clothes and settled ye in bed and figured ye'd sleep the day away, but ye slept through the night too. I started to worry when ye didn't wake up first thing this morning. So I decided to fix ye a tray and see did the food not draw ye back to wakefulness."

"Dawn," Emily murmured thoughtfully. "The storm started just before midday. That means I was strapped to that mast for—"

The woman nodded solemnly at Emily's dismay. "It took a lot out of ye. Ye needed yer rest. Eat up," she added. "It's rare enough I get the chance to cook fer someone and ye could use fattening up."

"You're the cook here, then?" Emily asked.

The woman blinked, then again slapped a hand to her

forehead. "Och! I've not even introduced myself, have I? I'm Mrs. MacBain, dear. Cook, housekeeper, and . . ." She shrugged, then glanced around the room. Embarrassment immediately covered her face as she took in its state.

"It must be difficult to keep so large a home clean if you're on your own," Emily said sympathetically, and the woman sighed.

"Aye. I don't generally bother with any but the main floor. Most of the rest of the castle is kept closed. We don't usually have guests." She turned her gaze back to Emily and took another pastry before moving the plate a little closer to her in silent invitation. "And now that ye know my name, who would ye be?"

"Emily." She took one of the offered pastries. Her mouth watered as she broke the soft bun and the fresh-baked, yeasty scent wafted to her nose. "Emily Wentworth Collins."

"Emily Wentworth Collins, is it?" Mrs. MacBain smiled as Emily bit into the pastry with a moan of pure pleasure, then added, "That's an important-sounding name. For an important lady?"

"Nay. I have no title, I'm afraid," Emily admitted, then cleared her throat and said, "My memory is rather vague, but I am sure I recall a man untying me from the mast."

"Aye." The woman heaved out a breath that sent little bits of powdery sugar flying. "The MacKay."

"The MacKay?" Emily echoed with interest. "Is he a handsome man? Pale? With sad eyes?"

"Aye. Keeran MacKay's a handsome devil and that's no lie. 'Tis a shame about him, really."

"A shame?" Emily queried softly.

"Hmm." The housekeeper's wrinkled face went solemn, then she seemed to shake off the mood and she turned a thoughtful gaze Emily's way. "I noticed ye wear no rings. Ye aren't married, are ye, dear?"

"No," Emily admitted, bewildered by the seeming change in subject. Being a naturally honest girl, she felt compelled to add, "Not yet."

"Not yet?" Mrs. MacBain asked, a question on her face.

"I was to marry an earl today," Emily explained, then corrected, "Well, I guess it would have been yesterday we were to wed. 'Tis why my uncle and I were traveling north. We were to arrive at the ancestral estate in the afternoon, spend the night, then the wedding was to take place the next day. I suppose I slept through the portion of time during which I was supposed to be married."

"Marrying an earl? And you not even a lady?"

Emily bit back a smile at Mrs. MacBain's shock over this idea, though she wasn't surprised by it. There was a time when such a thing would have been unheard of. However, times were changing, and commoners were no longer peons bound to their lords, but were free to perform commerce and amass great wealth. And with that change, impoverished but titled lords had begun to marry untitled but wealthy commoners to secure their place in society. Mrs. MacBain was obviously of an old-fashioned mind and didn't approve of such arrangements.

"Well, while not titled, I *have* had all the proper schooling. And I am told I'm quite wealthy. Then too, the earl wanted a healthy, young bride to beget an heir, and my uncle wanted the title and connections the earl holds, for business purposes." She frowned now and glanced up at the kind woman. "Uncle John was washed overboard at the start of the storm. I don't suppose—?" She stopped her question when Mrs. MacBain sadly shook her head.

"The master said ye were the last soul left alive, dear. I am sorry."

Emily nodded. She felt as much grief at the loss of the captain and sailors who had been strangers to her until the morning they had boarded the ship as she did at the loss of her uncle. In truth, he had been as much of a stranger to her as those other lost souls. She sighed unhappily at that knowledge.

"Ye've said yer uncle and this earl wanted the wedding. What did *ye* want?" Mrs. MacBain asked, watching her closely.

"Me?" Emily blinked at the very idea. What she wanted didn't really come into it, and she had never been foolish enough to think it did. The woman's wants were never important. Her duty was to do as she was bid with as much cheer and obedience as could be mustered. Men made the decisions in this world. She had been trained in that from birth. It was the way of things.

"Aye, ye," Mrs. MacBain said, drawing her thoughts again. "Did ye wish to marry the earl?"

Emily shuddered at the very thought of the ancient, leering earl of Sinclair. The one time they had met, he had eyed her hungrily and announced to one and all that she would bear him "fine fruit." Hardly an impressive first meeting. "No. But my uncle wished it."

"I see. Well," Mrs. MacBain said reluctantly. "I suppose we should send a message to the earl."

"No!" Emily herself was startled by the shout that ripped from her throat. Forcing herself to take a calming breath, she tried for reason. She had been numb with a sort of horror ever since learning she was to marry the aged and repulsive earl of Sinclair, but had known there was no way to avoid it. As her guardian, her uncle had every right to arrange her life as he saw fit.

Now, however, he was dead. Did she still have to carry out his wishes and place herself in the earl's hands? In effect, handing over the reins of her life to that—from all accounts—lascivious man? Or was her life now, finally, her own? It seemed to be her own, as far as she could gather. No doubt a barrister would be placed in charge of her finances until she reached the age of twenty-five—as stated in her father's will—but the barrister could not order her to marry anyone. No one could now. She was free. The thought was a new and precious one.

Free. That horrid, torturous storm had freed her. But freed her to do what? She wasn't sure what she could or wanted to do, and would appreciate the chance to figure it out without the earl haranguing her or the family lawyers hovering about her with disapproval. And this was probably her only opportunity to ponder what she wished to do, she realized. At least it was as long as no notice was sent informing everybody that she still lived.

Emily glanced at Mrs. MacBain. Encouraged by her kindly expression, she admitted, "I do not wish to marry the earl. I never have."

"Then surely ye don't have to now?"

"No, but—" She hesitated, then admitted, "I fear if you contact the earl and I am returned to him, I shall be pressured to honor the agreement and—"

When she hesitated again, Mrs. MacBain patted her hand with understanding. "Time is what ye need, deary. Time and space to sort the matter and decide how to handle it. And there is plenty of time and space here. It would be nice to have another woman's company for a bit."

Emily felt relief pour over her, then tensed again and asked, "But what of your employer?"

Mrs. MacBain shrugged that concern away. "It's doubtful his Lairdship would notice, let alone mind, if ye stayed on a bit."

"His Lairdship? Your employer is a lord?" Emily asked with surprise.

"Well, no. Not any more." Her gaze skittered away from the curiosity in Emily's face and she said, "Anyway, don't worry about the master. He's never about during the day and is often out at night, feeding. It's most likely you'll be sleeping while he's prowling about."

Feeding? Prowling? Emily was confused by the woman's odd choice of words and would have asked about them, but Mrs. MacBain distracted her by giving her hand a reassuring squeeze. Then the older woman stood and moved to the chest at the foot of the bed.

"Yer dress was quite ruined by the storm, but there is surely something suitable here for ye to wear." She began sorting through the contents of the chest as she spoke. The housekeeper fished out, examined, and discarded several gowns as apparently unsuitable before settling on a pale blue one with a matching girdle and long draping sleeves.

"Take yer time about eating, dear," Mrs. MacBain said as she set the gown across the foot of the bed. "Once ye've finished and changed, come below to the kitchens and I shall show ye to the library. The master is an avid reader, so there's quite a selection to entertain ye."

"About your master," Emily said as the woman moved toward the door. "I should like to speak to him, to thank him for rescuing me."

A cloud seemed to pass over the woman's face, then she forced a smile and waved a hand in an attempt at airy dismissal. "Oh, la. He willna be around until dar . . . dinnertime, but ye can speak to him then."

"Dinnertime?" Emily smiled. "No doubt it's your cooking that brings him home."

Another shadow crossed the woman's face at Emily's attempted compliment, but all she said was, "He prefers to dine out. Still, he'll be here then."

Leaving Emily to wonder why anyone with such a marvelous cook would prefer to seek his meals elsewhere, the housekeeper slid out into the hall and softly closed the door.

Emily peered around the room she had slept in, hardly aware of how gloomy it was anymore. She was free. That thought kept running through her mind, and yet Emily had been resigned to her fate for so long that she could hardly believe it had changed. She didn't have to marry the earl of Sinclair.

Smiling, she pushed away from the table and stood. She was quite full and finished with her meal, but there were things to do here. Emily was grateful to Mrs. MacBain for allowing her the time to sort out her situation, but wouldn't add to the woman's work. She was young and strong and would earn her keep by helping about the castle. And she would start by taking the breakfast tray below to the kitchen.

Keeran woke the moment the last rays of sunlight disappeared beyond the horizon. For a moment he lay quiet and still, listening to the activity in his home. There was a hum of energy on the fringes of his consciousness that he'd been aware of through his sleep, a stirring in the air that told him something was different. He usually awoke to the soothing awareness of the MacBains' calm presence somewhere in the keep, but this night was different. While he was aware of the older couple, their energy was less calm than usual, less soothing. There was an underlying excitement to their life force. There was also a third presence in his home. He knew it was the girl from the boat. She had been asleep when last he'd awoken, her presence quiet and undisturbing. Tonight, he could feel the energy pouring off of her in waves that permeated almost every corner of his castle. She was awake—that was obvious—and would now have to be dealt with.

Keeran tried to concentrate on her energy and sense exactly where she was in the castle, but found himself unable to. Her vibration seemed to fill his home. That realization made him scowl. He was usually able to sense where individual souls were, but this woman seemed somehow different.

He pushed the loose lid of his coffin aside and sat up, regretting that he had brought her here. Keeran hadn't intended to, but then he hadn't planned on rescuing damsels in distress in the first place.

He'd been returning to the castle after the hunt, eager to get in out of the rain and wind, when Keeran had heard her screams. They'd seemed distant at first. Recognizing that they were coming from the coast, he'd turned in that direction. Her cries had become louder the closer he'd got, until by the time he reached the shore it was as if she were screaming in his ear. She hadn't, of course, and he hadn't even been hearing her with his ears, but she had a strong mind and her distress had reached him clearly. Keeran had quickly taken in the situation. A ship was in trouble on the water. He'd known at once that she was the only one left alive and had sensed that the ship was about to shatter on the coral reef that had taken so many other ships over the years.

Before he'd even known what he intended to do, Keeran was on the ship freeing her. He had removed her to shore, planning to lay her beneath a tree on the beach for someone to find in the dawn. The villagers would have realized that she was from the ship, but would have assumed that she had somehow managed to make it ashore. As for the girl, she had been a drowned rat, already half-dazed when he'd reached her, but the blow she'd taken to the head as he'd untied her from the mast had knocked her unconscious. Keeran had felt sure she wouldn't recall his presence on the ship, or—if she did—would believe she'd imagined him.

However, Keeran's plan to leave her there on the beach had died when his drowned rat had stirred as he knelt to lay her in the sand. She had opened pain-filled eyes and peered straight at him with a sort of wonder that had made him pause.

"You saved me. Thank you." It was all she'd said before drifting back into unconsciousness, but he'd found himself staring at her, unable to abandon her. Then he'd peered down to see that her hand clasped his, holding him like a child clinging to her mother. Trusting that she would be safe.

Strangely reluctant to leave her alone and defenseless, he had straightened with her still in his arms and carried her home in the predawn hours to be left in his housekeeper's care.

When he had awoken last night, Keeran's first thought had been of her. He'd been concerned when Mrs. MacBain informed him that the girl had slept through the day and had yet to awake. Then he had thought she might perhaps awaken during the night and not know where she was. To prevent her suffering any unnecessary alarm, he had foregone his usual nightly hunt and watched over her through the night, disappointed when the approaching dawn had forced him from her side.

He now told himself that his disappointment had only been because he was eager to learn what he needed to know to see her back to her people and out of his home. Keeran preferred his life to move along in an orderly and routine fashion and knew instinctively that this woman's presence would disrupt that. And as he had feared, she already had. That realization filled him with irritation as he left the hidden room where he rested during the day. The energy pouring off of his guest was stronger than any he had felt in a long while. He found himself drawn to it and annoyed by it at the same time.

Keeran made his way to the stairs leading to the first floor at a quick clip. He had every intention of speaking to his unwanted houseguest, finding out who she was and where she belonged, and making the necessary arrangements to return her there as quickly as possible.

Chapter Two

Emily finished scrubbing the last little bit of the dining room floor, then sat back on her haunches and wiped her forehead with a sigh. She was hot and weary from hard work, but she was also deeply satisfied. She had gotten a lot done this afternoon.

It had taken a good deal of talking and cajoling, but Emily had finally convinced Mrs. MacBain to allow her to help about the castle. She had then taken a quick tour of the first floor of the castle before deciding on starting in the dining room. Mrs. MacBain had told her earlier that she only bothered with the kitchens, library, hallways, and the office, but still Emily had been dismayed at the state of the dining room, which obviously hadn't been cleaned in years, perhaps decades. It had taken little thought to decide that this room was where she should start her efforts, and she had set to it with a vengeance. In the one afternoon, she had swept and washed the stained and cobwebbed walls, cleaned the paintings, polished the oak table and chairs, and scrubbed the stone floor.

Her gaze slid around the now-pristine room, and Emily smiled faintly. A new coat of paint would have been nice, but the room was much improved. So much so that she felt sure that Mrs. MacBain's employer might see his way clear to joining her in dining there this evening. At least, she certainly hoped so. She would be pleased to have a word or two with the man.

Emily grimaced at that thought. Earlier in the day she would have liked to dine with him so that she might thank him for rescuing her. But after her tour of the castle, she wanted to discuss an entirely different matter altogether. Specifically, his lack of consideration for his staff. Emily could not believe the amount of work that the elderly housekeeper tended to on her own. Most castles boasted a chef concerned only with the daily task of cooking, their time taken up with baking bread and making the full-course meals the lords, ladies, and other wealthy employers demanded. Mrs. MacBain did this daily, plus all the other chores a full staff would be expected to do: dusting, sweeping, scrubbing. This castle was huge and old and even with only part of the ground floor to tend to, the task was herculean. The ground floor alone consisted of the kitchens, an office, two separate salons, a sitting room, a dining room, a long book-filled library, a ballroom, and various other miscellaneous chambers. Some of the rooms were obviously kept closed, the dining room among them, but the others were spotless, obviously dusted and scrubbed daily.

Then there was *Mr.* MacBain. While collecting the paraphernalia she would need to clean the dining room,

Emily and Mrs. MacBain had chatted. Along with learning that Mrs. MacBain's employer was "Laird Keeran
MacKay—who was no longer a lord" for reasons that the
older woman had somehow avoided explaining, Emily
had learned that while Mrs. MacBain had the duties inside the house, Mr. MacBain tended the stables, yard, and
everything else without help as well.

Emily had hidden her dismay from Mrs. MacBain, but
inside she was seething over the situation and could not
believe that Laird Keeran MacKay—who was no longer
a lord—could be so cruel. She could understand that financial setbacks might make the man thrifty, but this was
ridiculous. The couple were too old to be working this
hard, and she intended to tell the man so when he returned to the castle this evening. The only question in her
mind was whether she should do so before or after thanking him for saving her life.

"What the devil are you doing?"

Emily's heart leapt into her throat and she jerked
around on her knees at that sharp question from the doorway. She hadn't heard anyone approaching and was taken
completely by surprise to find herself staring at the handsome, dark-haired man with the sad eyes. However, his
eyes weren't sad at the moment, rather they were cold
with what might have been fury. And while he was handsome, the planes of his face were sharp and harsh as if
chiseled from marble, definitely not the softer face from
her memory. He looked more like an avenging angel than
the angel of mercy who had saved her. Still, there was no
mistaking this man as anyone but Keeran MacKay, the
man who was no longer a lord.

"Well?"

The sharp question startled Emily out of her temporary

paralysis and she blurted the first thing to come to mind. "Cleaning."

This answer only seemed to infuriate the man further. "I have servants for that. You are not expected to sing for your supper, nor clean for it. Get off my floor."

Flushing with embarrassment, Emily struggled to her feet, nearly losing her balance and falling when her legs cramped in protest at being on her knees for so long. Only the quick reaction of her host as he stepped forward to take her elbow in a hard grip kept her on her feet until she had regained her legs. This only increased Emily's humiliation. Where moments ago she had felt pride in her accomplishment, she now felt shame at her weakness and her rumpled condition. Her first meeting with her savior and host wasn't going at all as she'd planned. For one thing, she'd intended to clean up and make herself presentable before meeting him. For another, she had never imagined finding herself feeling at such a disadvantage. But then, she had never expected the man to be offended at her efforts to help Mrs. MacBain.

Reminded of the older woman and the unrealistic expectations of the man now glaring at her, some of Emily's embarrassment faded, being quickly replaced with righteous anger.

"Yes. You have servants," she agreed grimly. "*Two* servants expected to tend to this *entire* castle and its grounds. Surely you must realize that one poor elderly couple cannot tend to all this work on their own? They need help, and since you haven't seen fit to hire them assistance, I took it upon myself to do so to show my gratitude for how kind they have been."

She paused and huffed out a little breath, then sucked more air deep into her lungs, holding it there briefly in an effort to regain her temper. Emily had the mildest of temperaments. It was very hard to stir her anger, but she could not stand injustice of any sort and the situation the MacBains suffered here was ridiculously cruel in her mind. This man was working them into the grave. Though, she admitted to herself, he might not be wholly aware of the fact. Men seemed to be ever oblivious to domestic matters, and she realized his cruelty might merely be a matter of thoughtlessness. That possibility calmed her enough that she tried for a conciliatory tone as she said, "If it is a matter of financial distress—"

"I assure you I suffer no such distress," he snapped, obviously insulted at the suggestion, and Emily felt her temper shoot up again.

"Then it must be that you are simply a skinflint, my lord. Saving money on the backs of the MacBains."

A gasp from the doorway drew her attention to the elderly woman now standing there. The alarm on Mrs. MacBain's face and the direction of her gaze made Emily aware that—in her upset—she had been poking her host in the chest. Flushing, she withdrew her finger, cleared her throat, and stepped back, suddenly finding herself unable to look at the man she had just been berating.

Keeran turned away from Mrs. MacBain's alarmed expression and back to the woman before him. He had walked the earth for well over two hundred years and had never before met a woman like this one. Unless they were in his thrall, most females quailed before him, acting as skittish as spooked colts. But, while she was pale and stiff, this woman showed no signs of quailing any time soon. He was scowling his displeasure at this when it suddenly occurred to him why she was different from all other women. The girl was daft, of course. She'd been left strapped to that mast out in the wind and rain too long. Obviously all the banging about had shaken her senses. The waves had probably washed the brains right out of her head.

Satisfied with this explanation, Keeran felt himself relax until he peered back to his housekeeper and noted that she was still looking alarmed, as if she feared he might take a bite out of the woman right there in front of her. He hadn't seen that expression on her face in a good thirty years—not since she had gotten used to him and concluded that he would not harm her. To see it there now upset him almost as much as his guest's lack of fear discombobulated him.

"I—" Mrs. MacBain glanced from him to the tray she held, then to the woman who had been berating him just moments ago. "I was just . . . I thought—"

Irritated, Keeran waved her explanations away and moved past her out of the room. He was upset by both his housekeeper's anxiety and all these changes in his home. Keeran disliked being upset. He enjoyed peace and quiet. He preferred routine, the same routine day after day. That being the case, it was not surprising that at that moment he wished for nothing more than to send his unwanted houseguest home and—

Dear Lord, he had forgotten to find out where she belonged, he realized, and came to a halt. The woman had so overset him that he hadn't asked the questions he'd intended to. He turned to peer back up the hall and could hear the hushed conversation taking place in the dining room. Mrs. MacBain was asking rather nervously what had taken place. She also addressed the girl by name. *Emily.* A pretty name for a pretty girl who was now admitting that she had taken him to task for his lack of consideration in regard to his staff.

Shaking his head in wonder that she had dared to do so, Keeran turned away and continued up the hall. He would talk to the girl later, after he had fed. Every time she had blushed or flushed, a wave of hunger had rolled over him, making him almost faint. He would feed, calm down, then sit her down and talk to her. Hopefully by that time she would be calmer, and possibly would have those smudges washed off her nose and cheeks. She had been annoying, but she had also looked rather adorable with the smudges. It had been a long while since Keeran had found anyone adorable.

"Oh, child."

Emily felt her heart sink at Mrs. MacBain's expression. If she had looked alarmed, Emily wouldn't have worried, but Mrs. MacBain was shaking her head with sadness.

"It isna because he willna pay that we have no help. His Lairdship would be happy to pay. But none of the villagers will work in the castle. He even hired a couple from the south once to help, but the villagers scared them off. The couple didn't last a week."

"Scared them off?" Emily asked, dismayed to think that she may have been unfair in her attack on her host. "How? And why will the villagers not work here?"

"Fear mostly," the housekeeper admitted, then frowned and moved past her to set the tray on the table before glancing around. "Ye've done a fine job in here. Thank ye fer yer help."

"Why are the villagers afraid to work in the castle?" Emily asked, unwilling to allow her to change the subject.

Mrs. MacBain turned back to the tray. Emily suspected

it was to avoid looking at her as she muttered, "Oh, there have been stories about the master and this castle being cursed for years. Tales of . . ." She hesitated again, then firmed her mouth and shook her head. "I'll not betray m'laird by repeating them. 'Tis enough to say that the villagers are afraid and so won't work here. Now, ye should eat before the food gets cold."

"You aren't afraid," Emily pointed out, unwilling to let the matter drop.

"Nay. But I was at first," she admitted reluctantly. "Until I had been here for a bit."

"What made you come to work here if you were afraid?" Emily asked.

"I felt I owed His Lairdship. He saved my boy."

"Saved him?"

"Aye. My Billy got himself lost in the woods. I don't know how many times I told him never to stray into the woods, but he and a couple other boys were having an adventure, wandered into the woods, and got lost. His Lairdship found them. They would surely have died of exposure ere someone found them had he not taken up the search. I came up to the castle the next morning to tell him I was grateful and he asked if Mr. MacBain and I would work here." She shrugged. "I couldn't say no. He had brought my boy back to me."

"And the parents of the other boys? Did he ask them too?"

She shook her head. "They never came to thank him that I know of. Neither did any of the parents of the other children His Lairdship has saved over the years, and there have been many," she assured her with a firm nod. "Children who were swimming when and where they shouldn't have, playing when and where they shouldn't have, and so on. His Lairdship always finds them and brings them home safe."

"I see," Emily murmured, and she thought she did. The laird of the MacBains saved the lives of local children, yet was reviled and feared because of some silly supposed curse from decades ago. It seemed terribly unfair to her. Terribly unfair.

Worse yet, she herself was one of those he had saved and then had reviled him for first being too unthinking and then being too cheap to hire help for the MacBains, when the truth was that he had the money and was willing, but no one would work for him. She bit her lip as shame overcame her. "And I chased him away from his own table with my accusations when he was obviously planning to dine in for a change. He will go hungry because of my assumptions."

"Oh, well, don't ye worry none. He'll scare up something to eat somewhere," Mrs. MacBain said vaguely. "Come, sit down to your own meal."

Suddenly indescribably weary, Emily did as the woman suggested and moved to sit at the table, before asking, "Where is your son now?"

"Oh, he passed on some time ago. He was still just a lad, but was killed while in the king's army. He worked here before he was a soldier though." She smiled and patted Emily's shoulder soothingly. "You should eat. Ye've worked hard today, harder than ye've any right to have worked, and while I appreciate it . . ." She shook her head and left the room. She had tried arguing Emily out of helping her all day. It seemed she saw little sense in trying to talk her out of it again.

Emily ate her food alone in the fine dining room she had almost managed to return to its former glory. The wooden table shone from her scrubbing and buffing and there wasn't an inch of the room that was not better for her efforts. She, on the other hand, could now use a good soak. Her efforts—while satisfying—had been exhausting. If she'd had the energy, she would have taken herself off to clean up before eating, but Emily feared that should she do that, she might not find the energy to return below to eat. So, she forced herself to finish a portion of the food Mrs. MacBain had worked so hard on, unable to eat all of it only because her muscles didn't seem to have the strength to lift the fork over and over.

It made her doubly grateful that the lord of this neglected castle had gone out for his meal. Emily didn't understand why he would want to when he had such a wonderful cook, but supposed it was for the best, at least for tonight. She would have been embarrassed to have had to eat with the man after the way she had treated him. It was something of a relief to her that she was going to manage to avoid him. But this was only a temporary reprieve, she knew. Emily still had to thank him for saving her life. And on top of that, she now owed the man an apology for maligning him unfairly.

Sighing wearily, Emily pushed herself away from the table and left the room. She would have to make a quick washup, change, then return below to the library to wait for Keeran MacKay's return. She owed him an apology and wouldn't rest until she had given it.

Keeran stood at the foot of the bed and watched his guest sleep. Emily. She slept like an angel, her expression serene in repose. One arm bent, a lightly curled hand by her cheek, the other lying open on the bed. He watched her for a moment, then turned to peer around the darkened room, able to see it clearly in the moonlight with his nocturnal predator's eyes.

The room was coated in dust and filth. Her cleaning efforts obviously hadn't reached up here. He wondered briefly on that, then let it go with a shrug. He had returned home from the hunt, hoping to find her still awake. When he had found no sign of either the girl or the MacBains on the main floor, he'd made his way here to the room they had settled her in that first night. He'd intended to wake her and force her to tell him where she belonged so that he might return her there, but the sight of her sprawled across the foot of the bed, still wearing the rumpled gown from earlier and still bearing the smudges on her cheek and nose, had made him pause. It was obvious she had sat down for a moment to rest and then simply drifted off to sleep, exhausted by her efforts that day.

Emily made a small murmur, and Keeran turned his gaze back to her as she sighed and shifted in her sleep. She was beautiful in moonlight, a pleasure to look upon. Perhaps it wouldn't be so bad that he hadn't found out where she belonged and wasn't sending her home on the morrow. She hardly seemed unsettling in her sleep. Aye, he wouldn't disturb her and insist she tell him where she belonged. Tomorrow was soon enough, he decided as he pulled the bed coverings down from the top of the bed to cover her.

She was just one woman. How much trouble could she cause in a day?

"I shall expect you at the castle within the hour." Emily nodded at the small crowd around her, then turned to smile at Mrs. MacBain. The older woman's returning smile was a little uncertain, but she ignored that as she joined her to start back to the castle.

Emily had awoken that morning, upset to find herself curled at the bottom of the bed. She truly had wished to make her apologies to Keeran MacKay for her behavior the night before and had been determined to thank him for saving her. It seemed, however, that she had fallen asleep before she could manage the task.

Determined to speak to him first thing, Emily had thrown the covers aside and hurried out of bed and about her ablutions. She had then rushed below, only to learn that the master of the castle had already left for the day. Emily had no idea where he had gone and hadn't been rude enough to inquire, but Mrs. MacBain had claimed that she didn't expect him back until dark, so Emily supposed he had traveled to a nearby city on business or some such thing.

It was while she had sat over another lovely breakfast that Emily had decided to visit the village on her host's behalf. The man was in dire need of household staff, and it was obvious that he'd had little success in the matter. She decided to use her own powers of persuasion for him. The man had saved her life, and she had treated him abominably in return for it. Emily felt she owed him. It was as simple as that.

Armed with all the information she could gather, and with a protesting Mrs. MacBain trailing her every step, Emily had taken the short walk down into the village. She had been determined not to return until she had succeeded in employing several servants for the castle.

It hadn't gone quite as she'd expected. She'd started out approaching those who were unemployed, which seemed to be the better part of the village. The response was less than enthusiastic. But she hadn't changed her tactics until an elderly woman had actually dared to spit on the ground at her feet, splattering the lovely slippers Mrs. MacBain had given her to wear. Then Emily had been forced to regroup. She had taken Mrs. MacBain aside and asked her to point out those who'd had children or relatives saved by the master of Castle MacKay. She had hoped that, like Mrs. MacBain, they would feel they owed it to the man. However, the others didn't appear to suffer the same conscience as the housekeeper did.

Emily had then asked Mrs. MacBain for the names of those who were both unemployed and whose child or relative had been rescued by The MacKay. Armed with this further knowledge, she had set to work. Resorting to pestering, bullying, and shaming when necessary, she had managed to convince more than half a dozen people to agree to work up at the castle. It wasn't as grand a success as she'd hoped for. The castle was in a sorry state and in need of a lot of work. She would have been happier with twice that number, but Emily would take what she could get. On top of that, the few she had managed to cajole into the duty had steadfastly insisted that they would not even set out for the castle until after sunrise and that they were to be allowed to be away well before sunset.

Emily could only shake her head over the superstition this revealed. Obviously this demand was a result of the mysterious curse supposedly plaguing the castle and its owner. It made her curious about the curse again, but Mrs. MacBain was remaining steadfastly closemouthed on the subject, and Emily would not betray the woman who had been so kind to her by asking any of the villagers to explain this curse.

Letting the mystery of the curse drop from her mind, Emily began to plan what she would have the workers do first. All the rooms needed cleaning. They could also all use a coat of paint, but—

She stopped suddenly as an idea occurred to her. "Mrs. MacBain?"

"Yes, dear?" The elderly woman paused as well.

"You go on back to the castle. I need to return to the village."

"Oh, but—"

"Go on," Emily interrupted her protest with a smile. "I can find my way. The path is clear."

After a hesitation, the woman conceded and continued along her way, leaving Emily to return to the village alone. Her steps were quick and excited as she walked. She was feeling quite pleased with herself. She had no doubt at all that Keeran MacKay would be pleased with what she had accomplished so far, but what she hoped to do now would surely please him even more.

Dear God, she had to go! That was Keeran's first thought on arising. His sleep had been disturbed by the presence of strangers in his home all afternoon. They hadn't been threatening, but their very presence had poked and prodded at his awareness as he'd attempted to rest. Now, he stormed up the stairs out of the dungeon, prepared for battle. Were he a dragon, he would be breathing fire.

He stormed up the hall toward the dining room, aware of the subtle changes made here and there. The floor shining clean, the hall tables polished to a fine sheen, a vase of flowers in the entry. Dear God! She was bringing his home to life and he couldn't stand it. It had taken decades to get used to the filth and neglect of a nearly servantless castle. Was he now expected to get used to it being clean again, only to have to relearn life with it the other way all over again when she left and the new servants refused to return?

"Oh, my laird." Mrs. MacBain rushed up as he neared the dining room. It seemed the likely place to find his guest; it was nearing dinner and that was where he'd found her yesterday. But the room was empty. He turned to his housekeeper, a forbidding expression on his face. "Where is she?"

"Ah . . ." She hesitated, her suddenly wary expression making Keeran curse inwardly. He detested the frightened way people reacted to him, but he hated it most of all from the MacBains, who should know better by now.

"She was only trying to help, my laird," Mrs. MacBain excused the girl. "She hoped to please ye to thank ye fer rescuing her. She—"

"Mrs. MacBain," Keeran interrupted patiently. "I realize she didn't mean to upset me. But I like routine. I only wish to ask who her family are so I can arrange to return her home." Much to his amazement, the woman's face now went through several changes, starting with alarm and ending in a calculating look he had never before seen on her face.

"Ah . . . well, my laird—"

"I am no longer Laird, Mrs. MacBain," he reminded her.

"Of course, my lair . . . ah, sir." She smiled brightly. "Miss Emily's abovestairs preparing for the evening meal."

Keeran nodded and turned toward the room. "I shall wait for her in the dining room."

"Ye're joining her?" She seemed alarmed at the prospect.

"No. I shall wait for her and speak to her before she eats."

"She'll be a while," the woman warned, then added, "I'm guessing a long while. I told her the meal wouldna be ready for two hours."

"Two hours?" He turned on her with dismay.

The housekeeper's head began bobbing like a heavy flower on a slim stem in a breeze. "Well, she just quit working and went upstairs but a moment ago. She worked ever so hard today, my lair . . . sir," she interrupted herself to add, then continued, "I knew she could benefit from a nice soak. Then she shall have to dry her hair by the fire, and dress, and I knew she would rush through it all and weary herself unnecessarily did I not be sure she had the time she needed. And she was ever so weary already from all the work she was doing around here trying to make ye happy, so I told her dinner wouldn't be for—"

"Very well," Keeran interrupted her diatribe. When she fell silent, he eyed her hopeful expression with suspicion, then sighed and decided, "I shall speak to her when I return, then. I shan't be late. Please ask her to wait for me."

"Aye, my lair . . . sir." Her head was bobbing in that odd way again, but she was smiling widely, obviously relieved. Keeran considered her suspiciously for one more moment, then turned away and continued out of the castle.

As he had the night before, Keeran would have to find his meal closer to home than he liked. He preferred to travel far and wide, varying where he struck to prevent alarming anyone near to his home. Not that he ever killed anyone while feeding. Keeran fed a bit here and a bit there to prevent harming anyone unduly. Of course, this method of sustaining himself was a bit riskier than feeding off one person, but left his victims healthy and well, if a little weak. To him, the risk was worth it. The beast—Carlotta, he had since learned, was her name—may have stolen his life and damned his soul to hell that night over two hundred years ago, but she could not take his humanity.

A bitter laugh slipped from his lips as he moved into the night. Many would argue that he was anything but human now. Yet still he clung to what bits of integrity he had learned as a human. He had no idea *what* he was now, or rather, he knew but preferred not to think about it. A vampire, a soulless nightwalker, feeding off the lifeblood of those around him. And a coward. He had suffered this existence for two centuries and still he had not the courage to let the sun claim him.

Forcing these unpleasant thoughts away, Keeran set about his business. He wished to be back before his houseguest should retire again. Mrs. MacBain was acting oddly and he didn't trust her to tell the girl that he wished to speak with her.

As it happened, Keeran had underestimated his housekeeper's obedience. It seemed she had indeed passed along his message to Emily, for he found her in the library on his return. Unfortunately, while the girl had remained below to await him, she had been unable to remain awake. He found her curled up in his chair before the fireplace, sound asleep.

Pausing before her, Keeran found himself unable to disturb her slumber. She looked achingly innocent, and innocence was something he had known little of in the last two hundred years. Keeran found interaction with humans painful, knowing they had loved ones to go home to; that they lived, laughed, and loved as he never would again. So, other than the occasional servant he managed to convince to work for him, he had little interaction with the rest of society. What little contact the necessity to feed did force on him was usually with its less sterling members of society, ne'er-do-wells and drunkards he came across during his nightly hunts. Keeran preferred to avoid feeding on the innocent. Despite the fact that he left them mostly unharmed, he didn't care for the guilt that sullying them caused on the rare occasion when necessity had found him feeding on one.

Now, he found himself fascinated by the woman who, in rest, seemed innocence incarnate. Emily. Her hair shone golden in the firelight.

"An angel," he whispered. His hand moved of its own accord to caress one soft, golden tress. It felt as warm as he recalled sunlight to be and, had he a heart, he was sure it would have pained him at that moment. She was achingly beautiful. Keeran wouldn't have been at all surprised had she sprouted wings and begun to glow with heavenly light there before him.

"She couldn't stay awake. She worked herself to the point of exhaustion today."

Those soft words drew his gaze to his housekeeper, who had suddenly appeared to hover anxiously nearby. Keeran felt irritation sting him at her protective attitude. Did the woman yet not trust him not to harm the chit? If after knowing him for thirty years she did not, what hope was there for him in this world? To live eons without love or true friendship, to watch those around him age and die, one after another, endlessly. . . . Perhaps there *was* no hope for him.

Suddenly aware that his fingers still curled in the girl's fair hair, Keeran withdrew his hand and straightened. "We should put her to bed," he growled in a soft voice. "She cannot sleep here all night."

"I'll wake her and—"

"No," he said sharply when she started forward. "There is no need to wake her. I shall carry her abovestairs."

"But—"

"You will have to light the way," Keeran interrupted. He really didn't need her to light the path for him. As with all nocturnal beasts, Keeran's eyesight was exceptional in the dark. But, as he had hoped, his suggestion had soothed the old woman, assuring her that he expected her to accompany him, as was proper.

After a brief hesitation, Mrs. MacBain nodded reluctantly and picked up a candle from the table beside the door.

Satisfied that he would get his way, Keeran bent and gently scooped Emily into his arms. She was a soft and light bundle, her breath a warm caress against his neck as she sighed sleepily and cuddled against him. Keeran inhaled as he straightened, his chest squeezing at the scent of her. She smelt of sunlight and flowers, she smelt of life, and he felt a yearning stir within him. He wanted to drink of that life, to bathe in it and perhaps redeem the soul he was sure he'd lost.

Mrs. MacBain cleared her throat. Reminded of her presence, he turned toward where she waited by the door and carried Emily forward.

"I asked her if she was married," Mrs. MacBain said

as she led him out of the library and along the hall toward the stairs to the bedrooms.

To Keeran, that comment came out of the blue. The question had never occurred to him. Now that she had brought it up, however, he suddenly felt himself tense in anticipation of the answer. A murmur of protest from the girl in his arms made Keeran realize that his hold had tightened possessively around her. He forced his muscles to ease as he asked, "Is she?"

"Nay."

This news was something of a relief to Keeran, though he couldn't say why. What matter was it to him whether Emily was married or not? He had just convinced himself of this when Mrs. MacBain added, "Not yet."

"Not yet?" he echoed, this time unable to deny the fact that this news had an effect on him. He didn't at all like the possibility that she might belong to another.

"Aye," Mrs. MacBain answered. "She was on her way to marry the earl of Sinclair when the ship ran into the storm. It was her uncle's wish."

Keeran glanced down at the woman in his arms. The earl of Sinclair? His very skin crawled at the idea of that elderly degenerate touching this fresh young woman. He knew the man, had known him since the fellow's birth. The Sinclair had been a cruel, heartless child and had grown into no better of a man. The old bastard had already beaten several wives to death, yet persisted in finding new victims. Keeran didn't at all like the idea of the fragile young woman he carried being the next victim on The Sinclair's list.

"She doesn't wish to," Mrs. MacBain went on as she gripped a handful of the plain cloth of her long skirt and lifted it out of the way so that she could lead the way up the stairs. "And now that her uncle is gone, there is no one to make her. But she fears she may be forced into it does the earl learn she still lives. She needs somewhere to stay for a bit and sort the matter out."

Keeran was struggling with this news when she added, "I hope ye don't mind, my laird, but I told her she might rest here a bit till she sorted the matter out."

Keeran heard the trepidation in her words and knew she was concerned that he would be upset by her invitation for Emily to stay. Several hours earlier he might have been. He certainly hadn't been pleased with the chit in his arms when his rest had been disturbed by the work she had set into motion in his home. Now, however, holding her warm body close in his arms, he began to wonder why he had been so upset. So, the castle would be a pleasant home for a bit. He should enjoy it while he could, rather than bemoan that it would end soon enough. Besides, he didn't wish to see the girl married to The Sinclair. He would rather kill the man first.

"Ye did say some time ago that we were to think of the castle as our home, my laird," Mrs. MacBain hurried on. "And . . . well . . . if this were my home, I would allow her to stay, so I—"

"I am no longer Laird," Keeran reminded her grimly as he carried Emily up the stairs behind the housekeeper's swaying skirts. It was the only comment he intended to make on the woman's action.

Emily was dreaming of being encased in strong, hard arms that made her feel as safe as a babe. It was one of those rare dreams when you actually knew you weren't awake. In her dream, she was reading in the library when her host returned. She set the book aside and smiled a polite greeting. Keeran MacKay smiled back, a soft smile, his eyes warm as they took in the white gown she wore. Before she could speak, he had crossed the room and scooped her into his arms to hold her close against his strong chest.

"My lord! I mean, sir," she corrected herself on a gasp. "This isn't proper."

"Do not berate me, my little beauty. I cannot help myself. Your loveliness, your wit, the way you have set my home to rights. All of it has set my heart aflame. You are the perfect woman for me, my little dove. I want to marry you, cherish you, and keep you safe from the arms of the lascivious earl of Sinclair."

"Oh, my lord," Emily breathed, her heart full to bursting at his passionate proclamation.

"I am no longer Laird."

Emily blinked her eyes open and stared at the face mere inches from her own. Keeran MacKay. He was holding her in his arms. Only the warm expression was missing. His face was cold and hard. He could have been a marble bust. At least, he could have been were he presently as pale as he had been the first two times she had met him. At the moment, he was flush with color. Very flush, really. She hoped it wasn't from carrying her. Carrying her?

Emily realized they weren't in the library. Keeran was carrying her, not just holding her in his arms, but actually carrying her abovestairs. This wasn't part of her dream. Alarm suddenly coursing through her, she glanced a little wildly about to see that they were trailing Mrs. MacBain up the stairs. She wasn't dreaming anymore.

Chapter Three

"No."

Emily's gaze shot to Keeran's face. His expression was stern and his arms tightened around her as he shook his head. He must have guessed by the way she had tensed that she was about to struggle and request to be set down.

Realizing the peril she would put them both in by struggling now, Emily forced herself to remain quiescent in his arms. Still, she was terribly uncomfortable there. It was one thing to dream that he had swept her into his arms and quite another to actually be in them. The reality was that after years of having proper behavior drummed into her head, Emily was terribly uncomfortable allowing a virtual stranger to carry her about. In truth, she was even embarrassed by her dream now that she was awake.

Why on earth would her sleeping mind think she would welcome the attentions of her host? The answer to that was simple enough. Emily knew herself well. She was aware that she'd been terribly lonely every moment since the death of her parents. She had yearned and yearned for years for someone to love her.

At first, Emily had worked very hard to gain that love from her uncle. She had behaved herself at all times and worked hard at her studies, knowing that her nanny and tutor would inform him. She had hoped that he would be pleased, but if he was, he had never let her know. He had never even let her know that he realized she was alive. John Collins, her father's brother, had dumped her at her deceased parents' country estate, never to bother with her again until her twentieth birthday. That's when he had sent for her to be brought to London to attend her engagement party. To say that the news of her engagement had come as something of a surprise was an understatement. And it hadn't been a pleasant one. The earl of Sinclair didn't exactly live up to Emily's childhood dreams of the perfect husband. In truth, he was worse than her wildest nightmares. She could only be grateful that the negotiations had apparently taken two years, from her eighteenth birthday till her twentieth. It was the earl of Sinclair who had told her that. Licking his lips as he tried to peer down the neckline of her gown, he'd said her uncle was a greedy man who had dragged the marriage negotiations out over two years in an effort to keep as much of her inheritance as he could. The Sinclair had said the words in such a way that his admiration was obvious.

"Here we are, sir."

Mrs. MacBain's voice intruded on Emily's thoughts,

and she glanced to that kindly older lady to see that they had reached the top of the stairs and traversed the hall while she had been lost in thought. They now stood outside the door to the guest room she'd been using and Mrs. MacBain was holding the door open. The older woman's eyebrows rose as they landed on Emily. "Oh. Ye're awake."

"Yes." Emily flushed, once again embarrassed to be in her host's arms. But when she began to shift in his arms, he merely tightened his hold a tad and strode forward, carrying her into her room and directly to the table where Mrs. MacBain had served her breakfast that first morning. He bent to deposit her in a chair at the table, then straightened and turned to his housekeeper.

"Hot cocoa."

Mrs. MacBain blinked in confusion. "Hot cocoa?"

"I would imagine a cup of warmed cocoa would help our guest get back to sleep," he pointed out. "Make it two cups please, Mrs. MacBain."

"Two cups?"

Emily couldn't help but notice the suspicion that crossed the older woman's face and the way she hesitated. She seemed torn between obeying her employer and remaining in the room where she no doubt felt she was needed to maintain the propriety of the situation. Men simply weren't supposed to be alone in a lady's room. It wasn't done. Still, Emily would be glad of the chance to speak to her host and finally thank him for saving her life and offering her shelter. Also, she had no wish to see the woman annoy her employer in an effort to protect Emily, an effort that surely wasn't needed. Keeran MacKay didn't appear the sort to attack her at the first opportunity, else he would have done so already. She had been in his home for two nights now without coming to harm.

Offering a reassuring smile to the housekeeper, she patted her hand and said, "We shall leave the door open, Mrs. MacBain."

The housekeeper glanced toward Emily uncertainly, then nodded and left the room. The moment her footsteps faded down the hall, Keeran MacKay finally took a seat and turned his attention to her.

His gaze seemed almost a physical touch as it slid over her features. Emily found herself unable to meet it, and glanced around the room before recalling that she wished to thank him. "I am sorry I fell asleep. I did try to stay awake. I wanted to speak to you, to thank you for saving me."

"You are most welcome." He looked terribly uncomfortable with her gratitude, so Emily let that subject drop and moved on.

"I also wished to apologize for what I said yesterday. Mrs. MacBain explained that it isn't your fault that—"

"Apology accepted," he interrupted, apparently equally uncomfortable with her regret.

With that, Emily didn't really know what else to say. Silence descended upon them, enclosing them in an oddly intimate quiet that the lack of light in the room only seemed to increase.

Emily glanced toward the candle Mrs. MacBain had set on the table by the door. It and the light spilling in from the hall were the only illumination to be had, leaving most of the room in darkness. Standing abruptly, she moved to collect the candle and started lighting several of the other candles spread around the room as she tried to think of something to talk about. In the end, however, it was he who broke the silence.

"Mrs. MacBain informs me you were to marry The Sinclair," Keeran said abruptly.

Emily's steps slowed, a grimace crossing her face. "Yes. My uncle arranged it."

"But your uncle is dead."

"Yes," she agreed.

"Will you be able to bow out of the wedding without fear of scandal?"

A little sigh slid from Emily's lips as she lit the last candle. Then she retraced her steps to the table and sank back into the seat he had set her in earlier, letting her shoulders drop dejectedly. "I have pondered the matter and fear I may not."

That realization was an unpleasant one that she had been trying to ignore. Emily had been taught well. A young woman alone in the world could not hope to avoid scandal if she broke off an engagement that had been arranged for her and agreed to. It seemed her choices were between marriage to the earl of Sinclair or ruin. Neither event seemed acceptable to her. But she could see no other option open to her.

Emily glanced toward her host, surprised to see displeasure on his face. She had to wonder if he too disagreed with marriage between the classes. That seemed the only reason to her that he might be dismayed at her possible nuptials. Not wishing to think about the future she was struggling desperately to find an alternative to, Emily shifted the subject to the changes she had in mind for his castle. Her host seemed rather annoyed and reticent on the subject at first, but soon ventured his opinions and desires on what should be done. When that conversation expired, they moved on to another and another.

Keeran MacKay had a keen mind and a sharp wit.

Emily enjoyed talking to him So much so that once or twice the thought crossed her mind that she wished it were *him* she was supposed to marry, rather than the earl of Sinclair. Were she to marry a young, handsome, and kindly man like Keeran MacKay, rather than the unpleasant earl, she would have gone to her betrothed willingly and without reservation. And her future wouldn't have seemed so bleak.

Emily wasn't sure what made her glance toward the door. A sound perhaps, or simply movement spotted out of the corner of her eye? Turning her head, she spotted Mrs. MacBain standing in the doorway and she smiled at her in greeting, then tilted her head to peer at her curiously. The housekeeper appeared to be frozen to the spot, her expression stunned as she stared at her employer. Emily turned to glance at Keeran, bewildered to find that he was merely smiling softly. There should be nothing surprising in that. He had been laughing at a jest Emily had told him, when Mrs. MacBain had drawn her attention. It had taken a good deal of effort to get that laugh out of the man, but Emily had been determined to bring a smile to his lips. The sadness she had sensed in him from the first made her own heart ache somewhat and she had wanted to lessen it for him, if only for a moment or two.

"Well." Mrs. MacBain seemed to snap out of her amazement and continued forward with the tray bearing two cups of hot cocoa. She glanced around the chamber as she walked and scowled at the mess it remained. The woman had wanted to have some of the workers clean this room as well today, but Emily had argued against it. She would rather see the main floor set to rights first. She'd started this project in an effort to make things nice for her host as a thank-you, not to make herself more comfortable. Besides, she only slept here; most of her waking time was spent below, so she also benefitted more from concentrating on that part first. The guest room could be seen to afterward, though she might not be here to witness it by then.

"'Tis fine," she said now to the housekeeper and received an affectionate, if exasperated, look for her efforts.

"'Tis not fine, but ye're a stubborn lass, so I'll let it go," the woman said.

Emily saw the curiosity cross Keeran's face, but he didn't comment or ask what they were speaking of; he simply sat quietly as his housekeeper set the cups of hot cocoa down. The woman hesitated then and Emily knew she was considering what she should do next. Propriety required that she stay, but it was obvious from Keeran's expression that he would order her to go if she tried. Besides, Mrs. MacBain had worked just as hard as Emily today. The woman must be as tired as she was.

Reaching out, Emily patted the hand holding the empty tray and smiled at her reassuringly. "The door is open, and we know you are nearby. We will be fine."

What she really meant was that *she* would be fine. Mrs. MacBain nodded solemnly. "Aye. O' course ye will. And no doubt ye're so tired that ye'll drop right off to sleep once yer done with yer cocoa." The last was said with a speaking glance toward her employer.

Emily bit her lip to keep back her amusement at his disgruntled reaction to it. It was obvious he was unused to his employee speaking to him in such a way.

"She is only concerned about propriety," Emily said soothingly once the woman had left the room.

Keeran made a face, but didn't comment. Instead, he stood and moved toward the door.

Afraid he was about to close it after she had promised the older woman that it would remain open, Emily was on her feet at once and hurrying after him.

"Oh, but I said we would leave it open," she protested, catching at his hand to stop him.

"I was only going to be sure she wasn't lurking in the hallway outside the room," he assured her and continued forward, drawing her along with him.

"She was tired. I think she has probably gone to bed," Emily commented as they both peered out to find the hall empty. When Keeran didn't comment, she turned to glance at him and found him staring down at their still-entwined hands. She flushed deeply and would have released him, but he closed his fingers over her own, holding her.

"So warm."

Those almost reverent words raised curiosity in Emily, but she pushed it aside as she realized that, indeed, compared to him she was a raging furnace. The hand holding her own was cool in comparison. Not unpleasantly so, rather like a nice breeze on sun-baked skin, but it was surely a sign that the man had just returned from outdoors and had caught a chill on his journey back from wherever he had dined this night.

"And *you* are chill," she exclaimed. "Come. We should build a fire to warm you."

Tugging her hand free, she hurried away toward the fireplace and Keeran stared after her. Had she bothered to look, he knew she would have found amazement on his face, for that's what he was feeling at the moment—amazement at her concern and kindness in wishing to see to his well-being. Of course, Keeran was not feeling chilled and the fire would do him no good, but he was touched and even surprised by her concern for him.

She had given him one surprise after another tonight. Earlier, when Mrs. MacBain had been here, he had noted the affectionate way Emily touched and patted the hand of the older woman as she spoke to her and had actually felt jealous of those touches and the women's easy affection. But then she had touched him while they spoke as well, and he had realized it was in her nature. Still, he drank in every smile and touch like a flower soaking up sunshine, and he had felt himself bloom beneath it just as a flower might, his defenses unfolding and opening to allow her near. Dangerously near, he feared. It had been decades since he had found anything to smile about. As for laughter, he couldn't recall doing so since the night Carlotta had killed his father and changed Keeran forever. Yet tonight he had smiled several times and even laughed once or twice. He had also simply enjoyed talking to her.

Emily was an intelligent woman, with surprising wisdom for someone who had lived so few years. He found he liked her, and this was a sad thing to Keeran. Her life span would be just a blink of time in his life. Soon her beauty would fade, her body would begin to wear out, and then she would leave this life and pass on to her just reward. Keeran would most likely be alive long after she had turned to dust. It was heartbreaking for him to even consider this, which was why he usually avoided allowing people into his life.

Realizing that he was being most unchivalrous, Keeran roused himself and moved to join her in kneeling on the cold stone before the hearth. He took over the task of building the fire, loading several more logs into the fireplace, then using the candle she fetched to set the kindling alight. Within moments a cheery fire was burning, giving off a good amount of heat.

"There." Keeran glanced to Emily to see that she had sat back on her haunches to survey the results of their efforts. She smiled at him now with satisfaction. "That should soon warm you."

Keeran found a rusty return smile and offered it to her, then stiffened when dismay suddenly crossed her face.

"Oh. You have hurt yourself."

"No, I haven't," was his surprised response.

"Yes, you did." Leaning forward, she brushed one finger gently over his lower lip. Keeran was so startled by the action that he didn't move. Then he was so startled by his own reaction to that one brief touch that he simply stared at her as she examined her finger, turning it for him to see. "You must have bit your lip without realizing it."

Keeran stared at the drop of blood on the finger a bare inch from his face. The faint scent of it mingled with her own to make a heady perfume. Without even thinking, he found himself leaning forward that last inch and slipping his tongue out to lick the pearl of liquid off her soft flesh. Realizing what he was doing, he froze, then glanced to Emily's face. Her eyes were wide, but with surprise, not alarm, and even as he watched, he could sense the changes taking place within her as she curled her fingers closed as if to hold on to the sensation of his touch, letting her hand drop to rest in her lap. He could almost hear the blood suddenly rushing through her body as excitement stirred within her, and certainly could smell that intoxicating elixir as it rose to the surface of her skin to make her blush prettily. Her beauty in the flickering firelight combined with that mixed scent to make him almost dizzy.

"Keeran."

It was the first time Emily had spoken his name. It slid from her lips on a soft sigh, tinged with a heartfelt pleading that was echoed in the luminous depths of her eyes, and he knew instinctively that while she had not lived as long as he, she was certainly as lonely as he. Here was a kindred soul, yearning for love as he was, yet fearful it would never be given. Without considering what he was doing, Keeran gave in to his wants for a change and closed the last bit of distance between them, this time to press his lips softly over her own.

It was like kissing a sun-baked apple, warm and sweet, with a hint of tang. As a human, Keeran had always had a weakness for apples, and now he was like a starving man presented with a whole apple pie still warm from the oven. He devoured her lips. He licked them, slid his tongue out to urge them apart, then slid his tongue between them to taste her inner sweetness.

Emily moaned as his tongue invaded her mouth. She had never been kissed like this. In truth, she had never been kissed. But she liked it. She only wished he would hold her as he had in both her dream and when he had carried her up here. She longed to feel his arms around her, making her feel safe again, for at that moment, she felt rather as if she might be falling off a precipice.

As if reading her thoughts, Keeran slid his arms around her, tilting his head to the side as he drew her deeper into the kiss. Emily moaned again and allowed her own arms to creep around his shoulders, tightening the embrace they shared until her breasts were pressed nearly flat between them. That aroused a whole new series of sensations within her, ones that were overwhelming and frightening, yet exhilarating at the same time. Gasping a breath of protest when Keeran broke the kiss, Emily let her head drop and pressed her mouth to his neck. In her excitement, she nipped at the roughened flesh there. The sudden short, breathless laugh Keeran gave then confused her almost as much as his words when he teased, "That's *my* job."

Emily would have asked what he meant by that comment, but a startled look had come over his face as if he were stunned by his own teasing, and he started to withdraw. Desperate not to see this interlude end, Emily tightened her hold on his neck and pressed her lips to his again. When he stilled in surprise, but did not kiss her back, she moved her mouth across his, then shyly slid her own tongue out to brush it across his lips as he had done to her.

The response she got to this ploy was startling. Apparently she had done it correctly, she decided with pleasure, as he began to kiss her again with a sudden urgency. This time his arms did not remain still around her, merely holding her close. His hands began to roam over her back, then slid around to smooth up over the cool cloth of her gown to cup her breasts. Emily gasped, her back straightening in a jerk that lifted the generous mounds upward out of his touch. Fortunately, his lovely hands followed, and Emily shuddered and quivered as excitement began shooting through her, little bolts of lightning that centered at her nipples but ran down to her stomach and lower still, causing an ache between her legs.

"My lord," Emily moaned as he broke the kiss and his mouth began to travel down her neck.

"Yes," he groaned back, not bothering to correct her reference to his title as he had on the stairs. He continued to palm and knead at the tightening flesh of one breast, but his other hand slid away, encircling her to urge her lower body closer as he pressed her upper body away with his caress. Both of them were still on their knees, and Emily gasped as his knee nudged between both of hers. But she couldn't seem to draw breath at all when his hand dropped to catch her beneath her bottom and urge her upward until she rode his thigh. Their bodies came together like two pieces of a puzzle.

"Keeran." She breathed his name and let her head drop back, offering his nibbling lips better access to her throat as his thigh rubbed against her, building her excitement.

Keeran gave a low groan as she offered her throat to him and his hunger became confused. The sweetness she unknowingly offered was tempting and, had he not just fed, he wasn't sure he would have been able to resist a taste of her sweet-smelling blood. But he had just eaten and another hunger consumed him now, one he had not really suffered for many a year. Just the same, he withdrew his mouth from the area of her neck and the temptation it offered, allowing it to drop toward her breast. He could feel the hard, excited pebble her nipple had become and tongued it through the cloth of her gown, but soon became frustrated with the hindrance.

With a growl, he tore at the cloth, rending it downward to expose the flesh he hungered for. Emily gasped out what might have been an "oh" or a "no"—Keeran wasn't sure which. It was enough to make him hesitate, panting with effort as he struggled to regain control of himself. He could have wept with relief when she then slid her hands into his hair and drew his mouth hungrily back to her own. It had been a surprised "oh," not a request for him to stop.

Keeran wanted to roar with triumph as he reclaimed

her lips. He thrust his tongue deep and found one naked breast with his hand. The heat of her seemed to encompass him as he touched and kissed her. She felt like a living flame in his arms, and she seemed to grow warmer with every passing moment, with every new caress. She was searing his cooler skin with her heat. Keeran wanted to feel that heat everywhere. He wanted to feel her skin burn against every portion of his flesh. She made him feel alive.

Keeran knew she was innocent, that he had nothing to offer her. All he could do was take, but he couldn't help himself. Breaking their kiss yet again, he ducked his head down and caught the warm flesh of her breast in his mouth to suckle eagerly. Her skin was salty and sweet all at once, a pleasure to his palate.

"Ohhh." Emily tightened her grip on Keeran's hair and pressed herself into him as he suckled. The ruined gown was drifting off her shoulders, leaving half her back bare to be heated by the fire. Keeran's cool caress of her flesh had been an exciting counterpoint as he had palmed her breast and teased her nipples. Now he was driving her wild with his mouth, showing her pleasure as she had never known, while at the same time causing a yearning she didn't understand. She wanted more, but what more could there be? How much excitement could she stand? And what would happen when she could stand it no more?

Cool fingers slid under her gown and brushed along the flesh of her inner leg. Emily instinctively clenched her legs around his thigh, trapping his hand there. She was suddenly aware that she had been riding his leg for several moments, unconsciously grinding herself against him, but she had no chance to feel embarrassed at this boldness. His hand did not remain trapped for long and was already creeping upward again. Emily found herself clutching at his hair reflexively, then tearing his head away from her bosom so that she might find his lips again. She seemed suddenly to need his mouth on hers more than she needed breath.

Keeran obliged her, claiming her lips, then urging them open so that he could thrust his tongue deep even as his fingers finally reached the center of her, the spot where all of her excitement and yearning were pooling. His touch was ice to fire and she felt the moisture created between her legs, then all she was aware of was that she was burning up as he caressed her.

Emily arched against him, her hands now slipping from his hair to clutch the cloth of his shirt. She was hardly aware that she had done so and that she was tugging at the expensive material until it rent apart, baring his chest. Though she had ruined the item of clothing, she felt no regret since the action allowed their flesh to meet. Emily groaned her pleasure into his mouth as her burning nipples rubbed across his chest. And she reveled in an answering groan from Keeran, pleased to know that he enjoyed it as much as she. *His* pleasure hadn't occurred to her until then. Emily had been too swept away by the sensations overwhelming her to even consider his enjoyment, but now her mind was turned in that direction and she wished to please him as he was pleasing her. The problem was, she was unsure how to do so and it was most difficult to think with him touching her the way he was.

Emily never got the chance to come up with an idea— if her poor woolly mind could have at that point—for it was at that moment that a shriek came from the hallway.

"Oh! Get away, ye silly cat, or ye'll be tripping me up and sending me to an early grave." More was said, but in an incomprehensible mutter that Emily couldn't make out. Not that she was paying much attention by that point. She and Keeran both froze at the first sound of the house-keeper's voice, then jerked apart to stare in horror at the open door leading into the hall. Emily had forgotten her-self so much that the fact that the door was open had quite fled her mind. Not only had she behaved shamelessly, she had done so with the door wide open for anyone to see. Not that there was anyone to see but Mrs. MacBain and her husband. Still, Emily could not believe she could be-have so badly. Where had all her propriety gone? She was settling into a nice round of self-recrimination when Keeran reminded her of the more important matter at hand by releasing her from his embrace and attempting to draw the torn edges of her gown together to cover her nakedness.

Flushing wildly, Emily glanced down to avoid his eyes and noted the damage she had done to his shirt as well. Reaching out, she tried to repair that damage at the same time, but she simply got in the way of Keeran's efforts.

"Never mind," he said, suddenly turning her away and urging her toward the bed. "I shall stop Mrs. MacBain in the hall and tell her that you are tired and taking yourself off to bed. I'll order her not to disturb you."

Emily nodded, then just as quickly shook her head. "But what of your shirt?"

Keeran drew the two sides to overlap, then tucked the shirt more firmly into the top of his black breeches. "It will be fine," he assured her when she looked doubtful. He started to turn away, then paused and turned back, pulling her close for another kiss. She suspected he had intended it to merely be a quick goodnight peck, but their passions were close to the surface yet and rekindled swiftly. The peck became a passionate melding of mouths that had Emily moaning in a heartbeat.

"Silly kitty. Get along with ye now. I've no time to be standing here petting the likes of ye."

Keeran pulled away with a curse as Mrs. MacBain's voice intruded again. It sounded terribly loud to Emily, as if she stood just outside the door or was speaking in an unusually loud tone.

"I had better go before she comes in here."

"Yes." Emily offered him a tremulous smile. "Thank goodness for the cat or she might already have come in."

Keeran paused, blinked, then nodded slowly and turned away. He pulled the door closed behind him. The moment it clicked into place, Emily hurried forward and pressed her ear to the wood to listen to what took place in the hall.

Mrs. MacBain's voice was loud and clear as she said, "Oh, sir. I was just coming to see if ye would care for more cocoa."

Keeran's voice was less loud and Emily couldn't quite make out what he said, then Mrs. MacBain spoke more quietly so that she couldn't be heard, either. Presuming they had moved off down the hall, Emily heaved a sigh and turned back to her room. It was aglow with candlelight and appeared terribly romantic. The dirt and dust were hardly noticeable in this soft light. Smiling, she drifted around the room, blowing out candles. Then she removed the torn gown, donned a fresh one, and climbed beneath the bedclothes. It was only once she was there, warm under the blankets and wrapped in the safe darkness of night, that she allowed herself to think about what had just taken place.

Keeran MacKay was an exceptional man who had done exceptional things to her. She couldn't wait for morning to come so that she could see him again.

He would have to avoid her from now on. Keeran told himself that sternly as he stared into the fireplace in the library. He was sitting in the same chair he had found Emily sleeping in when he had returned earlier, and he fancied he could still feel a trace of her heat there. He could definitely smell the sweet soap she had used in her bath. It seemed to cling to the fabric of the chair, a gentle reminder of her presence.

Keeran would have to content himself with that reminder. He had learned tonight that he didn't have the control he had always prided himself on. For over two hundred years, control had been an issue of utmost importance to him. The hunger, when it struck, was almost crippling in its strength, and the urge to drink and drink until his victim was dry, rather than stop and find another to feed from, could be strong, but he had fought these urges for what seemed like forever. Yet tonight another hunger had overwhelmed his supposed control, and it had taken only a matter of minutes. Seconds, perhaps. The scent of her, the taste of her mingled with that drop of blood he had unthinkingly licked from her finger, the look of yearning in her eyes . . . All of these things had combined to leave him helpless before desires he hadn't felt since his turning, in ways he hadn't even realized he still *could* feel.

Keeran wanted to tell himself that it had been so long since he had even felt these desires that he was simply taken by surprise, that the next time he would be more in control. But he knew it wasn't so. While it was true he hadn't felt desire for several decades, he knew that the next time he would not be more in control. Even now his body still ached for her, and he was fighting the insane urge to return to her room, climb into bed with her, and take all the sweetness and innocence she had to offer. The problem was that he had nothing to offer her in return. Eternal damnation and a waking death hardly seemed a fair trade for the passion, companionship, and love he was sure he could have with Emily. No. He would rather see her married to the earl of Sinclair than make her his partner in death. He definitely had to stay away from her. It would be hard to resist her, and he doubted she would aid in the endeavor, but for her own sake he had to.

Chapter Four

Emily finished applying the last bit of paint to the wall of the dining room, then stood back to survey her efforts. This was the special chore she had returned to the village for, earlier in the week. She had gone to purchase paint for the castle. Of course, it'd had to be ordered from the south and carted up to the village, but she had convinced the store owner—with the promise of a generous bribe—to leave his store in his wife's care and travel down to collect the paint himself to get it here quicker. Emily had been sure to order colors as close as possible to those that had already been peeling off the walls of the castle. She hadn't wished to upset Keeran unduly with too much change.

Her mouth turned into a sad moue at the thought of her host. He had given her a glimpse at the heights of passion, then withdrawn from her, leaving her to sink slowly on her own. And he *had* withdrawn from her. Much to Emily's disappointment, Keeran had already been gone for the day when she had gone below the morning after their interlude in front of the fire. She had been even more disappointed when not only did he not seek her out that evening, but there was no sign of him at all. But Emily had convinced herself that he must just be busy. However, when he was absent all the next day and evening, she'd been forced to admit that he was deliberately avoiding her. Emily had blamed herself. She had been too forward and allowed too many liberties, and now he no doubt had a disgust of her.

It was three nights before Emily saw Keeran again, and when she finally did see him, she was sure it was an accident, that he hadn't intended to run into her. That night, she had worked later than usual and was making her way toward the stairs when he had entered the hall from the other end. He'd paused, seemingly startled by her presence, then had moved slowly forward to meet her as if drawn by an invisible string. Pausing before her, Keeran had simply stared down at her for the longest time, a smile growing on his face that had confused her until he had reached out to run a finger lightly over her nose and announced, "You are the only woman I have ever met who looks adorable with dirt on her face."

Emily had blushed at the compliment, then caught his fingers as he would have drawn them away. Pressing them to her cheek, she'd said, "I'm sorry. I know I behaved badly. Truly, I have never behaved so with another man. I know that may be hard to believe, considering how I acted, but it's true. I—"

"Nay." Shock had covered his face at her words and he

had moved his fingers to cover her lips, silencing her. "Nay. You have nothing to apologize for, Emily. I—"

"Then why have you avoided me these past days?" She'd been unable to keep the pain and bewilderment out of her voice.

Keeran had stared at her helplessly, then groaned and pressed his mouth to hers. Passion had exploded between them, and Emily had found herself pressed up against the wall as his mouth devoured her lips and his hands traveled her body. Then his mouth had dropped to her neck, and Emily had given a surprised cry at the sharp pain that had claimed her as he nipped her throat.

Keeran had pulled away at once, horror on his face, then turned and rushed from the house. Emily had stared after him in shock, one hand pressed to the side of her throat. He had pulled away from her so swiftly that she had seen the long, sharp canine teeth protruding out over his lower lip. She'd stood there staring at the door he'd disappeared through, her thoughts in a whirl. He was never around in daylight. He'd somehow rescued her from that ship in a storm too violent for a rowboat to traverse it safely. He never ate at the castle, but "fed" elsewhere, as Mrs. MacBain had put it. The rumors in the village, the fact that the servants would not work before dawn or after dusk. . . . Keeran MacKay was a vampire.

Emily had still been leaning weakly against the wall when Mrs. MacBain had found her. The older woman had taken one look at her pale face and had begun to defend her employer. She had sat Emily down and told her what she knew of the tale of The MacKay; how he had been turned, and how he had lived his life since that day. Despite the villagers' fear of him, by all accounts he was a decent man, if man he could be called.

Emily had listened to the woman's words a little vaguely. In truth, this revelation didn't frighten her so much as shock her. Keeran MacKay hadn't hurt her in all the time she had been there. Besides, she had seen the horror on his face when he realized what he had done. He hadn't meant to nip her, perhaps hadn't bitten her at all, but nicked her by accident with one of his sharp teeth. Still, she had let the woman talk, taking each story of his kindness and courage to heart. It meant something that, despite the poor treatment he received from the villagers, Keeran still went out of his way to search out missing children and such. It meant that he was a good man, a decent man, and that he loathed himself as much as the villagers did—else he wouldn't allow them to treat him as they did. Now she understood the sadness and torment in the depth of his eyes. He saw himself as a monster and, as such, denied himself any semblance of a normal life, neither allowing friendships nor love to blossom, even balking at having a comfortable home. Her heart had ached for him in that moment, and Emily had determined that she would be his friend if he would allow nothing else.

She had taken to spending her evenings in the library, dozing until she heard him return home, then seeking him out and insisting he join her in tea by the fire. He did join her, though he never drank the tea, but merely warmed his hands on the steaming cups she poured him. They had never once spoken of what had happened or the fact that she knew what he was. They had spent many an enjoyable night talking by the fire, but had not had a repeat of the passion they had previously enjoyed. Keeran was now holding himself at a distance. Emily suspected he was afraid to let her in. She had done everything she could think of to try to break through the barrier he had erected, but nothing had worked. She was beginning to lose heart.

Emily felt time weighing on her and knew she must make a decision about her life soon. No matter how much she enjoyed his company and the peace of his home, she could not remain here forever. At least not without an invitation.

"My."

Emily turned at that long drawn out word and forced a smile for Mrs. MacBain as the woman peered around the newly painted room.

"It looks lovely."

"Yes, but I fear I have completely ruined this gown," Emily said ruefully as she glanced down at the stains and paint spatters covering her borrowed blue dress. She had worn it for most of the hard work, saving the few other gowns from the chest for the evenings when she relaxed in the library.

"'Tis a fair trade, I should say," Mrs. MacBain informed her grimly, and Emily managed not to grimace at those words with their gentle reprimand. The housekeeper had wanted Emily to allow the servants to do the painting, but she hadn't wished to pull them away from their efforts cleaning the rest of the keep just yet. They were making such good headway, she hesitated to distract them.

"I hope your employer feels the same way."

Mrs. MacBain glanced at her sharply at those stiff words, then reached out to pat her arm. "Never mind, dear. He'll come around."

Emily wasn't sure what the older woman meant by that, so didn't comment. She merely began collecting the paintbrush and paint together, intending to clean up.

"Leave those. I'll tend to them," the housekeeper insisted. "Mr. MacBain has already carried the water up for yer bath. It'll grow cold if ye don't use it soon. It's why I came to find ye. Why dinnae ye go bathe and change into yer night things? I'll bring yer dinner up to ye. Ye've circles under yer eyes from exhaustion, and should rest this evening."

Emily hesitated, but allowed herself to be convinced in the end and murmured her thanks as she left the room. She had been working at a frenzied pace these last days, trying to avoid thinking about leaving and how to handle the earl of Sinclair if he should try to pressure her into marrying him as she feared. It was beginning to catch up to her. That wasn't the reason the housekeeper was trying to convince her to remain in her room tonight, however. At least, Emily didn't think it was. She suspected the woman feared her employer's reaction to her painting the dining room.

A glance out the windows as she walked into the entry to start abovestairs showed her that the sun was sinking into the horizon. Emily supposed that was why Mrs. Mac-Bain had fetched her to send her to her room: to get her out of the way before Keeran awoke and saw that she had painted his dining room. It was the one plan she had not mentioned to him, wanting to keep it as a special surprise. Mrs. MacBain was dubious about whether it would be a pleasant one.

Emily entered her room to find that the MacBains had indeed already prepared her bath. The tub sat before a roaring fire and several candles lit the room. Emily slid out of her dress and sank into the steaming water with a sigh.

She would have to leave all this soon. She would have

liked to stay. It was why she had delayed her decision so long, but Emily had come to the conclusion as she painted today that, though she wasn't looking forward to the prospect, she couldn't continue to delay leaving indefinitely.

Pushing the thought from her mind, she concentrated on scrubbing the paint from her skin and washing her hair, then stepped out of the tub, dried herself, and donned the nightgown and robe that had been laid out on the chair near the fire. Finally, she sat in that chair to brush her long hair. The golden tresses had nearly dried when the door to her room suddenly burst open and Keeran stormed in.

Startled at his sudden appearance, Emily stood slowly and faced him, alarm on her face. He hadn't been in her room since the night he'd carried her up from the library. He didn't look pleased to be here now. A scowl made him appear rather ferocious as he moved to her at a quick clip.

"You have to stop. Just stop!" he snapped.

Emily's eyebrows flew up on her forehead. "Stop what?"

"Stop everything. You cannot simply show up one day and begin cleaning and painting and disrupting my life like this."

He looked more pained than angry, she decided, and felt herself relax as understanding reached her. Her voice was gentle when she asked, "Why? Because you do not feel you deserve it?"

He reacted as if she had slapped him, his head jerking back in reaction to her words. He spoke through gritted teeth when he said, "I do *not* deserve it. I am a monster. A beast. I—"

She gave a derisive snort that silenced him and left

him staring at her blankly. Taking advantage of his silence, Emily said, "You are hardly a beast, Keeran. I have been here over a week and come to no harm."

"I nearly bit you," he reminded her grimly.

"Yes," she agreed. "But you didn't. Nor do you feed off your own people, from what I can tell, and those you do feed on suffer no lasting effects when they very easily could."

"You don't understand."

"But I do," she assured him. "I do understand. Beasts do not trouble themselves to hunt for lost children."

He stared at her silently for a moment, then said, "You shall depart and the servants shall follow and I shall be left to watch my home decay and fall into ruin again. It would be easier if you just leave it as is rather than give me this taste of life."

"Oh, Keeran," Emily breathed. Pained by what these words revealed of his life, she reached out and touched his cheek.

They stood frozen like that for a moment and she could see him struggle with himself, then he gave in with a groan and turned his mouth into her palm, placing a kiss there. Before her brain could quite register the gentle kiss, he turned back to her and pulled her into his arms. Emily went willingly, raising her mouth to be plundered even as she stepped into his embrace. He was hard and cool, handsome and tragic, exciting and passionate.

Emily opened to him like a bud, the petals of her mouth spreading to allow him in to taste her nectar. Keeran drank deeply of that nectar, his hands sliding over the soft, thin robe she wore and molding her to his body. But soon that wasn't enough and he knew he must have more. This, of course, was what he had feared, why he had tried to avoid her this last week. Not that he had succeeded. His much-vaunted control had deserted him with her entrance into his life, and, after those first two nights, Keeran had found himself seeking her out every evening, spending hours simply watching the glow of firelight on her golden hair and enjoying the way her lips moved as she spoke. But he had managed to maintain some restraint. He had not allowed himself to kiss or even touch her, keeping at least that distance between them. Now his sensation-starved hands were eager to feel more than the cloth of her robe. Tugging the sash loose, he dropped it to the floor, then slid his hands beneath the robe to spread over the warm flesh of her stomach. He encountered material again here, but it was the even thinner cloth of a nightgown, a gossamer web over her nakedness.

Keeran slid his fingers up over the material and groaned in his throat with pleasure as he caught her breasts in his hand. When Emily gasped, he caught the sound with his mouth as she pressed into his touch. As pleasurable as this was, he still yearned to touch her naked flesh. Reaching down, he caught at the long skirt of the gown and tugged it upward, gathering it until he could slip his hand beneath and across her warm skin. She felt as good as he recalled, her leg smooth and warm. Keeran let his hand drift around to her bottom, cupping the globe with one palm and urging her against his hardness, then let his hand drop and slid it around in front until he could trail his fingers up one inner thigh.

Emily cried out into his mouth and began to lean heavily into him as he reached what he sought. Keeran immediately eased them both to kneel on the fur that had been set before the fire. He had noticed when he first entered that this room had finally been seen to. It was now as clean as most of the rest of the castle and had several added comforts since his last visit. Keeran was grateful for this one as they came to rest on the soft fur.

Breaking their kiss, he trailed his lips over her throat, then quickly away as a new hunger tweaked at him. He had come directly here after awaking and seeing the newly painted dining room. He should have learned from the experience earlier in the week and fed first. He could still hardly believe that he had nearly bitten her then. But that hunger was threatening to make itself known and was held at bay only by his desire. Once away from the temptation of the pulsing vein in her throat, Keeran felt that hunger ease a bit and managed to push it out of his mind as he urged Emily further back over his arm and made his way toward the mound of one breast. That first night, desperate desire had made him mouth her through the cloth of her gown. Tonight that would not do. Tugging the scooped neckline to the side, he managed to force it far enough down her arm that one breast was revealed. Keeran immediately lowered his face and sucked one engorged nipple into his mouth, teasing it until Emily was shifting and making exciting little mewls of sound.

"Keeran . . . please . . . I want . . . " Her words ended on a gasp as he slid one finger inside of her, stretching and pleasuring her at the same time. His body tightened in anticipation as her wet heat closed around the digit. He could already imagine what it would feel like to be inside of her. He wanted to be there right then, but knew she wasn't ready. He would have to be patient. The fact that he could made him wonder if some bit of control didn't remain to him after all.

Emily was coming apart. Keeran's delicious touch was making her mindless. She wanted it to go on forever, but this time she wanted to touch him in return. Forcing his mouth away from the breast he had bared, she urged him back enough that she could reach between them and begin to tug at his shirt. She managed to free the cloth from his breeches, but then needed his cooperation to remove it completely. Much to her combined regret and relief, Keeran gave up caressing her long enough to tug the shirt up over his head. He didn't immediately return to caressing her again, but kissed her instead as she let her hands travel over his chest and shoulders, enjoying the feel of him.

She was aware that he was urging her backward as he kissed her. They were both still kneeling, so she was being forced back onto her haunches. She ended lying in an odd and even slightly uncomfortable position. But Emily forgot that discomfort when he suddenly straightened and pushed her gown up her thighs, stomach, then up further until her breasts were revealed as well. Shock took the place of confusion for a second, as she realized she was now splayed out before him like a buffet, her knees spread wide, her buttocks resting on her heels and raising the center of her as if in offering.

Uncertainty and shyness filled Emily then and she tried to rise back up, but Keeran held her in place by lowering his head to her breast again. The shock of sensation that shot through her as he suckled her was enough to make her hesitate, and when his hand slid between her open thighs once more, it was enough to keep her still.

If there was any discomfort now, Emily no longer felt it. She was aware only of the pleasure he brought her with his mouth and caresses. Disappointment drifted through her when he left her breast, but then the stretched muscles of her stomach quivered and jerked as he trailed kisses down over it. She had a moment's shock and embarrassment when he continued downward until his face disappeared between her legs. Then the sensations he awakened within her pushed those aside and she cried out with unbearable pleasure instead.

When his hands drifted up to catch both her breasts as he continued to caress her with his mouth, Emily caught at and covered them with her own, squeezing them tightly in place.

Keeran immediately pinched at her pebbled nipples, tweaking them and adding to her excitement until she thought she could stand no more. It was then that something burst within her, convulsing her muscles and making her cry out his name in mindless delight.

Keeran murmured soothing words and held her as she rode the crest of the ecstasy he had given her. Then he straightened and scooped her into his arms. Emily wrapped her own arms around his shoulders and pressed her face into his neck so that she could kiss him there with joy and gratitude. She felt as if she had taken an elixir and was now in some sort of drugged state, her mind floating loosely. She was glad he was carrying her, for the muscles in her legs—in her whole body, really—were trembling so that she didn't think she could walk.

Halfway to the bed he whispered her name and Emily lifted her head to peer at him. The moment she did, he bent to claim her lips in a kiss. Much to her amazement, the passion she'd thought had burnt itself out immediately burst back to life within her and she eagerly kissed him back.

He continued to kiss her as he crossed the room. When they reached the bed, rather than set her down, he settled on the soft surface with her still in his arms. Emily found herself seated in his lap, her arms clinging around his shoulders as he kissed and held her. Her gown had fallen to cover her breasts, but caught at her waist when he had picked her up. Now she felt him tugging it upward. They were forced to break the kiss so that he could lift it off over her head. He tossed it carelessly aside, then began to kiss her again as his hands slid unhampered over her body.

Emily allowed her hands to move over his chest and arms, then let them drop down over his stomach until they reached the top of his knee breeches. Keeran immediately groaned into her mouth and she felt the muscles in his stomach ripple. Feeling encouraged, she let her hand drop lower, but didn't get far before Keeran caught her hand and drew it away.

"But I want to touch you too," Emily whispered in protest when he broke their kiss to trail his lips over her cheek to one ear.

"Later," he assured her. "I am having enough trouble controlling myself."

Emily hadn't a clue what he was talking about when he spoke of control, but wasn't in the mood to question him. Contenting herself with running her hands over his shoulders, chest, and back, she sighed and arched and shifted into his caresses as his fingers slid between her legs and danced busily over her flesh, driving her to a fevered pitch. She was mindless with desire when he finally lifted her off of his lap to lay her back on the bed, and she shifted restlessly as he quickly removed the rest of his clothes.

Emily opened her arms in welcome when he rejoined her in bed, then dragged his head down to kiss him. She thought he would return to caressing her again and mentally prepared herself for the first shock of his touch. She wasn't quite prepared, however, when he suddenly slid into her. She cried out, more with surprise than pain, and stiffened beneath him at the unexpected intrusion, then realized that he, too, had stilled.

Emily opened her eyes to see his tense face, then shifted beneath him experimentally, wondering why there hadn't been more pain. Her nanny had said there would be horrendous pain the first time when she had spoken to her about the wedding night to come. But the small twinge Emily had experienced was far from horrendous.

A low groan from Keeran made her still her experimentation. She glanced at his face to see his agonized expression and wondered if she had misunderstood her nanny. Perhaps it wasn't the woman who suffered the first time. She was worrying over that when Keeran opened his eyes and speared her with a glance.

"Are you all right?" he asked gruffly.

Emily swallowed, then nodded solemnly.

"Thank God," he growled and immediately began to move. Emily almost protested when he withdrew from her, but the breath she had inhaled to speak with was expelled on a sigh as he immediately slid back into her again. Unsure what else to do, Emily slid her arms and then her legs around Keeran and simply held on, allowing her body to move, arch, and clench as it saw fit. Her body seemed to have a better idea of what to do than her mind did, which was perhaps a good thing, since her mind appeared to have decided to bow out of this undertaking. Emily was simply a mass of sensation now, her body singing to the tune he played.

Keeran drove into her over and over again, his body screaming with pleasure as her moist heat welcomed him. He had known it would be like this. Her body was a warm welcome on his return from battle, a flaming fireside after a cold ride through a blizzard. She heated him and made him feel as though his lifeless heart beat again.

Emily cried his name breathlessly, her nails biting into

his back as she urged him on, and Keeran growled with the excitement that was building to an unbearable level. Bending his head, he caught her mouth in a passionate kiss, then made a trail of kisses to her neck, where the scent of her excited blood was intoxicating. He inhaled the sweet scent, his growl growing in his throat, then felt his body buck and instinctively sunk his teeth into her tender flesh as pleasure engulfed him.

Emily's eyes flew open with shock as she felt his teeth slice into her throat. There was one moment of searing pain, then ecstasy replaced it and slid through her body. She felt that explosion of pleasure she had experienced earlier, only far more intense, and allowed it to overwhelm her as darkness closed in.

Emily opened her eyes and found herself peering through the open drapes at the predawn sky. She stared at the lightening sky for a minute, then a sound made her turn her head to find Keeran dressed and seated in a chair beside the bed. He sat in shadow, his expression obscured. It was then she recalled what they had done, and his biting her. Had he *turned* her?

"Am I—?"

"No," he assured her quickly and leaned forward to clasp her hands. "I stopped as soon as I realized what I was doing. I am sorry, Emily. So sorry. I never meant to . . . I shouldn't have . . ."

"It's all right," Emily said quietly, and meant it. She didn't mind that he had bitten her. She was only sorry that he had stopped before—

"Don't think that way!" he snapped harshly.

Emily blinked in surprise that he had been able to read

her thoughts. It seemed they had a connection now, and if that was the case, he knew she loved him. There was now nothing to be gained by not speaking of her love and the fact that she wished to stay with him, that she, in fact, would do whatever was necessary to be allowed to stay with him.

His hand squeezed hers almost painfully, drawing her gaze again. "Never think that way. You do *not* want to be like me."

"Perhaps not, but I *would* like to be *with* you, and if I must become like you to do so—"

"No." He covered her mouth to silence her blasphemy. But he was looking tortured now, almost desperate. "You don't know what you're saying. You don't understand."

"You are the one who doesn't understand," Emily interrupted, knocking his hand away from her mouth with sharp impatience. "Do you think I just let every man I meet make love to me? Nay. I love you, Keeran."

"No."

"Yes."

"No!" he roared, suddenly on his feet and pacing away from the bed, then back. "You cannot love me."

"I can and I do," she insisted.

"Emily." He bent to take her hands beseechingly. "I have nothing to offer you."

"You have yourself. That is more than enough."

"You can't mean that."

"I do."

"No. You don't, you *can't* know what you're saying." Keeran turned away, pacing several feet before stopping. He was tempted by her offer. To keep her with him for eternity, to have her to hunt with, to curl up by the fire in the library and read with on cold nights. . . . Keeran was tempted. Terribly tempted. He had never before wanted anything so much in this imitation of a life he lived. But he couldn't do it. Emily had crawled inside his heart. He didn't know how; he had thought that organ long dead, yet there it was. Not only had she cleaned and brightened his home, she had brightened his night and filled his heart as well. She was his sun and he wanted desperately to keep her with him. But the love that made him desperate to keep her by his side was the same love that wouldn't allow him to do it. Keeran had taken her innocence; he would not take her life. He could never condemn her to this eternal death, and damn her soul to eternal hell.

Emily watched Keeran's stiff back and waited breathlessly. She knew he was considering her words and making his decision. Her happiness depended on that decision. When he finally turned back to her, his expression held his answer, and Emily felt something begin to die within her. Her heart perhaps, or hope? He did not speak right away, but simply stood staring at her hard as if memorizing what she looked like. When he finally spoke, his voice was polite, as empty and polite as the words he mouthed.

"The dawn comes. I must leave you. I will arrange a carriage and outriders to take you home when I rise tomorrow night. With any luck you shall be able to leave first thing the morning after. You should sleep now." He didn't stay to wait for Emily's response, but strode from the room once the words had left his mouth.

Emily stared at the door he closed behind him and felt her heart breaking. She had lost. Her hopes of happiness had just walked out of the room.

Chapter Five

Emily did not sleep. For one moment, she considered bursting into weak tears and sobbing her broken heart out, but then she decided that would be a horrible waste of time, and time was something she now had very little of. The moment the sun set on this day, Keeran would make the necessary arrangements to see her out of his life. She had to think of a way to convince him to let her stay, to let her love him.

Tossing the bedclothes aside, she slipped out of bed and began to dress as she sought the answer to this problem. Several ideas occurred to her, but Emily discarded each of them for one reason or another. It was when she went down to join the MacBains in the kitchen that the perfect idea came to her. And it was prompted by Mrs. MacBain asking which room she planned to paint that day and if she wouldn't allow some of the new servants to help her this time.

Until that point, Emily had not even considered painting today. She had a more important matter to consider, but the housekeeper's question had made her decide that while she would not take the time, there was no reason she could not take a couple of the new servants off cleaning detail and put them to work painting. Then she had pondered which room to start with and the paint available. There was a sky blue to replace the faded blue in one salon, sunny yellow for the other . . .

Her thoughts had slowed as an idea began to niggle at her.

"Emily, dear?" Mrs. MacBain had said, rousing her from her thoughts. "Is something wrong?"

Emily had blinked and turned to glance at her. "No," she'd said slowly. "No. Nothing's wrong. In fact, you've given me a brilliant idea."

"I have?" the older woman asked with surprise.

"Yes." Emily's mouth widened in a glorious smile. "And if it works, you will have made me the happiest woman in the world."

"Oh . . . well . . . that's nice," she said uncertainly.

"Yes, it is," Emily agreed, and pushing away her untouched food, she stood excitedly. "I shall need your help. And all the servants. We shall need the paint too." She began pacing as she ticked off her list, then whirled and rushed forward to hug the housekeeper. "Oh, Mrs. MacBain, I think this might work."

Keeran woke to complete silence. He had become so accustomed to the activity and presence of others in his home that this silence seemed unusual and even ominous. Then he recalled what had happened last night and understood. Emily had probably told Mrs. MacBain that she was to leave tomorrow, and the new servants had already decided they were through with his home. This seemed the likely answer.

It was for the best, he told himself as depression settled over him. Now he could return to his routine. Endless days and nights of misery and gloom.

Impatient with his own morbid thoughts, Keeran sat up and slipped from his resting spot, telling himself that this had been his choice. Emily had offered to spend eternity with him. It was he who had turned her away, refusing to sully her any further than he already had.

Thoughts of Emily made him realize that her presence seemed somehow subdued this night. While he could feel her in his home, it was not the strong, vibrant presence he had become used to. It was quiet and tense, almost waiting. But waiting for what? he wondered as he mounted the stairs to the first level of his home.

There were no torches to light the way, and the MacBains were nowhere to be seen when he entered the kitchen. It was only then that he paused and closed his eyes, seeking them with his mind. He quickly realized that they were not there and felt concern grip him. Mrs. MacBain was terribly fond of Emily. Surely she wasn't so upset about his taking her innocence that she had quit his employ?

Nay, Keeran thought. The housekeeper couldn't know about that. Emily certainly wouldn't have told her. However, she might have told her that he was arranging tonight to send her away, he realized, and hoped that the older woman wasn't so upset with this news that she had quit. His next thought was that it didn't really matter. Once Emily was gone, he would hardly care if anyone else were there or not.

Leaving the kitchen, he moved silently along the dark hall, his steps slowing as he saw that candlelight was spilling from the open ballroom door ahead. Suspecting that he would find Emily there, Keeran hesitated, unsure he had the strength to resist her should he find himself in her presence. But in the end, he didn't have the willpower not to see her. Approaching the door cautiously, he peered into the room, then froze, his eyes widening at the display he found there.

His first thought was that Emily must have purchased every candle for sale in Scotland. And perhaps all those in England too. Hundreds of them littered the room. Some were in candleholders of varying sizes—seemingly every candleholder in his castle had been put to use—but most had simply been affixed to the floor by their own wax. None more than a foot apart, they littered the ballroom like a field of flaming flowers. And in the center stood Emily, a lone rose in her pink gown.

Keeran had never seen such a beautiful spectacle. Leaving his place by the door, he walked the wide path that had been left through the candles and joined her in the circle of light. Without a word, he took her in his arms and there in the field of flames he kissed her with the passion of centuries, then slowly stripped off her clothes and his own and lay her down on them. Her skin glowed opalescent in the candlelight as he made love to her, the small drops of perspiration that formed on her brow catching the light like diamonds.

Keeran's dead heart swelled and squeezed by turn, glory and pain battering him at once. This was a moment he knew he would remember into eternity and every time he recalled it, he would suffer both agony and exultation. This was a gift like no other.

"I love you," Emily whispered in the last moment of their passion, and Keeran squeezed his eyes closed, trying to memorize the sound and inflection of the words so that he could replay it in his head in the centuries to come. He was determined that memories were all he would allow himself to hold on to from this night.

When it was over, he rolled onto his back and pulled her to rest against him, cushioning her head on his shoulder and hushing her when she would have spoken. He just wanted to hold her for a moment and pretend that it could be for longer than that, that he needn't get up, redon his clothes, and make his way to the village to hire someone to see her home to England.

They remained like that until Keeran felt Emily shiver against him, and he became aware of the gentle breeze wafting around them. Opening his eyes, he glanced around and realized that every door leading out onto the terrace beyond was open. No doubt this was to allow the smell of fresh paint to escape, for Keeran could see that the walls had been painted the sky blue of a sunny day as he recalled it to look. Unfortunately, it was also allowing a cool evening breeze in.

He started to sit up, intending to help her dress lest she catch a chill, but she stopped him with a hand on his chest. "Please. Just a little longer."

Keeran hesitated, then pulled her closer in his arms and remained reclining, no more eager than she was for this interlude to end and reality to intrude. He slid one hand along her arm and stared up at the ceiling, his mind tortured with the fact that he would soon lose her . . .

until he noticed that the ceiling was freshly painted as well.

Emily held her breath. She had been waiting for him to notice the ceiling; it was her true gift to him, *and* her message. It was the idea that Mrs. MacBain's question had given her that morning.

"It's the sun," Keeran said suddenly, and she felt her throat constrict at his thick voice. He was obviously moved by the painting she and the servants had worked on for most of the day. While they had painted the walls the blue of a sunny day, the ceiling of the ballroom now sported a large, bright sun and fluffy white clouds on a paler blue sky.

"Yes," she managed to say past the lump in her throat. "The sun. Daylight. A sunny day, painted so that you can see it every night when you wake up, Keeran."

Easing her off his shoulder, he stood slowly and turned in a circle, his gaze drinking in this, his first sight of sunlight in more than two hundred years. "It looks so real."

He reached up as if to catch at a cloud, then let his hand drop slowly.

"Yes." Emily stood up beside him and touched his arm. "I can have the sun and you too, Keeran. This is enough for me."

He stared at her sadly, then shook his head. "But it isn't real."

"No," she admitted, then straightened her shoulders and prepared to argue for her happiness. While painting that day, she had considered very carefully what she should say, and now she took a deep breath and made her case. "No, it isn't real. But 'tis as real as my life will be if you send me away, Keeran, for I will always, until my death, only be pretending at living without you. I will be a pale portrait of the woman I could be, just as this is only a painting of daylight. There will be no passion, no husband, no family, no love, because none can replace you in my heart. I love you, Keeran. Do not send me away and damn me to a half-life without you."

"Ah, Emily." His voice was filled with regret, and she knew what was coming even before he said, "You will forget me. You will—"

"Learn to love another?" Emily interrupted with a sharpness that silenced him. "Do you see me as so fickle? Is my heart so weak and untrue to you? Then allow me to correct this mistaken impression of yours. *I will love no other.* I shall for the rest of my days sit and recall my time with you. I shall become a lonely old spinster, yearning for a lonely man who hides in his crumbling castle from the love of a woman who would explore the night world at his side and hold him in her heart forever, if only given the chance."

Dear God. Keeran closed his eyes. She was there, so close he could touch her if he had the courage. She was a flame of vibrant life that had brought laughter and joy to his empty home and light to his eternal night. She had stirred the dead ashes of his heart back to painful life so successfully that it now ached with his love of her. He wanted so badly to keep her with him, but—

"I am not a man," he argued desperately, having to fight himself and his own wants now, as well as fight her. "Carlotta took my soul and damned me to—"

"Perhaps she didn't," Emily interrupted.

"What are you saying? Of course she did. She turned me."

"Aye, she turned you, Keeran. But perhaps she couldn't take your soul with that act. Surely only you can give it away and damn yourself." Seeing the hope budding on his face, she took his hand. "Keeran, you told me that you wanted to stay on that bed and allow the sun to end your existence after she turned you. If that had happened, do you think you would have gone to hell or heaven?"

"Heaven. It was probably my only way to get there."

A smile blossomed on Emily's face. "Because you would have then been choosing your own death over others'."

"Yes." His expression was tormented. "But don't you see? I didn't have the courage to do so. I damned myself with my own cowardice."

"By choosing life?" she asked, then shook her head. "Nay, Keeran. According to the Church, it is a sin to take your own life."

"Murder is a sin, too."

"But you have never killed anyone to continue your existence," she pointed out, then asked worriedly, "Have you?"

"No." He shook his head slowly.

She beamed her relief at him. "Then you are not the monster you think yourself to be. Keeran, I think whether we go to heaven or hell depends entirely on our own decisions, not on those made for us or things done to us. The woman who is violated does not carry the stain of that sin on her soul; her rapist does. Carlotta took your life and turned you into a vampire. But you chose not to take life to sustain your own, and *never* to use your strength and powers to harm others. In fact, you have taken the time and trouble to save many a life, despite how poorly you were treated for it in return. Surely, you cannot be damned."

He was silent for several moments, digesting what she said, then a smile spread his lips. "When put that way . . ." His eyes found hers, then he reached for her hand. "Emily."

"Yes." She answered his unspoken question. "I still want to be with you. I will give up the life I have known for an eternity with you."

"It can be hard at times," he warned.

"Life is hard at times," she said simply.

"You will miss the sun, and have to watch those you care for go to the grave before you."

"So long as it isn't you I must watch go to the grave, Keeran. I can bear anything else but that."

"Oh, my love." He pulled her into his arms and held her close, hugging her as if he would never let her go. "You have given me so much in the short time since you entered my life. Love, laughter, sunlight, hope. And I have so little to offer you in return."

"Aye." Emily sighed, then leaned back to peer up at him and say, "Saving my life, saving me from marrying The Sinclair, a home, love, eternal life. Really, you have so little to offer, I should ask for a dower."

A burst of laughter slipped from his lips. It was followed by a surprised expression that made Emily smile. He was always so surprised to find himself amused. His existence must have been terribly gloomy and lonely all these centuries. She would see to it that it never was again.

Reaching up, she slid one hand into the hair at the back of his head and drew him down for a kiss that soon turned passionate, but after a moment, Keeran caught her hands and broke the kiss. "We should go to your room."

"Nay." She pressed a kiss to the side of his mouth, then the column of his throat, before leaning back to smile at him. "Here. In the sunlight."

Keeran glanced around at the candles and fireplace, then finally to the sunrise she had painted. "Yes. Here in the sunlight."

HEART OF
THE MUMMY

Saranna DeWylde

Dedication:

To Jess Hartley, Crystalrain Love, Arlene Bishop
Whitworth, and Colleen Thompson for helping me name
my heroine and get to know her.

To Angelee Van Allman, a brilliant artist and dearest
friend. There is no better tribute I have to offer than to
give you your own art museum.

To Deana Holmes, my platonic life partner. Love you!

Author's Note

Khepri is the name of a scarab-faced god in the Egyptian pantheon. I had already chosen that for the moon priestess's name when I learned of the deity. The scarab just happened to be the inspiration.

Chapter One

D r. Kalila Corazon Blake looked out across the sea of young, eager faces as they waited for her presentation on the Egyptology exhibit to begin. Aside from being on dig sites, this part of her job was her favorite. She loved sharing her knowledge and her experiences with kids. Each age group brought her different kinds of joys. Grade-school kids were always wide-eyed little sponges, ready to devour every bit of information she had to share. They were so caught up in the splendor of it all. They got excited about the pyramids and pharaohs the way they got excited about dinosaurs.

Middle-school kids were still pretty in to it, and they asked a lot of great questions. Kalila had to bring her A game to answer them all. But it was the high-school kids who were the biggest challenge, and secretly, she liked them best. They always pretended to be too cool to be interested. The prevailing attitude for a lot of them was that they were just there because they got to miss school. She had to work to engage them, but once they did, they were absolutely delightful.

Kalila could share certain things with the high-school kids that she couldn't with the younger ones. She didn't have to sanitize the royal intrigues, or the step-by-step mummification process that always burrowed into the older kids' imaginations. If she had enough time, she liked to use the mummy part from the *Tales from the Darkside* movie. It was definitely ridiculous, but it drew the kids in. It got them excited and open, and then they were just like the grade-schoolers again: little sponges ready to soak up any information she had to share.

Today, she had the high schoolers. Unfortunately, she didn't have the time to include that portion of the movie. She hoped having a real mummy for them to examine would make up for it.

"Hi, guys! I'm Dr. Kalila, and I'm the resident Egyptologist here at the Van Allman Museum of Art. I have bachelor's degrees in archaeology and classical studies, an MA in museum administration, and a PhD in Egyptology." She grinned widely and looked around at the faces once again. "And mummies are my jam."

More interest. A couple of kids who had been on their phones put them away.

"We have a big surprise for you today. You're going to get to see an actual mummy. Not a reproduction, like what we usually have on display."

Conversation and chatter exploded from the group. She motioned for them to quiet down, but her grin couldn't have gotten any bigger if she'd tried.

"I know, it's cool. I'm excited for you! For me, too. But before we go back and see the specimen, let's talk about rules. We don't know who he or she was, and we haven't gotten the carbon dating back on the fibers yet. We simply call them Pharaoh." She turned to lead the kids back toward the door of the conference room where Pharaoh had been laid out for their inspection. "We found Pharaoh in a trunk from an estate sale lot that had been donated to the museum. We assume Pharaoh made their way here back during that sacrilegious time of mummy unwrapping parties and the like in the Victorian era."

Several of the students mouthed "mummy unwrapping" at one another and then wrinkled their noses in disgust, yet they leaned in toward her slightly, obviously needing to hear more.

"We are going to respect Pharaoh. This is all that's left of someone who lived, breathed, loved, and died. That means no touching." She held up her hands as they sighed. "I will have things for you to touch. Just not Pharaoh. We will have casts of Pharaoh's bones—"

"Bone." One of the kids laughed.

Kalila knew just how to deal with him. "Absolutely. A name that you will be more familiar with is King Tutankhamen, or King Tut. When he was mummified, his penis was mummified erect."

"Eternal boner," one of the kids snickered.

"Exactly." She nodded sagely.

"That sounds like a curse," a boy from the back said. "I bet Morticia over there would know." He nodded to the quiet goth girl in the corner.

Kalila's gaze was drawn to the girl in question. She was wearing all black, her box-dyed burgundy hair falling in her pale face, and there was no mistaking the bright yellow binding of E. A. Wallis Budge's *Book of the Dead*, which she had clutched to her chest.

"And do you know about curses?" Kalila asked gently.

The girl's eyes were impossibly big, and Kalila could see that she was trying to parse out if this was a trick, if Kalila was going to mock her, too.

"I love talking about curses. They're mostly urban legends, but you can't deny the numbers. Of the men who opened Tut's tomb, or were involved, many fell to misfortune. One received a gift of a paperweight of a mummified hand that was supposedly wearing a bracelet inscribed with a curse. Shortly after, his house burned down. When he tried to rebuild it, he was hit with a flood. Another man died of blood poisoning from a mosquito bite. I could go on."

Everyone nodded at her. Even the teachers who were with them were eager for more.

She could tell that the girl had something she wanted to ask, and Kalila gave her another gentle smile. "You have a question?"

"What about He Who Endures?" she blurted.

Kalila's heart sang. This was really why she'd gone into archaeology and Egyptology. She saw some of herself in that girl, caught up in the legend.

"This is actually one of my favorite topics. Now, in most academic circles, He Who Endures is right on that same list with aliens, Bigfoot, and Atlantis. But the story is so compelling." She looked down at her watch and decided they had time for the quick version.

"Of course witch-bitch would know about that," one of the guys muttered.

Before Kalila could respond, one of the girls punched

him in the shoulder. "Shut up. I want to hear this. And stop using 'witch' like a bad word."

High-school kids had definitely changed since her day, and she had to say it was a good thing.

"His name was Menes Sethos Cepos Akhenaten, and he was a mighty warlord. It was rumored that he was the first to unite the tribes along the Nile, and his empire reached beyond any other before. It was his footsteps Attila and Alexander followed to conquer their known worlds. When, finally, he had all his heart could desire, he decided to take a wife. A priestess of Isis who called herself Handmaiden of the Moon. She refused him, even though he offered her gold, jewels, anything she desired. Yet the one thing she asked for was the only thing he would not give. His heart."

There were snorts in the crowd.

"You can scoff, but when he married her against her will, she cursed him, poisoned him, tore out his heart and interred it in a secret place, then had his body thrown outside the city walls for the jackals. With no earthly body, his spirit became immortal flesh, and he was forced to wander for all eternity searching for the heart he refused to give her, and being thwarted every step of the way by the Left Hand of the Moon, the descendants of the priestess's guards."

The goth girl sighed, and Kalila would admit, every time she heard the story she still sighed, too. Poor, tragic bastard.

"And Dr. Kalila?" the girl asked. "Aren't there mentions of He Who Endures in other cultures? Across dynasties centuries apart?"

"Yes," she answered. "There are. The tale of He Who

Endures is as universal as the creation myths and great flood stories."

She checked her watch again. "Okay, guys. Let's go in and see Pharaoh. Remember to be respectful."

She let them into the conference room, and the chaperones helped divide them up into groups and got them started at the various stations and activities she and the Van Allman staff had set up for them.

Just as she knew it would, all the spooky stories had motivated them to learn more about the culture, the history, and the truth about life in ancient Egypt. The same way her father's stories and Indiana Jones did for her.

It wasn't long before one of the museum staff, Lindy, brushed against her elbow and whispered in her ear, "There's a call for you."

"I'll call them back," she said.

"No, you are going to want to take this. It's the Menes Society."

Outwardly, she managed to keep her manner calm, collected, and professional. "Can you take over for me?" Inwardly, of course, she was a mess.

"Only if you tell me what they want over drinks later."

If she didn't incinerate with anticipation first. "You got it."

Kalila tried not to run full speed ahead to her borrowed office and settled for walking smartly. Her hands were shaking and her guts had turned themselves inside out.

The Menes Society was the only reputable organization that could even whisper the legend of He Who Endures and not be laughed into the sea. Their core tenets didn't posit that there was some immortal guy running around looking for his heart, but they were looking for proof that Menes existed.

She took a deep breath before she picked up the phone and pressed the Hold button on the landline to connect back to the call.

"This is Dr. Blake."

"Dr. Blake, I am Dr. Chenzira Hassan with the Menes Society. I assume you've heard of us?" He cleared his throat. "Through your father's work?"

"Of course. What can I do for you, Dr. Hassan?"

"You can go to Jordan."

She understood the words he'd spoken, but they weren't connecting in her brain. The Menes Society wanted her to go to Jordan? But why?

When she didn't speak he continued. "It's going to be all over the news outlets soon enough. A giant sinkhole has opened up in the desert and it's unlike anything we've seen there before."

"You think proof is there?" she blurted.

Way to go, Kalila. Don't ruin this. Be objective. Be professional.

"We *know* the proof is there. The first pictures from the walls are . . . stunning. And wall after wall is dedicated to He Who Endures. We need a team out there now, and we want you to head up the dig and coordinate the preservation efforts."

She had to bite the inside of her cheek to keep from simultaneously shrieking and shitting her pants. This was the opportunity of a lifetime. She fingered the small silver heart charm around her throat and thought of her father. If only he were here right now.

She breathed deeply. "I . . . when?"

"Now. If you're on board, you'll be flying out by private jet as soon as you can get to the airport. Time is of the essence and money is no object."

"Yes." As if there was ever the possibility of any other answer.

"We'll send a car. I've emailed you a briefing packet. Inside, you'll find my assistant's number. Text her your size and whatever incidentals you may need for a month of work. You will be arriving on site before the rest of the team. I trust you can set up your personal accommodations on your own? You've been on digs in the desert, correct?"

"Yes. I'll text her now." Her brain automatically began cataloging everything she could possibly need, and she didn't bother to try to go cheaply because he said money was no object. She would get her team the latest and best everything, from eco-friendly, self-cooling tents to decent bathing facilities.

"The car will pick you up at the museum in half an hour."

She needed to get her passport, but she was sure that wasn't going to be a problem. "I'll be ready."

Dr. Hassan hung up, and she quickly checked her email on her phone.

He'd been right. The first pictures were nothing short of stunning. The color pigments had somehow withstood the ages and seemed to be as bright and vibrant as if they'd just been painted.

The hieroglyph that was believed to represent He Who Endures was everywhere.

And so, it seemed, was a warning.

She enlarged the images until she could see every detail the camera had managed to capture.

The warning was repeated almost as often as the He Who Endures hieroglyph. The Left Hand of the Moon guarded this sacred place.

Her eyes widened as she made out the specifics of the warning. Those who disturbed the tomb would be cursed to be devoured by undead jackals and rot in their guts until Isis pulled them from the darkness with her own hand.

If she'd been a different sort of person, that might have fazed her. She'd have attributed that chill skittering down her spine like a sharp-footed scarab to that ominous curse, but Kalila wasn't afraid of dust, or curses, or even ancient deities. Not when it came to He Who Endures.

This was definitive proof to academia that Menes had existed. Not that she really expected him to still be tooling around, kept alive by an ancient curse, but he had been *real*. And his story had captured imaginations; it had traveled from culture to culture.

She had been right.

More importantly, her father had been right.

Tears stung her eyes and her throat was thick with emotion.

She couldn't wait to get on the ground in Jordan. Only first she had to let Lindy know about the offer and that she was definitely taking it. With only thirty minutes to get her things in order, the driver would simply have to run her by her apartment to pick up her passport.

Darting back to the museum tour, she saw that Lindy had handed the kids off to Chelle, who always did a great job with them.

"Is it what I think it is?" Lindy asked.

"A sinkhole has opened up in Jordan revealing a lost Egyptian city of the dead."

"And the Menes Society's involvement?" Lindy's strawberry-blond eyebrows crawled up toward her hairline.

"The walls are covered in his story, Lindy." Her lip quivered with repressed emotion. "This could make my career."

Lindy squeezed her hand. "I hope it does, and that you'll still come back and speak. The kids just love you."

"I love them, too. I'll definitely be back. Thanks so much for understanding."

"Of course! If you're able, take pictures and email them to me. We'll do an exhibit."

"That would be amazing."

"I know I don't have to tell you this, but be careful. A discovery like this could mean a lot of things to a lot of people, and not all of them are good."

"I'll be careful." Kalila took her words to heart and pressed her museum keys into Lindy's hands. "I have to come back for these, after all."

She double-timed it back to her office to get her belongings together before making her way to the front of the museum to wait for the car service. It wasn't long before a sleek, black Mercedes pulled up and the driver rolled down the window.

"To the airport?"

"To my apartment first. I need my passport."

He nodded and got out of the vehicle to open the door for her. Once she was settled inside, he offered her a bottle of water and cookies.

"They'll have a meal for you on the plane," he said. "You have your instructions?"

"I do. Thank you."

She leaned back in the plush, buttery leather seat and began making lists of the things she needed for the dig.

Kalila was still reeling that she'd been chosen not only to lead this dig, but that she was going to be there first.

Her hands and brushes and tools were going to be the first to touch those walls since the desert had swallowed the tomb whole. Her fingers would follow in the wake of the priests who'd buried him, of the priestess who'd cursed him.

And it would be her hands that typed the definitive paper on the subject of He Who Endures, and it would be published in various journals and passed around at conferences.

She would have the validation that her father always sought.

Kalila couldn't get to Jordan fast enough.

It took her little time to grab the things she needed, email Dr. Hassan her lists, and be ready to board the private plane at the downtown airport.

When she was finally on her way to Jordan, the plane somewhere over an endless, dark ocean, Kalila dreamed of a starless night, of a place where the air was thick with incense and flowers, where the taste of cardamom and figs were sweet on her tongue, and where a curse wrought in blood and shadow had been born.

In her dream, it was *her* blood. Her shadows.

Her curse.

The Moon Priestess wore *her* face.

Chapter Two

Menes Sethos Cepos Akhenaten Dakarai was not cur-rently entombed in a hole in the desert.

No, the hole in which "Dr. Seth Dakarai" had buried himself was much more civilized. It had all the modern amenities he required. The foremost being a decent ristretto and a comfortable chair in which to study the papers that had been strewn out on the desk in front of him.

The Vatican Archive housed the biggest collection from the ancient world since the Library of Alexandria. A tragedy that still made him weep openly if he thought about it for too long.

It had taken years to get access. He'd befriended a young priest by the name of Joseph Soldano, he'd told him his story. And then he'd waited. And waited. And waited some more. He watched as time marched across his friend's face, leaving her indelible mark with deep grooves and canyons, yet Seth had stayed the same. No new lines or grooves on his face. No thinning about his neck and shoulders, no sagging around his jowls. No, he remained exactly as he had been the day he'd met Joseph, with the same scars, the same lines around his eyes he'd gotten from staring long hours into the unforgiving Egyptian sun.

He'd not only stayed the same, he'd *endured*.

Seth had tried other ways. He'd stabbed himself before another priest, but the magic that healed him had also alerted the Left Hand of the Moon to his presence and they'd managed to interfere.

So he'd had to bide his time with young Joseph. Yet what was a human lifetime to him? It was nothing so much as a few days compared to the long years of his existence. He had nothing but time and could afford to be patient.

Yet, so far, while he'd found many vastly interesting papers, accounts, and other research to occupy his mind, he'd found nothing as it related to his own predicament.

A shuffle of feet echoing across the marble floors called his attention and he looked up to see Joseph coming toward him, dressed in his standard uniform of black wool cassock and the signature scarlet rabat tied above his waist.

"Ah, Cardinal Soldano. What brings you to the Archive this morning? Don't tell me I've worn out my welcome?"

"No, no, my friend. I have news."

Seth took a sip of the ristretto and let it fortify him, preparing him for whatever news Joseph had brought him.

"Something's happened. The Menes Society is dispatching a team to the Jordanian desert."

He put down the tiny glass carefully. Perhaps he hadn't heard correctly. Jordan? "What?"

"A massive sinkhole revealed an *Egyptian* tomb. The first pictures . . ." Joseph shook his head. "Seth, they're incredible."

He tried to quell the surge of hope that bloomed hot and almost rancid in his guts. After all this time, could it be? He'd thought perhaps his redemption lay in the newly revealed necropolis at Saqqara, only to have his fragile hopes disintegrate like ancient papyri in a flame.

"I'm sure they are." He took another sip of his ristretto.

"You don't understand, my friend. The walls are covered with hieroglyphs and warnings. All about He Who Endures." Joseph handed his cell phone to Seth and, when he didn't take it, shook it. "Look for yourself."

He finally accepted the phone, and what he saw lit that tiny ember of hope to a blazing bonfire that threatened to consume him. Row after row of vibrant, intact artwork told his story again and again. It bore a warning that those who should disturb the tomb would bring about the fury of undead jackals.

This was it.

It had to be.

His heart had been mummified and buried somewhere in that tomb.

"I have to get on this dig, Joseph." He looked up at his friend. "It's there. My heart is there, I know it." He shuddered as the curse of the jackals replayed over and over in his mind. It hadn't been a good death the first time around. Yet, if it meant peace after all this time, he'd face the ordeal again, gladly.

"I suspected as much. I've already put your name forward to Dr. Hassan as the art historian for the job. However, you won't be lead on the dig. It'll be Dr. Blake."

"Rafael Blake and I go way back. Not as far back as you and me, but far enough."

Thoughts of Rafael's daughter, Kalila, came unbidden. He remembered her wide-eyed curiosity. Her passion for the work they shared.

Her obsession with a myth.

He wondered if she was still following her father around, soaking up all the detail she could, putting her hands on as much history as she could hold while scrounging happily in the dirt and sand.

"Not Rafael. His daughter. She's the archaeologist in charge. You'll be assisting."

"Why not Rafael?" he demanded.

"You hadn't heard? He passed some time ago."

Fuck. He hadn't heard. He thought of Kalila and her wide, brown eyes filled with tears and all alone in the big, hungry world.

He thought of that same girl out in the wild desert and facing down cursed jackals and the Left Hand of the Moon. His first instinct had been to say that she was but a child, but as he mentally counted the years that had passed, he knew she wasn't.

She was a woman grown, not a child. Not even a young woman, now that he thought about it. Although, they were all young to him, and it was becoming easier and easier to see himself as something set apart from humanity. Something he knew Khepri had thought of him all along.

Seth wondered if that was the punishment she'd hoped to inflict with his curse? That he'd come to see himself the way she had? He supposed he'd even tried to make it so by denying he had feelings or a heart to give her.

"How did it happen?" he asked, bringing himself back to the present.

"He passed in his sleep. He was seventy."

Seventy. That wasn't so very many years at all when he thought of it. Too short a time to see everything there was to see, to experience all the people one would like to meet. No, it wasn't long at all.

And now Kalila was alone in the world, with nothing and no one to turn to but a memory. He supposed that made her sound helpless and fragile, and he knew she was none of those things. She was curious, passionate, and strong.

Not that it mattered. He couldn't afford to let Kalila Blake be a distraction.

"How soon can I be on a plane to Jordan?"

"Immediately. You're leaving out of Fiumicino. A car will take you. The Society will provide everything you need. Of course, there is the small matter of the nondisclosure, but . . ." He shrugged and lifted a brow.

"It is no matter." He stood and put his hand on Joseph's shoulder. "Thank you, Joseph."

"May it bring you the peace you seek." The cardinal put a hand to his heart. "Even though my heart will be sore."

How easily they spoke of his death.

In Seth's youth, death had been something to fear, something to fight. It was to be faced each day and fought back like a pride of lions. Yet now, he would go lie willingly in the jaws of the great beast, ready at last to surrender.

He'd admit there was part of him that wondered if he

was really ready for it to be over. There were still so many new things to be discovered. New frontiers. The deepest parts of the ocean, the far reaches of space . . . Regardless of what he chose, he wanted it to be *his* choice.

After saying goodbye to Joseph, he grabbed his go bag and let the service take him to the airport. The private flight to Amman was only about three and a half hours, and he spent that time going over the files Dr. Hassan had forwarded to him. He kept going over them again and again, even though he knew he'd soon see those images in person.

He was only loosely aware of the other members of the team who'd joined him, and that turned out to be his mistake.

Something sharp pressed against his spine through the seat, and hot breath washed over the back of his neck.

"You should be more careful in your friends, *ya Homaar*."

He recognized the dialect as Egyptian Arabic, and the speaker had called him a son of a donkey. No, his father had been many things. A donkey was not one of them. Seth did, however, curse himself for a fool for not being more aware of his surroundings. It had been so long and he had been through many incarnations since his last encounter with the Left Hand. He considered for a long moment. A knife wound obviously wouldn't kill him, but he'd have one hell of a time explaining how he was still walking around with a blade in his spine.

Yet this development, coupled with his assailant's words, led him to believe that either this man was no member of the Left Hand of the Moon or he had no idea who he was actually dealing with.

"Who is this friend and how has he offended you?" Seth asked.

"I'm not going to waste your time or mine. Get up slowly. Walk to the back of the plane."

This man had just signed his own death warrant.

Seth put his files away and did as instructed, slowly rising from his seat so as not to draw attention to him or his assailant. He headed back toward the galley, and this time he was careful to take in and catalog his surroundings.

The weapon would be no problem. He'd let the man stab him and then use his own blade against him. But where to put the body?

"I am not who you think I am," he said, trying to avoid having to kill him. Even though a bit of inconvenience now could save him trouble later.

"Let's not bother with that. I know you work for Him. I knew it as soon as I saw you board this flight."

Once they were in the galley and away from prying eyes, Seth turned to face him, and what he saw was a man haunted. His dark eyes were wild and his face gaunt, deeply grooved by something more heinous than the march of time.

"So what are you going to do, Left Hander? Are you going to kill me?" Seth asked casually. "There's only one way this is going to go for you, and that's poorly."

Something tickled just below his ear. He raised his hand to wipe it away but paused. It couldn't be what he thought it was. It just couldn't.

Except, when he saw the wild look in the man's eyes take on a new brightness, he knew it was.

Of course it was.

The giant scarab was Khepri's creature. A purple-and-gold-scarab hieroglyphic was as good as her name.

Fuck.

He inhaled deeply and found his calm as it skittered down the back of his shirt and its furry legs made purchase on his skin. One wrong move and it would bite him, filling his body with a paralytic venom that would cause his flesh to rot from the inside out.

If he were mortal.

The thing had to be as big as his hand. Jackals, flesh-eating scarabs . . . he wasn't about to ask what more could happen to him, but these things together strengthened his resolve that he would find his heart in the ruined city.

The scarab found its way over his shoulder and down into his sleeve, and then it scuttled out onto the top of his palm, where it rose up on its hind legs to look at him. He'd swear the thing recognized him. If only because he hadn't screamed his throat raw.

"I told you, I'm not who you think I am," he said with a whisper and tossed the giant scarab back at him.

It landed on his chest like the center jewel of some stunning necklace. The man froze and then slowly reached into his pocket and carefully pulled out what Seth assumed to be the beetle's carrier.

"Reap what you have sown, henchman." He blew a hot breath toward the scarab, and its long pincers slid into the man's skin. "And as you die, know that it will not be by your hand. *Because I endure.*"

His mouth went slack and an expression of abject terror washed over his face. His muscles contracted all at once as his body spasmed and went stiff, the scarab's venom doing its awful job.

Seth captured the thing in the carrier; he didn't want anyone else on the expedition to die in the utter agony his would-be assassin now faced, silent as the grave. The poor bastard couldn't even scream.

He'd free the little creature at the dig site after he'd gotten what he wanted.

Seth went back to his seat and sat down, but he didn't let down his guard this time. He stayed alert until they were on the ground in Amman. And his vigilance didn't waver when they were loaded into the all-terrain vehicles for the long drive across the desert sands to the dig site at the sinkhole cave-in.

Not until he saw *her*.

Then all sense and logic fled.

His first thought was: *mine*. It had nothing to do with the way her khakis hugged her generous hips and outlined the peach-sweet curve of her ass. Nor the way that her expedition shirt clung to the heavy globes of her breasts. Not even with the way her golden skin seemed to glitter in the harsh and unforgiving sun.

The sight of her roused the long-sleeping conqueror that lived deep in his bones. Something about her called to the warlord he used to be, and to the man he was now.

He wanted her.

He burned with need.

It was a fire he'd never felt before.

Not even with Khepri.

He dared a glance around him. For that thought alone would be enough to raise her from the dead to strike him down. She'd been a vain, vain woman. Yet, not without reason.

Seth reminded himself that Kalila Blake was not his, nor could she ever be. Not even for the fleeting moments that would comprise the whole of her human lifetime. It wouldn't be fair to do that to her.

Even though he knew that if he confessed his secret to her, she'd be one of few who would believe him. She was, perhaps, one of the only people on this earth he could be his true self with.

His fingers itched to delve into her masses of black hair. To see her naked under the hollow desert moon and to make her call his name in a language that no longer lived in human tongue.

She must have sensed his regard because she turned to look at him.

As soon as their eyes met, shock waves of lust ricocheted through him, and he almost had to look away. Only looking away would be denying himself this part of her that he could have.

Then she smiled, and it made him wonder if Khepri's beetle had bitten him after all.

"Well, damn," she whispered. "I swear, you haven't aged a day. Tell me, Seth, you bathe in the blood of your enemies, right? That's how you do it? Or do you sacrifice them to Isis in exchange for eternal youth?" She didn't give him a chance to answer. Instead, she said, "I'm thrilled they called you."

The hits just kept coming. He hadn't expected her to be so happy to see him.

Everything about Kalila Blake threw him off his game.

Especially when she pressed her delicious curves up against him and she smelled like ripe figs. There was no way she wouldn't be able to feel his body's response to her. For a moment she tightened her embrace, and he could do nothing but burn in a hell of need until she decided to release him.

Release.

Oh, he could definitely count the ways and means . . .

Her fingers lingered on his shoulders as she slowly pulled away.

He realized he hadn't given her any answer to her greeting. He was thousands of years old and a woman could still rob him of not only his tongue but of his sense.

"It's good to see you, too, Kalila." His hand was on her hip and he couldn't bring himself to pull away from her.

She turned away from him to issue more directives, and then, when she focused on him again, Kalila wore a mischievous expression. "I've been dealing with setup since I got here. I haven't had a chance to get down into the site yet. Why don't we drop your things in your tent and do some recon on the first room before nightfall?"

Her excitement was palpable, and Seth wondered again if maybe he should tell her. Because, suddenly, he didn't want her down in that tomb.

After his encounter on the plane with the deadly scarab, what horrors lay in store for Kalila once the Left Hand learned she was here?

Chapter Three

Seth Dakarai hadn't changed.

It was almost as if he'd been frozen in time. Not a single new line or groove marred his face. And she would know. She'd spent enough long hours staring at him adoringly. Kalila had committed every angle, every line to memory.

He hadn't changed, but she had.

Kalila looked at him with the eyes of a woman grown. She'd foolishly thought that her childhood crush would have flickered out like a candle that had burned down to the last, but no. That flame was now a bonfire.

How dare he still be so damn hot? The absolute nerve. Bastard.

He was beautiful not in the way of delicate things, but in the way of the furious power of nature. He was primal, and harsh, and to look at him, no one would ever expect his expertise to be as an art historian. A mercenary, or some kind of Special Forces discipline, like how to assassinate someone at a hundred yards with a toothpick and a coconut. He had a predatory grace in the way he moved, as if his body was always coiled and ready to strike.

Kalila had spent hours thinking about what it would be like to run her hands through his shoulder-length, wavy black hair that he kept tied at the back of his neck. He had these black lashes that were so thick, it made him look like he'd lined his eyes with kohl. His skin was tan and dark, kissed both by genetics and long hours under a harsh and unforgiving sun.

His goatee she was sure had been a gift from the devil, mostly because she imagined how it would feel rubbing against the inside of her thighs.

And he was hard. He was so hard everywhere.

Hugging him had been a mistake, and not simply because it felt so good. She'd learned he wasn't immune to her. The press of hot, engorged flesh had burned through their clothing and branded itself on her imagination.

She'd thought she wanted him when she was young. Innocent daydreams about first kisses, first touches, and first passions. Now, she wanted him with all the knowing of a woman who took her pleasure when and where she wanted.

Except she didn't want to be that same silly girl with a silly crush. He wouldn't see her as a woman grown, with her own power and her own agency. That in itself was a big turnoff when she thought about it. More importantly, this dig was hers. The work here was so important to her father's legacy, and to realizing her own dreams.

Kalila wouldn't throw it away on a man, even if that man was Seth Dakarai.

The heat of his appraisal burned through her back, and she was hyperaware of every step she took. Every moment. She suddenly didn't know what to do with her arms. When they finally reached his tent she pulled back the flap, not because she was being polite but because it gave her something to do.

"Thank you, Kalila."

The way his voice seemed to purr her name sent hot stabs of desire straight through her. Damn it, she was a professional and he was her colleague. She inhaled a deep breath to steady herself.

"Most welcome." She watched him drop his bags and grab his tools and digital camera. This was good. She knew as soon as they got down into the dig she'd be too worried about the work, and he'd be his condescending, know-it-all self, and these feelings would strangle themselves.

Then he surprised her by asking, "Do you think this is it? The tomb?"

She studied him carefully. Part of her wanted to share her excitement with him, but she remembered that time in Greece right after she'd turned twenty, when he'd finally started treating her like an adult with a brain, and as soon as talk had turned to the legend, he'd dismissed her. Kalila couldn't afford him undermining her. This could make her career and she wasn't about to let him take that away from her.

"I don't know what that place is. That's what we're here to find out, isn't it?"

"I saw what looked to be a bit of purple pigment in one of those first photos. I couldn't quite make out the symbol, but I'd swear it was a scarab."

"Since when have you been up on He Who Endures?" She arched a brow. "I thought it was all nonsense?"

"Maybe you convinced me." He cocked his head to the side and winked at her.

Instead of admitting just how much that affected her, she snorted. "I know you better than that. Further, why would I ever give you that kind of ammunition?" she blurted.

"What do you mean?"

"Greece?" She said this as if she were offended he didn't know. "You let me think you were really interested in what I had to say and then you crushed me."

Why had she confessed how that made her feel? She should have kept it to herself. Pretended like it never mattered. She'd gift wrapped her own downfall and handed it to him with a smile.

She'd sworn she wouldn't let him get under her skin, and now, just because she still wanted to get under his clothes, she'd left herself unprotected.

He was silent for a long moment, and the longer he didn't speak, the hotter her face burned, and it had nothing to do with the blazing sun overhead.

"It doesn't matter, does it? We'll know soon enough. Are you ready?" she asked.

"Kalila," he began softly.

For a moment, he seemed he was going to reach out to her. Touch her. She definitely couldn't have that. If his words wrecked her, his touch would be devastating.

"This topic is a hard one for me. I should have had more patience for your exuberance."

He met her eyes with a deliberate slowness.

Kalila knew with an absolute certainty he was trying

to tell her something. That there was some kind of subtext she wasn't quite catching, and she wasn't sure how she felt about it. Why couldn't he simply come out and say what he wanted her to know?

"So now you've changed your mind and believe He Who Endures was a real man?"

"I never said he wasn't a real man, only that we'd never had proof he existed beyond these stories. And I've seen too many talented archaeologists lose their credibility and their careers chasing a bedtime story."

"Yet here you are. And you're asking me if I think we've found him."

"And you still haven't answered me."

"I don't have an answer for you. All I have is the work. And we're losing daylight."

"You're right about that. Twilight is closer than you think."

She watched him as he reached for her, his hand moving through the space in a slow, fluid motion that was like watching him move through water. It was surreal, and it didn't quite compute as his hand, so very hot and real, closed over hers.

"I never meant to crush your imagination and enthusiasm. I was an asshole. Do you forgive me?"

Her brain short-circuited at the touch, but she managed to somehow find her way back to coherence.

"You can't ask me like that." She grinned. "Because then I have to say I forgive you. What if I don't?"

"Ah, see. I never said I wasn't *still* an asshole." He grinned back.

"Fair enough." She drew back her hand to gain some control of herself and the situation. "I think we need some asshole energy. Did you translate that curse? 'Eternity rotting in the bellies of undead jackals'? That's pretty serious."

"The Egyptians don't fuck around with their curses."

"I was explaining that to a bunch of high schoolers when I got the call about this project. They always like that part." She laughed. "I'll admit, it's still one of my favorite parts, too."

He walked back under the flap and out into the bright desert heat. "I bet that's part of what appealed to you about this project."

She shrugged. "Well, you know."

"I remember how you used to ask your father over and over for the darkest tales with the most horrifying curses." He met her eyes again. "I was sorry to hear of his passing."

"I miss him every day."

"I know he'd be so proud of you. Not just because you're here, but because of everything you've accomplished."

Her eyes teared up and she wiped at her face with the back of her hand. "Damn, that sand got me."

"It does that." Seth headed toward the access point with his tools in hand.

She took longer strides to keep up with him. Kalila didn't much care to feel like she was trailing behind him like a kid. She reminded herself that she was in charge. This was her dig.

Except when they descended through the access point and emerged into that first room, it was like Greece all over again. At least, it felt that way to her. She was trotting along behind him, excited to see everything, to take it all in, to immerse herself in this remnant of a civilization long passed.

Although it wasn't long before the ancient marks on the wall, their colors still so vibrant and vital, drew her away from Seth, away from her insecurities and longings, away from everything but the story that played out on the walls.

The purple scarab glyph seemed to glow, pulsing with color and light. She reached out to touch it, but paused before she made contact. She wouldn't touch these priceless walls with anything but her proper tools. Yet she felt the scarab glyph belonged to her somehow.

"Khepri," she whispered.

For a moment she was sure, if she could just touch it, that she'd feel the priestess through the ages that separated them.

She'd feel her, and know everything she knew. The river of time would drain away like the dry season on the Nile before the floods and, finally, Kalila would have the answers she sought.

She shook her head, as if she rattled herself hard enough, thoughts like that would cease to exist. Of course no one would take her seriously if she started talking about sensing, and her dreams of Khepri.

"You say her name with such reverence."

If she didn't know better, she'd say that his tone was almost accusatory.

"Why wouldn't I? I have respect for all the lives who have come before me. The people who lived, loved, fought, and died here. This work, for me, it's about honoring them, and bringing their stories to the modern world."

"I just would have thought," he said as he used a delicate trowel to clear some debris, "that because you were so enamored with He Who Endures that you'd not have any soft feelings for the woman who cursed him. Who had his heartless body flung from the city gates and left to be devoured by jackals. Legends say she also poisoned him."

She turned away from the hypnotic scarab. "I mean, it's not like he forced her into marriage or anything. It's not like he threatened her people and her homeland with the decimation of war. Sure, he was totally innocent."

"He was! He was a warlord. That was the way of things, then. He didn't threaten her people. He offered. He was respectful."

"How do you know? Were you there?" She shook her head. "The Scarab Papyrus says differently."

"The Scarab Papyrus hasn't been authenticated," he shot back.

"Ah! But the carbon dating matches the time period and the descriptions of the people and places match up," she argued.

He snorted. "Yeah, and they say Plato gave us a map to Atlantis, but no one's found it, have they? Because it's crap."

She snorted back. "You're so closed-minded."

"I prefer facts."

"Yeah, me too. And you know how we get facts? They start as hypotheses that are then confirmed with data." Kalila rolled her eyes. "You're so frustrating. First, you won't even admit that this guy existed, and now, you're ready to go to the mat over some imagined slight. What's going on with you?"

He looked over at her, and for the first time ever, Kalila felt she had the upper hand in the conversation. It didn't feel as good as she thought it would. She didn't like the haunted expression on his face, nor the way he seemed so incredibly vulnerable and breakable.

This took a wrecking ball to her worldview. She didn't like it.

"Seriously, Seth. What's going on with you? You can talk to me."

"I want to," he said softly. "But I don't think it's fair to you."

"Hey, I don't need you to save me. Or protect me. I'll decide what I can deal with and what I can't."

Just then, an awful, high-pitched howl rent the air. Followed by another. And then another. Until it was a chorus of screaming.

"Get behind me," he commanded, and pulled twin blades from his khakis, ready to fight off the threat.

"I have to protect my crew. They're my responsibility." She dashed toward the access ladder and scrambled up as quickly as she could to take stock of the situation.

Dusk had rolled in quickly, settling like a blanket around them, and at the edges of the camp, she saw jackals had surrounded them.

The locals they'd hired weren't staying to secure the camp; they were piling into vehicles and fleeing the scene. She managed to stop a man she'd worked with before, but he had only one word for her.

"Cursed."

He fled, too.

Leaving them alone in the falling darkness with the hungry predators.

Kalila knew what she had to do. She went for her tent and grabbed the riot shotgun. It had been loaded with less-than-lethal rubber buckshot. Kalila didn't want to hurt these animals—humans were guests in their territory—but she also wasn't of a mind to be dinner. She'd use live ammo next if she had to, but she hoped this experience would be enough that they'd avoid the camp and humans in the future.

She shouldered the shotgun, braced her feet apart, and racked the weapon, took aim, and unleashed the rubber buckshot on the pack, and, thankfully, they scattered. She watched as they retreated into the sand, and the darker it got, the more she noticed the eerie red glow of their eyes blinking like demon lights.

No wonder the locals feared them. Creepy little shits.

They yipped at one another, as if discussing the current situation.

"Go on, get," she yelled.

Kalila was suddenly aware of a presence behind her. Hot, hard, and solid. She turned to face him.

"You handle that thing pretty well."

"Thanks." She scanned the horizon again. "It's weird, though, right? I mean, I know jackals are opportunistic predators, but this was a big camp. They shouldn't have perceived us as vulnerable to attack."

"Maybe it's the curse. To rot for all eternity in the belly of undead jackals."

A sudden chill coursed down her back and she couldn't shake the overwhelming sense of dread that washed over her in unforgiving waves.

"Your crew is gone, Kalila. Maybe you should radio for help."

She stuffed the dread down deep and rallied. "Like hell I will. We've got more crew flying in soon. We'll be fine. You're welcome to go back to the city if you like. But I'll not be going anywhere."

"Did I ever tell you about that dig in Africa?" He scanned the horizon before turning his attention back to her, and the yips of the jackals began again in earnest. "They surrounded the camp, although it was much smaller than this one. That day, one of the archaeologists fell and fractured his leg. We were waiting on a Medi-Vac to the nearest city. The jackals smelled the blood, and they attacked the med tent as a single unit. Do you know what happened to him? They tore him apart, Kalila."

"That's awful. I'm so sorry that happened to him." She reached out and touched his shoulder without considering the fallout. It had only been to offer him comfort, but fire ignited inside her. She swallowed hard. "And to you, but I'm not leaving."

"Kalila, you don't understand what's happening here. Things are only going to get worse."

"How do you know?" She waited for him to answer, but when none was forthcoming, she added, "How do you know, unless you're the one making them worse?"

That wasn't something she wanted to believe, that Seth would sabotage her, but what other answer was there?

"You think I have pet jackals?" He snorted. "I'm trying to help you."

The fact that he didn't take her seriously, and that he deflected instead of actually answering her, fired her suspicions into overdrive. "I think you're trying to help yourself, Dr. Dakarai." She stepped away from him to put the physical distance between them she'd intended with her words. Kalila lifted her shotgun and rested it on the top of her shoulder. "I'm not leaving. No matter what you do."

She left him standing alone in the middle of the empty camp and retreated to her tent, where his warnings about the jackals were never far from her mind.

Nor was the curse.

Chapter Four

Agony ripped through him with jackal's teeth.

It was that comparison that caused Seth to realize he was dreaming. Their teeth tore at his flesh, and he knew there was nothing for it, no relief, no surcease; he must, as he had always done, simply endure.

Yet the scent of sweet, ripe figs wrapped around him, and the horrors began to fade as he found himself wrapped in Kalila. His head was cushioned against the soft swells of her breasts, her fingers were somehow cool on his forehead, and her hair a dark curtain, allowing him to hide his shame for the moment.

He tightened his embrace around her, if only to reassure himself that this was real. Whenever he was close to any measure of peace the nightmares returned, where he relived the terror of the jackals devouring his flesh.

He'd been dead, but the curse was the gift that kept on

giving, forcing him to live through it over and over again. Seth would say he'd paid the price for any crime he could have committed tenfold.

"Are you back with me now?" she whispered.

He clung tighter. She shouldn't be there with him. It was dangerous for her, but she felt so good. "Why did you come?"

"You were having a nightmare."

She must have heard him screaming. Shame hit him hard and fast. "You shouldn't have." When she stiffened he added, "The jackals have an advantage in the dark, Kalila. They could have moved on you."

"Hey, you know me. I've seen *Indiana Jones* enough times to know you don't go anywhere without a flamethrower." She pushed her hair back over her shoulder, and he saw the lighter and a can of hair spray on the folding desk next to the cot.

He knew he should untangle himself from her embrace, but it felt too good. She didn't seem inclined to move, so why should he give up something that brought him so much pleasure? Seth technically knew the answer to that, but he wasn't going to think about it. Instead, he'd lie here with her until dawn if she wanted to stay that long.

"I do remember. The Peru dig you came on with Raphael." He laughed. "I remember seeing your industrial hair spray and wondering just what in the hell you were going to do with that in the middle of the jungle and why he'd let you bring it."

"He didn't tell you?"

"Nope. He said your reasons were your own and if I wanted to know, I could ask you." He hadn't been able to fathom any practical use, so he hadn't asked.

She smoothed his hair away from his face and he wanted to turn into the caress like a cat. "Speaking of personal grooming, seriously, Seth. What are you doing for your skin? It has to be something. The souls of undergrads? You can admit it if you had work done. I won't tell anyone."

He snorted. "It's just good genes."

"You really don't look any different than you did twenty years ago. How is that?"

That part of him that wanted her to know him, to really know him, surged. It was on the tip of his tongue to tell her. She'd said she didn't need him to protect her, that she could decide what she could handle. So he could trust her to handle it.

In the end, he took the coward's way out. He wanted to see the wonder in her eyes when she realized the legend was true, but didn't want the disappointment when she realized that He Who Endures wasn't special. It was just him. And he could have saved her father years of disappointment if he'd simply confessed.

Maybe, the other thing he couldn't stand would be that she'd want him. Really want him, but it wouldn't be for who he was but *what* he was. Simply because he'd existed so long.

An ugly truth reared its head when he realized perhaps that had been his problem all along. He'd thought he deserved things simply for existing.

Instead of facing any of those things, he said, "It's definitely the souls of undergrads."

"Can I ask another question?"

"You're going to ask me whether I agree or not," he teased.

"Your face is still in my cleavage, so I think I get some leeway."

"Fine," he agreed, unwilling to move his face to safer territory.

"You apologized for Greece, but you didn't really answer why you treated me that way. Will you now?"

"I don't have a different answer for you." Yet, he did. They'd gotten too close to things that hurt him. That wide-eyed wonder and excitement over the very idea he existed. She'd had too much hope for a creature such as him. He hadn't done anything to make humanity better. He hadn't changed any lives with his great knowledge. He'd simply existed.

Again, his curse. He'd only endured.

Never, in all of the long years of his eternal existence, had he ever felt so unworthy, had he ever felt like such a failure.

So he'd lashed out.

"Make something up," she teased. "Or you can tell me how old you actually are. I thought you were my father's age, but you can't be."

"Maybe I'll tell you tomorrow."

"Why wait? Think I won't still follow you around making big eyes at you if I know you're an old man?"

"How did you ever figure it out?" He looked up at her. "It's the dye in my beard, isn't it?"

She reached out and stroked his chin, and all the playfulness from the moment was gone, replaced by a particular intensity, the moment suddenly out of time, and they were both frozen.

If he wasn't careful, this heat between them was going to explode into a flame that would burn them both. He wanted it too much to say no, even when he knew the fallout was going to be catastrophic.

It had been so long since he'd been with a woman. Since he'd wanted to touch and be touched. Since a woman who smelled like sweet figs had stirred his desires. Seth knew she wasn't Khepri, and he didn't want her to be, but everything about her seemed as if she'd been designed by the hand of Isis herself just for him. He knew he wasn't that lucky, that the esteemed goddess would take a personal interest in advancing his well-being.

Yet still, here she was, a soft and sweet woman, with a spine of steel and a brilliant but open mind. Her lips were full and pink and called to him like a sweet oasis. Her fingers pushed through the hair at his temple, slowly and with intention.

"I think I should stay with you tonight. Just in case."

"Just in case the jackals come back? They haven't left, Kalila." He shouldn't be here, lost in her soft body, stoking the fires of desire when danger was so near.

"I know. I need to stay here so you can protect me."

With a surprisingly fluid motion, she slid down his body and settled in against his chest as if they were long-time lovers and this intimacy was comfortable and worn.

This woman needed him to protect her? After the way she'd stood down the whole pack with a riot shotgun? No, she didn't need his protection. She was here, protecting him and his ego.

And he was going to let her.

Kalila had always been precious to him, with her wide eyes, her unflinching curiosity, and her passion for knowledge. Although, now that she was a woman, it was different. He felt privileged she wanted to be here with him.

Of all the people he could have chosen to spend his last days with, Kalila Blake was the best. Simply being in her presence had reframed his world. It was a peace that even the Left Hand of the Moon couldn't take away. After seeing Khepri's scarab on the wall, he knew without a doubt that his heart was down there somewhere.

He wondered what she heard with her face pressed against his bare chest. Did she hear a phantom heart pumping away? Or was it cold silence?

"When did you say the rest of the crew should be here?"

"Afraid of being trapped in the desert alone with me?" she teased.

"I can't protect you properly without all the information. I need to know when reinforcements will arrive so I know how to ration the food. How long we need to hold the perimeter. We need to be very careful with further excavation. If there's some kind of cave-in, no one will know where we went."

"I'm glad to see you're taking your job seriously."

"Kalila, I always take strategy and survival seriously."

"I know. When I first met you I was sure you were a government spook. My dad assured me that you were definitely *not* a government spook. It took him a long time to convince me that you were an Egyptologist and art historian."

How had she sensed that about him? He tried to change the subject. "These excursions can be dangerous. The black market is big money, and most of these people have very little care what happens to the people who get between them and their money."

"I do, actually, know that."

He considered for a long moment. "You do, don't you? I'm sorry I keep treating you like you've never done this before."

"You know what would help you?"

"This should be good."

"Call me Dr. Blake. Maybe that will remind you."

"Maybe it will, Dr. Blake." Why did it feel so illicit to say that to her while she was in his arms?

He knew she felt it, too, because she shivered against him, and he could feel the beat of her heart thudding faster as she pressed closer to him.

"You should try to get some sleep. Tomorrow is going to be a long day," he said.

"Who can sleep? I can't wait to get back down into that room. I'll admit, I'm obsessed with that scarab. It just calls to me."

That couldn't mean anything good, of that he was sure. He was suddenly afraid that this indulgence would lead to putting Kalila in danger. Yes, she'd said she could choose for herself, but she didn't have all the information.

He decided then that he would tell her. He didn't have a choice.

That was when he saw it. The venomous scarab had crawled onto Kalila's shoulder. It made him wish he'd crushed the thing under his boot when he'd had the chance. Instead, he'd had to set it free in the ruins. He was getting sloppy in his old age, and his nostalgia might well cost Kalila her life.

Kalila moved to swat at her shoulder, and he grabbed her wrist.

"Don't move," he whispered.

"Oh God, is it a snake?"

"No, it's a beetle, but it's Jurassic. It's the kind of scarab whose venom can liquefy your insides."

"I'm terrified and excited at the same time. What does it look like?"

He decided to be honest. "It's Khepri's scarab."

"Oh my God! You know what that means? We found it. This is the place. Legend says the heart was buried with an army of these things." She exhaled. "Shit, I hope it doesn't bite me."

"I will make sure it doesn't." He reached out to grab it, but she stopped him.

"What are you doing? Don't piss it off."

It looked up at him, and he wondered if this was to be Khepri's final revenge. To punish a woman who didn't deserve it just to make sure he knew no peace. He also realized this was not the scarab from the plane, either. While it was purple, and iridescent, this one had black-tipped pincers.

A low sound came from the thing, and it sounded almost like a purr.

Kalila sat up oh so slowly and held out her hand next to her shoulder.

"What are *you* doing?" It was his turn to ask her. "Are you actually insane?"

He watched with fascinated horror as it crawled into her palm and she brought it up to her face.

"You're so pretty," she cooed.

It wiggled this way and that, as if preening.

"Yes, that's you. So pretty. You're not going to bite me, are you?" She swung her legs off the cot and moved slowly to the tent flap. "Hey, can you open this so I can put her outside?"

He made quick work of the entryway and held it wide open for her. The scarab's attention was fixed on Kalila. As if it lived and breathed only for her.

"There you go, muffin." She rested her palm on the ground and it hopped off, wiggling its pincers at her.

Seth saw a dozen pairs of red eyes flicker around the campsite, and the howls of the jackals shattered the silence of the night.

The little scarab hummed, a lighter sound than that of what he'd thought might have been a purr, and an iridescent purple wave of the creatures flooded up from the depths of the dig and swelled toward the jackals.

As the waves washed over them, they left nothing of the jackals behind.

Not even their bones.

Then the giant scarabs burrowed down into the sand, gone, as if they'd never been.

"You saw that, right?" Kalila murmured. "It wasn't my imagination?"

"No, I saw it." He cleared his throat. "I don't know if I believe it, but I saw it."

"I wish I'd caught that on film."

"No. Can you imagine what would happen to them? And to the well-meaning scientists who wanted to come study them? They'd catch them. Put them in cages. Drain their venom. Destroy their habitat. We can't do that to them after what they just did." It was rather what he imagined would happen to him if the world should ever come to know of his existence.

She cast him a sly glance. "So you believe they chose to attack the jackals? They chose them as their prey to protect us?"

"Let's not be hasty. They're here to protect the hea— their home," he quickly corrected himself.

"Yes, but why would they not perceive us as threats? We're the ones digging it up. Unless there's something more?"

She'd always been too sharp for her own good. "We should sleep on it."

"I don't know, are you going to be able to sleep knowing just how many of them are below our feet right now?"

"I sleep in the city just fine and it's loaded with roaches and rats and all number of things living just below the surfaces of where we eat and sleep."

She rubbed her arms. "I guess it seems different somehow."

"You were the one baby-talking the damn thing like a kitten."

Kalila grinned. "Well, it did purr. It was stunning, and an honor to have been able to have that interaction. I just don't need tens of thousands of them, you know?"

Seth definitely knew. He knew a lot of things he had to tell her, but he wanted to hide in her for just a little while longer. "The desert night grows cold. Come to bed," he said as he tugged her hand to lead her back inside the tent.

Chapter Five

Come to bed.

It was her every fantasy come to life, and from the look on his face, he knew it. She allowed him to lead her into the tent, and to the cot where she fell into his arms easily, but even with the rush of desire between them, this was something else.

Kalila wasn't quite sure what it was, but it was special.

She wanted to talk about what had just happened, but it didn't seem like the right time. Although when would be the right time to talk about something that was impossible?

Something niggled at the back of her brain. Some awareness she wasn't quite ready to consider, so those thoughts sank into shadow and she sank into *him*. Kalila couldn't believe this was happening. How many nights in her twenties had she lain awake fantasizing about something exactly like these moments? About being in his arms, surrounded by him, sheltered in his embrace. Now that she was here, it felt familiar.

It felt like home.

But she couldn't let herself think those thoughts. She rather imagined he didn't want to be her home, and he didn't want her to be his, no matter what happened between them. He just didn't seem like the type. She couldn't fight what she felt, so instead, she let herself enjoy what it felt like to be where she'd dreamed of being.

After that sleep took her quickly, and she found herself once again in that place of myrrh, cardamom, and figs. The incense was heavy, the smoke thick. She was immersed in warm water, and the moon shone down in a waterfall of silver. Unfamiliar hands moved over her body, washing her limbs, and something sweet and smoky was placed on her tongue.

"Will you see your future tonight, my lady?" Those weren't the words that the slim, dark-haired girl had spoken, but that was what she came to understand them to mean.

"Tonight, the future sees me," she whispered. "Quick, bring me silvered glass!"

Kalila looked at herself through eyes that were not her own. This body was not hers.

And the giant scarab that had perched on the edge of the stone bath gave a deep, satisfied purr.

A ribbon of knowledge began to wrap around her. She began to hear Khepri's thoughts about the warlord who would claim her. She would settle for nothing less than love, and the Moon Priestess knew he had a wealth of it to give, but he was afraid of weakness.

How had Khepri gone from this to cursing him to walk

the earth for all eternity? Kalila didn't understand, and she wanted to. She *needed* to.

The river of time pulled at her, the undertow dragging her away from the place of palm fronds and sweet-smelling water, and back toward her reality. As she was plucked from the dream she heard Khepri calling her name and asking her to stay.

When she opened her eyes, she was alone on the cot and he was stuffing his feet into his boots.

"You're finally awake. The sun's been up for a while now. We should get to it before it gets too brutal."

He handed her a bottle of water and a plate with jerky, biscuits, and jam.

"Breakfast in bed. Thanks." She tried to act as if spending the night in his arms was a completely normal event.

She stuffed down her food and said, "I'll meet you at the access. I need to get dressed." Kalila darted over to her own tent and freshened up before putting on her work clothes.

It occurred to her again that simply sleeping in the same tent with him had been a fantasy come true. Yet, this morning, she was still the same Kalila. He was still the same Seth. It hadn't been some irrevocable change.

He was back down in the first room and intently working on clearing a wall piece for further analysis. She dug back in with her chosen piece, using a brush with fine hairs to clear away some of the dust debris. They worked side by side in companionable silence for some time, until the sun was high and angry above them.

Slowly, graffiti began to take shape across the bottom right corner of the hieroglyphic retelling of the tale of He Who Endures.

She laughed until she honked like a goose when she realized what it said.

He looked up from his work, pushing sweat away from his brow. "What?"

"There's graffiti here. Look." She pointed to the corner of the mural. "And it says, 'Amen was here.' People don't ever change, do they?"

Seth nodded. "Not really. I was in Rome when they called me to join the dig, and I was having similar thoughts. Have you ever been?"

"Not yet." She wanted to go. Kalila had been to many strange and wonderful places, but she hadn't seen a lot of the commonly accepted marvels. She'd camped out on Easter Island, as a child had gotten to swim with the turtles in a lagoon on the Galapagos Islands, gotten to spend a week in Machu Picchu, but she'd never been to Rome. Or Paris.

"So, there are ruins all about the city. Everywhere you go is a blend of ancient and modern. There is graffiti in some of those ruins dating back to the earliest days of Rome. And it's the same. *'Lucius Pinxit.'*"

She remembered her Latin well. "'Lucius wrote this'?" Kalila laughed. "I had a friend who went to Rome and said she was disappointed in how dirty it was in some places. So much graffiti. But it hasn't changed, has it?"

"No, I'd say not. The architecture is different, but people still face the same struggles. To be heard. To be seen. To try to make a mark that will be remembered."

"Something that will endure," she blurted, and then realized the connotation. The subject he hated most in the world, which of course begged the question why he was even there.

"Speaking of enduring, that purple used for Khepri's hieroglyph . . . it shouldn't be here."

The discovery thrilled her. It could mean any number of things, most of which were boring and banal, but it was the possibility that lit her fuse. "I know! It wasn't known in Egypt or Jordan until almost a dynasty later. What is it doing here? There's so much about this place. I feel like every time we get close to answering one question, it'll spark a hundred more. Which is both exciting and exhausting."

He put down his tools. "Given the chance, would you spend your career studying this place?"

She met his gaze. "As long as it kept yielding information, I can't imagine being anywhere else."

Kalila watched him take a deep breath, and his shoulders sagged under the weight of something unseen.

"What would you do if the heart were real?"

He couldn't be going where she thought he was with this. "I'm sure it's real."

"No, I mean, what if it had magic?"

He was! What had gotten into him? It didn't seem like this was a trick so he could taunt her. "I thought these were the kinds of suppositions you hated."

"Humor me." He looked away from her for a moment. "Please?"

"I don't know. If it had magic, I'd keep it."

"You want to live forever?" he asked softly.

The idea of living forever had been one she'd thought of often. One couldn't consider the possibility of He Who Endures without considering what it would be like to walk in his shoes.

"I wouldn't hate it. I mean, all my family has already

passed. So I don't have to worry about outliving anyone. I'd be able to read all the books on my to-read list. I'd get to learn so much. See so much. Explore every inch of this beautiful world." She smiled at him. "But that's not why I'd take it. It's not mine, so I wouldn't take it to use it. I'd take it to protect it until the owner comes for it. If it has magic, that would mean it belongs to someone else, regardless of what my father said about it."

"What did Rafael say about it?"

He came to sit next to her, and she could feel his body heat against her hip and her leg. She wanted him closer, wanted that electric frisson when they were skin to skin.

"You have to promise you're not going to laugh at me."

"I solemnly swear."

Looking up into his earnest eyes, she believed him. Kalila decided to take a chance and tell him.

"When I was a little girl I had these recurring dreams. Sometimes I still have them, but it was mostly when I was little. I'm sure it's just because the stories of the myth captured my imagination, and they still do."

She bit her lip. Waiting to see some kind of scorn or derision on his face, but there was none, so she continued. "In these dreams, I'm the Moon Priestess. I would live out days in her life in those dreams. Most often, it's in a place that smells like ripe figs, and myrrh, and maybe cardamom. When I'd tell my dad about those dreams, he would tell me that I had to find He Who Endures, or at least the tomb that held his heart, because it belonged to me." It was one of Kalila's happiest memories because he'd encouraged her to search, to believe, to trust her own perceptions, no matter how wild they seemed.

"Is that your price for everyone?" Seth asked.

"My price? What do you mean?"

"Khepri's price for Menes was his heart. Is that the price you want me to pay?"

"No, I know you don't have it to give." She gave a dull laugh. "It's probably buried in some tomb somewhere, too."

"Harsh." Seth smiled, but it wasn't one of joy or ease. It was sad somehow.

"But am I wrong?" She knew that she wasn't. In all the years that Kalila had known Seth, he'd never been in any kind of meaningful relationship.

"No." Except even as he answered, he'd wrapped his big hand around the back of her neck and pulled her gently toward him.

He was going to kiss her, and in that moment she wanted his kiss more than she wanted concrete proof that Menes and Khepri had walked the earth.

"*My* price," she whispered against the hard slash of his mouth, "is pleasure."

It was inevitable then, the crashing together of their mouths like their bodies had their own gravitational pull. She'd wanted this for so long, and when his mouth took hers, it was everything she'd ever hoped it could be.

Kalila wrapped her arms around him, and she couldn't seem to get close enough. She couldn't touch enough of him. She wasn't sure if she'd crawled into his lap or he'd pulled her there, not that it mattered. The only thing that did matter was the fire between them. The friction when she rolled her hips that send fireworks exploding through her body.

It was fanciful, she realized, to think that he tasted like eternity. When she tried to quantify eternity, and how it should taste, where she'd gotten such a silly idea, still, all she could think of was him. Seth had become as immutable as a mountain in her imagination.

Yet he was not immutable. He was a living, breathing man who was made of flesh and bone, just like her. He was no monolith. He had hopes and desires, pain and loss, just as everyone did.

His hands moved to the buttons on her shirt. "With your permission?"

Goddamn, if still asking for consent even when she was clearly into it wasn't the sexiest thing she'd ever heard come out of a man's mouth, she didn't know what was. It spoke to the kind of man he was. His integrity. His decency.

It made her want him even more.

"God yes!" And then, while his hands made short work of those buttons, she nuzzled into his neck, her lips pressed against the pulse of his heartbeat. "Will you give me the same, Seth? Do I have your permission?" Her palms rested flat against his chest, waiting for his consent to strip him bare.

"Ah, *Kalila*." He said her name with reverence, almost as if her name itself were an endearment.

And at one time, it had been. Her name meant beloved.

"I can't give you my heart, but my body is yours," he said.

The passion in his words, the sincerity twisted sharp thorns into her heart. She knew she should be experiencing this moment with every part of her except her heart, but she couldn't shut the thing down. It had a mind and a will of its own.

It had decided, for better or worse, that this was a man she loved. Regardless of whether or not he had those same feelings for her. Of course she wanted his love, but the point of loving was to give, and do it freely, with no expectation of anything in return.

It was on the tip of her tongue to tell him how she felt, but Kalila was sure that he already knew, and to give the words life and breath would only make him feel guilty about what was happening between them.

While Kalila knew she wasn't responsible for his feelings or his actions, she knew that if he felt guilty about it, he would stop, and she wanted his touch more than she wanted him to hear her confess something he already knew.

Yet she couldn't keep the reverence out of her touch. It was in the way she mapped the topography of his body with her hands, committing every curve of muscle, every angle of his flesh to memory. It was in the way she worshipped him with her mouth, her lips embossing his skin with her devotion with every kiss.

"Let me taste you," he said against her throat. "I want your pleasure on my tongue."

He spread his shirt on the hard ground for her, and she leaned back on her elbows and splayed herself open for him.

"By Osiris, you're the most beautiful thing I've ever seen."

Osiris? It had seemed like a spontaneous utterance, not an affectation. Only, before she had time to consider the implications of what he'd said, he was bent between her thighs, and his silky hair brushed against her skin, sending waves of need through her.

His goatee barely brushed her cleft, and the actuality of the sensation was better than anything she'd ever imagined. The first touch of his tongue sent her spiraling into a mindless bliss where nothing existed except ecstasy.

It was only moments before he had her on edge, but he pulled back.

"Not yet," he whispered against her skin.

It was as if he knew what she wanted before she spoke the words. She'd wanted this to last. Kalila didn't know what was on the other side of this pleasure, but she had the distinct feeling that it would never be like this again.

She wanted to wring every moment, every sensation from this encounter that she could.

He moved up her body until he rose above her, looking into her eyes while his hand replaced his tongue, his thumb gently strumming her clit while he pressed two fingers inside her heat.

Her eyelids were heavy with desire, but she wanted to look into his eyes. She had to, to know that this was real.

He whispered something to her in a language she didn't understand but that was familiar somehow.

"I want you, Seth. Now," she demanded.

"Patience, Kalila." He pressed a kiss to the edge of her mouth that was somehow the most devastating thing he could have done. "I want to watch you first. I want to feel you clench around my fingers, and I want to taste your cries of pleasure."

His words were poetry, his lips were a song, and his body was art. Everything about him seemed crafted by the divine, and for this moment he was hers.

Suddenly, he pulled back, but this time, it wasn't for any sort of erotic purpose. His shoulders tensed and she watched as all his muscles coiled and prepared to strike.

"What is it?"

"I don't think we're alone."

"We're definitely alone. Unless the crew got in early, but we'd have heard them long before they arrived."

He was on his feet in a single leap, unmindful of his nakedness. And, in truth, it was her opinion that he should never, ever wear clothes. In fact, it should be considered an international crime to cover up a body like his.

"Get dressed. Arm yourself. Just in case."

Damn. She'd been cockblocked by a curse.

He grabbed twin blades from his discarded clothing and crept out of the room, toward the access.

She exhaled heavily and began to dress, mentally cataloging where all the weapons in the camp were located and how she'd need to move to access them, depending on the threat.

Kalila wondered just what was next, because it had been jackals, then a wall of flesh-eating scarabs, and now what? Besides her raging case of blue bean.

At this point she wouldn't be surprised if He Who Endures himself walked into their camp.

Chapter Six

Seth didn't want to leave her like that, sweet and wanting, and oh so close to orgasm.

But it was possible that the Left Hand had been behind the jackals, and he wouldn't put it past them to hurt Kalila simply to keep him from his goal.

Yet he wondered about the giant scarabs. They'd protected him, and Kalila. They seemed to even . . . like her. When coupled with her dreams, Seth's logic could lead him to only one conclusion, but that was even more insane than his existence.

Could Kalila be Khepri?

No. He wouldn't say it wasn't possible, but it wasn't likely. Considering Kalila didn't demand anything from him he couldn't give her, and she wasn't inclined to punish him for it either.

Dusk was already falling again. How could that be? It

hadn't seemed like they'd spent that much time down in the first room. He had the strangest thought that they'd been kept down there until they made the choices someone wanted them to make.

But that was insane. It wasn't as if, after all these years, Isis or Osiris were going to puff up from the ether and meddle in his life.

Seth crept forward, silent and alert, taking in everything around him. He looked for the small details of someone's passing—items having been moved, shifts in the sand—and he found nothing.

Not until he got to his tent, and there saw the hieroglyph that loosely translated to "demon" had been painted on his tent in something red that definitely was not paint.

"Someone really doesn't want us here," Kalila said, and handed him his clothes.

He dressed quickly, all the while scanning the horizon, searching for any possible threat. Seth had to get Kalila out of there, but he was faced with two insurmountable problems. She wouldn't go, and even if he could convince her, there was no way to go until the rest of the crew was on-site. He couldn't expect her to start out on foot in the open desert. Not that she would. He knew with a certainty she wouldn't leave this site, and she definitely wouldn't leave him.

"Someone really doesn't want *me* here," he began.

"Let me guess. You think I should leave."

He turned to look at her, really *look at her*. She stood at the ready, with her makeshift flamethrower, the riot gun, and determination in her eyes.

"Of course I think you should leave. I don't want you to get hurt." He allowed himself the luxury of reaching out to touch her face. "It's not that I don't think you're competent, or strong. I care about what happens to you, Kalila."

"And *I* care about what happens to *you*. I know you're about to say something like how you couldn't live with yourself if something happened to me, but what about what I can live with? Do you think I'd be able to forgive myself if I left you here, alone?" She held up her hand to stop him from speaking. "Not to mention one of the most significant finds of the century? Not a chance." She looked out at the sandy horizon. "Plus, I'm not tromping through the desert on my own. That would be even more dangerous. At least here, we can protect each other."

Seth considered arguing with her because he didn't need her protection. Or want it. He'd come here to die.

But he couldn't very well tell her that, could he?

Except, looking into her eyes, he realized he trusted her. He trusted her more than he'd ever trusted another living soul. He wanted to tell her the truth. He ached for it. Keeping it from her had become a physical pain. But the question remained whether he should. Seth realized he was hot and cold when it came to telling her or not, but he needed to know he wasn't only telling her for himself. Lessening his own burden while adding to hers.

Seth also knew if he told her who he was, there was no chance this side of the afterlife she'd leave. Not that there was much to begin with.

"So, in the stories," she began carefully, as if her words were shards of glass on her lips. "They speak of a religious sect called the Left Hand of the Moon. It seems surreal to ask this, but do you think this could be their work?"

The question was like a punch in the face.

When he didn't speak she continued. "I know what

that would imply if we agreed it could be this sect, but I have no answers that don't have some kind of supernatural root cause. Looking at this as a woman of science, I can allow that the jackals might have been a coincidence. Even though the scarab behavior was unlikely, it's still possible the jackals emitted some pheromone or something that drew them as prey over us, but the passage of time, Seth. I know we didn't spend more than a few hours down in the dig. There's no way it should be dusk, and it's not a sandstorm. So what is it?"

He nodded slowly. "Okay. What if it is the Left Hand of the Moon? If it is, they seem to only have a problem with me. Not you."

"If you say one more word about me leaving you here, I'm going to actually . . . I don't know what I'm going to do, but you won't like it."

He couldn't help but laugh. "Fine. I won't bring it up again, but how are we going to fight off the Left Hand until the rest of the crew gets here, and when they do, how are we going to protect the site and whatever we find?"

"I think you're forgetting the most important thing here, Seth."

"What's that?" He was quite sure he hadn't forgotten it at all.

"If we allow that these strange occurrences can be attributed to the Left Hand of the Moon, we have to allow that the heart is here, and its owner will be coming for it."

He cocked his head. "Why would you assume he'd want it?" Seth cleared his throat. "Granting such a thing, such an existence, were possible?"

"That's a lot of power to have over someone. If someone else uses it before he can get it, he has to live *forever*.

Even if I wasn't ready for the dirt nap, I wouldn't want someone telling me I could never have it." She bit her lip, obviously considering something.

"Okay, so now that we know it's here, we have to find it. If it wasn't, they wouldn't be trying so hard to keep us from it," Seth said as a cold twinge of guilt skittered down his back. He'd spent so long trying to root the myth of him out of her head, and now he was preying on her fantasies to get her to help him find the heart he'd told her didn't exist.

He was a bastard. Maybe he'd deserved his punishment after all. It occurred to him that he'd always put his own wants and needs above everyone else in his life. Even those he'd claimed to love.

Everything he'd ever done had been with some kind of end goal in mind. He'd been a conqueror, he said, to unite the people, but it had been for his own insatiable lust for power. When he'd taken Khepri he'd not forced himself on her. He'd seduced her. Their pleasure had been mutual. Only he'd demanded to marry her because she was the best. The most beautiful. He couldn't have given her his heart if he'd wanted to, because he did not yet know what it meant. In his friendships, they'd never been for the sake of getting to experience the other person. They'd all been motivated by some selfish desire.

The revelation had found the weakness in his armor and had split it apart like a cracked egg. He was bare and vulnerable not to anyone else, but to the truth. And it cut with a thousand blades.

Seth supposed it was fitting that he'd finally learned the lesson he'd been meant to learn all those long years ago.

"We're taking a chance going back down in the dig. I

mean, we were before, but now that there's someone who will do anything to stop us, we need to take some more precautions. Should we search in shifts? One person is the lookout, while the other looks for the heart?"

"We're safer together." There was no way he was going to let her stand watch. "We can rig alarms around the camp with fishing wire and we stay strapped."

"Won't they see us?"

"No. I can find my way in the dark. You're going to stay down in the first room, lanterns high. If it looks like you're only interested in the hieroglyphs, you should be safe, at least until I get back."

He didn't want to leave her, not even for those few moments it would take to string the line around the perimeter, but he had no choice. They couldn't get down in the dig without some kind of protection topside.

Seth wanted to finish what they'd started earlier, but there wasn't enough time.

How odd, for a man who'd had millennia to get his fill of the world and what it had to offer that now he'd run out of time. The irony of the situation wasn't lost on him.

It occurred to him that he could choose.

He didn't have to be done.

Part of him had wanted to die simply to spite his curse. But there was that other part of him that still had things he wanted to experience. After all his long years, it hit him just now that he still had living to do. Why should he deny himself anything he wanted when it was so obvious that she wanted him, too? Being happy would be the best rebellion.

He allowed himself to imagine a future with Kalila. What did his happiness look like?

It shocked Seth that it didn't look much different from

where he was right now. The only thing he'd change would be the Left Hand of the Moon putting Kalila in danger. Otherwise, being out on some discovery mission with her, strolling through the pages of antiquity, and bringing the ancient world to the modern, there was nothing better.

"What?" she asked him. "Why are you looking at me like that?"

He offered her a crooked grin. "Just thinking."

Only then, the scene changed. She wouldn't stay young. She'd grow old; she'd die. While he . . . he would simply have to endure.

Unless he found the heart.

Then he could still have his happiness, and he could leave this world when she did. Because with Kalila gone, the world would finally have nothing left to offer him.

"Well, you'd better think faster. It's almost dark."

"Remember what I told you."

"Crank the lanterns. Work on the hieroglyphics. Situational awareness. Got it."

"I'll be back in less than ten minutes."

He dashed to his tent and pulled some lengths of fishing line from his bag. He'd packed enough to rig the whole camp, but Seth was most worried about keeping the dig site safe. It didn't matter if they vandalized his tent, or took his belongings. What mattered most was seeing their enemy coming, and being ready to launch a counterattack. He tried to work out a more feasible plan as he rigged the line around the camp. If only he could be sure that the scarabs would still protect her. He considered for a moment offering a prayer to Isis.

He had never prayed to her before. Never honored her temples or her days. He'd never bowed to any power but his own.

Yet, he'd do it for Kalila.

In times past, he'd only have had faith in what he could see and touch, in the actions he could take. This was a leap for him, and he wondered if any of the old gods were left, or if he'd outlived them, too.

"Hear me, Oh Great Isis, Queen of Heaven." He spread his arms wide as he beseeched the sky and fell to his knees. "I, Menes Sethos Cepos Akhenaten Dakarai, am on my knees in supplication." He bowed his head. "I am He Who Endures and I beg your blessing. I have done all that mortal hands are capable of doing and I ask your protection, not for me, but for *her*."

The night was silent and still, no breeze rustling the encroaching darkness around him. Yet, still, something shifted in the great expanse of sky overhead, and the moon's silver light fell in a diamond-dusted waterfall on his face.

He wanted to believe that she heard him, he wanted to believe she'd grant him this one boon.

The moment was over and the clouds crashed together, blocking out the silver light, which was just as well. He didn't need his enemies seeing him traipsing about the camp, yet if they had been watching, they would have seen him surrendering to their goddess, entreating her aid. They'd think him mad.

Maybe he was.

Maybe the long years of solitude had finally taken their toll on him and he was nuttier than squirrel shit, as Rafael had loved to say.

Except Seth couldn't help looking up at the sky again, and it seemed to him there was now no moon at all. No clouds. It was as if it had all been a figment of his imagination.

He scanned the horizon one last time and, not sensing any movement or that there was anyone in the camp but him and Kalila, he went to the access point and descended to where Kalila was working with the first mural of hieroglyphics.

"Find anything interesting here?"

She looked up from her work. "I did, actually." Kalila stepped down from the ladder. "So, as you can see in this entryway," she motioned to the four walls and the ceiling, "it looks as if the tale of He Who Endures is basically copy/pasted around the whole area. Look here at the third mural. Instead of Khepri's scarab, we have what might be a representation of the god Set. See the saluki-shaped creature wearing the headdress?"

He leaned in to examine it, and it pulsed the same strange purple that Khepri's scarab glyph had earlier.

"I'd swear that wasn't there yesterday."

"I know. Me too." She nodded. "It's strange the things our eyes want to see, and how easily we miss what's right in front of us."

He felt like that had deeper meaning, but they didn't have time for him to analyze it.

"If that's the thing that's not like the other, it must be a code," he said.

"So we need to look for other examples," she instructed. "What progress have you made on the piece you were working on?"

"Not much. It looks like a portrait of some kind."

"Which is highly unusual, don't you think?"

He nodded. "From the markings, I think he might be a priest."

"I'm racking my brain, but I can't think of a time when anything like a portrait has been on the wall in any of these tombs or the lost cities. Carvings, yes. Stories with body figures, but never anything like a portrait. That has to mean something."

"I think it means that this place was not lost for as long as we originally thought. The painting style, even the pigments, I think are more modern." He shrugged. "Eh, Italian Proto-Renaissance modern, not airplane modern. For example, this blue? If it's what I think it is, I'd have to have it tested to be certain, but it's some kind of ground gemstone. Lapis, maybe? I can't remember off the top of my head, but it was first used in Giotto di Bondone's *The Lamentation of Christ*. So I would date this portrait between 1304 and 1400."

"The Left Hand of the Moon," she whispered, with something like awe tinging her voice. Kalila grabbed her electric lantern and shone it next to the portrait. "Do you think this is a self-portrait? Or a warning?"

"It could be both," he agreed easily.

"Bastard," she whispered. "Defacing this place with his modern nonsense."

"I have to wonder what caused the sinkhole." Suddenly, he wondered if this was a trap. But to what end? They couldn't kill him and they didn't want him to die.

She nodded. "How long have they been using it, and are they using it still? We need to go deeper." Then she leaned in closer to the wall. "Hey, look. There's another of Set's glyphs."

"Set was a trickster god, which means his glyphs are no use to us."

"We just haven't figured out how to use them yet, but we will." She crept forward down the long hall with her lantern held aloft, and it stretched shadows down those vividly painted halls.

There were too many choices, too many opportunities for deadly traps.

"Don't go any farther!"

"What, why?"

"Just like we rigged our camp, this place must surely be rigged, too, if they were using it as some sort of headquarters. Or if the heart is here."

While he didn't expect fear from her, rather a healthy sense of caution, he was surprised at her grin. "Do you think there might be some big-ass boulder that might chase us down these hallways like *Indiana Jones*?"

"It's probably snakes, if we're honest." Because what would be worse than giant, flesh-eating scarabs? Of course snakes.

She positively cackled. "Unlike Indy, I like snakes."

And suddenly, there was an answering cackle, yet it was not made by a human voice. It was the high-pitched keening of a jackal.

Chapter Seven

"It's fine." Kalila shook her head. "It's all *fiiiinnne*. That absolutely was *not* a jackal I heard."

"No. Totally not," he agreed much too easily.

She looked around, half expecting to see the wave of scarabs again, but no such savior presented itself.

Kalila laughed nervously. "The curse did say they were undead."

"It did," he answered, but there was no teasing in his voice. No lighthearted banter.

For someone who'd spent much of their time together trying to convince her that all of this—the story of He Who Endures, the Left Hand of the Moon, and curses— was all tripe, he'd sure changed his mind in a hurry.

It didn't add up.

Most people didn't let go of their long-held belief systems so easily. Not even in the face of blatant and over-whelming evidence to the contrary.

Things began to snap into place in her mind. Each and every experience she'd had since she'd been in Jordan had somehow magnetized the pieces of the puzzle and they rearranged themselves until they fit.

She watched him in the warm glow of the lantern light, and she knew now why it had seemed like he'd hated her in Greece.

Why he'd tried so hard to convince her and her father that they were wasting their lives searching for a myth.

Kalila knew why it seemed he was a hardened soldier rather than an art historian.

She even knew why he was here now.

Why he wanted the heart.

There was only one answer that fit with the evidence.

The man standing before her, his face unmarred and ungrooved by the relentless march of time, the man who had touched her so intimately, this man that she loved, he was none other than Menes Sethos Cepos Akhenaten.

He Who Endures.

Her own heart stuttered in her chest. How could she have missed it? Those questions he'd asked her about what she'd do with the heart—that had been as close as he could come to telling her the truth. He wanted to know if he could trust her.

She swallowed hard as the implication of what this all meant struck home.

Well, shit, she had no hope of capturing the man's heart now. The goddamn thing had calcified in a jar. Kalila had to bite her lip to keep from surrendering to hysterical laughter.

She was determined not to freak out or lose her shit. She knew now that she could never share any of what she'd discovered here with the academic world. She'd had this mad hope of validating her father's legacy, her own. Making a name for herself with this dig. She couldn't do that. Not now.

Especially not now…because he was here to die.

Her eyes stung and her throat constricted.

Swallow it. Stuff it down, she commanded herself.

What replaced her grief was the burning plethora of questions she wanted to ask him about the things he'd seen, the things he'd done, and what it had been like to watch humanity move through time without him.

More than ever, Kalila wanted to tell him what he meant to her. Not as the myth, but the man who'd touched her, kissed her, and held her in his arms.

One more connection sparked in her brain. Why they'd used Set's glyph. Set. Sethos. *Seth*. She'd thought some of it had been simple graffiti, but it wasn't. They were a map!

"What?"

"I know how to find it!" she blurted.

For a single moment, less than that, she'd been sorely tempted to keep her revelation about the glyphs to herself. If he couldn't find the heart, he couldn't leave her. If he couldn't find the heart, he couldn't die. She wanted more time with him. Why was there never enough time?

Not enough time to see everything she wanted, do everything she wanted, or hug as long as she wanted. What she wouldn't give for one more minute with her father. Her mother. Seth.

Only those thoughts weren't in line with the person

she wanted to be. Or the person she believed herself to be. Regardless of how the outcome might hurt, Kalila had to do what she knew to be right.

"How?"

"It's the Set glyphs. I saw more down another of those halls, and it looked like graffiti, but it's not. It's a map."

"That could lead to a deadly trap. Big-ass boulder, remember?" he teased her, but it fell flat.

"No, Seth. I know it's the way." She put her hand over her heart. "I know, because it's only on those particular murals that the Khepri scarab glows for me."

Another revelation hit her. Had she already *had* a lifetime to love this man? Had she thrown it away into the jaws of jackals? The thought turned her stomach.

Kalila desperately wanted to know what he thought of her; that was, if he thought of her as Khepri 2.0? Did he see the Moon Priestess in her, and was that why he wanted her? She took a deep breath. She'd drive herself insane if she kept following that train of thought.

He nodded. "Lead the way."

She lifted the lantern, grabbed her tools, and headed down into the pitch-black of the left hallway. There it was, just as she'd remembered. The Set graffiti. Only that hallway ended with no other branches to follow.

"Where now?"

"There has to be a hidden passage. Help me find it!"

He used his own lantern and his fingers to feel along the edges of the wall, and she sank to her knees to search the area beneath the graffiti.

"Look, Kalila!"

She turned and looked to where he pointed. It was a single loose stone in the floor.

"Snakes or boulder?" she asked him.

"Poison arrows?" He shrugged.

"One way to find out." She launched herself over to the stone and pressed it with the heel of her hand.

The floor beneath them gave way to some kind of chute, and they were sent careening down into a heavier darkness beneath the lost city of the dead. Kalila wasn't sure how she managed the trip down without screaming, but she did, and she kept her electric lantern pressed tight against her chest.

She hit the bottom with a thud, and Seth was close behind. Kalila scrambled out of the way because being dropped via some slide from hell onto a stone floor from at least a story above was not something she cared to repeat.

At least not until she figured out where they were, how they were getting out, and if she'd found what they were looking for.

Seth groaned as he got to his feet and dusted himself off. He turned up his lantern, as did she, and they realized the walls had been painted with gold.

They were in some kind of sacred space because treasures lined the walls. Gold, silver, emeralds, rubies, and other precious stones and coins filled the room. There were piles and piles of them from wall to wall.

"The heart is a prize beyond treasure. So there must be another door," she mused aloud.

"Many would be tempted here, but you're not?"

"No. Even if I were so inclined, this would all belong to the people of Jordan. Not to me." Yet something glinted in the light and called her attention away from her task. It was a crown of hammered silver, and it had been fashioned in the shape of a scarab, inset with amethysts and emeralds. The purple-green of Khepri's scarabs. "Except for that. That might have been mine in another life," she whispered before she could stop herself.

"Maybe you should wear it, then. Maybe the scarabs would answer your call if we're attacked again. I doubt the jackals can use tools and levers to get down here, but you never know. Especially if they're undead. They'd have had a lot of time to learn," he teased her.

"Or if someone lets them in," she said softly.

"I was trying not to think about that."

"I have to tell you something."

"What? Now?" he asked, seemingly incredulous.

"Yes, now. If not now, when?" She took his face in her hands and pressed her mouth to his. "I'm not asking you for anything—"

Suddenly, he looked haunted, and it made her doubt her decision.

"Kalila, you can't—"

"I can do whatever I please." She released him. "And what pleases me is that you know I love you."

Lucky for her, inspiration struck and saved her from his awkward silence. Even though she didn't want him to say words he didn't feel, she didn't want to sit there with him while he fumbled for a kind way to say *no, thank you*, either.

"Come on. The heart is *beyond* treasure." She pointed at the far wall, where a door they hadn't noticed had opened and no glow from gold or jewels issued forth.

They moved forward as a unit, careful to stay on what looked to be a marked path through the mountains of treasure.

When they entered the room, long rows of old torchères burst to life, illuminating the burial chamber of He Who Endures.

On a giant, round slab in the middle of the room were twelve mummified jackals.

"Oh fuck me," she whispered.

"I don't think I could here, sorry." His eyes were on the jackals, as if he waited for them to burst to life just as the torchères had and devour him.

At this point it wouldn't surprise her if they did.

"That's just creepy. Are those the ones that . . ."

"I think so," he answered.

There was something in the middle of the jackals. It looked to be a small jar.

The reality of where they were, what they had found had started to set in. This was it. The mummified heart so many had spent so long looking for.

Yet the only seeker that mattered was right here next to her. "Go on," she said. "Take it."

He shook his head slowly. "I can't."

She realized then they were guarding it. The Left Hand knew he wouldn't be able to pass the pack to claim it.

Well, they hadn't counted on her, had they? Mother-fuckers.

She scrambled up onto the stone, and just as she was about to snatch the coveted jar from its eternal rest, she paused and looked at him.

He nodded along. "Big-ass boulder," he said, referencing the scene from the movie once again.

"Here goes nothing," she said as she lifted the jar.

Nothing happened. No ancient devices whirling to begin sealing her doom. No howling, zombies, mummy jackals. Nothing.

Almost to her disappointment.

She hopped off the stone, and as she did, she saw three more tableaux set up much the same way.

"Uh, did the guy have more than one heart?"

"Oh hell no," he said when he tilted his head in the direction she pointed.

"How do we know which one is the right one?"

"We don't. We take them all."

That was not the answer she'd been expecting. She'd thought he'd know his own heart, but it was right in front of him, and he didn't. . . .

Now she understood the lesson.

His heart, the Moon Priestess, had been right in front of him all along. Yet he'd been too stubborn, too prideful to see it.

Kalila wanted so badly to tell him, but she knew that revelation was for him to figure out on his own, if there was time.

"I think that's going to end badly," she said, regretting her earlier disappointment that nothing awful had happened when she'd snatched the first jar.

"What else can we do? What if we only take this one and we find our way out and discover it's not the one?"

"What if it is the right one and the wrong one triggers a big-ass boulder?" she shot back.

"Then we'll escape and you'll have quite the story to tell, won't you?"

"Okay." She sighed, as if she was entirely put-upon. Although she knew she was going to grab those other jars.

Kalila stepped carefully over to the other displays. She removed each jar in turn, waiting for something to happen. Yet each jar was removed with no consequence.

The air was suddenly redolent of her dreams: the scents of ripe fig, of cardamom, and of myrrh.

"Do you smell that?"

"Besides the must of ten thousand years? No."

A low growl startled her, and she turned to see the jackal mummies had begun to move. They were stretching, shaking their cotton-wrapped heads, and their eyes had all started to glow an eerie red.

This, this was the curse. To rot in the bellies of undead jackals for all eternity.

"Seth?" She swallowed hard. "I think I need saving now."

Except he couldn't save her, could he? These jackals were his weakness. He couldn't even move among them to grab the heart he'd searched eons for. It was right in front of him, and their corpses had frozen him solid. He wouldn't be able to help her. Her gun would be no use, but maybe her makeshift flamethrower—

The eyes of a jackal narrowed, as if it knew what she was thinking, and it leaped at her. Kalila drew her hair spray and her Zippo lighter to spray flame across the dried tinder of his wraps, and then feinted to the right, out of its bite radius.

Only instead of taking the thing out, her action simply made it more horrible. It landed and shook its flaming head, its slavering jaws snapping, and it leaped again.

Kalila had nowhere else to go. It had her cornered.

Yet the burning bite never came.

Seth had somehow bent space and time to put himself between her and the jackal. Its flaming jaws closed over his arm, and then it was gone, as if it had never been.

One by one, the undead jackals that had so recently come to unlife disappeared, as if they'd never existed. The only concrete proof of the reality of what they'd just seen was the deep, bleeding bite in his forearm.

"You're not going to turn into a zombie, are you?"

"Shit, I might."

She exhaled a deep sigh of relief and leaned against him. "That was insane."

"Like the rest of this night, eh?" He kissed the top of her forehead.

"Thank you."

"For what?"

"Saving me. That had to have been terrifying for you."

"For me? You're the one who almost got eaten."

It was on the tip of her tongue to say he was the one who actually had been eaten, but she bit it back.

"We need to figure out how to get out of here. I'm pretty sure back the way we came is a no-go."

She nodded. "Most of these cities of the dead have an exit route. It's quick and simple." She looked around. "I imagine there should be some stairs around here somewhere that lead to the surface. And I'm so glad I just put new batteries in these lanterns."

Just then, a great roar echoed through the tunnels and rattled the foundations like a great storm.

Only it wasn't a storm.

It was an explosion.

Chapter Eight

The walls around them came down like dominoes folding in on one another.

Seth's first thought was to protect Kalila, and he wrapped her in his arms and dove with her under one of the tilted slabs as half the ceiling rained down in rubble on top of them.

When the dust and detritus had settled, he saw the slabs had built them a tiny, makeshift room. Enough that they could move around. Enough that they had a few hours of air.

A few hours of air if he slowed his life-functions and he didn't breathe.

In the warm glow of the lantern light, he saw horrible knowledge in her eyes. At first, he thought that it was only about their situation, but when she slowly extended the jars to him, he realized she knew everything.

He didn't accept them. Instead, he said, "I swear I'll get you out. I will."

A madness took hold of him, then. Some kind of panicked rage he'd never felt before. Not even when he was reliving what those damned jackals had done to him. She couldn't die down here. He wouldn't let her.

It wasn't fair.

Fuck, but when had life ever been fair for anyone? Why should it be fair for her?

Because it just had to be. Because in all his long years of existence, he'd never done any of the things he should have. Because if anyone deserved another breath, it was Kalila. She could do all the things he was supposed to.

She was the one with the pure heart.

She was the one who wanted to drink the world down and wring it for all it was worth.

She was the one . . .

He'd started clawing at the rubble with his bare hands, and the more he pulled down, the more came to take its place.

Her hands were on his and her voice was soft in his ear. "Stop."

He couldn't stop. If he stopped, she was going to die.

"Stop," she said again.

Something in her voice made him pause, made him turn to look at her.

"It's not your fault, Seth. It's okay."

No, it wasn't okay. Nothing would ever be okay again. It *was* his fault. He should have made her leave. He should have done anything except what he had done. Any deviation at so many points along this road and they wouldn't have ended up here.

He'd fucked up again. He'd put his own wants and desires over someone who loved him.

Someone he . . . cared about.

"Your poor hands," she said, pulling strips from her own shirt to wrap around his hands. "They're ground beef."

"They'll heal. I can do it. I can get you out. Let me."

"You can do a lot of things, Seth, but moving literal tons of earth and stone is not one of them."

"I swear by Isis you're not going to die down here."

She exhaled on a shaky breath. "And what can you do to stop it?" Kalila swallowed hard. "Doesn't matter. Because I achieved what I dreamed about most."

Oh, he didn't want to look at her. He didn't know if he could stand it. Him? Finding him was what she'd dreamed about most, wasn't it? What a useless goddamn thing that was. Only he couldn't tell her that. Not here. Not now.

"You did," he said quietly. "You always believed."

"How stupid you must have thought me," she said quietly. "I get it now. I really do."

"You weren't stupid. As a child, you were a treasure. As a woman, that and more." Looking in her eyes and seeing that love for him shining there cut him deeper than any knife. "I'll tell you now why I was angry at you in Greece. I owe you that."

"You don't owe me anything."

"I want to tell you," he said finally.

She squeezed his hand.

"It was because I wasn't anything like the way you imagined me. I haven't done anything special. I haven't changed the world. I haven't done anything but exist."

"You don't think you've changed the lives of the people you've met? Those you've helped?"

"Not in any measurable way."

"Maybe not to you. Have you heard the starfish allegory?"

"The one with the child throwing beached starfish back in the sea?"

"Yeah. She may not have been able to save all of them, but don't you think she changed things for the ones she did?"

"We shouldn't be using up our air talking," he said. "Especially me. I don't need to breathe. If I don't, you'll have more."

"Why? To suffer longer? It'll be at least two days until the rest of the crew can get here once I don't check in by radio. There isn't two days' worth of air in here even if you don't breathe."

"Why do you seem so goddamn eager to die?" he snapped.

"I'm not. I'm scared, I'm pissed. I'm not ready to be done with this world. This life. I want more. God, I've always wanted more of everything, but mostly what I want is time. Time with my mom, my dad, you . . . but I'm not going to get it. I don't want to spend my last breaths afraid. I'd rather spend them in awe. Even knowing I'd end up here, I don't think I'd choose any differently. I got to find you. To know you. You don't know what that means to me."

"It means too much, Kalila. Your life? Not worth this," he said as he smacked his chest.

"Tell me the history of the world, warlord. Tell me the stories of the things you've seen. Please tell me you've written down your memoirs somewhere so that someday those stories will be read. Even if people have to believe they're fiction."

"I hate to tell you, sweetheart, I'm just like Rome. I'm graffitied, dirty, and not much different from when I was young."

"Then maybe that's the beauty of being mortal. It's that it ends. To feel alive, to really feel it, it has to have an expiration date. When you were young, acquiring lands and resources, you felt alive. Giving your heart felt like a kind of death, didn't it?"

"Why would you say that?" Seth didn't like how her words made him feel, but there was no more room to hide from himself. Or from her.

"Hear me out. Giving your heart meant you didn't need to take anymore. You didn't need to fight. There was no more striving for anything. You would have had to admit that there was nothing left to conquer."

"Maybe you're right."

"Do you think this is my karma?"

"What could you have possibly done to deserve this?" He was pissed that she'd even think that.

"Well, I guess I poisoned you, ripped out your heart, put it in a jar, and fed you to jackals."

He cupped her face. "You are not Khepri. You don't deserve to pay for her sins."

"That's the thing, Seth. I'm pretty sure I am."

Even if she was, he didn't care. He couldn't stand the thought of Kalila suffering for any reason.

"If your soul is hers, your penance is long over." Seth found words springing to his lips that he never thought he'd say. He'd been angry with Khepri for a long time. Yet Kalila didn't deserve his rage or his pain. She hadn't hurt him. All she'd done was love him. He was the one who deserved to suffer. "I forgive you. Can you forgive me?"

"Only if you tell me a story," she teased.

"Will you give me the words?"

"Of course," she said, now serious. "I forgive you."

Something inside him changed. It was as if he'd been carrying chains around in his bones and they were gone now, turned to smoke and ether. That was when it hit him hard. He'd spent the gift of time worrying about how he was going to die instead of how he should be living.

He thought again about the future he'd imagined with Kalila. There was no hope for that now.

"You know what's stupid? I've been trying to call the scarabs to come dig us out. I think their help might have been a onetime thing."

"I'm actually okay if I'm not devoured by some creature a second time."

She laughed. "I shouldn't be laughing, but I can't help it."

"It's the dry delivery of my gallows humor."

"Oh God, I'm not ready for this life to be over." She sniffed and wiped at her nose. "Quick, tell me something. Anything."

At that, his mind went completely and utterly blank. "Sorry, I've got nothing."

"You leaped in front of undead jackals to save me. You can save me from this, too. Come on. Dig deep."

"Oh, well. Because you're asking to be saved, I guess I can come up with something. Actually, no. I know you. You have a million questions. Start asking."

"Where were you born?"

"A tiny settlement on the Nile. It had no name. It was simply home."

"How many languages do you speak?"

"A thousand or so. But I can read and write in all of them."

"Where is the most unexpected place you've been?"

"Atlantis."

"Now you're just fucking with me." She raised a brow.

"No, seriously. I have been to Atlantis. It was a beautiful country that was decimated by war. Before you ask, Iceland."

"Iceland?"

He loved the wide-eyed wonder on her face. He found himself wanting to tell her everything he'd seen, everything he'd done, but they didn't have the breath for that.

Or the time.

"They harnessed a new power source from a meteor and built an awful weapon. It disrupted our atmosphere and caused massive flooding and an extinction event worldwide."

"Where is the best place you've ever been?"

"Best is relative."

"What was the first thing that popped into your mind when I asked the question?"

"Anywhere with you," he confessed softly.

"I've loved you all my life."

This time, her confession didn't sting. He still felt unworthy, but it was different somehow. Perhaps because he'd let go of his hatred and his rage? He didn't know.

"I remember you used to follow me around, asking me so many questions. By Osiris, the questions."

"You always seemed to have the answers, though. My father answered questions, but not like you. The way you told history, I always thought you had a unique way of making me feel like I'd been there. Probably because you had been."

He remembered specifically the story she was talking

about. "Peru again. Raphael was pissed at me about the volcano sacrifices. He said I'd give you nightmares."

"You did," she agreed easily. "But I never told him that because then he wouldn't let you talk to me anymore."

"He probably shouldn't have let you talk to me at all if we're being honest. I used to get after him about bringing you on digs. I thought it was too dangerous."

"I know. He told me, and it made me even more determined to go." She was quiet for a long moment. "I understand why you didn't tell us, but do you think my dad had some idea?"

"I don't know, but I'm grateful you understand why I didn't tell him or you."

"This whole Khepri thing is actually really comforting because I can imagine that in some way, he does know. He's back with my mother. Maybe they'll get another turn on the wheel. Or they're in their own paradise." She leaned into him. "What happens? What's it like?"

He didn't want to tell her that. He couldn't. "I'm sure it will be a different experience for you than it was for me."

"Oh, right. Yeah, that's fine if you keep that to yourself," she teased.

He still didn't understand how she could be so calm.

Or why she hadn't asked him for his heart.

Seth could give it to her; then she'd have all the time she wanted.

All the time left in the world.

But it would mean giving up his escape hatch. The one he'd fought to find for so many years.

It would mean eternity. The whole and true definition of that word didn't sum up the actuality of unending existence.

In the 1980s, at the end of the Cold War, he'd had to ponder what it would mean for him after nuclear war. Would he be left wandering a dead planet alone? To never again know the pleasures of the flesh? Not only those of an erotic nature, but the taste of a good wine, the sound of a particular piece of music, the sound of another human voice. It had been too awful to bear.

Yet, when he'd made his vow that he wouldn't let her die, she'd asked him what he was going to do to stop it, and he'd not been able or ready to give an answer.

So what was he going to do?

Could he finally put someone else first?

It was one thing to talk about nobility, and sacrifice. He was reminded that dying for someone was the easy part. Living for them—well, that was the hard part.

Could he live for Kalila Corazon Blake?

The simple fact that he had to ask himself the question made him doubt himself. Just as he had all those lifetimes ago with Khepri.

Seth was afraid he was going fail again, and this time, it would be unforgiveable.

Chapter Nine

It was getting harder to breathe. The air was getting thin. Kalila's time was running out.

She refused to feel the fear that coursed through her veins. She reminded herself that she was lucky. She knew that these would be her last moments and she got to choose how to spend them.

Kalila didn't want to go on to whatever was next with fear in her heart, although she knew it would be there no matter what she did.

However, that didn't mean she couldn't fill it with other things, too. Like her love for this man.

"I have two requests."

For a moment, he seemed afraid. He thought she was going to ask for his heart. As if she'd take his final peace away from him so she could have a few more moments. It wasn't worth it. She'd tried to imagine what eternity would look like, how lonely it must be.

"I'd ask that you wait just a little to reunite with your heart. Only a few moments." Kalila took a shuddering breath. "I don't want to be in the dark alone."

"I . . . No. I won't leave you," he said. "What's the other?"

His words brought her a small comfort. She knew it probably wasn't fair of her, but she couldn't help it.

"I want to use the last of this air on something spectacular." Kalila leaned in and kissed him.

"The idea that this is the last time I'll touch you is so unfair because I just found you," he murmured against her lips. "That doesn't sound like peace. It sounds like hell."

"Maybe we'll meet again like this time." She made quick work of her own clothes, baring herself to him. "Make me come so hard that I'll feel it in my next life, and I'll know you instantly."

"I think you knew me instantly in this life, too."

He pulled her closer and kissed her lips, the taste of him bittersweet as pleasure warred with grief.

"I need you inside me, Seth."

He eased her back on the pile of their clothes and rose above her. "Will you call me by my name?"

"Which one?" She cupped his cheek. "Warlord? He Who Endures? Menes?"

"That's the one. I haven't heard it spoken by another tongue actually addressing me since that night."

"Menes," she began.

He closed his eyes for a long moment, and his breathing was ragged and harsh.

"Menes," she said again, "give me your body because in the next life, your heart is mine."

With that, he thrust home, pushing his girth deep inside her wet heat and she clenched around him, pulling him ever deeper. She clung to him, hips rocking in a rhythm even more ancient and primal than the man inside her.

This symbiosis between them was how she knew the divine was real. Nothing could be so perfect otherwise.

He reached between them, his fingers ghosting over her clit while he pumped into her, and she wanted ever more. Yet, just like when she'd been on edge before, she wanted it to last longer. She wanted to feel more.

Always more.

Yet there wasn't more. This was it.

So she surrendered to a wave of pleasure and rode it up into the stars where her body was not her own but belonged to sensation, to ecstasy. To earthly delight.

In a blissful haze, Kalila felt his body tense, his muscles coil while he fought his own release. "Come for me, Menes."

Her words sent him over the edge and he spilled inside her, all the while whispering words to her in that language he'd spoken earlier. Whatever he'd said to her, her brain didn't recognize the words, but her heart did.

This would have to be enough.

As she lay in his arms in the aftermath, Kalila decided, all in all, it could be.

"I hope you don't think that was it," he said. "We're going again."

A dreamy, hazy fugue had begun to overtake her, and she knew it was more than simply the afterglow of a good round of lovemaking.

"I don't think we are," she managed to whisper.

"No, Kalila. No." He cupped her face. "Open your eyes for me. Don't go. Not yet."

"I'm sorry I'm too scared to go alone. Sorry I'm leaving you in the dark alone," she murmured.

"I don't care about that. It's all dark without you."

He was so warm, and she suddenly felt so safe, and infinitely loved. The dark wasn't scary at all. It was home. Well, as home as anywhere could be without her ancient warlord.

"Is okay," she mumbled. "Okay."

"Not okay." His hands smoothed her hair away from her face. "Ask me."

His words made no sense to her foggy brain. Ask him for what?

"Ask me, Kalila. I'll give it to you."

Understanding sparked. He wanted her to ask for his heart. "No."

"Don't you want to stay with me?"

"You're just scared. It's okay." She was hit with a dose of sudden clarity. "I don't want anything you haven't decided to give."

"But I have," he swore.

"You don't even know which of the three it is."

She didn't know if it was a shadow on his face, or if it was simply the shadow of her life as it faded, but his mouth set in a grim line.

"Yes, I do. It is you, Kalila Corazon, my beloved heart." He kissed her. "Right in front of my face, all this time."

A nuclear bomb exploded inside her chest, filling her body with a power unlike any she'd ever felt before. Kalila sensed it building ever higher, until she realized it was going to burst from her in a concentrated force.

The explosion destroyed the tomb and everything

around it for a five-mile radius. The blast incinerated the walls, the rubble, the dirt, the sand, leaving only a giant crater and an insane, melted mass of gold and silver dotted with caches of jewels.

The sand slowly swallowed it down until it, too, was gone.

There was nothing under that hard, unforgiving sun but Kalila and Seth.

And she remembered everything.

"Khepri didn't mean for you to die," she said, giving voice to Khepri's memories as they bloomed fully formed in the back of her mind.

The betrayal on his face stabbed her in the guts, but she deserved it. "It's me. I'm still me, but I remember being Khepri. I remember what I did to you, and it was awful."

He schooled his expression. "I already told you, I forgive you."

"How can you?"

"The same way you forgave me," he said.

"I didn't poison you. I didn't throw you to the jackals. The curse—well, it was grief given voice," Kalila said.

"I don't want to talk about it because it doesn't matter. You're here. You're mine. And you're not going to die for me, you're going to live for me." He swept her up into his arms. "Say you understand."

She almost couldn't believe this was real. For a moment, she was sure this was some hallucination induced by lack of oxygen to her brain, but if it was, Kalila didn't care. This was where she wanted to be. This was the ending she wanted because it wasn't an ending at all.

It was a beginning.

Where she'd have enough time. She was going to learn

all the languages he knew, plus ten more. She was going to go back to Greece, to Peru, to Iceland, everywhere on her to-see list. She was going to taste everything there was to taste. Drink down every experience to be had.

And she was going to get to do it with the literal man of her dreams.

"Hey, beloved heart. I'm not hearing those words I want to hear. Behave or we're not going to play warlord and priestess when we get back to the city."

"Yes, we are. I get to be the warlord this time," she teased him.

"Whatever you say. But first, give me those words." He kissed the top of her head. "I need them."

She draped her arm around his neck. "Are you going to carry me all the way back to civilization?"

"Probably."

"Okay. Then, yes, Menes Sethos Cepos Akhenaten Dakarai, I would have died for you, but I'd much rather live for you."

"And you understand, you can't give it back? This is forever."

"Forever," she agreed happily. "You're not really going to carry me all the way, are you?"

"Of course I am. Now that I've got you, I'm not letting you go."

"I suppose I'll just have to *endure* it."

"As must I," he said with a heavy sigh.

"We Who Endure sounds pretty great."

"You know what else sounds great? You. Naked. As soon as we get to a city."

"That really was a short performance earlier. Not that I'm complaining. Danger boning is usually quick and dirty. But next time I want less quick and more dirty."

"This was why we didn't get married. You already think you're in charge."

"I absolutely am."

"You absolutely are, beloved heart." He kissed the top of her head again.

But instead of carrying her off into the sunset, he carried her into the sunrise. It was the dawn of a new day, a new life, and a happily ever after that Kalila Corazon Blake had only ever dared to hope for in her dreams.

Chapter Ten

The Water Lily Resort and Spa was a far cry from a crater in the middle of the desert, and Seth was happy to be there.

He watched as his wife glided through the sparkling, blue saltwater of the pool, with little care for anything but pleasure for the sake of pleasure.

She sank down to the bottom of the pool and didn't come up. Seth knew she was testing out her new abilities, and so he didn't worry. He let her enjoy herself without interference.

When Father Joseph showed him the pictures from the dig, Seth had known that something about the place would change him irrevocably. He hadn't realized it would be like this, that he could be so happy.

Content.

When Kalila decided to come up from the bottom of

the pool, he had to tell her that she'd been right and wrong about striving. She'd been right in that he'd been afraid of not having anything to fight for, yet now that he knew peace and contentment, he did have something that needed protecting at all costs.

Her.

She hadn't fixed what was broken inside him; he'd done that himself. She hadn't changed him. He'd changed because it was what he wanted. He'd learned the power of love. That was what had taught him how to change: love.

Something sparkled in the distance on the crest of the ocean waves. He looked back to where Kalila had finally bobbed to the surface in the pool.

"Did you see that?" she asked.

"I did. What do you think it is?"

"Oh! There it is again."

That was when he realized it was the tip of a crown. A woman began to emerge from the water, and he could tell even from that great distance that she was not human.

She was tall—had to be seven feet at least—and she was cloaked in a gown that glinted between gold and silver in the rays of the afternoon sun, and was immediately dry as she stepped onto shore. Her black hair was in a plait over her shoulder, and in it, he could see the working parts of the universe from supernovae to the vast endlessness of space.

The woman beckoned to them, and Kalila didn't even question it. She was already headed down the beach before he could rouse himself from his chair. He followed her quickly, and when he saw that two great jackals emerged from the water behind her, Seth broke into a run.

Fear unlike any he'd ever known clamped down on him like massive jaws.

The woman held out her hand to him, even though he approached at a dead run.

"Don't tell me you don't recognize your goddess, Menes."

Isis? Was it possible?

He supposed after the events of . . . well, always, anything was possible. Seth slowed to a stop and linked his hand with Kalila's.

"Do you remember that you prayed to me in your hour of need? Do you remember my answer?"

He'd long thought himself to be abandoned by the gods. He'd thought they were all dead.

Her laughter was like the sound of tinkling bells. "Oh, sweet boy. Do you think you're all that endures?"

He had, actually.

"I have a gift for you both. One, a confession. Khepri was not responsible for your suffering. It was me. Yes, she did request a curse, but it was from a broken heart. Normally, I don't grant those. We know what is pain and what is a sincere request. Sometimes, they're the same, but oftentimes, the wishes of a broken heart are but the cries of grief. Yet you were both too full of pride. Too stubborn. Too selfish."

He knew she was right, but he didn't think he deserved so many years of suffering. Of course if he hadn't paid that price, he wouldn't have Kalila.

"Oh, I know what you're thinking. I had nothing to do with how long it took. That was all both of you."

"You said there were presents?" Kalila grinned.

In every story Seth had ever read, Isis did not take

kindly to impertinence. She'd been known to smite even gods to dust.

Yet she reached out and put a motherly arm around Kalila and squeezed her tightly. "Yes, you're going to love this one. I have a gift for you, and a mission."

"More adventure! I'm ready!" Kalila cried.

"I knew you would be." Then she turned to Seth. "What say you, warlord?"

"I go where Kalila goes."

"Of course you do."

The jackals eyed him from behind her long dress and he showed them his teeth, and they bent their heads.

"Stop harassing Peanut and Butter. They're nervous already. All I need is jackal vomit on my new slippers. The ride up from the underworld is rough on them." She pulled out a large, glittering golden stone. "The Left Hand of the Moon has gone rogue. Chenzira Hassan has taken control. I need you to find their new headquarters and install this where it goes."

"That's not what I think it is, is it?" he asked.

"Well, if you think it's the Eye of Horus, you'd be right. He's been turned to stone and they're using his divine vibration to locate all the ancient places. To what end, I'm not yet sure."

"Chenzira Hassan?" Kalila asked. "Dr. Chenzira Hassan of the Menes Society? That can't be the same man."

"He's the one who staged the original sinkhole at the city of the dead. He orchestrated the jackals. No one knows his end game but him," Isis replied.

"What about the rest of the Menes Society? Are they part of it?" Kalila questioned.

"I'm sure someone could find out." Isis gave him a direct stare. "After all, they spent their lives trying to find proof that you lived. You could go to them under the ruse of being a descendant." She shrugged. "Or as yourself. Whatever you're comfortable with."

The idea of that sounded like another tour in hell, but he'd do whatever the goddess asked of him. However, he wanted to be prepared.

"So when we plunk this thing home, what happens?"

"Why, Horus wakes up, of course," Isis said, as if he were the stupidest creature on two legs.

"And waking up Horus is a good idea why?"

She huffed, exasperated, and scratched the jackals behind their ears. "So he can get away from them."

"Why don't you just . . . you know?" he asked as he waved his hands in the air.

"If she could just, you know, she would have already," Kalila said. "Obviously."

"Yes, you're right." He nodded. That had been a stupid question, but Seth had to wonder why a being such as her would need human help. "What I meant to say is, why can't you?"

"I don't know. I've tried. But that's what I have you two for. Are you ready for your next adventure?" She held out the stone and dropped it in Kalila's hand.

"I know I am."

"It's always an adventure with you," he said to Kalila.

The goddess was gone, and all that was left was *his* goddess, who was already excited to go traipsing off into some wild unknown all over again.

"Do you think there'll be a big-ass boulder?" She flashed him a lopsided grin.

"This time, there might be," he encouraged.

"Good." She stood up on her tiptoes to kiss him. "However, I'm looking forward to some hours in that decadent master suite before we take off. What do you say, war-lord? Think you can conquer me?" Kalila winked at him and dashed back up the beach toward the hotel.

The warlord in question gave chase, but he was happy to say that he was the one who'd been conquered, and he'd be thanking Isis for that gift every day.

Because Seth was no longer He Who Endures.

He had endured, but now it was time to really live, and he was lucky enough to get to do it with the woman who was his beloved, his heart, his forever.

THE YEARNING

Hannah Howell

Prologue

Scotland, A.D. 1000

"Nay!"

Morvyn Galt woke shaking and sweating with fear. The scent of magic was thick in the air. She scrambled out of her bed and yanked on her clothes. She could feel her sister's anger, feel how Rona's broken heart was twisting within her chest, changing into a hard, ugly thing that pumped hate throughout her body instead of the love it once held. Morvyn knew she would not be in time to stop the evil her sister stirred up, but she had to try. She grabbed her small bag and raced toward Rona's cottage, praying as hard as she could despite her fear that her prayers would go unheeded.

When she reached Rona's tiny home, she tried to open the door only to find it bolted against her. The smoke coming from the house was so heavy with the scent of herbs and sorcery that her eyes stung. She banged against the door, pleading with Rona as she heard her sister begin her incantation.

"Nay, Rona!" she screamed. "Cease! You will damn us all!"

"I damn but one," replied Rona, "and well does he deserve it."

Placing her hand over her womb, Rona stared into the fire and saw the face of her lover, her seducer, her betrayer. He was marrying another in the morning, forsaking love for land and coin. She would make him suffer for that, as she now suffered.

"Rage for rage, pain for pain, blood for blood, life for life." Rona swayed slightly as she spoke, stroking her belly as she tossed a few more painstakingly mixed herbs into the fire.

"Rona, please! Do not do this!"

"As mine shall walk alone, so shall yours," Rona continued, ignoring her sister's pleas. "As mine shall be shunned, so shall yours."

Morvyn scrambled to find something to write with. She needed to record this. As she sprawled on the ground to take advantage of the sliver of light seeping out from beneath the door, she realized she had no ink. From beneath the door she could see the smoke curling around her sister and saw Rona toss another handful of herbs upon the fire. Morvyn cut her palm with her dagger, wet her quill with her own blood, and began to write.

"Your firstborn son shall know only shadows," intoned Rona, "as shall his son, as shall his son's son, and thus it shall be until the seed of the MacCordy shall wither from hate and fade into the mists."

Morvyn scattered her blessing and healing stones in front of the door, praying they might ease the force of the spell.

"From sunset of the first day The MacCordy becomes a man, darkness will take him as a lover, blood will be his wine, fury will steal his soul, yearning will devour his heart, and he will become a creature of nightmares." Rona felt her child kick forcefully as if in protest, but continued.

"He will know no beauty; he will know no love; he will know no peace.

"The name of the MacCordys will become a foul oath, their tale one used to frighten all the Godly.

"Thus it shall be, thus it shall remain, until one steps from the shadows of pride, land, and wealth and does as his heart commands.

"Until all that should have been finally is."

Morvyn sat back on her heels and stared at the door. She could not believe her sister had acted so recklessly, so vindictively. Rona knew the dangers of flinging a curse out in anger, knew how the curse could fall back upon them threefold, yet, in her pain, she had ignored all the dangers. Morvyn placed her hand over her heart, certain she could feel the pain and misery of countless future generations, those of their blood as well as those of the MacCordys.

The cottage door opened and Morvyn looked up at her sister. In the light of the torch Rona held, Morvyn could see the glow of hate and triumph in Rona's blue-green eyes. Rona thought she had won some great victory. Morvyn knew otherwise and was not surprised to feel the sting of tears upon her cheeks.

"Rona, how could you? How could you have done this?" she asked.

"How could *I*? How could he?" Rona snapped, then frowned when she saw the blood upon Morvyn's palm. "What have you done to yourself, you foolish child?"

Morvyn began to pick up her things and return them to her bag. "I had no ink to mark down the words."

"So you wrote in blood?"

" 'Tis fitting. The Galts and the MacCordys shall be bleeding for ages after what you have done this night." She felt the heat in her stones as she put them away and hoped the power they had expended had done some good.

"You cannot keep such a writing about. Not only is it considered a sin for you to write at all, but those words could condemn me, condemn us all."

"You have condemned us, Rona. You knew the dangers."

"Unproven. *That* is proof of sorcery, however," she said, pointing to Morvyn's writing.

"I shall write the tale upon a scroll and hide it. Mayhap one of our blood will find it one day, one with the wit and strength to banish the evil you have stirred up this night."

"He had to pay for what he has done!"

"He was wrong, but so were you. The poison you have spit out tonight will infect us all, the venom seeping into our bloodline as well as his. To do such magic on this night, at the birth of a new century, only ensures the power of the evil you have wrought." Morvyn stood up and looked down at what she had written. "I fear you have stolen all hope of happiness for us, but I will not allow this to endanger your life. It will be well hidden. And every night for the rest of my life I shall pray that, when it is found, it will be by one of our blood, one who can free us all from the torment you have unleashed this dark night."

Chapter One

Scotland, 1435

Sophie Hay stumbled slightly as another fierce sneeze shook her small frame. A linen rag was shoved into her hand, and she blew her nose, then wiped her streaming eyes with her sleeves. She smiled at her maid, Nella, who watched her with concern. Considering how long she had been scrambling through this ancient part of her Aunt Claire's house, Sophie suspected she looked worthy of Nella's concern.

"I dinnae ken what ye think ye will find here," Nella said. "Old Steven said her ladyship ne'er came in here; thought it haunted, and he thinks it may not be safe now."

"'Tis sturdy, Nella." Sophie patted the stones framing the fireplace. "Verra sturdy. The rest of the house will fall ere this part does. The fact that that stone was loose," she pointed to the one she had pried away from the wall, releasing the cloud of dust that had started her sneezing, "was what told me that something might be hidden here."

"And ye dinnae think this place be haunted?"

Sophie inwardly grimaced, knowing she would have to answer with some very carefully chosen words or Nella would start running and probably not stop until she reached Berwick. "Nay. I sense no spirits in this room." She would not tell Nella about all the others wandering in the house. "All I sense is unhappiness. Grief and a little fear. It was strong here by the fireplace, which is why I was searching here."

"Fear?" Nella's dark eyes grew wide as she watched Sophie reach toward the hole in the wall. "I dinnae think ye ought to do that. Fear and grief arenae good. God kens what ye might find in there."

"I am certainly nay sticking my hand in there with any eagerness, Nella, but," she sighed, "I also feel I must." She ignored Nella's muttered prayers, took a deep breath to steady herself, and reached in. "Ah, there *is* something hidden here."

Sophie grasped a cold metal handle on the end of what felt like a small chest. She tugged and felt it inch toward her a little. Whoever had put it into this hole had had to work very hard, for it was a tight fit. Inch by inch it came, until Sophie braced herself against the wall and yanked with all her might. The little chest came out so quickly, she stumbled backward and was only saved from falling by Nella's quick, bracing catch.

As she set the chest on a small table, Sophie noticed her maid edge closer, her curiosity obviously stronger than her fear. Sophie unfolded the thick oiled leather wrapped around the bulk of the chest, then used a corner of her apron to brush aside the dust and stone grit. It was a beautiful chest of heavy wood, ornately carved with runes and a few Latin words. The hinges, handles, and clasp were of hammered gold, but there was no lock. She rubbed her hands together as she prepared herself to open it.

"What are all those marks upon it?" asked Nella.

"Runes. Let me think. Ah, they are signs for protection, for hope, for forgiveness, for love. All good things. The words say: *Within lies the truth, and, if it pleases God, the salvation of two peoples.* How odd." She stroked the top of the chest. "This is verra old. It must have just missed being discovered when the fireplace was added to the house. I wouldnae be surprised if this belonged to the matriarch of our line or one of her kinswomen."

"The witch?" Nella took a small step back. "A curse?"

"I doubt it when such markings cover the chest." She slowly opened the lid and frowned slightly. "More oiled leather for wrapping. Whoever hid this wanted it to last a verra long time." She took out the longest of the items and carefully unwrapped it. "A scroll." She gently unrolled the parchment and found another small one tucked inside. When she touched the erratic writing upon the smaller parchment, she shivered. "Blood. 'Tis written in blood."

"Oh, my lady, put it back. Quickly!" When Sophie simply pressed her hand upon the smaller parchment and closed her eyes, Nella edged nearer again. "What do ye see?"

"Morvyn. That is the name of the one who wrote this. Morvyn, sister to Rona."

"The witch."

"Aye. No ink," she muttered. "That is why this is written in blood. Morvyn had naught else to write with and she was desperate to record this exactly as it was said." Sophie opened herself up to the wealth of feeling and knowledge trapped within the parchment. "She tried to stop it. So desperate, so afraid for us all. She prays," Sophie whispered. "She prays and prays and prays, every night until she dies, sad and so verra alone." She quickly removed her hand and took several deep breaths to steady herself.

"Oh, m'lady, this is no treasure, is it?"

"It may be. Beneath that despair was hope. That would explain the words carved upon the chest."

"Can ye read the writings?"

"Aye, though I dinnae want to."

"Then dinnae."

"I must. That chest carries the words 'truth' and 'salvation,' Nella. Mayhap the truth as to why all the women of my line die as poor Morvyn died—sad and so verra alone. I willnae read it aloud." Sophie's eyes widened and she felt chilled as she read the words. "I cannae believe Morvyn wrote this. She feared these words." Sophie turned her attention to the larger scroll. "Oh, dear."

"What is it?"

"I fear Rona deserves her ill fame. She loved Ciar MacCordy, The MacCordy of Nochdaidh. They were lovers, but he left her to marry another, a woman with land and wealth. He also left her with child."

"As too oft happens, the rutting bastards," muttered Nella.

"True. Rona was hurt and her pain twisted into a vindictive fury. One night she cursed The MacCordy and all the future MacCordy lairds. Morvyn tried to stop it, but failed. Her fear was that the Galts would pay dearly alongside The MacCordy, if in a different way. She writes out the curse again and, trust me, Nella, 'tis a bad one. She expresses the hope that some descendant will find this and have the courage and skill to undo what Rona did. Ah, me, poor Morvyn tried her whole life to do just that, with prayer and with healing spells. She wrote once right after the curse was made, and again when she was verra old. She leaves her book of cures and spells as well as her stones. The use of the stones is explained in the book.

"Morvyn says she thinks she has discovered the sting in the tail of Rona's curse. A Galt woman of their line will know love only to lose it, to watch it die or slip through her grasp. She will gain land and wealth, but such things will ne'er heal her heart or warm her in the night and she will face her death still unloved, still alone." Sophie wiped tears from her cheeks with the corner of her apron. "And she was right, Nella. She was so verra right."

"Nay, nay. Your ancestors just chose wrong, 'tis all."

"For over four hundred years? This is dated. It was written in the year 1000. The verra first day." Sophie muttered a curse. "That fool Rona sent out a curse on the eve of a new year, a new century. It was probably a night made to strengthen any magic brewed and she stirred up an evil, vindictive sort."

Nella wrung her hands together. "There isnae any of that evil in this house, is there?"

Sophie smiled at her maid. "Nay. I sense that magic has been stirred in here, but nay the black sort."

"Then from where comes the fear and sadness?"

"Heartache, Nella. Lost love. Loneliness." Sophie cautiously picked up the two small bags inside the chest and gasped. "Oh my, oh my."

"M'lady, what is it?"

"Morvyn's stones." She gently placed one bag back inside the chest on top of what she now knew was Morvyn's book of cures and spells. "Those are her healing stones.

These," she clasped the small bag she held between her hands, "are her blessing stones."

Nella stepped closer and shyly touched the bag. "Ye can feel that, can ye?"

"Morvyn had magic, Nella, good, loving, gentle magic." She put everything back inside the chest. "How verra sad that such a woman suffered heartache and died unloved because of her own sister's actions." She closed the chest and started out of the room.

"Where are ye taking it?" asked Nella as she hurried to follow Sophie.

"To my room where, after a nice hot bath and a hearty meal, I mean to read Morvyn's wee book." She ignored Nella's mutterings, which seemed to consist of warnings about leaving certain things buried in walls, not stirring up trouble, and several references to the devil and his minions. "I but seek the truth, Nella. The truth and salvation."

It was late before Sophie had an opportunity to more closely examine her find. The house, lands, and fortune her Aunt Claire had bequeathed her were welcome, but carried a lot of responsibility. Aunt Claire had been ill during her last years, mostly in spirit and mind, and there was a lot that had been neglected. Although wearied by all the demands for her attention during the day, Sophie finally sat on a thick sheepskin rug before the fire, sipped at a tankard of hot, spiced cider, and looked over what her ancestor had left behind.

A brief examination of the book revealed many useful things, from intricate cures to simple balms. Sophie only briefly glimpsed the spells, few and benign, before turning to the explanation of the stones. She considered them a wondrous gift, having long believed in the power of stones, which were as old as the world itself. Sentinels and possessors of the secrets and events of the past, Sophie was sure all manner of wonders and truths could be uncovered if one understood the magic and use of them.

Still sipping at her drink, Sophie next turned her attention to the scrolls. She read both Morvyn's letter and the curse several times before replacing them in the box. The truth was certainly there, but Sophie was not sure she could see the salvation promised. Nothing in Morvyn's writings or the words of Rona's curse seemed to indicate a way in which to end the despair suffered by so many Galt women.

Staring into the fire, she grimaced, for she could feel the spirits of those who had gone before, including poor old Aunt Claire. Generation after generation of Galt women, who briefly savored the sweet taste of love only to have it all go sour, had returned to this house to die or spent their whole sad lives here. Each one had spent far too many years wondering why love had eluded them, why they had held it for so short a time only to see it trickle out of their grasp like fine sand. Although she had only been at Werstane for a fortnight, several times she had felt the despair of all who had gone before, felt it weigh so heavily upon her that she had come close to weeping. If Aunt Claire had felt it too, had spent her whole life feeling it, it was no wonder she had become a little odd.

And now that she understood the curse Rona had set upon the MacCordys, understood the "sting in its tail," as Morvyn called it, Sophie knew her fate was to be the same as Aunt Claire's, as that of all the lonely, heartbroken spirits still trapped within Werstane. Her own mother had suffered the sting of their ancestor's malice, but had let that despair conquer her, hurling herself into the sea rather than spend one more day in suffering. As Sophie faced her twentieth birthday, she was surprised she had not yet suffered the same fate, but love had not yet touched her. Most people considered her a spinster, an object of pity, but she was beginning to think she was very lucky indeed.

Sophie finished her drink, stood up, and set the tankard on the mantel. She would not join the long line of heart-broken Galt women. If it took her the rest of her life, she would end the torment her vindictive ancestor had inflicted upon so many innocent people. If it was God's wish that the Galt women should suffer for Rona's crime, surely four hundred and thirty-five years of misery was penance enough. Perhaps He wanted a Galt woman to put right what a Galt woman had made so wrong. It was her duty to try. And, she mused, as she crawled into bed, there was only one proper place to start—Nochdaidh.

"Nella isnae going to like this plan," she murmured and almost smiled.

"I dinnae like this, m'lady. Not at all."

Sophie glanced at her maid riding the stout pony at her side. Nella had not ceased bemoaning the plans Sophie had made in the entire sennight since she had made them. It had been expected, but Sophie was weary of it. Nella's fears fed her own. What she needed was confidence and support. Nella was loyal, but Sophie wished she was also brave, perhaps even a little encouraging.

"Nella, do ye wish me to die alone, sad, and heart-broken?" Sophie asked.

"Och, nay."

"Then hush. Unless Rona's curse is broken, I will suffer the fate of all the Galt women of her bloodline. I will become just another one of the sorrowful, despairing spirits roaming the halls of Werstane."

Nella gasped, then gave Sophie a brief look of accusation. "Ye said there werenae any spirits at Werstane."

"Actually, I said there werenae any spirits in the room we were in when ye asked about them." She grinned when Nella snorted softly in disgust, but quickly grew serious again. " 'Twill be all right, Nella."

"Oh? The woman in the village said the laird is a monster, a beast who drinks blood and devours bairns."

"If he devours bairns, he obviously has a verra small appetite, for the village was swarming with them. And that village looked far too prosperous for one said to be ruled by some beast." She looked around her, noticing how stark the land had grown, then frowned at the looming castle of dark stone before her. "That place does look a wee bit chilling, however. The boundary between light and dark is astonishingly clear."

"Do ye feel anything, m'lady? Evil or danger?" Nella asked in an unsteady whisper.

"I feel despair," Sophie replied in an equally quiet voice. " 'Tis so thick, 'tis nearly smothering."

"Oh, dear. That isnae good for ye, m'lady. Nay good at all."

Sophie dismounted but yards from the huge, ominous gates of Nochdaidh and placed her hand upon the cold, rocky ground. "Rona's venom has sunk deep into this land."

"The verra ground is cursed? Will it nay reach out to infect us as weel?"

"Not ye, Nella. And what poison is here is for The MacCordy, nay ye and nay me."

Nella dismounted, moved to stand at Sophie's side, and clasped her hand. "Let us leave this cursed place, m'lady. Ye feel too much. What lurks here, in the verra air and the earth, could hurt ye."

"I am hurt already, Nella, and I face e'en more hurt. Long, lonely years of pain, the sort of pain that drove my mother to court hell's fires by taking her own life. The MacCordys also suffer. The pain should have been Rona's alone, and, mayhap, her lover's. Yet she inflicted it upon countless innocents. Aunt Claire did no wrong. My mother did no wrong. The mon behind those shadowed walls did no wrong. One woman's anger has tainted all of us. How can I ignore that? How can I but walk away? I am of Rona's blood and I must do all I can to undo this wrong. If nay for myself, then for the Mac-Cordys, for my own child if I am blessed with one."

"So, if ye can break this curse, ye will love and be loved and have bairns?"

"Aye, that is how I understand it."

Nella took a deep breath, threw back her thin shoulders, and nodded firmly. "Then we must go on. Ye have a right to such happiness. And I can find it within me to be brave. I have protection."

Thinking of all the talismans, rune stones, and other such things Nella was weighted down with, Sophie suspected her maid was the most protected woman in all of Scotland. "Loyal Nella, I welcome your companionship. I shall be in sore need of it, I think." Sophie took the reins of her pony in her hand and started to walk toward the gates of Nochdaidh.

"'Tis as if the verra sun fears to shine upon such a cursed place," Nella whispered.

"Aye. Let us pray that God in His mercy will show me the way to dispel those shadows."

Chapter Two

"A visitor, Alpin."

Alpin MacCordy looked up from the letter he had been reading. His right-hand man Eric stood across from him at the head table in the great hall. There was no hint of amusement upon the man's rough features, yet he had to be joking. Visitors did not come to Nochdaidh. Anyone traveling over his lands was quickly and thoroughly warned to stay away. The dark laird of Nochdaidh was not a man anyone came calling on.

"Has the weather turned so ill that it would force someone to seek shelter e'en in this place?" he asked.

"Nay. She has asked to speak to you."

"She?"

"Aye." Eric shook his head. "Two wee lasses. The one who calls herself Lady Sophie Hay says she *must* speak to you." He suddenly turned and scowled at the doors. "Curse it, woman, I told ye to wait."

"My lady is cold," said the thinner of the two women entering the great hall, even as she pushed the other woman toward the fireplace.

"I am fine, Nella," protested the other woman.

That soft, husky voice drew Alpin's attention from Eric, who was bickering with the woman called Nella. He felt a slight tightening in his belly as the lady by the fireplace pulled off the hood of her cloak, revealing a delicate profile and thick, honey-gold hair. At the moment she was distracted by her maid's efforts to get her cloak off and the argument between Eric and Nella. Alpin took quick advantage of that, looking his fill.

Her beautiful hair hung in a long, thick braid to her tiny waist. The dark blue woolen gown she wore clung to her slim, shapely hips and nicely formed, if somewhat small, breasts. Her face was a delicate oval, her nose small and straight, and her mouth full and inviting. She was tiny but perfect. Her maid was also small, dark haired, somewhat plain, bone thin, and plainly not at all intimidated by the burly Eric's harsh visage or curt voice.

Alpin rose and moved closer to his uninvited guests. When the lady looked at him, he needed all his willpower not to openly react to the beauty of her eyes. She had eyes the color of the sea, an intriguing mix of blue and green, and just as mysterious. Her eyes were wide, her lashes long, thick, and several shades darker than her hair, and her equally dark brows arced delicately over those huge pools of innocent curiosity.

For a moment he thought this beautiful young woman had somehow made it to his gates without hearing about him, then he looked at the woman she called Nella. That woman's dark eyes were filled with fear and horror. She clutched one thin hand tightly around what looked to be a weighty collection of amulets draped around her neck. The women had obviously been thoroughly warned, so why were they here, he mused, and looked back at Lady Sophie. That woman shocked him by smiling sweetly and holding out her small hand.

"Ye are the laird of Nochdaidh, I assume," she said. "I am Lady Sophie Hay and this is my maid, Nella."

"Aye, I am the laird. Sir Alpin MacCordy at your service, m'lady."

When he bowed, then took her hand in his and brushed a kiss over her knuckles, Sophie had to swiftly suppress a shiver. Heat flowed through her body from the spot where his warm lips had briefly touched her skin. She started to scold herself for being so susceptible to the beauty of the man, then decided she should have expected such a thing. They already shared a bond in many ways. They were caught in the same trap set by the vindictive Rona so long ago.

And he was beautiful, she thought with an inner sigh. He was a tall man, a foot or more taller than her own meager five feet. He was lean and muscular, his every move graceful. His hair was long and thick, gleaming black waves hanging past his broad shoulders. Even his face was lean, his cheekbones high and well defined, his jawline strong, and his nose long and straight. He had eyes of a rich golden brown, thickly lashed, and nicely spaced beneath straight brows. His mouth was well shaped with a hint of fullness she found tempting. If this was how Rona's lover had looked, Sophie could understand the pain and anger of losing him to another, even if she could never forgive the woman for how she had reacted to those feelings.

"Why have ye come to Nochdaidh, m'lady?" Alpin asked as he reluctantly released her hand.

"Weel, m'laird, I have come to try to break the curse the witch Rona put upon the MacCordys."

The disappointment Alpin felt was sharp. She was just another charlatan come to try and fill him with false hope. As too many others had over the years, she would ply her trickery, fill her purse with his coin, and walk away. She but hoped to slip her lovely hand into his purse using lies and fanciful spells or cures.

"The tale of Rona the witch and her curse is just that—a tale. Lies made up to explain things that cannae be understood."

"Oh, nay! 'Tisnae just some tale, m'laird. I have papers to prove 'tis all true."

"Really? And just how would ye have come to hold such proof?"

"It was left to me by my aunt. Ye see, Rona was my ancestor. I am one of a direct line of Galt women—"

She squeaked when he suddenly pulled his sword and aimed at her, the point but inches from her heart. The fury visible upon his face was chilling. Sophie was just thinking that it was a little odd to still find him so beautiful while he looked so ready, even eager, to kill her, when Nella thrust her thin body between Sophie and the point of Alpin's sword.

"Nay!" Nella cried in a voice made high and sharp by fear. "I cannae allow ye to hurt my lady."

"Now, Nella," Sophie said in her most soothing voice as she tried and failed to nudge her maid aside, "I am sure the laird wasnae intending to do me any harm." A sword through the heart was probably a fairly quick death, she mused.

"Are ye? Weel, ye would be wrong," Alpin drawled, but sheathed his sword, the surprising act of courage by the trembling maid cutting through the tight grip rage had gained on him. "There would undoubtedly be some satisfaction in spilling the blood of one of that witch's kinswomen."

"Mayhap, but that wouldnae solve the problem."

"How can ye be so sure?"

"Why dinnae we all sit down to discuss this?" said Eric, pausing to instruct a curious maid to bring food and drink before grabbing Nella by the arm and dragging her toward the head table. "Always better to sit, break bread together, and talk calmly."

"Fine. We will eat, drink, and talk calmly," Alpin said in a cold, hard voice, "and then they can leave."

This was not proceeding well, Sophie mused as she watched Alpin stride back to the table. It was not going to be easy to help someone who, at first, wanted to strike you dead, then wanted you to leave. She should have suspected such a reaction. She had not sensed one good feeling since entering the shadows encircling Nochdaidh. Despair, fear, and a bone-deep resignation to the dark whims of fate were everywhere.

The laird was filled with the same feelings and much darker ones. When he had touched her hand it was not only attraction Sophie had felt, his and her own. There was anger in the man. It was there even before he had discovered exactly who she was. She had also felt dark, shadowy emotions, ones she had only felt on the rare times she had somehow touched the spirit of a predator, such as a hawk or a wolf. Alpin MacCordy was fighting that part of him, the part born of her ancestor's curse. As she collected the chest with Morvyn's things and started toward the table, Sophie hoped she could convince Sir Alpin that she could be an ally in that battle.

"What's that?" demanded Alpin as Sophie took the seat to his left and set the small chest covered in runes on the table.

"The truth about the curse," Sophie replied, opening the chest to take out the scrolls. "Rona's sister Morvyn wrote it all down and, just before she died, she hid it. I found it whilst cleaning the cottage left to me by my aunt."

"So, to help me ye thought it wise to bring more sorcery into my keep?"

Sophie was prevented from responding to that by the arrival of the food and drink. When Sir Alpin asked if her men needed anything and she told him no men traveled with her, the look he gave her made her want to hit him. She was pleased, however, when he cleared the great hall of all but the four of them as soon as the food and drink were set out.

"Ye traveled here alone? Just ye and your maid?" he demanded the moment they were alone.

"I have no men-at-arms to drag about with me," she replied. That was close to the truth, she mused, for the men guarding Werstane were not yet her men, not in their hearts. This scowling laird did not need to know that she had slipped away unseen to avoid having to take any Werstane men with her. "I have a cottage, sir, and nay a castle like this." It was another half-truth for, although she was determined to stick to her plan to hide her wealth, she found she did not really want to lie to this man.

"But your maid calls ye her lady."

"Good blood and a title dinnae always make for a fat purse. I am a healing woman." She unrolled the scrolls. "Now, about the writings Morvyn left—" She tensed when he touched the smaller one.

"This was written in blood." Alpin studied the hastily scrawled writing. "Rage for rage," he murmured then scowled. "Curse it, my Latin isnae so good."

"Allow me, m'laird." She saw how the other three at the table all tensed. "Without the herbs and all, they are but words." She began to read. "Rage for rage, pain for pain, blood for blood, life for life. As mine shall walk alone, so shall yours. As mine shall be shunned, so shall yours. Your firstborn son shall know only shadows, as shall his son, as shall his son's son, and thus it shall be until the seed of The MacCordy shall wither from hate and fade into the mists.

"From sunset of the first day The MacCordy becomes a mon, darkness will take him as a lover, blood will be his wine, fury will steal his soul, yearning will devour his heart, and he will become a creature of nightmares. He will know no beauty; he will know no love; he will know no peace. The name of the MacCordys will become a foul oath, their tale one used to frighten all the Godly.

"Thus it shall be, and thus it shall remain, until one steps from the shadows of pride, land, and wealth and does as his heart commands. Until all that should have been finally is."

Sophie nodded her agreement with the action when both Eric and Nella crossed themselves. The laird stared at the scrolls, saying nothing, but she could feel his anger. She knew he wanted to deny the curse, but that a part of him believed in it.

"Why write such filth down?" he finally asked. "Why not let the words die with the bitch who spoke them?"

"Because Morvyn needed to ken exactly what was said if the curse was e'er to be broken," Sophie replied. "Morvyn spent her whole life trying to undo the evil her sister had created. She failed, but hoped someone who came after might succeed."

"And ye think ye are the one, do ye?"

His sarcasm stung. "Why not? And what can it hurt to at least let me try?"

"What can it hurt? I believe your ancestor Rona showed what harm can be done by letting a Galt woman practice magic. Ye must excuse me, but I cannae help but view any offer of aid from a Galt woman with mistrust."

"Then view my offer as utterly self-serving. Curses carry a price for the one who makes them, m'laird. When Rona cursed your family, she cursed her own. 'Tis said that a curse will come back threefold upon the one who casts it. As every MacCordy of Ciar's blood has suffered, so has every daughter of Rona Galt's blood."

"Ye look fine to me." Too fine, he mused, but tried to ignore her beauty.

"Rona cursed your soul, your heart. In doing so, she robbed all women of her line of any happiness. The moment a Galt woman finds love, tastes the sweetness of having her love returned, 'tis stolen away from her. No Galt woman of Rona's blood can hold on to her heart's desire. She grasps it just long enough to ken the pleasure of it, to gain a need for it, and then it dies."

"It sounds like a tale spun to explain poor choices in a mate."

Sophie inwardly cursed. "Do ye really think every

woman born in Rona's line for four hundred and thirty-five years chose wrongly, gave her heart foolishly? *Every* woman, m'laird, ended her days gripped tightly by despair. The heart's ache was deep and everlasting. 'Twas worse for the ones who actually married the men they loved, for they were bound forever to a mon they loved, one who had once loved them, but would ne'er do so again. Many lived to a great age burdened by that loss. Others couldnae bear it, and, despite the threat of suffering in hell's fires for such a sin, took their own lives. My mother hurled herself into the sea, unable to bear the pain another day, a pain e'en the love of her children couldnae ease."

It was Eric who finally broke the heavy silence. "Ye believe we are cursed then? That the ill fate which has befallen the MacCordys for so verra long is born of the curse of this one angry woman?"

"Are ye nay shunned?" Sophie asked softly. "Do ye nay walk alone? Do ye nay live in the shadows? Although the sun shines o'er the village, this place sits in the shadow. Do ye think that natural?"

"If this Morvyn couldnae end this curse, what makes ye think ye can?" asked Alpin.

"Weel, Morvyn ne'er came here," Sophie replied. "I doubt any Galt woman has e'er come here. That could make the difference. I have the strongest feeling that I will be the only one to e'en try since Morvyn hid this chest. Ye may not believe in curses, m'laird, but I do, and I wish to try and end this one. I wish no more Galt women to hurl themselves into the sea out of despair," she added softly.

Those last words killed Alpin's refusal on his tongue.

He could deny *himself* hope, but not her. Hope was a paltry thing to cling to; bitter, fruitless, and painful, but she needed to discover that hard truth for herself.

"Stay then, and play your games, but ye best not trouble me with such nonsense."

Before she could protest that, he had called in two maids to take her and Nella to a room. Sophie decided she had pushed him hard enough for now. She had succeeded in getting permission to stay and try to find a way to end the curse. There was a chance she would not need his complete cooperation, but, if she did, there was now time and opportunity to sway him. As she and Nella went with the maids, Sophie prayed the hope that had stirred to life inside of her was not doomed to be crushed.

Alpin glared at the door Lady Sophie and her maid had disappeared through. He took a deep drink of the wine mixed especially for him, a thick mixture of sheep's blood and wine. It fed the need which grew stronger every year and he doubted some wide-eyed lass could effect a cure. He wanted to feel pleased that the women descended from Rona Galt had suffered as his family had suffered, but could not. None of them had deserved the misery visited upon them. He also wanted to hold fast to his previous scorn concerning the possibility of a curse, but found himself wavering, and that angered him.

"Mayhap she can help," said Eric, watching Alpin closely.

"So ye believe me cursed?" drawled Alpin. "Ye think our troubles caused by some woman long dead who danced about a fire one night, uttering those fanciful words as she sprinkled some herbs upon the flames?"

Eric grimaced and dragged his hand through his roughly cut dark hair. "Why do ye resist the idea of a curse? What besets ye and has beset every MacCordy laird before ye for hundreds of years isnae, weel, normal."

"Not every disease affects so many people it becomes common. Just because an affliction is rare doesnae make it the result of some curse or sorcery."

"Then, if ye truly believe 'tis nay more than bad blood, why have ye let the lass stay?"

Alpin grimaced. "A moment of weakness, or insanity. It was her wish to nay see any more Galt women hurl themselves into the sea out of despair. I have no hope left, but I couldnae bring myself to kill hers. 'Twill die soon enough."

"I sometimes think that is some of our trouble. We have lost hope."

"Only a fool clings to it for four hundred years," Alpin drawled.

"Mayhap." Eric stared out the window, seeing only another of the many shades of darkness he had spent his whole life in. "I often wonder if that loss of hope brought on this never-ending shadow we live under."

"Ye grow fanciful. And, if it is born of the death of hope, then we best be prepared for it to grow e'en darker."

"Why?"

"Because our little golden-haired Galt witch will all too soon be burying hers."

Chapter Three

"Eric, wait!" Sophie ran the last few feet toward the man she had been hunting down and grabbed him by the arm. "If I didnae ken better, I would think ye are trying to avoid me." She did not need Eric's glance behind her to know Nella had caught up to her; she had heard the rattle of her maid's many amulets. "I just wish to ask ye a few things, Sir Eric."

"M'lady, ye have been here but a sennight and have spoken to near everyone within the keep, outside the keep, and probably for near a dozen miles around," Eric said. "I cannae think that I can tell ye anything that ye dinnae already ken."

"If I am to break the curse, I need all the knowledge about the MacCordy laird that I can gather. I am certain the grip of this curse can be broken if I can just find the right key. Morvyn failed, but she ne'er came to see exactly what the curse had done. That might be why she failed. So, I am gathering all the truth I can and recording it. The answer is in there, I am certain of it. I can feel it within my reach."

Eric leaned against the side of the stables he had been trying to escape into when she had caught sight of him. "The lairds of the MacCordys grow to monhood watching their fathers change into some creature from a nightmare. They then become men and begin to change themselves."

Sophie crossed her arms beneath her breasts. "That isnae verra helpful. How do they change? A lot of what I have been told is difficult to believe. I do ken that the laird cannae abide the sun."

"Nay. The light of the sun fair blinds him. Alpin finds it increasingly painful as he ages. Three years ago he spent but an hour in the sun and it was as if he had been dropped into boiling water. If not for the heavy clothing he wore, I think he would have died. He hasnae ventured beyond the shadows since that day, except at night, or, if heavily cloaked, on sunless days."

"And he needs blood."

"Aye," Eric snapped, then sighed and dragged a hand through his hair. "That need grew slowly. He now eats naught but nearly raw meat, seared just enough to warm it, to make the juices flow. His usual drink is now an even mix of wine and blood."

"Do ye ken if he felt the change immediately, or if it was a slow awareness?"

"Since this affliction has been visited upon every laird, 'twas expected, so I cannae say. The first hint comes when the heir becomes a mon and when next he becomes angry. The eyes change to those of a wolf and the teeth become sharper. After so many years we have learned to watch for the change, to guard against that first attack of anger. There were some tragedies in the early days ere we learned what to expect. Alpin was little trouble, for he, too, had studied the matter and was prepared." Eric shook his head. "He has great strength, m'lady, and fights to control this affliction, but the change cannae be stopped."

"What if one ceased to feed the need for blood?" she asked.

"Och, nay, ye dinnae wish to do that. 'Twas tried and the need grows to a near madness, endangering all who draw too near."

"Restraint willnae work?"

"Nay, not e'en if one finds the means to hold him in a way he cannae break free of. The strength of these men can be terrifying to behold. So can their ability to persuade, to beguile, be beyond compare. E'en if ye find chains strong enough to bind them, they can eventually get some poor fool to set them free."

Sophie stared down at her foot as she tapped it slowly against the hard-packed dirt of the bailey, her hands clasped behind her back. Most of what Eric told her matched what she had learned from others. He told her the truth without any gruesome elaborations or tales of the devil, however. The truth was not good. No normal restraints or cures had worked. It had been foolish to think the MacCordys had left any stone unturned in the course of over four hundred years. Rona's curse refused to be denied its victims.

"None of the lairds lives to a great age, aye?" she asked, looking back at Eric.

"Sadly true. A few have killed themselves, a few died in battle, some are murdered by their own people."

"But nay until they have bred an heir."

"Aye, and after the son is born, the change often happens more quickly. The old laird, through sheer strength of will, held back the worst of the affliction for thirteen years, but I believe seeing the curse appear in Alpin broke his spirit. The verra next battle he fought, he died, and I think he planned to do so. In battle, the beast within the lairds bursts free in many ways. Their strength is that of many men, their ferocity unmatched, and their skill at laying waste to the enemy a source of legends. 'Tis why we are so often sought out by men who wish us to fight their battles for them."

"Has there been a laird or two who was seduced by such power, began to welcome it?"

"Oh, aye, a few. But nay Alpin," Eric said firmly, "if that is what ye think. Alpin has more strength of will than any mon I have e'er kenned or heard of. If any mon could beat this, he could, but there isnae any sign that he is winning that battle. Nay, at best he but slows the tightening of the grip of this affliction."

"Then he doesnae grow worse as quickly as his father or grandfather?"

"Nay, but his father was married by now and had bred the heir. His grandfather, weel," Eric shrugged. "He was verra bad from all that I hear. I dinnae ken if he was weak or one of those who reveled in the fear he could stir. He was killed by the villagers after he killed his wife. Tore her to pieces, 'tis said. Her and the lover he found her with."

Sophie ignored Nella's muttered prayers and nodded. "The rage. Catching one's wife with another mon would certainly stir it up." She suddenly smiled at Eric and rubbed her hands together. "I think I have a plan." She briefly scowled at Nella, who groaned, then looked back at Eric, pretending she did not see the smile he quickly hid. "I shall immediately start doing all I can to help Sir Alpin fight this curse. I ken all manner of things to shield him, protect him, strengthen him. Rowan branches, rune stones, herbs," she muttered, trying to recall all she had and to think of what more she might need.

"Er, m'lady—" Eric began.

Caught up in her thoughts, Sophie started toward the keep. "I dinnae suppose the laird would wear an amulet or two. Nay, he is being most uncooperative. He avoids me as if I am some toad-sucking demon waving a dead mon's hand at him," she mumbled to herself.

"Arenae ye going with her?" Eric asked Nella, who just stood there frowning after Sophie.

"She is muttering," replied Nella. " 'Tis sometimes best nay to hear what she is saying when she mutters. She only mutters when she is angry, and though she be a sweet, big-hearted lass, when she is angry she can have a verra wicked tongue."

"She willnae give up, will she?"

"Nay. She is a stubborn woman, and I think she is weighted with shame o'er what her ancestor did. Aye, and she was sorely grieved by what happened to her mother. M'lady will keep at this 'til she joins the angels."

"Nella?" called Sophie, suddenly realizing she was alone.

"Coming, m'lady." Nella hurried to Sophie's side.

"Good. We must change and go to collect some rowan branches."

"For what?"

"I intend to place as many as I can around this keep to try to weaken the power of the curse," Sophie replied as she entered the keep and hurried up the stairs.

"The laird isnae going to like this," Nella said quietly as she followed Sophie.

"Then we shallnae tell him."

Alpin knew he should not go to the great hall even as he found himself walking toward it. Sophie would be there with her smiles, her undampened hope, and that innocent beauty that made him ache. Avoiding her did not work, for he found himself trying to catch glimpses of her like some besotted youth. She also had a true skill for appearing around every corner. It was time to stop hiding in his own keep, he mused, as he strode into the great hall and straight into something hard.

Cursing softly, Alpin was just wondering what fool had placed a stool upon a chair right inside the doorway when something soft landed on him. His body immediately recognized Sophie, and he quickly wrapped his arms around her to stop her fall. Despite his best efforts, however, he lost his balance. Knowing he could not stop his own fall, he turned so that he took the worst of it, sprawling on his back with the sweet-smelling, viciously cursing Sophie sprawled on top of him.

He quickly became almost painfully aware of how good she felt in his arms, her gentle curves fitting perfectly against him. The scent of her filled his head, a stirring mixture of woman, clean skin, and a hint of lavender. When she shifted slightly on top of him, he tightened his grasp, unwilling to let her go. He could hear her pulse quicken, sense a building heat within her, and was sharply disappointed to find that she, too, feared him. Then he took another deep breath and realized it was not fear but desire that was stirring within her. Alpin beat down the strong urge to toss her over his shoulder and run to his bedchamber. He met her wide-eyed gaze with a hard-won calm, idly noting that desire made her eyes appear more green than blue.

"Might I ask what ye were doing?" He glanced at the stool and the chair, then looked back at her.

"I was hanging a few rowan branches o'er the door," she replied.

"Ye could find no one to help?"

"I didnae ask. I was trying to do it secretly. If I got someone to help me, then it wouldnae have remained a secret, would it?"

Alpin looked at the branches nailed over the door to the great hall, and sighed as he returned his gaze to her face. "Why?"

"For protection. Ye are fighting the curse," she hurried on before he could protest, "and I decided to do what I can to help. I plan to surround ye with protection, shields against evil, and things to help strengthen your will to fight, or, at least, keep it strong." She sighed. "I ken ye dinnae like such things so I thought to do it secretly."

"So ye planned to lie to me."

"Nay! I planned on telling ye nothing at all. Ye need such things to help ye hold firm whilst I search for a cure, but since I kenned ye would deny that or argue against my plans, I decided 'twas simplest to just boldly grasp the reins and charge ahead."

"And ride right o'er me."

"Weel," she grimaced, then smiled at him, "more like ride *beside* ye."

It was all nonsense, of course, Alpin mused. Rowan branches, magical stones, special herbs, and all such trickery could not save him. The earnest hope in her lovely eyes both attracted and annoyed him. He wanted to savor the sweetness of it and crush it with the cold, heartless truth. She was going to drive him mad long before his affliction accomplished the deed.

Then he found himself asking when had anyone at Nochdaidh last felt any hope at all? When had anyone worked so hard to try to help him? Never in his memory was the answer. Alpin did not share her hope, but her desire to help touched some deep need within him. He put his hand on the back of her head, tangling his fingers in her long, soft hair, and pulled her mouth down to his. The feel of her slender body, the scent of her, and even her foolish plots to help him shattered his resistance. He had to kiss her, had to steal a taste of her sweet innocence, of her precious if fruitless hopes, and of her desire.

Sophie tensed as he brushed his lips over hers. Heat flooded her body and she gasped. Alpin's kiss grew fierce and demanding as he invaded her mouth with his tongue. Such a sudden assault should have frightened or angered her, but it did neither. It inflamed her. Each stroke of his tongue coaxed forth a deep, searing need. She did not need to feel the telltale hardening of his lean body to know he desired her. She could feel it in his kiss, could taste it upon his tongue. That desire fed her own. The passion flaring to life within her was so heady, so sweet, she had no will to fight it.

"'Tis a strange place ye have chosen for some wooing," drawled a deep voice, "and nay verra private, either."

The kiss ended so abruptly, Sophie felt lost and unsteady. Alpin gracefully stood up with her in his arms, and set her on her feet. She swayed a little, then, realizing Eric stood there, nervously tried to tidy her appearance.

Not only was she severely disappointed that the kiss was over, but she suddenly wished she were alone. After experiencing something so stirring, so shattering to her peace of mind, she would like a little privacy to sort out her feelings and thoughts. It would be easy enough to leave, but she did not want anyone to think she was fleeing out of embarrassment or shame.

"Sophie fell and I caught her," Alpin said, giving Eric a hard look that dared the man to argue.

Eric met that gaze for a moment, then shrugged and moved to pick up the stool and chair. "What are these doing here?"

"The stool was upon the chair and Lady Sophie was upon the stool. I walked into them."

"Why would ye do something like that, m'lady?" Eric asked, only to have Alpin silently reply by pointing to a spot above the doors. "Oh, I see. Rowan branches."

"Aye," replied Sophie. " 'Tis said they protect against witches."

" 'Tis about four hundred and thirty years too late for that," murmured Alpin, and met Sophie's cross look with one raised brow. "Do ye plan to do a lot of this?"

"In every place I can. I have a few other ideas as weel. I dinnae suppose I can convince ye to wear an amulet or two, can I?"

"So I might rattle about the place like Nella? Nay, I think not." He looked up at the rowan tree branches. "I must resign myself to the constant sight of dying greenery, must I? I think this might count as sorcery."

"I consider it healing." Seeing the look of amused disbelief in his eyes, Sophie decided it was time to retreat. "I shall just go and clean up," she murmured as she hurried out the door.

Alpin was surprised when Nella glared at him before following Sophie. He shook his head and looked at Eric, only to find that man eyeing him with an uncomfortable intensity. Kissing Sophie had been an error in judgment. He had succumbed to a weakness, and, he mused, being caught at it was probably a just punishment.

"What ye saw was a moment of utter madness," Alpin said before Eric could speak.

"Are ye certain that was all it was?" asked Eric.

"Aye, and that is all it ever can be. A woman like Lady Sophie Hay can ne'er be for me. She is all hope, sweetness, and smiles."

"With a hearty serving of tartness, stubbornness, and passion."

"Aye. A perfect mixture," Alpin murmured and shook his head. "Sophie needs laughter, sun, and love. She cannae find any of that with me. Although I am drawn to her, the first woman to show no fear, to offer help, I must turn from her. When she realizes nothing she does will help, she will lose that innocent faith that is so alluring. If I try to hold her, she will see me become the creature my forefathers did. 'Tis cowardly, mayhap, but I find I cannae stomach the thought of watching her begin to fear me, revile me, to watch me become more beast than mon."

"But she might be able to help you," protested Eric.

"Nay, I doubt that verra much," said Alpin as he picked up the chair and took it back to the table. "I dinnae doubt for one moment, however, that *I* will destroy her. If I try to hold her, I will simply smother all that sweet light with my own darkness. I am not yet beast enough to commit that sin."

* * *

"Nella, I need some time alone," Sophie said, halting her maid when the woman tried to follow her into the bedchamber they shared.

"But, m'lady," Nella began to protest.

"I need to think, Nella. Just give me a wee while alone, then come help me ready myself to dine in the great hall."

"Because the laird hurled ye to the floor and tried to ravish ye?"

"Actually, Nella, I fell, knocked him to the ground, and he kissed me. That is all. Now, go. Please. I will be fine."

The moment Nella left, Sophie hurled herself face-down on the bed. She knew she had been attracted to the laird from the first moment she had set eyes on the man. Now, with one kiss, he had shown her that what she felt was far more than an interest in a mysterious, troubled, handsome man. She loved him. She loved a man who could not abide the sun, drank blood, ate raw meat, and could tear his enemies apart with his bare hands. Sophie doubted she could have handpicked a man more certain to ensure that she continued to walk the sad path trod by far too many Galt women before her.

Chapter Four

The curses were bellowed so loudly Sophie was surprised they did not shake loose a few of the stones in the thick walls of Nochdaidh. She was strongly tempted to ignore Alpin when he shouted her name. After all, he had ignored *her* very thoroughly for the last week. If not for the times she and he had crossed paths and she had caught a look in his eyes that could only be described as passionate, she could easily think he hated her. The only other times he had taken note of her existence was to flay her with his temper. She was only trying to help the ungrateful fool. It was hardly her fault he kept stumbling upon her shields and protections in ways that tended to cause him some minor injury. Did the man never sleep? she thought crossly.

"Sophie Hay!"

It was a little astonishing how that deep voice could

penetrate such thick walls, she mused, as she rose from the pallet she slept on. Although it was not the most comfortable of beds, she far preferred it to the one she had been given. That bed had been the site of far too many trysts. Sensitive to such things, she had felt the ghostly remnants of passion, lust, pain, and even fear; had been unable to shield herself completely from all the lingering memories of so many strong feelings. Nella now slept in the bed. Fortunately, Nella was so accustomed to Sophie's ways, she had not questioned the why of such an unusual arrangement. Sophie could not tell her very protective maid that those memories of lovemaking had caused her to have some very shocking and sensual dreams concerning herself and Sir Alpin.

As she hurried out of the room in response to a snarled demand that she best be quick or be prepared to suffer dark, but unspecified, consequences, Sophie was a little surprised to see that Nella still slept soundly. The sight that met her eyes as she turned toward Alpin's bedchamber had her feeling both aroused and a little amused. Sir Alpin, the much-feared laird of Nochdaidh, was wearing only his hose and a loose shirt that revealed a great deal of his broad, smooth chest. He was also sitting on the floor grimacing and rubbing one of his bare feet.

When he looked at her, she understood why he inspired such fear in people, even though she felt only a brief flicker of unease. His eyes resembled those of a wolf, the golden brown having become more yellow in color. The lines of his face had changed slightly, giving him a distinctly feral look. She could feel his anger, feel the wildness of it. Then he ran his gaze over her and she felt his emotions shift from anger to need. Her body quickly responded to that look, but he seemed unaware of that. His control was admirable, even somewhat astonishing, but she was beginning to heartily dislike it.

"Ye roared, m'laird?" she asked, crossing her arms and inwardly grimacing when she realized she wore only her thin linen nightshift.

"What are these?" he demanded, pointing to the stones lined up outside his bedchamber door.

"Rune stones," she replied. "Since ye had retired for the night, I set them there to shield ye as ye slept. I had planned to collect them ere ye woke. I hadnae realized ye were in the habit of slinking about in the dark of night."

"Nay? Perhaps I felt the need to feast upon some innocent bairn?" He noticed she had begun to tap her small, bare foot against the floor. "I am, after all, a creature of shadows, comfortable beneath the cloak of night, which so many others fear."

"Ye dinnae help matters by saying such foolish things." She gasped in surprise when he suddenly grabbed her by the arm and pulled her down until she was sprawled in his lap. "My laird, this is undignified and improper."

Sophie had wanted to sound imperious, but even she could hear the breathlessness in her voice. It should not surprise her that she was so weak-willed around this man. She had spent the last week dreaming of that first kiss, aching for another, and for so much more. Falling in love with this man had to be one of the most idiotic things she had ever done, but her heart refused to be swayed by good sense. Instead of learning how to fight his allure, she found herself hurt and angered over how easily he could fight the attraction between them.

He gave her a faint smile that barely parted his lips, then nuzzled her throat. Sophie trembled and wrapped her arms around him. When she felt the light touch of his teeth at the pulse point in her throat, she supposed she ought to be a little concerned. Instead, she curled her fingers into his thick hair and held him closer as she tilted her head back. The feel of his tongue upon that spot where her blood pounded in her veins, the damp heat of his mouth as he lightly suckled her skin fed her nearly desperate need for him to place those soft lips against her own. When he kissed the underside of her chin, then her cheek, she turned her face a little, trying to press her mouth to his.

"I can hear each beat of your heart, Sophie," he said against her temple, his voice deep and seductive. "I can hear the blood rushing in your veins. I can smell your desire," he whispered and lightly nipped her earlobe. "I can taste it upon your lips." He teased her lips with fleeting kisses.

"And I can feel your desire, Alpin." She nipped at his bottom lip and smiled faintly when he growled low in his throat. "It feeds my own." The way his narrowed eyes glowed, his nostrils flared, and his features tightened into a predatory expression should have frightened her, but Sophie only felt her passion soar. She suspected she might look nearly as feral as he did as she ran her tongue between his lips and said, "So taste it, Alpin. Drink deep."

Alpin did, holding her tightly as he kissed her. She met his growing ferocity with her own. It was astonishing to him that this delicate woman did not flee his raw desire, but welcomed it, equaled it. A flicker of sanity pierced the madness seizing him. It would be easy to simply revel in what she offered, but he had to resist. Instinct told him that Sophie would not give herself lightly, and he could offer her no more than a bedding.

He ended the kiss, pulling back from her until his head hit the wall. He closed his eyes against the sight of her flushed face, her passion-warmed eyes, and the rapid rise and fall of her breasts. When he felt his control return, he looked at her again only to catch her staring at his bared chest with a look so heated he almost lost control again.

"Cease staring at my chest, Sophie," he drawled, pleased at how calm he sounded, no hint of the need tearing at his insides to be detected in his voice.

For a moment Sophie did not grasp the almost cold tone behind his words, then she felt the sting of the abrupt ending of their passionate interlude. She felt anger push aside her desire and glared at him, saying with an equal coldness, "I wasnae staring at your chest, ye vain mon. I was but noticing that your laces are badly frayed."

She was good, Alpin thought, as he watched her stand up. If his senses of smell and hearing were not so acute, he might believe she was as unmoved by the kiss as he pretended to be. He could still scent her desire, however, still hear it pounding in her veins. Pride led her now, and, he realized, he could use that to keep her at a distance, to stop her from tempting him with her warmth.

"Best collect your rocks ere ye hurry away," he said.

"They are rune stones," she snapped as she picked them up.

He shrugged as he stood up slowly. "They are nonsense, foolish superstition. I begin to lose patience with all these games."

"And I begin to lose patience with the air of defeat that fair chokes the air at Nochdaidh!"

"After so long, ye must forgive us for no longer believing in cures. And if the air here is so foul to ye, mayhap ye ought to go do your breathing elsewhere."

"Oh, nay, ye willnae get rid of me so easily. Fine, go and wallow in your self-pity. *I* am nay ready to quit. If ye dinnae wish me to fight for you, so be it, but I will continue to fight for myself and for the sake of any children I am blessed with." Seeing the look of fury upon his face, Sophie decided she had pushed him hard enough and she started back to her room. "And best ye get those weak laces seen to ere they snap. Ye could put an eye out, ye ken."

She shut her bedroom door quietly, resisting the urge to slam it shut. Seeing that Nella was still asleep, Sophie shook her head and put her rune stones away. She crawled into her bed and closed her eyes, knowing sleep would be slow to release her from the tumultuous feelings still gripping her. As she struggled to calm herself, she decided it was not the despair of holding love too briefly and losing it that she needed to worry about. If she was not careful, Alpin would drive her utterly mad long before then.

"M'lady, what troubles ye?" asked Nella as she walked through the village with Sophie. "Ye have been verra quiet." She cast a fearful glance at Sophie's throat. "Did the laird drink too much of your blood?"

Sophie was abruptly pulled from her dark thoughts and stopped to gape at Nella. "Ye think the laird has been drinking my blood?"

"Weel, there is that mark upon your neck."

Clasping her hand over the mark upon her neck, Sophie grimaced. "I hadnae thought it so obvious." She sighed and told her maid about the confrontation between her and Alpin last night. "I assume 'tis something men like to do and, at that moment, it was quite, er, pleasant. I had thought I had hidden it."

Nella moved to adjust Sophie's braid as well as the collars of her gown and cloak. " 'Tis better now. Keep your cloak tied at the neck and it should remain hidden. Dinnae want too many catching a peek at it. If they ken 'tis a love bite, your reputation will be sorely marred, though I suspect most will think what I did."

"I fear so." She frowned as she caught sight of a crowd of people at the far end of the road. "A meeting?"

Two men ran past her and Nella, rushing to join the crowd. Sophie caught the word "murder" in their conversation and froze. This was the very last thing Alpin needed. Sophie was about to turn back toward the keep when one of the women in the crowd saw her, called to her, and drew everyone's attention to her.

"M'lady, ye must come see this," Shona the cooper's wife called. "This will make ye see the danger of staying within the walls of such a cursed place."

"I really dinnae want to see this," Sophie murmured to Nella even as she started to walk toward Shona, Nella staying close to her side. "For them to cry murder means 'tis nay a clean death. No death is pleasant to witness, but murder can leave a verra untidy corpse."

"Ye fret o'er the oddest things," Nella said as she nudged her way through the crowd. "Dead is dead. Aye?" Nella abruptly stopped and shuddered. "Oh, dear."

Sophie took a deep breath to steady herself, stepped around Nella, and looked down at what had once been a man. She felt her gorge rise and took several deep breaths to calm herself, her hand cupped over her nose and mouth to shield herself from the scent of death. Aware that the villagers were all watching her closely, she carefully studied the corpse. She knew what they believed, knew the accusations and questions that would soon be spoken aloud, and she searched out every clue she could find to be used to proclaim Alpin's innocence.

" 'Tis Donald, the butcher's eldest lad," said Hugh the cooper. "Weel, nay a lad. A mon with a wife and bairns. The poor woman found him like this. Said he often came here to sleep if one of the bairns cried too much in the night. Since their wee laddie is cutting teeth, he was setting up a fair howl all night long. The laird must have been on the hunt, and poor Donald was easy game."

"The laird didnae do this," Sophie said, her voice steady and firm.

"But his throat was torn out."

"Nay, 'tis cut." She crossed her arms and waited as Hugh crouched down to look more closely. "A verra clean cut it is, as weel. Swiftly done with a verra long, verra sharp knife."

Ian the butcher wiped the tears from his ruddy cheeks and looked closer. "Aye, she be right. I couldnae have done it neater myself. But that just means the laird used his sword."

For one brief moment, Sophie considered the fact that the laird had been awake and wandering about last night. Then she felt both guilty and ashamed. Alpin would never do this. Even if he turned into a beast, she had the sad feeling he would cut his own throat before he attacked some innocent. The trick would be in convincing these people who considered every MacCordy laird cursed, or a demon.

"Did anyone see the laird last eve?" she asked. "I did—in the keep, barefoot, cross and bellowing, and with nary a drop of blood on him. Now, I ken what ye think the laird is, that ye think he feasted upon poor Donald last eve. Look ye at the ground beneath Donald's neck. 'Tis soaked in his blood. If the laird did this, acting as the demon ye think he is, do ye truly think he would let all that blood go to waste?"

"He gutted the lad," said Hugh. "Mayhap the innards were what he craved this time."

Even as Sophie opened her mouth, Ian shook his head. "Nay. 'Tis another clean cut and I didnae see aught missing," he added as he covered his son with a blanket someone handed him.

"And that wound bled verra little," Sophie said, "as did the wounds to his head and face. Do ye ken what that means, Master Ian?"

"I think so. My poor lad was already dead and fair bled dry ere the other wounds were made. But why?"

"To make all of ye think the laird did this." Sophie patted the grieving Ian's broad shoulder. "If the laird had come a-hunting, had become the beast of the night ye all claim he is, he would not have left such an intact body. He wouldnae have let all that blood sink into the dirt. Nay, if he had become the demon ye fear is within him, he would have torn this poor mon apart, drank the blood, and nay cared if ye caught him bathing in the gore. This was done by someone else, someone who crept upon Donald as he slept, for there is nary a sign of a struggle, cut his throat, and then desecrated the body to try to hide their crime. Nay, worse, to try to fix all blame upon the laird. Poor Donald made someone verra angry."

"She just tries to protect her lover," spoke up a buxom young woman who suddenly appeared at Ian's side. "He has already made her one of his slaves. Look ye at her neck! He has been feasting upon her!"

Sophie felt herself blush deeply and clasped her hand over her neck. "Nay!"

"Och, aye," said Shona, and laughed softly. "Someone's been feasting on the lass, true enough. 'Tis a love bite, Gemma, ye foolish cow. Now cease your nonsense and help your mon. He has a son to bury."

"I thought ye said it wouldnae show if I kept my cloak tied," Sophie grumbled to Nella.

"Weel, it would have, if ye didnae have such a wee skinny neck that pokes its way out of anything one tries to lash to it."

Sophie's response to that insult was lost as her gaze became fixed upon Gemma. It took all of her willpower not to cry out in accusation, to remain calm. She knew who had killed Donald, although she could not yet even guess why.

"Ian," she called, drawing the man's attention back to her, "until we ken who murdered your son and why, 'twould be wise to guard his widow and bairns."

She held his gaze and inwardly sighed with relief when he nodded. The brief look of fury that touched Gemma's round face only confirmed Sophie's suspicions. The problem was going to be proving the woman's guilt without revealing any of her own special gifts. She shook her head, then noticed Shona remained although everyone else had left, and the woman was watching her with an unsettling intensity.

"The laird didnae kill Donald," Sophie said.

"I ken it," replied Shona. "I dinnae ken what to think about the mon who lives in that shadowed place, but I *do* believe he didnae do this. Ye shouldnae hope that many will share my opinion, however." She smiled faintly. "Ye ken who did it, dinnae ye? Do ye have the sight?"

A scowling Nella stepped between Shona and Sophie before Sophie could reply. "Aye, she does, but if ye tell anyone I will take a searing hot poker to your rattling tongue."

"Nella," Sophie protested.

"Fair enough," said Shona, grinning at Nella. She stepped a little to the side, reached out, and touched the mark upon Sophie's neck. "Mayhap I have the sight, too, for I am that sure 'tis the laird himself who has been nibbling on ye. Best ye push the rogue away."

"He willnae hurt me," Sophie said.

" 'Tisnae him ye need worry on, but them." She nodded toward the keep.

Sophie stared at the people, horses, and carts entering the gates of Nochdaidh. "Who are they?"

"The laird's betrothed and her kinsmen."

"His what?"

"The marriage was arranged years ago. The deed will be done in a fortnight. He didnae tell ye?"

"Nay, he didnae." Torn between pain and fury, Sophie spoke through tightly clenched teeth, then started to march back toward the keep.

"Wheesht, she looked verra angry," murmured Shona.

"Aye, she did," Nella agreed in a mournful voice.

"Will she put a curse on him?"

"She isnae a witch," Nella snapped, then sighed as she started to follow Sophie. "Howbeit, she is so angry that the laird may begin to think another curse upon The Mac-Cordy is the lesser of two evils."

Chapter Five

It was going to be a long night, Alpin mused as he sprawled indolently in his chair. He surveyed all the people seated at his table and decided it was going to be a very long night indeed. Except for Eric, who sat on his right and looked too cursed amused for Alpin's liking, everyone else did not appear to be feeling the least bit congenial. Since he had long ago lost the art of pleasant conversation, if he had ever even possessed such a skill, silence reigned.

Alpin looked at Sophie as he sipped his wine and inwardly winced. She had returned from the village to find him greeting his newly arrived guests. One look at her face told him she knew exactly who these people were. He was not accustomed to the look she had given him. People usually eyed him with wary respect or fear. She had looked at him as if he were no more than some impertinent spatter of mud that had soiled her ladyship's best dancing slippers. He had wanted some distance between them and now he had it. Alpin was not sure why he felt both guilty and desolate. He suspected she would leave now, just as he had been wanting her to, yet he was fighting the urge to hold her at Nochdaidh even if he had to use chains.

He looked at his bride next and watched her tremble so badly the food she had been about to eat fell from her plump white hand. Lady Margaret MacLane was pretty enough with her brown hair and gray eyes, her body rounded with all the appropriate curves most men craved. At the moment, she was ghostly pale, her eyes so wide with fright they had to sting, and her body shook almost continuously. She had already fainted once, and Alpin dared not speak to her for fear she would do so again.

And then there were his bride's kinsmen, he thought with a sigh. Most of them seemed oblivious to the tense quiet, their sole interest being in consuming as much food and drink as possible. The only time any of them was diverted was when he felt a need to cast a lecherous glance Sophie's way. Margaret's father also kept looking at Sophie, although curiosity was mixed with the desire in his gaze. A strong urge to do violence to the MacLanes was stirring to life within Alpin, but he struggled to control it. Slaughtering many of his bride's kinsmen was not an acceptable way to celebrate a wedding, he mused.

Unable to resist, he looked at Sophie again and tensed. She smiled at him, then smiled at Sir Peter MacLane, Margaret's father. Although Alpin had hated her silence, felt wretched over the hurt he knew he had inflicted upon her, he felt her sudden cheer was an ominous sign. She was planning some mischief. He was certain of it.

"There was a murder in the village today," Sophie announced. "Donald, the butcher's eldest son."

He was going to beat her, Alpin thought, and took a deep drink of wine.

"Are ye certain 'twas murder, m'lady?" asked Eric.

"Och, aye. His throat was cut. Ear to ear." Sophie ignored Margaret's gasp of horror and blithely continued. "His belly was cut open, too." Margaret groaned and her eyes rolled back in their sockets. "Oh, and his poor face was beaten so badly 'twas difficult to recognize him." Sophie calmly watched Margaret slide out of her seat to sprawl unconscious upon the floor. "If she is to make a habit of that, Sir Alpin, mayhap ye ought to scatter a few cushions about her chair." She smiled sweetly at Alpin.

Perhaps he would strangle her, Alpin thought. Slowly.

"Why was the laird nay called to make a judgment?" asked Sir Peter.

"Weel, most of the villagers thought he had already come and gone, that 'twas his work," Sophie replied, then looked at Alpin again. "Of course, I convinced them that ye didnae do it, at least those of them who would heed sense."

"How verra kind of ye," Alpin drawled.

"Aye, it was. I pointed out that all his blood had soaked into the ground and that, if ye were what they thought ye were, ye wouldnae have let it go to waste like that."

"Nay, I would have supped upon it."

"Exactly. And I pointed out that all his innards were still there, plus the wounds were done with a knife, nay with teeth or hands. He was also killed as he slept and I was fair sure ye wouldnae do that, either. Aye, I made it verra clear that ye were a noble warrior, too honorable, too forthright, too—"

"I believe I understand, Sophie," he snapped, feeling the sting of her reprimand even though he knew it was well deserved.

"How nice." Sophie stood up and smiled at everyone. "And, now, if ye gentlemen and the laird will excuse me, I believe I will seek my rest. It has been a most exhausting day, full of blood, tears, and treachery." As Sophie passed behind Alpin's chair, she reached over his shoulder and dropped the amulet she had made for him on the table in front of him. "For ye, m'laird."

"What is it?" he asked, fighting to ignore the hurt and anger he could sense in her.

"An amulet for protection. Ye can wear it or ye can keep it in your pocket. 'Tis why I was in the village today, to gather what I needed. I heard ye are planning to ride off to battle in three days' time. I wanted to be sure ye returned."

"And ye still give it to me after what has occurred today?" he asked softly.

"Why not? And who can say? Mayhap it will prove a charm as weel. Mayhap it will make your bride see ye as a charming, noble knight." When he looked at her over his shoulder, she met his angry gaze calmly.

"I should beat you."

"I shouldnae try it."

"How can I be sure this thing carries no curse?"

"As I told ye, a curse comes back upon the sender threefold. I believe I have enough trouble to deal with already. And I also told ye that I am no witch. Ye should be verra glad of that, m'laird, for, if I were and I were the vengeful sort, I would be weaving one for ye that would make Rona's look like child's play." Knowing her anger was escaping her control, Sophie strode away.

Alpin watched her leave, Nella quickly following her. He picked up the tiny leather bag strung on a black cord and sighed. As he held it, he could feel her hope, her prayers for his safety. Despite her anger and her hurt over what she saw as a gross betrayal, Sophie still wanted to save him, still wanted to help and protect him. He ached to grasp at that support with both hands and hold tight, but was determined to resist that temptation. Sophie deserved better than he had to offer.

Looking at his bride as she pulled herself back up into her seat, he supposed she deserved better as well, but he would not stop the marriage. Margaret had no care for him. She feared him and would undoubtedly be terrified by the changes that would come, but she would not be saddened by them. Margaret would not be hurt when he did not give her a child or come to her bed. There was a chance he might even escape truly consummating the marriage, and that weighed heavily in her favor. It was a dismal future laid out before him, but he had never held any hope for another, better fate, and he would not condemn a sweet sprite like Sophie to share it with him.

Recalling her parting words, he almost smiled. Mayhap not so sweet. She had strength, spirit, and a temper. Even when she was threatening to curse him, he knew she was perfect for him. Alpin considered the fact that he could not hold tight to her; the hardest part of the curse to endure, and the cruelest.

"Who is that lass?" demanded Sir Peter.

The first words that came to mind were *my love* and Alpin was stunned, so stunned it took him a moment to compose himself before he could reply with any calm. "She is who she said she is—Lady Sophie Hay."

"Nay, I mean what is she to ye?"

"Ah. Just another in a verra long line of people trying their hand at curing me of my affliction."

"So she is a witch."

"Nay, a healer."

"Then what is that she just gave ye?"

Alpin slowly placed the amulet around his neck. "Something she made to bring me luck in the coming battle."

"Then she is a witch."

"Many people, e'en the most godly, believe in charms for luck, sir. Lady Sophie is a healer, nay more."

Before the man could further argue the matter, Alpin drew him into a discussion concerning the upcoming battle. In some ways Sophie did practice what many would consider witchcraft, and those who feared such things were usually incapable of discerning the difference between good and bad sorcery. Alpin had the strong feeling she had other skills many would decry as sorcery, such as the sight, or some trick of knowing exactly what a person felt. One thing he was determined to do for her was shield her from the dangerous, superstitious fears of those like Sir Peter. It might even, in some small way, assuage the hurt he had inflicted. Or, he mused, he could allow himself to fall in the coming battle, ending her pain as well as his own. He sighed and forced himself to concentrate on the conversation. Fate would never allow him to escape his dark destiny so easily.

* * *

"That Lady Margaret is a worse coward than I, and that be saying a lot," muttered Nella as she sat before the fire in their bedchamber sewing a torn hem upon one of Sophie's gowns. "I wonder she hasnae washed her eyeballs right out of their holes with all the weeping she does."

Sophie lightly grunted in agreement, never moving from the window she looked out of, or taking her gaze from the activity in the bailey. For the three days Lady Margaret had been at Nochdaidh, the girl had done little more than cry, swoon, or cower. Not one thing Sophie had said or tried had calmed the girl. At times, Sophie had wondered what possessed her to try to help a woman who would soon lay claim to the man Sophie herself wanted so badly. She just could not abide being around all that self-pity and abject fear. There were enough dark, somber feelings thickening the air at Nochdaidh without Lady Margaret adding more by the bucketful. That very morning Sophie had finally given up on trying to help the girl.

"I tried to give the lass one of my amulets," said Nella, "but she just sobbed and crossed herself."

"Ah, aye. Despite the denials of everyone at Nochdaidh, as weel as our own, Lady Margaret is certain we are witches."

"Such a fool." Nella frowned at Sophie, set her mending down, and moved to stand beside her. "What is going on?"

"The laird prepares to ride away to battle. He must fight the men who have been pillaging Sir Peter's lands. A wedding gift, I suppose."

"I am sorry about that, m'lady," Nella said quietly.

"So am I, Nella." Sophie sighed. "My anger has faded, but my unhappiness lingers. I have come to understand that Alpin believes he is doing what is best for me by pushing me away."

"'Tis best for ye to have your heart broken?"

"So Alpin believes. He think 'tis easier for me now than if I stay at his side whilst the curse devours his soul."

"Mayhap he is right," Nella whispered.

"Nay. I believe I have finally figured out how to break this curse. 'Tisnae amulets, rowan branches, or potions that will save him. At best they but slow the change from mon to beast."

"Then what *can* save him, m'lady?"

"Me." She smiled briefly at an astonished Nella. "Aye, 'tis me. I am the key to unlock the prison of pain Rona built."

"I dinnae understand."

"Rona's words were: 'Thus it shall remain until one steps from the shadows of pride, land, and wealth and does as his heart commands. Until all that should have been finally is.' Until MacCordy weds Galt, Nella. Until a MacCordy laird chooses love o'er profit." Sophie shrugged. "That wouldnae have to be me in particular, but I begin to feel that that is how it has come to be. Alpin cares for me, of that I have no doubt. Yet he turns from that and goes to Margaret, who will bring him land and wealth. He may do so for verra noble reasons, but 'tis still the wrong choice. Again. 'Tis Ciar and Rona all over again. I fear that the curse will ne'er be broken if Alpin does marry Margaret."

"Then ye must tell him. Wheesht, ye have wealth and land aplenty, too, if that is what the mon seeks."

Sophie shook her head. "He willnae heed me. Alpin denies there is a curse at work here, e'en though, deep in his heart, I think he kens the truth. He willnae allow me to enter what he sees as his private hell, to share in his damnation. And if I tell him of my wealth to make him choose me, will the fact that his heart welcomes that choice end the curse, or will it become just another choice of wealth and land? I dare not risk it, for I truly believe he must choose between wealth and love, turning away from one to embrace the other."

"It makes sense, yet how can a curse tell the difference? It has no thoughts or feelings."

"Something keeps it alive, year after year. Something keeps each MacCordy laird alive, keeps them breeding that heir to carry on the curse, and something keeps killing the love in the hearts of the men chosen by each daughter of Rona's bloodline. I dinnae understand how, just that this curse somehow keeps itself alive and will continue to do so unless Rona's demand is met."

"So what can ye do?"

"Weel, I have a wee bit more than a week to make Alpin love me enough to want me to stay."

"Aye. Unless, of course, he already loves ye and that is why he will make ye leave."

"That is the dilemma I face, aye. Not an easy knot to untangle."

Nella stared down into the bailey. "What is that strange cart? Do ye ken, it looks a wee bit like a coffin on wheels."

Chilled by the image, Sophie wrapped her arms around herself. " 'Tis what poor Alpin must shelter in if he cannae find and defeat the enemy ere the sun rises. 'Tis made of iron with holes at the bottom to let in the air and some light, yet keep out the sun's rays. Once beyond the shadows, heavy cloaks arenae enough protection any longer."

"Odd that none of the lairds simply walked out into the

summer sun and let death take them. It would have freed them."

"I think the curse wouldnae allow it. It needs the heir. So a hint of hope, a sense of self-preservation, and the poor mon survives long enough to fulfill his sad destiny. Rona set her trap weel. Her magic was verra strong indeed."

"Yours be strong as weel, m'lady, but 'tis a good, kindly magic. Ye must try to have more faith in it."

"I think 'tis more important that Alpin have some faith in it. His surrender to a dark, sad fate runs deep, Nella, and I truly fear it will condemn us all."

"She watches ye," said Eric as Alpin mounted his horse. "I believe her anger has eased."

Alpin glanced up to see Sophie's pale face in the window of her bedchamber. "Then I shall have to think of something to fire it again."

Eric cursed softly. "Alpin, that beautiful lass cares for ye. Why dinnae ye—"

"Nay," Alpin snapped, glaring at his friend. "Cease shoving temptation beneath my nose. Look ye," he pointed at the iron cart as it rolled by, "I must carry my coffin about with me. 'Tis the rock I must crawl beneath if the sun rises whilst I am still afield. I go now to kill men because the father of my bride wishes them dead. And we both ken how I will revel in the slaughter," he added in a low, cold voice. "The scents of blood, fear, and death rouse the beast within me. I breathe them in as if they are the sweetest of flowers. It will take all my will nay to feast upon the enemy like the demon all think me to be.

"I can hear your heart beat, Eric," he continued. "I can

hear the blood move within your veins." He nodded to-ward a young man several yards away. "Thomas had a woman recently. Dugald has dressed too warmly and be-gins to sweat. Henry's wife has her woman's time," he nodded toward a couple embracing by the wall, "but he bedded her anyway."

"So ye have gained a sharp ear and a keen nose."

"I have grown closer to the wolf than the mon, Eric. I have resisted marriage longer than any MacCordy laird, but duty beckons. The bargain my father made must be honored. And despite my plan to seed no woman, to breed no child, I am nay longer sure I can defeat my fate so easily. As the wedding draws nigh, I feel something stirring within me that can only be called an urge to mate. 'Tis as if I am descending into a state of rut."

"Then mate with the woman we both ken ye really want."

Alpin shook his head. "There is a coward within me who trembles at the thought of Sophie watching me de-scend into madness, become a beast who needs caging or killing. There is also a strangely noble mon within me who cannae condemn her to watching her child step into monhood and begin the fall into this hell. I will wed Mar-garet." He took one last look at Sophie, then kicked his horse into a gallop, fleeing her and the friend who tried so hard to weaken his resolve.

Chapter Six

Alpin strode into his great hall, saw who waited there, and cursed. Now was not a good time to face his timid bride and her family. The battle had been fierce and bloody, the smell of it still upon him. He knew how such ferocity, such bloodletting, made him look. His people were accustomed, but his bride and her family were not. He had retained enough of his senses to wash his hands and face, but it was obviously not enough, not if the wide-eyed looks of his bride's family were any indication. As he approached the head table where most of them sat, Margaret gave out a small sob, her eyes seemed to roll back in her head, and she slipped from her chair in a swoon.

"Considering the fact that I spend a great deal of my time in battle," he drawled as he stared down at his unconscious bride, making no move to lift her up off the floor, "this could prove to be a problem."

He heard a faint rattle and knew Nella approached. The woman looked at the men, who did not move, then looked at the girl on the floor. Nella crouched, grasped Margaret under the arms, and looked at Alpin. Her eyes widened, but then she frowned.

"M'laird, did ye ken that your eyes look just like a wolf's?" she asked, glancing around in surprise when several people gasped.

Leave it to Nella to simply blurt out what everyone else pretended not to see, Alpin mused. He felt a tickle of amusement creep up through the bloodlust still thrumming in his veins. A smile touched his mouth, much to his amazement, but he knew it was a mistake the moment he did it. Several muttered curses cut through the silence and he saw a number of the MacLanes cross themselves. Nella's eyes widened even more, but she looked more curious than afraid.

"Your teeth have grown, too, havenae they?"

"Aye. 'Tis what happens when I have been in a battle."

"Ah, aye, the beastie comes out. All that killing, maiming, and blood spurting stirs him up, eh? Are ye going to sit in your chair, m'laird?"

A little startled by her abrupt change of subject, Alpin shook his head. To his utter astonishment, the small, bone-thin Nella easily lifted up the several stone heavier and half a foot taller Margaret. Nella set the woman in his chair with little care for any added bruises or concern for Margaret's appearance. His betrothed was sprawled in his chair like some insensate drunk.

And what was this talk of a beastie? he wondered. The moment he asked himself the question, he knew the an-

swer. It was how Sophie had explained his affliction to
Nella. Nella believed in the curse as strongly as Sophie
did. Sophie had obviously told Nella that the curse had
put a beast inside of him. It was a nice thought, far better
than the truth. The truth was that the beast *was* him and
he could not exorcise it. Soon, he suspected, he would not
be able to control it, either.

"Your food and drink are in your bedchamber, m'laird,"
said the buxom maid Anne, pulling him from his dark
thoughts.

"Good," he said. " 'Tis time I sought my solitude."

"Shall I—" began Anne.

"Nay."

Knowing she was offering him the use of her body, he
wondered at his reluctance. It had been far too long since
he had had a woman and his body was taut and needy.
Anne had serviced him in the past when he had returned
from a battle, so he knew she could endure the wildness
in him at such times. Then he saw the glint of fear and
disgust in the woman's eyes, visible beneath the arro-
gance and anticipation. Whatever her reasons were for
offering herself, one of them was certainly not desire. Inwardly shaking his head, he headed for his bedchamber.
He wanted only one woman anyway, and he could not
have her. Not only did she probably not understand how
to prevent a child from taking root, but he could not subject her to a bedding by the beast raging inside of him.

A bath awaited him and he took quick advantage of it,
scrubbing the scent of death from his skin. Although he
ached to find the strength to turn away from the meal set
out for him, he could not. His hunger was too great and
he feared what he might do if he did not slake it in some
way. Alpin tore into the meat barely seared on either side,

his speed in finishing it born of both need and revulsion. He poured himself some of his enriched wine and stood by the window, staring down into the torch-lit bailey. A little of the ferocity within him eased as he fed the craving that so disgusted and terrified him. When would enriched wine and raw meat cease to be enough? he wondered.

He tensed as he heard someone slip into his room. The fact that the scent he picked up was Sophie's did not ease his tension at all. This was a very bad time for her to come to his bedchamber. He listened to her take a few hesitant steps toward him, then stop. Slowly, he took a deep breath, closing his eyes as he savored her scent. She had bathed; her warm skin smelled of woman, with a hint of lavender. To him she smelled of laughter, of warm sun and wildflowers, of hope. He could almost hate her for that.

Another scent tantalized him and he grew so tense his muscles ached as he opened his eyes to stare blindly out of the window. Sophie smelled of desire. Alpin hastily finished his drink, but it satisfied only one hunger. There was another now raging inside of him, fed by the hint of feminine musk. He breathed it in, opening his mouth slightly to enhance his ability, and the blood began to pound in his veins.

"Go away, Sophie," he said. "'Tisnae a good time for ye to be near me."

It took Sophie a moment to realize he had spoken to her. From the minute she had entered the room to see him standing there wearing only a drying cloth wrapped around his lean hips, she had been spellbound. She had cautiously moved closer to him, her palms tingling with the need to touch that broad, strong back. He was so beautiful, he made her heart ache.

"I felt ye return," she said, taking another step toward him. "I wished to see that ye had come to no harm."

"I am still alive, if ye can call this living."

She sighed, but decided not to try to dispute his words this time. "I felt—"

"What? The beastie in me? The ferocity? The blood-lust? Or," he looked at her over his shoulder, "just the lust?"

Alpin realized his error the moment he set eyes upon her. Her hair was down, hanging in long, thick golden waves to her slender hips. She wore only a thin linen chemise, the delicate curves of her lithe body easy to see. Her wide eyes were fixed upon him, more green than blue. Sophie was all soft, womanly sunlight, and he craved every small inch of her.

Sophie shook her head. "I felt that ye needed me, but, mayhap, that was just vanity."

He turned to look at her more fully. "Nay, not vain. I *do* need ye, but I willnae allow myself to feed that hunger."

"Because of Lady Margaret?"

"Nay."

"Then why?" She forced herself not to reveal how his sudden move toward her startled her, knowing how easily he could read it as fear.

"Why?" He nearly snarled the word, standing so close to her he had to clench his hands into tight fists to keep himself from touching her. "Look at me. I am more beast than mon."

He did look quite feral, she mused, with his eyes more yellow than golden brown, and they had changed in that odd way again to look more like an animal's than a man's. His teeth had also changed a little, looking far more predatory. Subtle though the changes were, they were alarming, but not because she feared he could hurt her. She had seen such changes in him before, although not this clearly. The changes were proof, however, that nothing she had done so far had lessened the tight grip of the curse.

"The mon is still there, Alpin," she said quietly.

"Is he?" He strode to the table and picked up the plate that had held his meal. "Does a mon eat naught but meat, meat barely cooked, simply passed o'er the fire until it becomes as warm as a fresh kill?" He poured the blood that still pooled upon the dish into his tankard, then filled it with more wine. "Does a mon drink wine heartened with blood?" He took a long drink before setting the tankard down. "And the mix grows more heartened with each passing year. The craving grows stronger."

He walked toward her again. "And what mon, save the most bestial, takes such delight in battle? I have blood upon my hands, Sophie. I have washed them but I can still smell it. From the moment I first swung my sword this night, my bloodlust raged. The smell of blood and death were a heady perfume to me. I ken not how many men I killed, and I care not. I can kill as fiercely with my bare hands as with my sword. And, this night, I killed a mon with my teeth," he continued in a hoarse voice. "I fell upon a mon and tore his throat open with my teeth. For a moment, as his blood heated my mouth, I was filled with a savage hunger. I wanted to drink it all. It was sweet and the mon's fear made it taste even sweeter. Is that the act of a mon?"

It was a particularly gruesome tale, and a very bad sign, but she placed her hand upon his arm and quietly asked, "Was the mon unarmed? Was he offering his sword in surrender? Was he crying out for mercy?"

His gaze fixed upon that small, soft hand that touched his skin, Alpin shook his head. "Nay. His sword was about to take Eric's head from his shoulders. That doesnae matter," he began.

"It does. Aye, the manner in which ye killed the mon is worrisome, for it means the curse still holds ye firmly within its grasp. Yet ye had to kill him or he would have killed Eric. This mon was armed and your enemy. Any mon would have killed him. And none of what ye have said truly answers my question, for I have kenned what ye are from the verra beginning."

"The *why* is because ye are a virgin, and so ye cannae ken the ways to stop my seed from taking root and use them. The why is because I can smell your desire and it has the blood pounding so fiercely in my veins, I near shake with need. 'Twould be no gentle bedding I would be giving ye. Nay," he continued in a softer voice, "I want to sink myself deep into your heat, Sophie Hay. Sink deep and ride hard. That isnae the way to take a virgin." He started toward the door. "And 'tis wrong to take a lass's maidenhead when I cannae wed her."

"Where are ye going?" Sophie was not surprised to hear how husky her voice had become, for his words, his seductive tone of voice, had stirred her almost as strongly as the sight of his strong body so meagerly covered.

"To one who kens how to keep her womb clean. Anne may not desire me, but she is always willing to service me."

"'Tis the wrong time for me to conceive," Sophie said, desperate to stop him from going to another's bed. She would lose him to another soon enough.

His hand tightening on the latch of the door, Alpin hesitated. "How can ye be sure?"

"I am a healer, Alpin. There is also a potion or two I can drink." Something she had no intention of doing, but he did not need to know that. "And when was the last time The MacCordy bred a bastard, or e'en a second child?"

Alpin slowly turned to face her. "Never," he replied, feeling somewhat shaken by the realization.

"Of course not. For the curse to continue unthreatened, there can only be one heir. Each Galt woman has but one daughter. Or, as was shown by my mother and aunt, one birth producing a female or twin females. Thus the curse can continue in us as weel. If there was a brother, then the firstborn son of The MacCordy could have been slain ere he bred an heir, thus ending the curse. E'en a bastard son could have done so. Mayhap e'en a girl child."

"Bairns can die," he said as he started to walk toward her. "Many do. Too many."

"When Rona cursed your ancestor, she changed the fate of The MacCordy and of the Galt women of her bloodline. The curse was upon the firstborn son, the legitimate heir, therefore ye couldnae die or that fate would be altered. Mayhap, if a Galt woman of the line had died young, another would have been born to satisfy the curse, but I dinnae think it e'er happened."

"Ye speak as if the curse is a living thing."

She shrugged. "After so long, it may be in some ways. 'Tis our fate, our destiny, and such things willnae be denied, unless I can find the key to unlock its grip upon our lives."

He reached out and slowly dragged his fingers through her hair. Closing his eyes, he could hear the tempo of her blood increase, could smell her desire return and begin to grow stronger. By making him see that there would be no child born of their union, she had cut the only real tether upon his control. He could have her now. He *had* to have her now. Alpin grasped the hem of her shift and swiftly pulled it off her.

It happened so quickly, Sophie had no time to cover herself before he picked her up in his arms and carried her to his bed. He set her down and tore off his only covering, staring at her body all the while with a fierce hunger that made her feel beautiful. For the moment or two he stood there looking at her, Sophie took the opportunity to have a good look at him. That only added to her need for him. He was glorious, all smooth skin and taut, sleek muscle. And rather impressively manly, she thought, her gaze fixed upon his erection. She felt the rise of a virginal unease and ruthlessly smothered it.

Sophie was shocked when he settled his long body on top of hers, but not by the fact that she held a naked man. The feel of his skin against her, the hard contours of his body fitting so well with her soft curves, had her trembling from the strength of her desire. The feel of his mouth against the pulse in her throat did not frighten her, not even when she felt the light touch of his teeth. It made her breath catch in her throat as her need for him swiftly increased. As she ran her hands over his broad back, savoring the feel of his warm skin, she wondered if all of the heated dreams she had had were the reason why her passion was rising so swiftly and fiercely.

Then she frowned and tensed slightly, realizing that she had forgotten to shield herself from whatever memories and emotions were trapped within his bed. She did not want other passions Alpin had stirred in the bed affecting what they felt now. Sophie began to try to shield herself, only to realize there was no need. The only person she could sense had used this bed was Alpin.

"Um, Alpin?" She studied him when he clasped her face in his long, elegant hands and began to touch hot, soft kisses to her cheeks. "Ye have done this before, havenae ye?"

He smiled against her forehead. "A time or two, aye." He kissed the corners of her beautiful eyes. "It was a need I tried to ignore, for I feared breeding a child. The few times I weakened I went to the woman, or took her elsewhere. I didnae want the scent of mating upon my bed, for it would torment me, making it harder for me to subdue my monly hungers." He thought of one place he had taken Anne, inwardly grimaced, then began to tease Sophie's full lips with soft kisses and gentle nips. "Once in the bed ye now sleep upon," he heard himself confess and wondered what had possessed him to do so.

"Weel, ye arenae the only one. I think there have been many matings in that bed." She opened her mouth, inviting the deep, passionate kiss she ached for. " 'Tis why Nella now sleeps in the bed and I use her pallet. The bed was, er, unsettling." She twined her arms around his neck, threaded the fingers of one hand into his thick hair, and tried to hold his mouth to hers. "Are we going to go elsewhere soon?"

"Nay." He slid his hand up her rib cage and over her small, perfect breast, then savored her gasp of pleasure as it warmed his mouth. "I want your scent here. I want the scent of our loving to penetrate so deep that it will be years ere it fades. When I am again alone, I want to be able to breathe deep of it and remember."

Sophie was glad he kissed her then, and not simply because she so desperately wanted him to. She had been about to ask him where he intended to put his wife. Then she forgot all about his marriage, the uncertain future, and the dark past. Sophie was aware only of the feel and taste of him, the touch of his hands and his mouth, and the need he stirred within her. She sensed that he practiced some restraint, but she had none.

When he finally joined their bodies, she was barely aware of the brief, stinging pain signaling the loss of her maidenhead. She was so immersed in the joy and pleasure of feeling his body joined to hers, that it was a moment or two before she realized he was not moving. Looking up at the man bracing himself over her, Sophie mused that she had never seen him look so feral, nor so beautiful and arousing.

"The pain?" he began, finding speech difficult, as his every sense was fixed upon the feel of her, her heat, her scent, and his own blinding need.

"Was quickly gone." She slid her hands down his back and stroked his taut buttocks, sighing with delight when he convulsively pushed deeper within her. "Oh, my, ye do feel good." Sophie wrapped her legs around him. "More, please."

He groaned and kissed her even as he began to move. Sophie opened herself up fully to the pleasure he gave her. Soon it was questionable as to which of them was fiercer in their passion. Then, she shattered, swept away to a place of such intense pleasure that she lost all awareness. Just as she began to recover, Alpin drove deep within her, crying out as his own release gripped him. To Sophie's delight and astonishment, the feel of his seed, of his intense pleasure, sent her racing back to the blinding heights of desire. When he collapsed in her arms, she held him close, and felt sanity slowly return to them both.

Sophie was a little frightened by how deeply she loved this man, then told herself not to be such a fool. There was no controlling the heart in such matters. At the moment, she could see no future in loving him. She would leave, alone and heartsore, he would marry Margaret, and they would all remain prisoners of the curse.

The thought of such a cold future made her hug him closer, and she kissed the top of his head. When he lifted his head and smiled at her, she smiled back and knew she would love him always, no matter what the future held. She would hold that love close and cherish it. Unlike so many of her ancestors, however, she would not wallow in grief over what she had lost. She would find joy in her memories and she would continue to fight the curse, to try to find a way to break it.

Sophie kissed him, felt him harden within her, and silently swore that she would turn her love for him, returned or not, into a strength. With that strength she would find a way to end the curse, to give him the full, natural life he deserved, even if it was not a life he would share with her. It was what her love demanded of her, the least she could do in return for the joy he gave her, no matter how briefly it lasted.

Chapter Seven

Sophie sat before the fire to brush dry her newly washed hair and wondered what she should do next. As far as she was concerned, last night had set her course for her, but she was not sure if Alpin felt the same. He had not turned cold toward her, but there had been no opportunity or time to even speak to him. The MacLanes and the coming wedding had taken up most of his attention. She had caught a look in his eyes now and again, one of such passion it had caused her blood to run hot, but that did not mean he intended to make her his lover. Last night could have been seen by Alpin as no more than a weakening of his control, something he would now fight to regain. Sophie found that possibility very painful, but also understood it. He sought to protect her.

What she needed to decide was whether or not she would go to him if he did not seek her out. That would re-

quire her to swallow a great deal of pride, perhaps even
subject herself to a harsh rejection as Alpin sought and regained his control. Then again, time was swiftly running
out for her to make him love her enough to choose her, to
have enough faith in her to know she would never turn
from him no matter how dark the future. If she was right
about the way the curse could be broken, then such cowardly behavior as fearing how he might hurt her or damage her pride was almost as great a sin as Rona's. All of
their futures could rest upon his choice of bride and, if
she allowed him to set her aside, that choice would definitely be Margaret. If she failed, she would have years to
nurse her bruised heart and stung pride.

For one brief moment, she felt guilty. Margaret was his
betrothed bride and a betrothal was as sacred as a marriage. She was not only trying to take Margaret's soon-to-
be husband away from her, but, in the eyes of many,
committing a sin very close to adultery. Then she shook
her head, telling herself she had no cause for guilt concerning Margaret. The woman did not want Alpin. She
was doing as her father commanded, but made her despair painfully clear to all. And if there was a penance for
giving Alpin all her love when they were not married and
might never marry, Sophie knew she would pay it gladly.

A sound at the door made her heart skip with anticipation. Alpin was coming to her. She turned and gaped, the
sharp sting of disappointment swiftly pushed aside by a
wary fear. It was not Alpin but one of Sir Peter's men entering her room and hastily barring the door behind him.
She did not need to ask why he was there; the reason was
clear to see in his expression. It was a chillingly lustful
look, the sort of lust that he would satisfy whether she
agreed to service him or not. She had seen that look upon

his face a few times, but had foolishly thought he would never dare to act upon it.

"I suggest ye leave, Sir Ranald," she said, pleased with the calm tone of her voice, for inside she was trembling. "My maid will soon come and will be sure to set up a cry if the door remains barred."

"That bone-thin bitch Nella?" Sir Ranald chuckled. "Nay, I dinnae think so."

"What have ye done to Nella?" she demanded, suspicious of his certainty that they would not soon be disturbed.

"Just a wee tap to send her to sleep. Sat her up against the wall outside your door. Anyone sees her, they will think she nodded off to sleep whilst guarding your door."

"She sleeps in here and all ken it."

"Just as they all ken ye are far more than the laird's healing woman, aye?"

"Dinnae be such an idiot." As he approached, she started to step away, wondering if she had any chance at all of reaching the door, unbarring it, and fleeing before he could grab her. "And if I am more than that, attacking me isnae verra wise. 'Tis certain ye have heard all that is said of Sir Alpin. Such a mon isnae a good one to insult or anger."

"Ach, he willnae do anything about a mon helping himself to a wee taste of a whore. And he cannae do too much to me, can he? I am cousin to the bride."

He lunged at her and Sophie darted out of the way. Several times she managed to elude his grasp, throwing everything she could get her hands on. It all barely made him stumble in his relentless pursuit. She managed to get to the door, felt a tiny flicker of hope as she began to lift the bar, only to have it painfully doused when he grabbed her by the hair and yanked her back.

Although she fought with all her strength, Sir Ranald soon had her pinned to the bed. The sound of her nightshift tearing sent a chill of panic racing through her veins. She had only enjoyed one night of passion in Alpin's arms. She could not allow this man to defile her, possibly damage her ability to feel desire ever again, or, worse, cause shame to cool Alpin's passion for her or hers for him. Sophie cursed Sir Ranald, desperately tried to break his hold on her, and screamed for Alpin in her mind.

Alpin sipped his wine and calmly watched Sir Peter talk. It was hard to conceal his contempt for the man. Sir Peter spoke of the vanquishing of his enemies as if he had done it all himself, even though all knew he had waited out the battle safe at Nochdaidh. The man was a coward willing to toss his daughter into the lair of the beast so that someone else would do his fighting for him.

"Alpin!"

He tensed and looked around, certain he had just heard Sophie call to him. A tickle of superstitious fear ran through him when he could see neither her nor Nella. No one else showed any sign of having heard her call, either.

"Alpin!"

It was in his head, he realized in shock. There was a touch of fear in the way his name was being cried out. Alpin did not know how Sophie got into his mind, but he felt every instinct he possessed, those of the man and those of the beast, come roaring to life. Something was wrong.

Sophie was in danger, he thought as he slowly stood

up. He was certain of it. Then he saw that Sir Ranald was missing from the great hall. The man had often stirred Alpin's anger with the way he looked at Sophie. Alpin looked at the man who always sat with Sir Ranald, but that man refused to meet his gaze.

"Sophie," was all Alpin said as he ran out of the hall.

Eric had noticed the change start to come over Alpin, and, vaulting over the table, raced after him. He had no idea what had set Alpin's beast loose, but the way the man had said Sophie's name had sent a chill of alarm down Eric's spine. If some fool was hurting Sophie, Eric feared he was about to be faced with the awesome task of trying to stop his enraged laird from killing a man.

Alpin halted before the door of Sophie's bedchamber. He saw Nella slumped against the wall, but the sound of her heartbeat told him she was only unconcious, and he turned his attention back to the door. A cry of pain from within spurred him on. He slammed his foot into the door, twice, and heard the bar crack. Then he rammed his shoulder against the thick wood, breaking the door open so fiercely it crashed against the wall.

He scented Sophie's fear and the hot lust of the man pinning her to the bed. With a soft growl, he leapt toward the bed just as Sir Ranald looked to see what had caused the loud noise. The man screamed and tried to flee, but Alpin grabbed him by the throat and the crotch. He held the cursing, praying man over his head and then threw him against the wall.

A hand grabbed his arm and he easily shook it off. A small, still sane part of his mind recognized Eric's voice, but Alpin ignored his friend. He hoisted the now weeping Sir Ranald over his head again.

"Alpin, ye came in time."

That soft, husky voice calling his name cut right through Alpin's rage. The bloodlust still roared in his veins, however. He ached to kill this man who had touched Sophie, had hurt and frightened her. Yet, he could not do so in front of her. Still holding Ranald, Alpin walked out of the room to the head of the stairs and tossed the man into the crowd of MacLanes hurrying up the steps. He then returned to Sophie's bedchamber, walked to the bed, and reached for her.

Sophie did not hesitate. She flung herself into his arms, wrapping her arms about his neck and her legs about his waist, clinging to him like a small child. She sensed the fury and bloodlust which still pounded in his veins, but she felt only the comfort of his arms, the protection he offered her. As he walked out of her bedchamber, she caught sight of Nella and made a soft sound of distress.

"She lives. E'en now she wakes," Alpin said and continued on to his own bedchamber. "Eric will see to her care." He stepped into his room and barred the door behind him.

Eric helped a slowly rousing Nella to her feet, putting his arm around her to steady her. "Ye will be fine, lassie."

"Oh! My lady!" Nella cried, suddenly recalling who had attacked her and easily guessing why.

"The laird has her."

"Ah." Nella slumped against Eric, finding comfort in the burly strength of the man. " 'Tis a wonder, as I ne'er thought such words would cross my lips, but I am glad he has her." She squeaked in alarm, although she did not move, when Eric suddenly drew his sword and held it out to stop Sir Peter's advance on Alpin's bedchamber.

"He nearly killed my nephew!" snapped Sir Peter, but he made no further move toward Alpin's room.

"Ye are lucky the fool still breathes. He was after raping the Lady Sophie."

"So he tried to have a wee tussle with the laird's whore. 'Tisnae worth breaking near every bone in his body."

Eric felt Nella stiffen with outrage and tightened his grip on her. "Ye should try thinking ere ye speak, Sir Peter."

"Curse it, he shames my daughter, insults her by carrying on e'en whilst the wedding preparations are made." He took a step toward Alpin's room, only to stop and draw a sharp breath when Eric pressed the tip of his sword more firmly against his chest.

"If ye take another step, I will gut ye where ye stand. Ye will leave the laird and Lady Sophie alone, and, if ye are wise, ye will say naught. Your lass has made it verra clear she doesnae want this marriage, so I doubt she cares what the laird does as long as he doesnae come too close to her. Still, I suspect there will be a marriage done. E'en if the laird comes to his senses, ye can probably make some other arrangement to ensure he still fights your battles for ye." Eric met the man's glare calmly and watched him stalk away, back down the stairs. "A fool as weel as a coward," he muttered.

Nella looked up at Eric. "Did that bastard hurt my lady?"

"Nay," replied Eric. "Alpin reached her in time, although I cannae say how he kenned she needed help."

"There are a lot of things I dinnae understand about all of this, about the curse, e'en about some of the things So-

phie can do. Dinnae think I e'er will." She looked around
him, her eyes widening when she saw the battered condition of the door. "The laird did that?"

"Aye. The bloodlust was running high in him. If your
lady hadnae spoken to him, I think he would have torn
that fool Sir Ranald apart." He saw Nella frown in the direction of Alpin's bedchamber. "He willnae hurt her."

"I think I begin to believe that. Weel, at least that he
willnae hurt her in body, but I think he will sorely bruise
her heart." She sighed and looked back at Eric. "She
loves him, ye ken."

"Aye, and I think he loves her. Unfortunately, that will
probably ensure that he sends her away."

Nella nodded. "And thus doom us all."

"I thought we were all doomed anyway."

"My lady thinks she kens how to break the curse, but I
shouldnae tell ye. There cannae be any help given. It has
to be by free choice, unaided and undriven."

"I swear I will hold fast to what ye tell me," vowed
Eric.

"She thinks she is the key to unlock the curse. She
thinks he has to choose her o'er Margaret with her lands
and her dowry."

Eric stared at Nella for a moment, then cursed. "Of
course. 'Tis there to see in the last few lines of that bitch's
curse. 'Tis so clear, I wonder that we didnae all see it the
moment we heard it. Heart o'er gain. Sophie o'er Margaret. And ye are right. It must be *his* choice, one made
without prodding or trickery. Wheesht, lass, ye have set a
heavy burden upon my shoulders."

"Aye, 'tis a hard thing to ken and nay be able to act
upon," Nella said.

"Exactly. I can see hope within our grasp, but I must stand silent. All I can do is pray that Alpin acts as he must to free us all."

Nella looked back at Alpin's door. "Pray that as he holds her close, he comes to need that verra much, indeed, so much that he decides to cast aside that noble plan to free her for her own sake." She shook her head. "Pray, for all our sakes, that your laird has one blinding moment of selfishness which lasts long enough to ensure there is nay turning back."

Alpin watched the firelight caress Sophie's skin as she stood before the fire and washed herself. Each time she dampened the rag in the bowl of water and ran it over her skin, he felt desire tauten his insides. She was so beautiful, so graceful, it made him ache. He was not blind to the bruises upon her skin, however, and had to fight back a strong urge to hunt Sir Ranald down and kill him.

That rage and bloodlust had still held him firmly in its grip when he had first brought her into his room. Alpin could vaguely recall stripping them both and climbing into his bed with her in his arms. He had held her while she had wept. At some point during that emotional storm, she had fallen asleep. Still holding her close, he, too, had dozed, waking when she had slipped from his arms. And, despite the fact that he wanted her back in his arms, he was thoroughly enjoying the view.

Sophie blushed when she dried herself, turned to go back to bed, and caught Alpin watching her. She hurried to the side of the bed, gasping with surprise when he suddenly moved, grabbed her, and pulled her into his arms.

The man could move with astonishing speed, she thought, as he tucked the bedcovers over them both. She wrapped her arms around him as he nuzzled her neck.

"I can still smell him," Alpin muttered, then tightened his hold on her when she tried to move away. "Stay."

"But if the smell troubles you," she began even as she relaxed in his arms.

"It but restirs the urge to tear him apart."

"He didnae, er, finish."

"I ken it. I fear I would be able to smell that, too, and that would stir a rage I couldnae control."

"Oh. Do ye ken, I think having such a keen sense of smell must be a burden at times. Some of the scents wafting through the air arenae verra pleasing."

He smiled against her neck, then lightly nipped the life-giving vein he pressed his lips against. There was a dark part of him that hungered for a taste of what pulsed through that vein, but he did not fear it. He knew that, as long as he retained even the smallest scrap of sanity, he would not hurt Sophie. She was his sunlight, that bright warmth he so yearned to enjoy again, but which would only bring him death now. She was the flowers that no longer grew in his shadowed world, the laughter that so rarely echoed in the halls of Nochdaidh, and the hope they had all lost but yearned to regain. And, he realized, she could reach the man still inside of him even at the height of his bloodlust.

"I am sorry I wept all over ye," Sophie murmured. "'Tis odd, for, whilst that fool was attacking me, I was mostly furious. Then, ye came, and I was safe, yet I wept."

"He hurt you." Alpin raised himself up on one elbow and began to gently touch each bruise upon her silken skin. "And, 'tisnae how one acts after the danger has passed that matters. 'Tisnae unknown for men to collapse, trembling and terrified, after the battle is done. I heard ye call to me," he said quietly as he lightly kissed a bruise upon her throat. "In my mind I heard ye call my name."

"How wondrous strange. I did call your name—inside my head. Weel, our families have been bound together by Rona's curse for o'er four hundred years. Mayhap that has something to do with it." She threaded her fingers through his hair, holding him close as he kissed the bruises upon her breasts. "They dinnae hurt," she said when he frowned at a bruise as he traced its shape with his long fingers.

"The bastard left his mark upon your skin."

Sophie placed her hands on either side of his head, turned his face up to hers, and brushed a kiss over his mouth. "So I stink of him and am marked by him. There is a solution to that problem."

Alpin settled himself between her slim legs and gently nipped her chin. "And what would that be?"

"Ye could replace his scent with yours," she replied softly as she stroked his long legs with her feet. "Ye could put your own mark upon me."

"Such a clever lass. Ah, but it could take a wee bit of time and effort."

"Oh, I do hope so," she whispered against his mouth before kissing him.

Chapter Eight

It took every ounce of Alpin's will to leave Sophie while she still slept. Today was his wedding day, and knowing he could not hold her in his arms all night again made him want to crawl back into the bed and cling to her like some frightened child. He should make her leave, but he could not bring himself to say the words. Alpin feared the darkness in his world would be complete if he could not at least see her now and again. There would be no more lovemaking, however, he swore as he forced himself to walk out of his bedchamber. Today marked the end of their stolen idyll and he had to draw that line deeply and clearly.

Once in the great hall, he fixed his attention upon the final wedding preparations. Since the priest refused to enter the gates of Nochdaidh, they would have to go into the village. That had required Alpin to gain special per-

mission to be married after sunset, claiming some difficulty with sensitive skin. Embarrassing, but it had worked.
A heavy purse sent along with the request had helped.
That money had undoubtedly helped the church dismiss
the dark rumors about him as well. So, he mused as he
looked at his pale, trembling bride, he was free to marry.

As the day dragged on, Alpin fought the urge to go to
Sophie. His mood grew darker with every passing hour,
every badly smothered sob of his distraught bride. Alpin
did think it odd that Eric seemed to share his mood. It was
not until they gathered in the bailey to begin the ride to
the church that Alpin realized he had not seen even a
fleeting glimpse of Sophie or Nella all day.

"Where is Sophie?" he asked Eric as the man rode up,
leading the horse Alpin would ride to the church.

"Gone," Eric replied while Alpin swung himself up
into the saddle.

"Gone? Gone where?"

"She and Nella left to return to their home a few hours
ago. Lady Sophie said 'twas best, for ye would be tied to
Lady Margaret by vows said before God and that was a
line she didnae want to cross. Feared she might be
tempted if she stayed here. I sent three of the lads with
them. Couldnae let them travel alone."

"Nay, of course not," he muttered, blindly nudging his
mount into following the others to the village.

Alpin was stunned. He had wanted Sophie to leave,
had thought it for the best. Yet, now that she was gone, he
felt more desolate than he ever had before. This was how
it should be, yet it felt all wrong. He certainly did not feel
noble. When a man gave up what he wanted for the greater
good, for the benefit of someone else, should he not feel
some pride in himself, some warmth in the knowledge

that he had done the right thing? All he felt was cold; chilled to the very bone.

It made no sense, he thought as he blindly obeyed someone's command to kneel next to his weeping bride. Sophie had only been in his life for a month. Most of that time he had tried to avoid her or he had been yelling at her. How could the loss of one tiny, irritating woman make him feel so shattered inside?

He took his bride's sweaty, shaking hand in his and looked at her. She was desolate and terrified, yet he had barely spoken two words to her in the fortnight she had been at Nochdaidh. Sophie had seen him at his worst and had never faltered. Could he have wronged Sophie in a way by thinking her too weak to endure what might yet come?

"Sir Alpin?" called the priest. "Your vows? 'Tis time to speak your vows."

Alpin looked at the priest, then looked back at Margaret. "Nay," he said as he slowly stood up. "Not to this lass."

"This was agreed to with your father," yelled Sir Peter as he glared at Alpin. "Your sword arm for her dowry, the land, and the coin. Ye cannae simply say nay."

"Aye, I can. I suspect we can come to some agreement if ye feel a need for my sword arm. But not this way."

"But, the land, the wealth? Your father was eager for them."

"I dinnae want the land or the coin. I want," Alpin thought of Sophie, "smiles." He looked at Margaret, who had prostrated herself at the feet of the priest, kissing the hem of his robe as she muttered prayers of thanksgiving. "I want courage. I want someone who will stand beside me, nay cower or faint each time I enter the room. I want to be loved," he added softly, a hint of astonishment in his voice. "I intend to be a selfish bastard and go get what I want and hold fast to it."

"Thank God," said Eric. "She rode southeast. She and Nella refused to ride anything but those ponies, so they should be easy enough to catch if we ride hard."

Although he was curious as to why Eric looked so elated, Alpin decided now was not the time to discuss that. "I thought to leave ye here to make sure the priest will still be here and ready when I return."

"Nay, I ride with ye." Eric ordered a man named Duncan to watch the priest, then turned back to Alpin. "Ye will have to ride hard to get her, bring her back here, wed her, and get back within the walls of Nochdaidh ere the sun rises. Thought I would ride with Nella and leave the lads to follow at a slower pace."

"Nella, is it?" Alpin grinned when Eric blushed, then started out of the church, idly noting that his people looked uncommonly cheerful. "Nella who rattles because she wears so many amulets and charms? A bit timid."

"Aye," agreed Eric as he and Alpin mounted their horses, "but, if ye recall, 'twas timid, wee Nella who put herself between your sword point and her ladyship's heart that first day."

"Ah, so she did. Timid, but no coward." Alpin nudged his horse into an easy pace for, despite his sense of urgency, he had to go through the village with care.

"And, nay matter what happens, she is now, weel, accustomed to Nochdaidh. She will stay."

"Do ye think I am being too selfish?" Alpin asked quietly.

"Ah, m'laird, mayhap, but isnae every mon? But, 'tisnae some weak miss ye go after. She kens it all, e'en a lot of our dark history. Why dinnae ye just let her decide?"

Eric was right, Alpin thought, as they reached the edge of the village and kicked their mounts into a gallop. Sophie was a strong, clever woman who knew exactly what he was and what he could become. She even knew they would have to make some hard decisions concerning a child. It was time to place the decision in her small, capable hands.

"I am sorry, m'lady," Nella said as she sat next to Sophie near the fire the men had built.

"Aye, so am I." She glanced at the three young men from Nochdaidh who stood to the far side of the campsite deciding how they would divide up the watch. "At least this time we travel with some protection."

"True. 'Tis a comfort of sort." Nella sighed and idly poked a stick into the fire. "I had hoped the laird would see the truth."

"Weel, what *we* understand to be the truth."

" 'Tis the truth. I ken it deep in my heart. The words at the end of that vile curse say it clear. And I believe the fact that 'twould be a Galt woman and a MacCordy mon would make the curative power of the match e'en stronger."

Sophie nodded. "It was verra hard to say naught, but that also had to be." She smiled slightly when she saw how carefully Nella watched her. "Dinnae fret o'er me. I may have hoped for something different, but I anticipated such an ending. And, aye, I suspect I shall trouble ye with some bad days, but, at the moment, I am numb. 'Tisnae just that I have lost the mon I love, but I fear I have lost all chance of ending Rona's curse. And mayhap my pain is already eased by the knowledge that I will still have his child to love."

"His what?!"

"Hush, Nella. His child," she whispered.

"Nay. How can ye tell so soon?"

"Trust me, Nella. I am certain. I felt it the moment the seed was planted. 'Tis odd, though, for Alpin was certain no MacCordy laird had e'er bred a bastard. Who can say? Mayhap the end of the curse will come through this child. Mayhap 'tis fate at work here."

"And mayhap your kinsmen willnae bring the roof down with their angry bellows?"

"Ah, there is that. Weel, we shall deal with that trouble when it presents itself. Best we get some sleep now," Sophie said as she moved to the rough bed of blankets arranged for her and Nella. "We didnae cover much distance this day and I should like to get an early start in the morning."

"Alpin?" Sophie heard herself say as she abruptly sat up.

"M'lady? Is something wrong?" asked her guard, Angus.

"A dream, I think."

Since Angus had chosen the first watch, Sophie knew she had only slept an hour or two. She looked around but saw no sign of Alpin. Yet she could not shake the strong feeling that he was near at hand. Just as she was deciding that she was letting false hope lead her, Alpin and Eric rode into the camp. She sat stunned as Alpin dismounted and walked to her bed to stand over her.

"What are ye doing here?" she asked. " 'Tis your wedding night."

"Nay, not yet," Alpin replied and held out his hand. "I have come to give ye a choice, Lady Sophie Hay."

"A choice?" she asked as she put her hand in his and let him tug her to her feet.

"Me and all the darkness that surrounds me, or freedom and the sunlight."

"What of Lady Margaret?"

"The last I saw of her, she was kissing the hem of the priest's robes and thanking God for saving her from an unholy union."

"Then I choose you," she said, so choked with emotion that her voice was barely above a whisper.

Alpin's only outward reaction was to nod and brush the back of his hand over her cheek. The look on his face, however, told Sophie he was deeply moved, as did the faint tremor in his hand. She knew she would get all the emotion she could handle later when they were alone.

There was little time for her to think about the big step she had just taken. She and Nella were told to collect their cloaks and mount the horses. The three young men from Nochdaidh were ordered to return at their own pace. Then they were racing over the countryside, Sophie clinging to Alpin and Nella to Eric. A little unsettled by how swiftly they moved through the night, she closed her eyes.

The promise of dawn was in the sky when they reined in before the tiny stone chapel in the village. Sophie was so unsteady when they dismounted, Alpin had to carry her into the church. She nearly laughed when he roused the people sleeping in the church with a lot of yelling and a few well-placed kicks. It became even harder to hide her growing amusement as a yawning priest married them, Alpin briefly kissed her, and she was hurried out of the church. The sight of the rapidly lightening sky sobered her quickly, however, and she said nothing as she was tossed into the saddle, Alpin mounted behind her, and they raced to the keep.

"Why is Nella crying?" Alpin asked the moment they were safely within the walls of the keep. "I had thought she had come to trust me, or, at least, nay fear me."

Sophie ached to tell him what she thought this marriage might accomplish, but bit back the words. She could be wrong. It would be cruel to convince him all would be well now, only to discover nothing had changed. One look at Nella's wide-eyed expression told her that her maid was thinking much the same.

"My arse hurts," Nella blurted out.

There was a moment of heavy silence. Sophie could feel that Eric and Alpin were struggling as hard as she was not to laugh. She finally croaked out the word "bath" and headed toward her bedchamber, Nella quickly following. If she understood Alpin's strangled words correctly, he was also going to bathe and wanted her to join him in his bedchamber in one hour. Just the thought of what would ensue when she joined him in an hour had Sophie's blood running so hot she doubted she would need the fire to heat her bathwater.

Alpin stared at the meal set out upon a table near the fire. Coward that he was, he had eaten the meat prepared for him and had quickly had his plate removed. Sophie might understand and accept him for what he was, but he still shied away from complete exposure. It was one of the things he had been reduced to that he himself found hard to bear.

Sensing her approach, he turned to face her as she entered the room. She looked beautiful in her thin, lace-trimmed nightshift, and he found her scent to be a heady perfume. She also looked delicate, soft, and innocent, and he felt doubt assail him. Surely it was wrong to drag such a warm, gentle soul into his world of shadow and blood?

"Ye cannae change your mind now," Sophie said as she moved to the table and helped herself to a honey-sweetened oatcake.

"Ye dinnae belong here, locked into the darkness," he said.

"I belong with ye, Alpin, be it in shadow or in sunlight so bright it makes our eyes hurt." She looked at the food on the table, then back at him. "Ye cannae eat any of this?"

"Nay. There is nay longer a taste to it for me, and the act of eating it only serves to stir up a strong need for the other."

"Do ye miss it?"

"Och, aye. I yearn to sit at a table weighted with food of all kinds and eat until I cannae move. I yearn to stand in the sunlight and nay fear the warmth of its light. I yearn to have people look at me without fear, without crossing themselves or making the sign to ward off evil. I yearn to see the flowers grow in the bailey."

Sophie moved to wrap her arms around his waist and rest her cheek against his chest. "Ye shall have those things again."

He gently gripped her by the chin and turned her face up to his. "Ye sound so sure of that."

"One of us has to be."

Alpin smiled faintly. "When I knelt beside the Lady Margaret, that undying hope of yours was one of the things I thought of. I may ne'er share it, but I wanted it. I thought of smiles, your smiles and your sweet laughter. I thought of how ye dinnae fear me, e'en when I am bellowing and ranting. And when the priest asked me to speak my vows, I looked at my trembling and weeping bride, and realized I couldnae say them to her. She was terrified of me and repulsed. If ye hadnae come into my life, I probably would have accepted that, for 'tis what I have become accustomed to. But ye gave me a thirst for more, Sophie. I suddenly kenned that I yearned to be loved," he added in a near whisper.

"Oh, ye are, Alpin." She hugged him tightly and rubbed her cheek against his chest. "I love ye."

He felt the warmth of those words flow through his veins. Holding her close, he rested his chin on the top of her head. He started to smile when, after a few moments of silence, she began to grow tense. His smile widened to a grin when she slipped her hand inside his robe and pinched his waist. It was probably a little unkind to tease her so, but he was sure that she knew exactly how he felt.

"Alpin," she muttered crossly.

"I love ye too, Sophie mine. Ye are the sun that warms the cold shadows of my prison." He frowned slightly when he felt a slight dampness seep between her cheek and his chest. "Are ye crying?"

" 'Tis just happiness, Alpin."

"Ah, I thought your arse might hurt." He laughed at her startled look, picked her up in his arms, and carried her to his bed.

"Time for the wedding night? Or, rather, dawn?" she asked with a smile as he set her down on the bed and shed his robe.

After tugging off her shift, he sprawled in her arms. "With ye in my bed, my wee wife, I think I could actually grow to like the dawn."

* * *

"What are ye doing awake?" Eric asked Nella as she joined him at the table in the great hall.

She cut herself a thick piece of bread. "Hungry. I shall get some rest after I eat." Nella cut a thick slice of cheese, set it on the bread, and stared at the food in her hand. "Do ye think it will work?"

"Ah, fretting about that, are ye?"

"Arenae ye?"

"Some, aye. It seems as if it ought to, but this trouble has plagued us for so long, I find hope a hard thing to grasp."

Nella sighed. "So do I. I have heard all the tales of the sad lives of the Galt women and, though it makes sense that this is the answer, it just seems too easy."

"Ye think there ought to be some spell done, herbs and smoke and magic words?"

"Aye. A ceremony of sorts, I suppose. Ah, weel, mayhap the marriage itself was all the ceremony needed."

"It has its own power, true enough. Weel, ye eat and then rest, lass. Ye will need your strength."

"Oh? Why?"

"Because if Sophie is right and this ends the curse, there will be a wild celebration. If it doesnae, if she is wrong, she will be needing a lot of comfort."

Chapter Nine

Alpin stretched, poured himself a tankard of cider, grabbed a couple of honey-sweetened oatcakes, and walked to the window to stare down into the bailey. He felt at peace for the first time in his life and it was a good feeling, one he savored and prayed would continue. A day and a night spent in the arms of his passionate little wife undoubtedly had something to do with that, he thought as he washed down the oatcake with a drink of cider and started to eat another one. He was loved and it soothed a lot of the pain he had suffered in his life. There were troubles ahead, but he no longer feared the future as much as he had.

As he finished his third oatcake and washed it down with the last of the cider, he realized there was a lot of activity in the bailey. It looked as if every resident of Nochdaidh were out there. He nearly gaped when he saw what he was sure were Eric and Nella dancing around like fools. It was a little late to still be celebrating his marriage, he thought as he turned to look at Sophie, thinking to rouse her to come and see what was happening.

The sight of her distracted him for a moment, even though only her head was visible above the covers. She looked so young, sweet, and delicate as she slept, but he well knew the strength beneath that soft beauty. Her thick hair was splayed out over the pillow and coverlet, looking more golden than ever with the morning sun gilding its length.

His empty tankard slipped from his suddenly nerveless hand as Alpin realized what he had just done, what he was seeing. Alpin stared at the tankard as he accepted the wonder of having eaten oatcakes and drunk cider. The only hunger the act of eating had roused in him was one for more oatcakes and more cider. The sunlight was filling his room. He had seen all his people so clearly because they had been hopping and twirling about in the sunlight.

"Sophie," he called, realized his voice was little more than a soft croak, and cleared his throat. "Sophie!" he yelled.

When she just groaned and turned over, he ran to the side of the bed. He yanked the covers off her, grabbed her by the shoulders to pull her into a seated position, and shook her slightly. This time he was not finding her inability to wake quickly and be alert very endearing. Alpin knew he was in a precarious state of mind when he got a clear view of her lithe body and did not crawl back into bed with her, just snatched up her nightshift and yanked it over her head. He ignored her muttering as he dragged her over to the window.

"Look out there and tell me what ye see," he ordered.

Sophie struggled to do as he asked. As she slowly woke up, she realized Alpin was acting strangely, could feel his tense agitation. She frowned down into the bailey, wondering just what she was supposed to be looking at.

"Weel, I have to say that the people of Nochdaidh are some of the worst dancers I have e'er seen," she muttered and heard Alpin both laugh and curse. "And your mon Eric is the worst of all. He is leaping about in the sun like some sort of drunken—" Sophie's next words became locked in her throat. "Jesu, Alpin, the sun is shining on Nochdaidh," she whispered after a moment, then looked at him. "Did ye get hurt by it?" she asked worriedly as she looked him over.

Alpin sagged against the wall and put a shaking hand over his eyes. "Nay. I but sought to get ye to tell me whether I was dreaming or not." He reached out and yanked her into his arms. "The sun is shining o'er Nochdaidh, Sophie."

"Aye, and your people are hopping about like toads on hot sand," she murmured and held him tightly, feeling almost as unsteady, disbelieving, and elated as she sensed he was. A minute later, she jumped in surprise along with Alpin when the door to their bedchamber was flung open so hard it crashed into the wall.

"Alpin, the sun shines again!" yelled Eric, then grunted as Nella ran into the back of him.

Nella stepped around Eric. "Did ye see, m'lady? It worked! Praise God, it worked! I kenned ye were right." Her eyes slowly widened when she suddenly realized Alpin was naked. "Oh, my." She cursed when Eric clapped a hand over her eyes.

"For mercy's sake, Alpin, put some clothes on," Eric grumbled.

Even as Alpin moved to yank on some clothes, he eyed Sophie with a growing suspicion. "What worked, Sophie?"

"That ye chose her o'er the Lady Margaret," Nella replied and gave up trying to remove Eric's hand from her eyes.

"Sophie," Alpin pressed. "What plot or trick have ye been weaving?"

"No plot or trick, Alpin," she replied, then sighed. "I was fair certain I had puzzled out the key to unlocking the curse." She repeated the last lines of Rona's curse. "Do ye see? 'Twas right there, right before our eyes."

"And ye didnae think I ought to be told about what ye had learned?"

"Nay learned, Alpin, only suspected. It had to be your free choice, and I feared that if I told ye about it, the choice might not be so verra free. I also feared I might be wrong, and, if I convinced ye that I had found the answer only to have naught change, it would be cruel."

Alpin stared at her for a moment, then yanked her into his arms and heartily kissed her before striding out of the room. Sophie grabbed his shirt, yanked it on over her nightshift, and hurried after him. When she, Nella, and Eric reached him, Alpin stood unmoving, staring at the doors leading outside with his hands clenched tightly at his sides. Sophie stepped closer and took one of his hands in hers.

"The last time the sun's light touched me, it nearly killed me," Alpin said quietly.

"I dinnae think it will this time, my love," Sophie said,

then drawled, "We will pull ye back inside if ye start smoldering."

"Wretch," he murmured, then, taking a deep breath and keeping a firm grip upon Sophie's hand, he strode outside.

Sophie stayed close by his side as he went down the steps and cautiously moved out into the bailey. She stood quietly, feeling his tension and fear fade as his exaltation grew. His grip on her hand grew tight enough to be a little painful and she looked at him. His face was turned up to the sun, his eyes closed, and tears seeped from beneath his eyelids. Sophie moved to hug him, pressing closer when he wrapped his arms around her and rested his cheek against the top of her head.

"I fear to believe it," he said as he fought to compose himself, since nearly all of the people of Nochdaidh were there watching him.

"Weel, how do ye feel?"

"I think I might actually be feeling something that has long been missing from Nochdaidh—hope."

"Trouble, m'laird," said Eric, moving to stand beside Alpin.

Looking at the crowd of villagers rushing in through the gates carrying torches and crude weapons, Alpin drawled, "Mayhap I spoke too soon." He kept his arm around Sophie's shoulders as she turned to face the crowd.

The embarrassment Sophie felt over being seen so strangely attired by so many people faded quickly as she realized what had brought the villagers to Nochdaidh. Several smiles and small waves from a number of the women in the crowd told Sophie she would have allies if she chose her words carefully. The confusion that had beset so many of the crowd as they realized Nochdaidh was no longer shrouded in shadow and the laird was standing before them looking nothing like a demon would also aid her.

"This is my fault," she told Alpin. "I neglected to solve poor Donald's murder. I shall see to this."

"Shall ye now?"

He had to bite back a grin as she stood straighter and frowned at the villagers. She wore only his loosely laced shirt over her nightshift, her feet were bare, and her hair was hanging loose and obviously unbrushed. Her appearance seemed to have taken some of the fight out of the mob, who were already confused by the sunlight warming the bailey, so he decided to let her rule for a while. She knew more about the incident than he did, and all his men were subtly moving into a defensive position around the crowd, ready to act if the mood grew dangerous again.

"I suspect ye havenae come to congratulate me on my wedding," she said, crossing her arms over her chest.

"M'lady, we have come seeking justice," said Ian the butcher as he stepped to the fore of the crowd. "The killer of my son must pay."

"Did I talk to the wind that day? I believe I said the laird had naught to do with it."

"If ye will pardon me saying so, 'tis clear ye are under the mon's power. Who else could have murdered my lad? He had no enemies. We cannae find a single mon who disliked him."

"Then he will be kindly remembered, and that should comfort ye. But what about a woman?"

"My lad was true to his wife and, ere he wed her, he was a lad of strong morals. And he was a big, strong lad. What lass could kill him?"

Sophie shook her head. "One cutting his throat as he slept, just as I told ye was done. Aye, and one of those strikes upon his head may have come first to make sure he didnae wake whilst he was being murdered."

"But, he wasnae one to play with the lasses," Master Ian protested.

Although Gemma felt no guilt over her crime, Sophie sensed that the woman was afraid and her rage had not been satisfied with the spilling of poor Donald's blood. That was the woman's weak point and Sophie prepared herself to strike at it hard. "That doesnae mean there was no lass who wanted him to play." She sighed and shook her head. "A vain woman he turned aside, mayhap? Some woman who couldnae accept that he, or any mon, could resist her charms. Or that Donald would resist her allure to hold fast to his sweet, loving, beautiful wife—"

"Who couldnae satisfy any mon!" Gemma yelled, then paled as she realized what she had done.

Sophie could not believe the woman had broken so quickly, then stepped behind Alpin as chaos ruled. Only the quick, occasionally rough intervention of Alpin's men kept Gemma from paying for her crime at the hands of the mob. As she was dragged off to the dungeon to await judgment, she screamed out enough confirmation of her guilt to hang her. Sophie slowly approached a desolate Master Ian, noting out of the corner of her eye a plump widow of mature years who was having difficulty resisting the urge to do the same. Master Ian would not be alone for long.

"I am verra sorry, Master Ian," she said, patting his arm. "Did ye love her then?"

He shook his head. "Loneliness and lust, m'lady. The

downfall of many a mon, I suspect. Only, my weakness cost my lad his life."

"Nay, Master Ian, ne'er think that. Ye did no wrong, nor did your son. The guilt is hers alone." She leaned closer to him and cast a pointed glance toward the widow tentatively edging closer. "Learn from your weakness if ye must. I think the lesson might be that a good cure for loneliness isnae always to be found in the young or the bonny." She squeaked with surprise when Alpin suddenly grasped her by the arm and pulled her back to his side. "I was comforting the poor mon."

"Ye were matchmaking," he murmured, but frowned out the gates as a troop of horsemen came riding into view. "A busy day."

Sophie noticed that the villagers quickly slipped behind the men of Nochdaidh, then she looked at the approaching men and softly groaned. She should have taken time during the long, lusty night she and Alpin had just spent together to tell him a few of the truths she had kept to herself. Recognizing the four young men leading about a dozen others into Nochdaidh, she knew a lot of those truths were about to be revealed.

"Ye ken who these people are?" asked Alpin, feeling Sophie tense as the four handsome young men leading the others dismounted but a yard from them and eyed Sophie with a mixture of annoyance, shock, and amusement.

"My brothers," she said and pointed to each as she introduced them. "Sir Adrian, Sir Robert, Sir Gilbert, and Sir Neil." She took a steadying breath, knowing things could become a little chaotic, and took Alpin's hand in hers. "This is my husband, Sir Alpin MacCordy, laird of

Nochdaidh." She winced when they all stared at her for a moment, then all cursed.

"Ye married this mon?" demanded her brother Adrian. "Do ye ken the tales we have heard about him?"

"Aye," Sophie replied. "He lives in shadows, he drinks blood, he is a demon, he can change into a beast, and other such things."

"Ye left without a word—"

"I left a note."

Adrian ignored her and continued, "And Old Steven was sure that ye had been abducted. He had the men of Werstane searching and sent us word. We have spent weeks in the saddle looking for ye, going to Dobharach and e'en Gurby, then back to Werstane where we heard a chilling legend that made us think ye might be fool enough to come here." He put his hands on his hips and scowled at her. "And we were right."

"I had a plan," she ignored the groans of Nella and her brothers, "to solve our troubles. Weel, my possible future troubles. 'Twas no legend, Adrian. Ye see, our ancestor—" She gasped when Alpin suddenly clamped a hand over her mouth.

Although shocked and wondering just how many secrets his wife had, Alpin kept enough of his wits about him to stop her tale. A bailey crowded with curious and avidly listening people was not the place to start speaking of magic, witches, and curses. It would be too easy for people to start thinking Sophie was a witch as well.

"I think we'd best go inside," he said. "Eric, is there room for everyone?"

"Aye," Eric replied. "The MacLanes left yesterday."

Sophie grabbed Nella's hand and hurried to her room

to get dressed. By the time she joined the men in the great hall, however, she knew by the look upon Alpin's face that she was too late to soften the shock of some revelations. She grimaced and took her seat at his side.

"I believe there are a few things ye neglected to tell me, wife," Alpin drawled.

"Weel, mayhap one or two wee things," she murmured.

"Wee things like Dobharach, Werstane, and Gurby— your lands? Or that ye have enough money to build a gilded cathedral? Or that ye have enough men to raise a small army? Ah, and let us not forget the eight brothers."

" 'Tis all that bounty which made us fear she had been abducted," said Adrian. "She is a rich prize. Of course, since she lied to ye—"

"I didnae lie," protested Sophie. "I just didnae tell him everything." She waited a moment for the men to stop rolling their eyes and muttering insults about a woman's trickery, then proceeded to tell them all about Rona's curse and how she had been determined to find a way to end it. "And, so," she put her hand on Alpin's, relieved when he turned his hand to clasp hers, "I couldnae tell the truth or he may ne'er have made the choice, or would have made it for all the wrong reasons. If I was to be the choice o'er wealth and land, then he couldnae ken that I had any." She breathed a sigh of relief when Alpin lifted her hand to his mouth and kissed her knuckles.

Adrian shook his head. " 'Tis so difficult to believe, yet hard to argue against. Too much of the history of both families follow the paths set out by the curse." He looked at Alpin. "Do ye think the curse has truly been broken?"

"It would seem so. I think 'twill take more than one sunny day for me to feel certain, however."

Those words troubled Sophie for the rest of the day, even as she enjoyed the company of her brothers. Even the pleasure of watching Alpin eat a normal meal, openly savoring each bite like a child given a sweet, did not fully ease her growing tension. It was not until she eased into bed beside Alpin that she realized he had noticed her troubled mood. He did not immediately pull her into his arms, but turned on his side and watched her closely.

"Why do I get the feeling ye are keeping another secret?" he asked. "More lands? More wealth? More brothers?"

"Nay, I believe I have enough of each, dinnae ye?" she asked, giving him a weak smile.

"Aye, more than enough. So, what are ye hiding?"

Sophie sighed and stared down at the small ridge beneath the blanket made by her toes. "I am with child." She winced when she felt his whole body spasm with shock. "And, aye, I am sure, e'en though 'tis verra early in the game."

Alpin flopped onto his back and stared blindly up at the ceiling. "Ye said ye had potions ye could take."

Moving to sprawl on top of him, Sophie framed his face in her hands. "Do ye truly wish me to rid my body of our child?"

"Nay," he said quickly, his heart in his words, but then he grimaced. "But, the curse—"

"Is gone. Think, Alpin; I conceived ere ye chose me." She saw the glimmer of hope return to his eyes. "And I think ye also ken that I, er, feel things. I feel no taint in this child I carry. Have faith, Alpin."

He wrapped his arms around her and held her close. "I do have faith in ye. Ye will just have to have patience if I waver. After all, 'tisnae easy to forget four hundred and thirty-five years of darkness."

"The darkness is gone now. Ye chose love, Alpin, and drove the shadows away."

"Aye, I chose love." He tilted her face up to his. "And I shall teach our children the importance of all I have learned."

Sophie brushed a kiss over his lips. "And what would that be?"

"That a mon's real wealth isnae measured in lands, coin, or fighting men, but in the giving and receiving of a true and lasting love."

CITY OF DEMONS

Richelle Mead

Chapter One

There is a time and a place for a skimpy white night-gown. A misty island in the middle of winter is not one of them, but I'd certainly done stupider things to get a guy's attention.

"Hey," I yelled for the third time. I leaned one hip against the doorway, hoping to offer a better view of my figure. "You're going to freeze to death out there."

The man I addressed was sitting back in a lawn chair, posture easy and relaxed, with his long legs propped up and a laptop balanced in front of him. In the distance, early morning fog hung across the still water, nearly obscuring the dark shapes of other islands. After several more moments, Seth Mortensen—who dubiously carried the title of my boyfriend—slowly looked up from the screen and focused on me. Soft sunlight glinted on his brown hair, giving it a slight coppery glow.

"I don't know," he said thoughtfully, eyes lingering on my chest. "You look like you're the one who's freezing."

I petulantly crossed my arms, careful to leave my breasts and their attention-seeking nipples visible. "Are you coming inside or not?"

"I have a coat. I'm fine."

"You promised me breakfast."

"I just need another half-hour to finish this chapter."

"That's what you said a half-hour ago."

"I mean it this time." He looked back down. I was losing him. Damn it. This nightgown was one of my best. "Half-hour."

"Fine," I snapped. "Take all the time you want. I don't care. I'm going to go take a shower. A really long, slow, and sensuous shower."

No response.

"With lots of hot water and soap to make sure I get *every inch* of me clean. I'll probably have to do a lot of rubbing."

No response.

With a huff, I spun around and went back inside the bedroom, slamming the door loudly behind me. The cottage we were renting on Orcas Island only had this one bedroom, and it was small, with a messy, quilt-covered bed taking up most of the space. The front of the house had a kitchen smaller than my closet at home, and the bathroom here was tinier still. But this place had been ours for the weekend, and it was cozy and quiet and romantic. The kind of place you and your beloved could go to escape the world. To grow emotionally closer. To have mad, passionate, back-breaking sex.

If, of course, you could actually have sex with said beloved person without dire, soul-altering consequences.

With a sigh, I turned on the shower and waited for the water to heat up. I tossed my nightgown onto the bed and paced around naked, pondering not for the first time how an award-winning succubus could be so ineffectual—especially around a guy that was allegedly in love with me. Of course, the fact that said guy and I couldn't touch in any meaningful way kind of made things difficult. Being a succubus meant I was immortal and could shape-shift into any form I chose. The cost of that was that I had to steal energy and life from other people—through sex. So, yeah, that sort of put a damper on our romantic escapade here since I refused to consummate our love and shorten his life.

Halfway through my shower, the curtain jerked open. I yelped and saw Seth standing outside. He still had that same casual posture, but there was a glint of something very warm and very male in his brown eyes as he surveyed me.

"After writing *white nightgown* ten times, I decided it was time to quit."

"Well. You're too late. I took it off."

"I can see that." He didn't sound disappointed.

With deliberate slowness, I let my slick hands run down my body, wiping away the last of the soap. His eyes followed. Then, with feigned haughtiness, I snapped the curtain closed in front of him.

"Go away. I need another half-hour."

He opened the curtain right up again and reached into the tiny stall to shut the water off, oblivious to his own clothes getting wet. "You're done."

"Am not."

"Are too."

I pointed to the towel hanging on the bar. "Look,

you've displeased me this morning. Immensely. But, if you apologize profusely and beg my forgiveness, I might let you dry me off. Might."

A wicked, playful look shone in his eyes, and I loved it. Seth was normally pretty shy and introverted. Seeing his dark and passionate side surface was always a treat. He grabbed the towel and stepped back, waving it tauntingly, like a matador.

"You aren't the one making demands here, Thetis." Thetis was his nickname for me, in honor of a shapeshifting nymph from Greek mythology. "If you beg, then I *might* let you have the towel."

"What kind of a threat is that? I can just shape-shift—"

"Is this a bad time, Georgie?"

My mouth clamped shut as I stared beyond Seth. There, standing on the other side of the small bathroom, was my boss. Jerome was a demon—*arch*demon, in fact—who controlled all hellish activities in the greater Seattle area. He also looked like . . . well, John Cusack. Seriously—if you gave him a boom box to hold over his head, he would have been a dead ringer for the star of *Say Anything*. Out of instinct, I wrapped my arms ineffectually around my nakedness. It was very Garden of Eden.

"Please," Jerome said, rolling his eyes. "You have no idea how uninterested I am in your body."

Seth meanwhile had noticed my deer-in-the-headlights expression. He looked at me, glanced back to where I stared, and then turned back to me. "What's wrong?"

Jerome was invisible to mortal eyes. Only I could see—or hear—him.

"So what are you doing here then if you aren't spying?" I demanded. Seth opened his mouth to say something else, and I waved him off with my hand. He stayed quiet, suddenly realizing something immortal was afoot.

Jerome pulled a large manila envelope out of his black suit jacket. "I'm here to give you your plane ticket."

"My—what?"

"You're going to Los Angeles for me."

"Am I?" I attempted a little cockiness, but mostly I sounded confused. Because I was.

"Yes," he replied. "I was summoned for a tribunal. You're going to go in my place."

"What kind of tribunal?"

He waved his hands in a dismissive gesture. "Fuck if I know. Some duel. A demon got destroyed or some such idiocy, and they're having a hearing to figure out who did it."

I fell silent, processing the implications of what he was saying. "So . . . what? You got jury duty and you're pushing it off on me?"

"I'm reminding you that you work for me. And I'm telling you that you're going to Los Angeles."

More moments of silence. "They summoned *you*," I argued. "They aren't going to use me instead."

"They will. Hugh filed the paperwork this morning." The demon tapped the envelope, indicating the appropriate forms were inside.

"Why? Why me?" I asked.

"Because I have better things to do. And you always seem to be so interested in other people's business." He paused, face suddenly thoughtful. "And you might actually have something useful to offer."

That last sentence piqued my curiosity, but I didn't pursue it. "When am I supposed to go?"

"Tonight."

"I can't."

Jerome's dark eyes narrowed. "I'm sorry, Georgie. It almost sounded like you were defying me."

"I was. I can't go. Not tonight." I threw my hands up, indicating the cottage as a whole. "We have this for the entire weekend. It wasn't cheap."

He closed his eyes, and I had the distinct impression he was counting to ten. Jerome holding his temper was a rare thing. This might be a more serious affair than I realized. Meanwhile, Seth was simply watching and listening, no doubt trying to parse what was going on based on only hearing one side of the conversation.

Jerome's eyes opened. "Your weekend in a shit cottage on a shit island is none of my concern."

"I see," I said angrily. "So, it's okay for you to inconvenience me so long as it's convenient to you."

"Yes."

"No. I've done a lot for you lately. You owe me."

"I owe you nothing, Georgie. You're an unruly employee, and you're lucky I tolerate you."

That wasn't entirely inaccurate. Not only did I feel guilty about sleeping with Seth, I also didn't like to sleep with nice guys in general. They didn't deserve to lose their life energy and get wiped out. Of course, those were exactly the kind of guys Hell wanted damned, so my employers didn't appreciate me only going after corrupt men. I had "improved" recently for the sake of my career, but Jerome really had put up with a lot from me in the past.

"It's not fair," I growled.

Jerome snorted and spoke in a simpering voice. "Oh, oh. You're right, Georgina. It isn't fair. Thank you for helping me see the error of my ways."

I glared. "You're a real asshole, Jerome."

"That," he said seriously, "is the first reasonable thing you've said since I got here." He tossed the envelope onto the toilet lid. Seth jumped as it became visible. "This is neither an option nor a request. You *will* go to L.A. tonight."

Jerome turned, and I knew he was about to disappear. Anger and frustration flared inside me, mainly because there was nothing I could do. Suddenly, he stopped and sighed. He glanced back at me, annoyance all over him. A rectangular piece of white paper materialized in his hand. A plane ticket. He tossed it on top of the envelope.

"Take the human with you."

Jerome vanished.

After almost a minute of silence, Seth finally figured out that our visitor was gone. "You okay?" he asked.

"Yeah," I said shaking my head to clear it. "I think so."

Seth pointed to the papers. "What is that? What's going on?"

I took the towel from him without challenge and wrapped it around me. "This trip's about to take a different direction."

"Oh? How?"

"We're going to the City of Angels." I paused and reconsidered. "Or rather, the City of Demons."

The great thing about Los Angeles, at least, was that it was warm. And when you were just starting December in Seattle . . . well, even smog and urban sprawl seemed like small sacrifices for sun and surf.

Our flight down was uneventful. Seth worked on his laptop. I browsed through the papers in the envelope, trying to figure out what I'd gotten myself into. When we'd landed and retrieved our baggage, I hailed our cab and gave the driver the address. Seth, still engrossed in whatever novel he was writing, didn't pay much attention to the ride. So, he was kind of surprised when we arrived and he stepped out of the taxi.

"A Marriott?" he asked, looking up at the building in front of us.

"Yup."

"But . . ." He frowned and took a suitcase from the driver. Seth's reticence in conversation usually came from a need to choose his words carefully. I could tell this particular moment called for special care. "You're going to some kind of demonic council, right?"

"Yes."

"And it's at a Marriott."

"Yes."

"Why?"

Luggage in hand, we walked into the lobby. It was wide and round, with a faux marble floor and a huge, gaudy chandelier that looked shabby and cheap. I was willing to bet its sparkling shards were made of plastic, not crystal.

"Why not?" I returned. "They've got to hold it somewhere."

"Yeah . . . but why not around a bonfire in the middle of the woods? Or at least a Masonic temple."

I walked toward the desk and crooked him a grin. "No room service."

Our room was nothing special, but that didn't matter. I'd gone into this weekend wanting to spend time with Seth, and now we could have it. Sort of. In fact, depending on how long this absurd tribunal went, we could be spending a lot of time together. But, the trial didn't start until tomorrow, so for now, it was just me and him. The thought filled me with happiness, and I was almost able to forget I was here against my will.

Feeling saucy, I patted the bed. "Want to break it in?"

Seth raised an eyebrow, and I immediately felt stupid. Of course we couldn't break it in. The joke had risen to my lips without thinking. Suddenly, like that, the bubble of joy burst, and reality slammed into me. It didn't matter if I was on a cold island or a queen-size bed with a plaid comforter. Seth and I could never reach the intimate levels we both craved. I don't know why it hit me so hard just then, but that's how it was. Sometimes I could deal with the hands-off nature of our relationship; sometimes it killed me. But, regardless, it was better than killing *him*.

Seth, noticing my mood change, smiled gently. The physical limitations we faced saddened him too, but he dealt with them with infinite patience. I'd told him he was welcome to get cheap sex anywhere since I was certainly busy myself with succubus "duties," but he never took me up on the offer. He always said he wanted to be with me and me alone. He wouldn't be budged. His strength continually amazed me.

Ignoring the awkwardness created by the joke, he shook his head. "I'm too tired to break it in. But you, Georgina . . . well, if you want to . . ."

The dangerous smile was back on his face, and I could feel a similar one coming onto my lips. We might not be able to touch each other without serious repercussions, but I could touch myself without any sort of loss.

And Seth . . . well, Seth loved to watch.

Chapter Two

The next morning, Seth and I headed downstairs to the trial. I stifled a yawn in the elevator and leaned my head against his shoulder. He slid his hand down to my lower back and brushed an absentminded kiss into my hair.

"This is going to be a long day," I sighed.

"Did you read up on the . . . case?" The catch in his voice showed how weird he still found all of this. I didn't blame him. When I nodded, he asked, "What's it about?"

The elevator reached the lobby, and I waited until we had stepped outside and were away from the other occupants.

"Murder," I said, yawning again.

Seth looked at me.

"Murder," he repeated flatly.

"Yup."

We started walking toward the hotel's meeting rooms. After several moments of silence, he finally spoke again.

"I can't believe you just yawned while saying that."

"It's not very exciting."

"It's *murder*. And aren't we . . . aren't we dealing with immortals here?"

We reached a long corridor and suddenly slammed into a wall of people. There were a few humans mixed in with the bunch, but most were immortals. Demons. Vampires. Imps. Even a few succubi and incubi. I rarely spent time around this many immortals, however, and nearly staggered from the force of all those signatures—auras, if you will. It was heady and oppressive. Like breathing in too much perfume.

I peered around them. "Jesus. This is the line to get in." I hated lines.

"Georgina."

I turned back to Seth. "Huh?"

"Murder? Immortals?"

"Oh. Well. It can happen. You know that."

"Yeah, but the last time it happened, you weren't this calm."

He had a point, and I shivered involuntarily, recalling the incident he referred to.

"Well . . . that time involved a serial killer taking out immortals at random. And who, um, had a crush on me. No one knew what it—he—was. This time, it's pretty obvious what happened. A demon destroyed another demon."

It was something demons did from time to time. And honestly, when you considered demons' selfish and prickly natures, it was a wonder it didn't happen more often. Sometimes demons would set up formal duels. Sometimes one would just get pissed and incinerate the other. Demons varied in strength, and two who were matched in power mostly just tended to circle and scuff each other up. When the power levels varied wildly . . . well, things ended pretty quickly.

Regardless of how it went down, destroying each other was *not* looked upon favorably among our masters. It was disorderly and annoying and created a lot of paperwork for the personnel department.

"If it's obvious, then why are you here?" Seth wanted to know.

"Because they don't know which demon did the, uh, smiting. All the evidence shows a demonic attack; there's no question about that. What they have to figure out here is who the murderer is, so they can make an example of him or her."

"An example? Like capital punishment?"

"Not exactly. But trust me, you're really happier not knowing any more than that."

An imp standing in front of us turned around. He'd apparently overheard us.

"She means torture." He grinned at the two of us, revealing a mouth full of gold fillings. With his green suit and feathered derby, I think he was going for some kind of pimp look. Mostly it put me in mind of a porn star Robin Hood. *Robin of Cocksley*, maybe. Or perhaps *Friar Suck*. "Me? I'm guessing flaying, but my buddy Roger swears it's going to be disemboweling. I was just talking to this other guy in the bar last night, and he thinks Noelle's pissed enough that they'll actually flay *and* disembowel the poor bastard. Thinks they might even get some wraiths to do it—and you know how *those* little buggers are. They really get into ripping out intestines. Fuck, I don't even think they care about eating the entrails. They just play with them half the time. Spin 'em like lassos. Wear 'em like boas." He winked at me. "We're starting a pool. You want in, sweetheart?"

"No, thanks." I glanced over at Seth, who wore the kind of shocked look accident survivors had. "Demons heal," I said hastily. "None of it's permanent."

He swallowed. "And so, they flay . . . or whatever . . . this guy, and that's that?"

Our new friend the imp answered before I could. "Well, you gotta understand that the flaying or disemboweling takes a long time."

"How long?"

The imp narrowed his eyes thoughtfully. "Oh, I don't know. Three, four centuries. Maybe five, depending on how bad a mood the judge is in."

"Five centuries?" Seth exclaimed. "And that works? Stops repeat offenders? Discourages others?"

"No." The imp and I spoke in unison.

"But it certainly makes them think twice," I said.

The imp stood on his tiptoes, trying to see the front of the line. "Yeah, some of the punishment's public, so it sets a pretty harsh example. Pretty cool, really. Too bad we'll have to wait days to see it. It'd be a lot easier if they just did a reading and got it over with."

"Reading?" asked Seth. "What's that?"

"It's something immortals can do to each other. It's a way of . . ." I grasped at words for something I barely understood myself. ". . . viewing someone's mind and soul. More than a viewing . . . it's almost like a union with them. You can see their experiences, know if they're telling the truth. You *feel* them."

"Whoa. Wouldn't that be a lot less trouble then?" he

wanted to know. "And wouldn't it make sure the wrong person wasn't flayed?"

"It's soul rape," said the imp.

Seeing Seth's puzzled look, I explained more delicately. "Letting someone look into your soul is pretty invasive. It completely exposes you—opens up everything inside of you. And from what I hear, it's a pretty horrible experience, so no one does it willingly. A more powerful immortal could force it on someone else, but even demons don't like to cross that line. It'd be like . . ."

"Soul rape," repeated the imp.

I could tell from his expression that Seth still didn't quite follow. "And so, even though that would reveal the truth right away . . . it's still easier just to go through this whole process?"

"Yeah," I told him. "Demons want to hide their souls. Besides, with the way they lie, one could look inside another and swear they saw something that wasn't actually true. So then they'd have to get more demons to find out what's real. Makes everything a mess."

"This is going to be some trial," muttered Seth, shaking his head.

"Technically," I said, "this won't be a trial at all—at least not in the sense you're used to. It's more like a . . . a tribunal, I guess. There are suspects—but they don't get lawyers. They just get examined by the prosecution and the jury. The jury decides who they think is guilty. A judge keeps everyone from killing each other in the meantime."

"No lawyers?" Seth considered. "Let me guess. You guys are the ultimate guilty-until-proven-innocent group."

"No. Well, I mean, yes, but that's not why. Really, in the grand scheme of things, this is kind of a small dispute. Anthony—the guy who got killed—was a minor demon. They threw together this tribunal because no one wanted to go to the trouble of having a formal hearing. If they did, then *that* would have a lot more procedure and whatnot. It'd probably take place in Hell itself too. Not a Marriott."

"I hear that," said the imp in disgust. "This place is a dive. Last time I went to one of these, it was at a Hyatt." He shook his head, clearly appalled at the collapse of Hellish civilization. "Fucking cheapskates."

When we finally made it to the head of the line, the demon working the door gave me a hard time. His eyes flicked coldly over the paperwork I handed him. He promptly handed it back.

"You aren't Jerome."

"I'm his proxy."

"A succubus can't be a proxy."

He started to turn to the person behind me, but I jabbed him in the arm with my finger. He glared.

"Well, obviously I can, or he wouldn't have sent me. Read it again."

I actually hadn't read the document. When Jerome had given it to me, I'd assumed everything was in order and devoted my attention to actually figuring out what this case was about. I had, however, seen my name on the last page and figured that was the important part. I opened to that sheet and pointed.

"See?"

"It's invalid."

"You didn't even read it!"

"I'm sure he read it," a voice nearby suddenly said.

"Because surely, *surely*, Marcus, you wouldn't offhand-edly dismiss a potential juror—particularly one sent by one of the more powerful archdemons in the country. Not only would that be rude and likely incur *his* wrath, it would also create chaos here when we realized we were down a juror. And that, my friend, would incur *my* wrath. Now, surely, *surely*, that isn't what you want."

All three of us turned to the speaker. He was a demon, like Marcus the bouncer, but even a mortal like Seth—without the benefit of reading signatures—could immedi-ately assess the difference in strength. The newcomer radiated power, and it wasn't just his six-foot-five height and broad shoulders.

"Er . . . well . . ." Marcus jerked the papers away from me, suddenly unable to read them fast enough. He practi-cally dropped them in the process and stared at the bundle a full ten seconds before realizing he held the sheets up-side down. He flipped the stack upright, scanned through it, and then handed it back. "My mistake. You're cleared."

Seth and I walked into the crowded meeting room, the largest one the hotel had. It was one of the ballroom-size ones that wedding receptions were often held in. My benefactor fell into step beside us.

"My, my," he said pleasantly. "What is this world coming to when they let succubi sit on juries? It's like we have no standards left at all. Might as well put the sus-pects' names in a bag and draw a victim—er, culprit—at random."

We stopped walking, and a grin crept over my face. "They're trying to add a little class to these things, Luis, that's all."

He grinned back. "'Class?' Is that what the kids are calling it these days?" The giant demon leaned down and hugged me. "Nice to see you again."

"You too," I said.

Luis' gaze fell on Seth. "It's apparently a sign of the times too when succubi have human minions."

"He's my boyfriend."

Luis shrugged. "Same difference."

Rolling my eyes, I introduced them. "Luis used to be my boss," I explained. "Like Jerome. Only more fun."

"And sterner with unruly succubi," Luis added.

I thought about Jerome's recent behavior. "Debatable."

"Well, we can battle it out later." He glanced at his watch. "Right now, I've got to go take my place."

"Are you a juror too?" I asked hopefully. It might make this thing a little more entertaining.

He gave me an incredulous look, like I'd just insulted him. "Me? On a jury? Come on, you know me better than that. I'm the judge."

Chapter Three

The other jurors had reactions similar to Marcus the doorman's when they saw me.

"This isn't the Junior League, doll," one of them told me. "You can't just sit here and look pretty. This is serious business." The demon who told me this appeared to be drunk. Considering demons could sober up at will, he was purposely staying inebriated. Serious business indeed.

A few made uncomplimentary remarks about Jerome. One expressed jealousy over not thinking of sending a proxy herself. Most simply ignored me. The only one who treated me in a semi-friendly way was a guy who followed up his greeting with a proposition involving a whip, a waterbed, and peanut butter.

"I only use the organic kind," he added, as though that would make a difference.

Hoping he referred to the peanut butter, I ignored him

and turned my attention to the rest of the room. Blue linen covered small round tables set with pitchers of water and surprisingly cute flower arrangements. I'd left Seth at a table with a bunch of incubi, figuring that would be safest. Most incubi (and succubi) swung both ways, but the incubi would be more interested in hitting on human women. I hoped. I'd mainly wanted to keep Seth away from vampires and imps. The former would go after his blood, the latter his soul.

The jury of thirteen sat at the front, facing the crowd from a long rectangular table. Luis sat at a raised table to our left, looking bored. On the other side of him, another long table held three very unhappy-looking demons. A few empty seats separated them from a demoness and an imp that I believed to be the prosecution.

After scanning the room, my gaze fell back on Luis. He had an elbow propped up on the table, letting his chin rest in one hand as he too studied the room. His chin-length black hair fell forward and shielded his face like a curtain. Seeing him stirred a number of memories, most of which were good. He'd been my archdemon long ago, back when I lived in colonial Massachusetts. I'd gone there because I'd liked the idea of moving to a fledgling group of settlements; it had seemed like an adventure.

Luis had been a good boss, ready with a smile and scrupulously fair. He did not tolerate any slacking, however. That easy smile could turn fierce in the space of a heartbeat, and those who angered him didn't get second chances. Fortunately, I'd performed my job well.

But in the end, even a cool boss like him couldn't change my mind on one thing: colonial America was a dive. I'd soon lost interest in it and requested a transfer back to Europe, deciding I'd check back on the New

World in a few centuries or so. Luis had been sad to see me go, but he knew a happy employee was a good employee and had expedited my transfer.

Watching him now, I saw that same instant transformation take place. One moment he was slouching and bored; the next he was straight in his chair, banging the gavel and demanding attention.

The hearing started.

I realized then what Jerome had meant when he said I might have something useful to offer. It soon became clear that I was the only juror paying attention. One leafed through a copy of *Harper's Bazaar*. Another played sudoku. Two talked in low whispers, falling silent like guilty schoolchildren when Luis barked at them to be quiet. One demon at the end of the table had his eyes open, but I was pretty sure he was actually asleep.

As I had told Seth, this was mostly an opportunity for the prosecution to lay out their suspicions and evidence. The demoness I'd spotted at the end of the table was indeed Noelle, poor Anthony's supervisor. Beauty among demons meant little since they could change their shape as easily as I could. Nonetheless, Noelle had chosen an especially gorgeous form in which to walk the mortal world, one I paid attention to for future shape-shifting inspiration. Not that I had plans to copy her identically, of course. Demons weren't big subscribers to imitation being the sincerest form of flattery.

Her face was a perfect oval, framed by tumbles of jet-black ringlets that fell almost to her waist. Her skin was smooth and clear, a coppery tan color that set off the blue-green of her large, long-lashed eyes. She wore an ivory skirt and jacket, stylish yet professional, matched with gold-buckled high heels I very much coveted. After Luis, she was probably the most powerful demon in the room. Something about her reminded me of him, like perhaps she too was eager to smile and laugh. But also like Luis, business came first. She certainly wasn't smiling now, nor did she seem likely to anytime soon. Those lovely eyes were narrowed with anger as she studied the three suspects. I'd heard that Anthony had been a particularly prized employee of hers.

Noelle did little talking, however. She left that to her imp, a shrewd-faced little woman named Margo. Imps were the administrative assistants of the demonic world, and I was willing to wager good money that Margo had been a real estate agent when she was human. She had the look of someone willing to say—and do—anything to get you to buy that haunted fixer-upper on the fault line.

Margo called up the first suspect, a demon slimmer than Luis but every bit as ripped. He had a shaved head and skin so dark there was no way he could walk out among humans without getting double-takes. Definitely not natural. Still, he made a striking, handsome figure, and I was a bit disappointed to learn his name was Clyde. It didn't fit. I wanted him to be named Nicodemus or Shark or something cool like that.

"So, Clyde," began Margo, "do you know why you're here?" She spoke in a voice of utter boredom, like he was so beneath her as to barely deserve notice. I raised an eyebrow at this. She might technically be in the position of power here in the courtroom, but at the end of the day, he was a demon and she was an imp. There was no question about who sat at the top of the universe's food chain.

From the look on Clyde's face, I wasn't the only one who'd noticed the condescension. The look he gave Margo would have sent me running.

"Yeah," he said in a rumbling baritone. "I'm here because you guys have no clue who took out Anthony and need a scapegoat."

Margo's smile was thin and utterly fake. "Oh, I see. So, you're here for *no* reason at all. It's completely unfair. You have no connection whatsoever to Anthony that would make you a possible suspect. No reason at all that you would have wanted to kill him. You were just plucked out of your everyday life and dropped into this room because the world is cruel and unjust. Poor, poor Clyde."

"Margo," said Luis, his smooth voice sliding through the room like a blade. He didn't even need the gavel to get attention. She jumped. "Stop your posturing and get on with this. If you want to get melodramatic, you can go join the community theater's production of *Our Town*."

I heard a few snickers, and Margo blushed. She turned back to Clyde, face sober as she became brisk and businesslike.

"You work here in Los Angeles?"

"Yes," he said.

"Noelle's been your archdemoness for almost a century?"

"Yes."

"Which is about the same time Anthony worked for her?"

"Yes."

"So," she continued, a bit of that swagger returning, "when Noelle needed to appoint a new lieutenant, it was pretty clear to everyone that it'd be either you or him, based on seniority."

The set of Clyde's face turned hard. "Yes."

"And when the time for her decision came and she picked *him*, that must have been terribly disappointing."

He didn't answer.

"Particularly since, by all accounts, you are—were—much, *much* more powerful than him. Am I right?"

Clyde remained silent, and I didn't blame him. An acknowledgment of how much stronger he was than Anthony just proved how easily Clyde could have destroyed his rival.

"Answer the question," said Luis in a firm voice.

Clyde grimaced. "Yes."

Margo made a great show of flipping through some papers, but I had no doubt she already had everything in them memorized.

"So . . . let's see." More paper flipping. Down the table, the juror I'd suspected was sleeping began snoring. The demon beside him hit him in the arm, jolting him awake. "Okay," said Margo. "According to what I have here, you had nearly double Anthony's power. That would have been a neat, easy kill. Over before anyone noticed it—which, from what we can tell, was exactly what happened."

"I wouldn't have destroyed him for that," growled Clyde, his temper clearly rising. "Noelle made her decision. That was that."

"Not exactly." Noelle spoke for the first time, and heads turned. She had a sweet, lilting voice. Like music. Even some of the other jurors started paying attention. "You came to me after I appointed him, and you were *not* happy. In fact, I recall you saying some very . . . ugly things to me." She spoke crisply, all business-like. Even in the heat of an event like this, it was clear professionalism and calm were important to her. I admired that.

Although it was impossible to tell, I got the impression Clyde was blushing now. "I . . . was out of line, Noelle. I shouldn't have said what I said, and I apologize for it. I apologized then, after the fact." The words came out stiffly, but I got the impression they were sincere. Demons apologized. Who knew? "Although . . . not to place blame, but you were already upset when I walked in. You were in a bad mood, and it fed mine . . . and made what I said far worse than it might otherwise have been. Made me angrier than I normally would have been."

"You admit you were angry." Margo seized on this, a mongrel with a bone in her mouth. "Angry enough to insult and talk back to your archdemoness. Angry enough—according to witnesses—to 'exchange words' with Anthony too."

I could see Clyde's chest rise and fall as he took a few deep breaths before speaking. There was a temper there behind those dark eyes—again, not surprising for a demon—but he was working hard to stay calm.

"Yes. I had a few . . . confrontations with Anthony. He wasn't exactly humble about the promotion. We got into a few arguments."

"Because you were angry," reiterated Margo. "Angry enough to explode. Angry enough to kill him. You probably couldn't blow him apart fast enough, could you? Or maybe you ripped him up . . . tore him limb from limb or something before incinerating him. Anything to sate the bloodlust inside of you, right?"

He narrowed his eyes. "Honestly? It's been centuries since I had any bloodlust to sate. Funny thing, though . . ." He gave her a cold smile. "You're inspiring me to maybe rip something apart after all."

Luis sighed heavily and gestured to Margo. "Do you have anything else to add?"

The imp smiled smugly. "I think I've proven my point."

Luis glanced over at us. "Does the jury have any questions for the suspect?"

We all sort of sat there a moment, squirming under the room's attention. Then the demoness beside me raised her hand. Luis gave her permission to speak.

"So, did you call Noelle a bunch of names or something? What were they?"

"Yeah," piped up another demon. "Did you call her a ladder-climbing, self-serving cunt? That'd be a good one." While I admired Noelle's professional demeanor, it was obvious that others among us did not. I had the distinct impression my fellow jurors wanted to get a rise out of her.

Clyde's angry face registered momentary surprise. Luis snorted.

"Don't answer that," said Noelle, nodding to Clyde. Her face was still composed.

"Ooh," said my neighboring juror. "Then he *must* have called you a cunt, if you don't want us to know."

"I don't care if you know what he said," explained Noelle in exasperation. "But I'd rather you ask questions that are actually useful. This isn't *The Jerry Springer Show*."

"I agree," said Luis, giving my neighbor a censuring look. "Does anyone have any questions that will actually facilitate this matter?"

Silence. I have to admit, I felt kind of appalled. Demons were demons, evil by nature. But they also tended to be very efficient and business-like. The apathy around me was disheartening, even among our ranks. Whoever had thrown together this jury had picked low-ranking demons, ones who were completely self-absorbed and would never rise up in the ranks. They weren't shrewd like Jerome or commanding like Luis. They were bottom-feeders who'd be doing crappy jobs in Hell for the rest of eternity. They didn't care about this case. They were probably only here for the free food.

Tentatively, I raised my hand, needing to ask a couple of things that I honestly couldn't believe hadn't come up yet.

I thought I saw amusement in Luis' eyes when he noticed me. "Go ahead, Georgina."

The silence in the room grew even heavier. I don't think many of them had noticed there was a succubus on the jury until now. Even the center stagers—Noelle, Margo, and Clyde—seemed surprised to see me.

I put on my customer service face, hoping I looked as calm and confident as Noelle. "Where were you when Anthony was killed?"

Clyde didn't answer right way, and I could tell from his gaze that he was appraising me in a new way. I don't think he'd expected any sort of reasonable questioning in this courtroom. I don't think anyone had.

"I was at home, watching a movie."

"Was anyone with you?"

"No."

"No alibi," said Margo happily.

She was right, which didn't help his case. On the other hand, I felt pretty confident a demon like Clyde could have gotten some low-ranking vampire or imp to lie for him and play alibi.

"Any other questions?" asked Luis.

"What movie did you watch?" asked the drunk juror.

Luis glared at him, then flicked his gaze back to me. "Any *other* questions?"

I thought about it. "When was the last time you saw Anthony?"

"That morning. He was leaving Noelle's office while I was coming in."

"Did you talk?"

"No. Well, cursory greetings . . . and even that seemed to piss him off. He was angry and in a hurry. Was kind of an asshole." I had a feeling he might have elaborated, but Clyde probably realized trash-talking the guy he was accused of killing wasn't too smart.

I nodded and looked back at Luis. "That's all I've got."

"Why did no one ask those questions right away?" Seth asked me later, back in our room. There'd been a little more procedure, and then the court had recessed for the day. "Those are, like, the most basic courtroom questions ever. 'Where were you when this happened?' etc., etc."

I shrugged. "I know. None of them care."

"Yeah, but there's a five-century disembowelment on the line."

"They're demons," I told them. There wasn't more I could offer by way of explanation, and Seth seemed to understand.

"So, what about the other suspects?" he asked. "When will they be examined?"

"Tomorrow and the next day. Nobody wants to work too hard at these things, so they spread it out. In fact, most of the people watching are only here for the social aspect. It's the party of the century."

"Literally," muttered Seth.

I laughed and brushed my lips against his cheek.

"Well, speaking of parties, there's one right now up in the penthouse. Wine and appetizers for dinner."

A wary look crossed his face. "And you want to go."

"It's a party. And not everybody here sucks. Luis is cool."

Seth was silent a moment, and I could almost see the wheels turning in his head. "Luis was . . . nice."

"So, you want to come with me?" I asked. "It'll be fun. I saw you packed your Moon Patrol shirt, so you can even dress up."

He gave me a wry look at the shirt joke. "You know how I feel about parties *and* groups of immortals. This would be like . . ."

"A five-century flaying?"

"Yes. Exactly."

"Coward."

He caught me in his arms, pulling me to his chest. "Around this sort of thing? Yes. I make no pretense to bravery."

"What are you going to do instead?" Like I didn't know the answer.

"Are you kidding? There are five coffee shops around the corner with free WiFi. I'll have a new novel done by the time you get back from the party."

I didn't doubt it. And honestly, I couldn't believe Seth had gone this whole day without getting any sort of writing done. It was truly a sign of his love for me.

But then, a wistful look appeared in his eyes, one that indicated that *maybe* writing wasn't the only thing on his mind. "But I'd much rather spend time with you," he said.

A pang of guilt thudded in my chest, and suddenly, I felt bad. This was supposed to be our getaway, and here I was, blowing him off for a party. But I did want to get a feel for this case and knew there'd be other opportunities for us to hang out.

So, I let him go on his way, with promises to get in touch later tonight. As for me, I set about figuring out what to wear to this shindig. I might not respect most of the demons here, but I wanted to be respected. I wanted to look like I could actually add some value to that jury. And, yeah, I just also wanted people to think I was hot. Demons are selfish. Succubi are vain.

I'd packed lightly on this trip so I wouldn't have to check luggage, figuring I could just shape-shift on whatever I needed. Standing in front of the mirror, I conducted my own fashion show, trying on and dismissing a dozen different combinations. As much as I would have liked for Seth to go to the party with me, I was kind of glad he wasn't here to see me trying on more outfits than a teenage girl.

Finally, I decided on a white charmeuse trapeze dress, the kind of dress that looks like a bag on anyone except a model. I had a model's body but still cinched the dress with a wide, black leather belt that better defined my waist. Part of my light brown hair I pulled up into a high bun, the rest I let hang down my back. I was admiring the effect of black stilettos when I decided the white was too stark. I shifted the dress red, decided that was overkill, then settled on a pale gold shade that complimented the hazel-green of my eyes.

"You should have stuck with the white one," a gravelly voice suddenly said behind me. "It made you look angelic."

Chapter Four

I spun around, swallowing a yelp. Who the fuck was in my room? I peered into the darkness. There, practically blending into the corner shadows, stood Clyde.

"Holy shit," I said, as the demon stepped forward.

He smiled. "Sorry to startle you."

"It . . . it's okay." I forced a smile of my own, trying to play cute succubus and not act like I was freaked out that a demon—possibly a demon murderer—had materialized in my room.

Then, it hit me.

"How can you be here?" I exclaimed. "Aren't you under arrest?" I took a step backward. "Oh, Jesus. You didn't break out, did you?"

Still smiling, he shook his head. "They don't keep me behind bars, Georgina. They—" He paused thoughtfully.

"Do you go by Georgina? Or do you prefer Gina? Or Georgie maybe?"

"Georgina," I said. Bad enough there was already one demon in the world who called me Georgie. I'd told Jerome a hundred times not to call me that, but he never listened.

Clyde nodded, pleasant and cordial. There was no sign of the angry and frustrated demon I'd seen earlier. It was like we were already at the party, making small talk.

"Okay, Georgina. As I was saying, they don't lock me up. I'm bound to this area, though. I've got about a three-mile radius around this hotel that I'm confined to. I try to leave, and believe me, they know."

"Do they cut you off from your powers too?" I asked, by no means comfortable with this situation.

"Some, not all. If you're worried about me blowing you up or something, don't. Aside from the fact that I can't, it would really hurt my case if I destroyed one of the jurors."

Fair point.

"Okay," I said, feeling only a little better. I still had my arms crossed in a weak attempt at protection. "Then what are you doing here?"

"Just thought it'd be nice to get to know you," he said with a shrug. "Seeing as we've never met. A little chat to pass the time. I was very impressed with your performance in the courtroom today. I appreciated that you didn't ask my underwear size or my favorite color."

Disdain replaced the last of my fear. "You having chats with all the jurors tonight?"

I swear, that grin grew almost twice as wide and was reflected in his dark eyes. "You're too smart to be here, Georgina. You might be the only one who actually cares about how this turns out. Well, aside from me and the other two."

I shook my head. "If you're here to bribe me, it won't work."

"No?"

"No."

"Everyone can be bribed," he countered. "It's how you sold your soul in the first place. It's just a matter of finding out what you want now. The other jurors? They have plenty of things they want, things I can deliver on once I'm free and back in power."

"So, what? They're all on your side?"

"Depends on what Starla and Kurt offer them. Believe me, every demon on the jury who casts a vote will do it based on a bribe. The question is, which bribe will each one take?"

"That's . . . horrible."

"We work for Hell, Georgina. You want fairness, go to the other side."

"Luis is fair." I spoke without thinking.

Clyde tilted his head, studying me from another angle. "If you're thinking about running to him and telling on us, forget it. He knows what's going on, knows he can't stop it."

I chewed on my lower lip. I *had* been thinking of going to Luis.

Clyde came closer. "So, what do you want? What'll it take to get you to acquit me?"

"I told you, I don't want anything—nothing badly enough to free you if you're the one who did it."

His face hardened, a serious look crossing his features. "That's the point. I didn't do it, but that doesn't mean anything out there. They want someone to hang—literally and figuratively—and they'll take whoever's convenient."

He sounded sincere again, but I wasn't fooled. Demons were superb liars.

"Please go," I said, hoping he hadn't been lying about being unable to hurt me. That too had been convincing. "I'm not taking your bribe."

"You're a succubus," he mused. "You don't need money—that's what Starla'll probably offer you, by the way. But I'm guessing you've got plenty of your own—or can get it from some dying old man. Kurt . . . he's smart. He might offer something good. Not sure which way he'll go. But me . . . let's see. Pleasure. That's what you want."

I choked on a laugh. "Pleasure? Baby, do you know how often I get laid?"

He waved his hand dismissively. "Probably more than me. But that doesn't mean you like it."

It was true. I didn't always like it. Sometimes the act did it for me; sometimes not. But there was one part I always liked.

"I get my life from it," I said honestly. "And when that happens—that rush—that transfer. That's pleasure. That's amazing. Better than the sex."

"But wouldn't it be nice to experience sex that was better than the transfer?"

I stared incredulously. "You're trying to bribe me with sex? You're trying to bribe a *succubus* with *sex?*" Maybe he was the killer. He was clearly deranged enough. "That's the most—"

Clyde reached out and touched my forehead with his fingertips. I gasped at the jolt of power that shot through me.

Suddenly, I wasn't standing in the hotel room anymore. I was in another room, a room from antiquity, on a bed covered in plump pillows and silk sheets. The silk slid against my back, and Clyde's body slid against the bare skin on my front.

Our limbs were entwined, his mouth on mine in a kiss that was all fire. *He* was fire. His skin was literally hot—so, so hot. It was a demon thing. I seriously thought it would scorch mine, but my skin stayed whole and unmarred. He moved against me, bringing his mouth down and trailing more of those burning kisses down my neck. His lips found my breasts, taking turns with each nipple. He sucked hard on them, his teeth biting in a way that danced a very thin line between pleasure and pain. For now, it just barely kept to the pleasure side.

But his mouth and the fire of his skin weren't what drove me wild. They weren't what made me moan and arch my body up to his, pushing as much of myself forward as I could.

It was his hands.

Because everywhere they touched, they poured life into me—that beautiful, blissful silver life energy I stole each time I slept with a human. It was the glittering energy that filled the soul, the power that usually coursed into me at the end of sex and sustained my immortality.

But now, that energy was coming from the palms of his hands as he ran them over my body. He moved slowly too, dragging out that ecstatic agony. It was almost like he was massaging oil into my skin. That life covered me, saturated me, and soaked in. It was more than I'd ever gotten from a human—even the purest, noblest soul. Ten times more. Maybe a hundred. Who could tell? My body became one enormous erogenous zone. Really, there's no way to describe that energy to anyone who hasn't directly experienced it. It's, well, life. The universe. The touch of God.

One of those glorious hands danced down between my thighs. His fingers slid along my flesh, slipping through my wetness. His skin still burned against mine, and coupled with that continued flow of life, I almost couldn't handle it. I writhed under his touch, whimpering as his hands teased and taunted, promising much but not yet delivering.

I knew this wasn't *really* happening, but I also knew he wouldn't show it to me if it wasn't a possibility. This was his bribe.

"How . . ." I gasped out. "How . . . can you do this? How can a demon have this much life . . . ? Energy and souls . . . that's only for humans and angels to deal in."

He removed his hand so that it and his other one rested on my hips. Shifting onto his knees, he pushed into me. The pleasure and pain line blurred for me again, and it wasn't just because of his size and hardness—both of which were considerable. Nor was it the fierceness with which he thrust away—which was also considerable. It was that fire again, the heat that coursed through a demon's skin. It was like a flame spreading up and into me.

It hurt, yet I exulted in it. And as that fire continued to sear me, his hands stroked my breasts and upper body with that glittering energy. It was pure delirium, cool and crisp in a way that compensated for the heat of his body. We were fire and ice.

"How can a demon have this much life?" he asked, echoing my question. He continued moving forcefully into me, each powerful stroke pushing me closer and closer to being suffocated by all that lovely life. The rapid pace appeared to take no toll on him. His dark face watched me thoughtfully, and if I squinted just right, I could barely discern horns on his head and flames in his eyes. They shimmered in and out, like a mirage. "You don't know? Haven't figured it out?"

Some part of my brain said if I thought hard enough, I *could* figure it out. But I didn't really want to think too much just then. "No . . . no . . ."

The words came out as a moan, and I felt only a little embarrassed at my loss of control. Wasn't I supposed to be the sex professional here? Fuck it, I decided. There was so much life energy in me now that I doubted any more could even make a difference. I was drowning in it, high on it. And I could tell by his motions that he was going to come soon. A demon exploding inside of you is like fire too, and while it hurts horribly, it's also insanely pleasurable at the same time—so much so that it almost always triggers an orgasm in return.

I was going to come, and it was going to be *good*. My body was practically ready on its own, but I wanted to wait for him to finish it.

"You're forgetting something," he said softly. His strokes were long and controlled. Very purposeful. He was close, and I had no clue what he was talking about anymore. Fire and ice. That was all I knew.

"Forgetting . . . what . . . ?"

He leaned over me, putting his face right next to mine, and I cried out as the shift in position allowed him to take me at a different, deeper angle. Fire and ice.

"The reason demons can have this much life . . ."

I was almost there. So close, so close. His voice was low. It was velvet on my skin.

". . . is because . . ."

I was on the edge, ready to fall over. Fire and ice.

". . . we used to be angels too."

Fire and—

He pulled out and sat back on his heels. Suddenly, all that pleasure, all that bliss . . . it was gone. Bam! I was empty and aching. It was like being thrown into cold water. All ice now, and not even the good kind. No more fire. I jerked upright.

"What the fuck are you—"

I blinked and looked around. No silk-covered bed. No Clyde, even. I stood alone in the hotel room, still in front of my mirror. The dress was white again.

"Remember this," a voice whispered through the air. "We can finish it . . ."

Chapter Five

I went to the party, a bit dizzy on the idea that I'd just had virtual sex with a suspected murderer. Naturally, I had had sex with actual murderers in the past . . . but, well, this wasn't something I wanted to make a habit of.

Luis found me right away and handed me a drink. "You okay? You look like you've seen a ghost. And I know that can't be true since they stay away from these kinds of soirees."

I shook my head and took down the drink. Appletini. A bit froofy for my tastes, but hey, it had alcohol in it. I wasn't about to knock that after what I'd seen today.

"Long story," I said evasively.

"Okay." He sipped his own drink. "So, how'd you like your first day in court?"

"It's . . . depressing. Nobody cares. Someone was asleep on the jury."

"Only one?"

"Luis, I'm serious."

"I know," he said unhappily. "And so am I. That's how these things work."

I stared off across the room, absentmindedly watching a couple of demons who seemed to be . . . very close friends. One appeared to have an astonishingly long tongue. Like, Gene Simmons long. I looked away with a shudder.

"I realize we're evil and all that." I recalled Clyde's comment about me and my nature. "And yeah, I'm here because I gave in to temptation. So is everyone, even you guys. But, well, I don't know. I'd like to think there's some nobility in all this."

"There is, here and there. Some have given up and completely given in to their dark sides. Some are like you, still in possession of an annoying yet adorable sense of right and wrong. Semi-good people who only made one mistake, a mistake they regret, so they still try to live with some semblance of their old selves."

I frowned. "Are you like that? Regretting your one mistake?"

He laughed, finished the drink, and set it on a nearby table. "Oh, it's different for us. Mortals are faced with daily temptation—as well as the uncertainty of what's *really* out there in the world. Is there a God or gods? Is human life all there is before oblivion? Are you alone in the universe? I'm not saying that justifies falling, but it's certainly easy to do. If you believe there's no real higher calling in life, why not give in to temptation? Why not take the easy way out and seize your deepest desires? Maybe damnation won't be that bad . . . then, you realize it *is*. Some embrace it. Some, like you, hope that maybe holding on to that one spark of goodness will redeem you. Get you salvation."

"I don't think that," I said obstinately.

He winked. "Don't you, though? Somewhere, buried deep inside, is a hope that maybe things can change. Because again, mortals—or mortals turned immortals—just don't know for sure. Now us . . . higher immortals . . ." The brief amusement faded. Darkness clouded his features. "We know. We know the truth, what's out there, what's beyond life and the universe. We've seen divinity, seen the rapture . . . and we still turned away from it. It's lost to us. It's a fleeting dream, the kind you wake up from in the middle of the night, one that leaves you gasping and mortified because it's only a phantom . . . a fading memory that's forever denied, blocked by a wall through which there is no passage."

A chill ran down my spine. I was used to lighthearted Luis and all-business Luis. This Luis—troubled, philosophical Luis—was frightening. I could see the longing in his eyes, the remembrance of that which he still longed for and could never have again. It was a haunted look, a look filled with things too big and too powerful for a succubus to understand.

He blinked, and some of that otherworldliness faded.

"And that, Georgina," he informed me, bitterness in his voice, "is why so many demons have completely given themselves over. When you lose what we've lost, when your hope is gone . . . well, for most of us, there's no point in trying to reconcile our old selves with our new selves. It's too late."

"But not you. Not entirely."

"Hmm . . . I don't know. I don't know if there's anything good in me anymore."

"But you want to see this trial conducted fairly," I pointed out.

His smile returned. "Wanting to know the truth isn't necessarily being good. Maybe it's just curiosity."

I didn't believe that. I liked to think there was some glimmer of that angelic nature left in Luis. *We used to be angels too.* Clyde had proven that they still burned with the power of life. But maybe I was just being naive.

"And some of us," Luis continued, "seek the truth simply for vengeance."

He inclined his head over to a table set with food. There, Noelle and Margo conferred about something. From the grim look on the demoness' face, I could only presume it was about the murder.

"Don't be fooled by her alleged concern for a fair trial," Luis murmured in my ear. "And don't be fooled by her pretty face. She's dying to punish someone, dying to rip someone's head off with her own hands. Destroying one of her demons is an insult—and whatever other fancies you want to believe about us, never doubt for a moment that we're controlled by pride. Hers has been slighted, and she wants someone to pay."

"But does she want the *right* person to pay?"

"She'd certainly like that, less because of fairness and more because she hates the thought that whoever did this to her might walk away unpunished. But if we can't figure out who did it . . . well, she probably wouldn't be too picky so long as she got to watch *someone* suffer." He paused. "Plus, I think she . . . 'liked' Anthony. If you catch what I'm saying."

"Ah." Noelle's anger suddenly took on a whole new meaning for me.

He nodded. "That's also why she didn't ask to simply look inside them, I think."

He was referring to the same "soul reading" that Seth had asked about. If Noelle, who had brought this case to court, really pushed, she could have maybe convinced the authorities to force readings on the suspects. It might be taboo, but sometimes Hell resorted to it.

"She claimed something about how they didn't need to go to those extremes and how the jury would decide in an efficient way," he added. "It sounded quite noble. But I think that's bullshit."

I thought about it. "Because if it turned out none of the suspects had done it and there were no other leads, she wouldn't get to take her revenge out on someone."

"Exactly."

Wow. He wasn't kidding. She really was out for blood.

I spent the rest of the party socializing with Luis and others, smiling and flirting in a way that came second nature to me. I had become something of a novelty—the only lesser immortal on a demonic jury—and a lot of people wanted to talk to me.

I also received a fair number of solicitations, but that was pretty common for a succubus. We were viewed as the call girls of the immortal world. Fortunately, none of tonight's offers involved peanut butter.

After the party, I found Seth in a diner a few blocks away, a place I never would have suspected of having Wi-Fi. He sat in a corner, focused entirely on the laptop in his usual way. His devotion to his work was infuriating at times, but it was adorable too. Watching him, I felt a sudden desire to run my fingers through his hair and make it messier still.

He hadn't noticed me entering, and when I had almost reached him, one of the waitresses stepped up to the table. She was young, lower twenties, with her blond hair pulled up into a high ponytail. Underneath the blah uniform, I could see a perfect hourglass figure. She had the good looks of a struggling actress, but I half-suspected she wasn't anorexic enough to meet today's starlet standards.

"You want more?" she asked, holding up a pot of coffee. The orange rim signaled decaf. Typical of Seth.

I waited for him to ignore her, but to my surprise, he looked up right away. He smiled at her. It was the cute half-smile that always made me melt.

"Sure."

She filled the cup, leaning over to do so. And then—I swear it—Seth's eyes hovered briefly on her cleavage before looking away. Impossible. Seth almost never checked women out. I stiffened.

"What chapter are you on now?" she asked.

"Thirteen."

"Thirteen? Are you taking speed with that decaf? You were on eleven last time I checked."

His smile twitched. "The muse is in a good mood tonight."

"Well, send her to my place. I've got a ten-page paper due tomorrow."

"Is that the history one?"

What kind of question was that? Had he learned her life story after only a few hours?

She shook her head, ponytail swaying. "English. Gotta analyze *Dracula*."

"Ah, yeah." Seth considered. "Vampire stories. Slavic dualistic concept of life and death, light and darkness. Harkening back to pre-Christian myths of solar deities."

Both the waitress and I stared. Seth looked embarrassed.

"Well. Not that Stoker used much of that."

"I wish you could write this for me," she said. "You could do it in five minutes. I can't believe you wrote all that. Where do you get all those ideas?" She grimaced. "That's probably a stupid question, huh?"

"Nah. Someone I know thinks that, but honestly, it's a good question. I just don't have a good answer, I'm afraid."

That "someone" he referred to was me, and I didn't really appreciate being delegated to a non-specific pronoun. The appropriate designation would have been, "My stunningly brilliant and beautiful girlfriend whom I adore beyond all reason . . ."

She laughed. "Well, if you figure out the answer, let me know. And let me know if you need anything else."

I swear, there was a subtle inflection in her voice when she said that, like she was offering more than just coffee. And Seth, amazingly, was still smiling at her, even regarding her admiringly. He'd also been almost comfortable in chatting with her. Usually his shyness took over with new people, and you could barely get two words out of him—and even those came with a heavy dose of stuttering.

I swallowed back my jealousy. Seth and I had our arrangement. He was perfectly entitled to go after cheap waitresses if he wanted. Besides, I was above such petty insecurities.

The waitress passed me on her way back to the kitchen. *Beth*, her nametag read. Alliterative with bitch.

Okay. Maybe I had a little pettiness.

I strolled over and sat down across from Seth.

"Hey, Thetis," he said. He smiled at me, but it was a leftover smile from Beth.

"Hey," I returned. "Think you can drag yourself away?"

"Let me finish this page, and I can. Cady's about to figure out who the culprit is."

"Too bad she can't help me with this trial."

He looked up from the screen. "No insights at your party?"

"Someone tried to bribe me." No need to get into specifics. "And Luis concurs that the whole thing is corrupt." I smiled. "You going to come back tomorrow to see more antics?"

He typed a few words. "No . . . if it's all right. That whole thing freaked me out. And I'm kind of on a roll here. This place has a good vibe."

"Yeah," I said carefully. "That waitress seems pretty nice."

"She is," he agreed, eyes still on the screen. "She reminds me of you."

I kept smiling, but I wasn't entirely sure if I should feel complimented or not.

Chapter Six

Whatever resentment I held toward Seth and the waitress faded pretty quickly when we got back to our room. He held me as securely as ever, kisses light on my skin and affection radiating around him like an immortal signature.

I let him sleep in the next morning as I blearily dressed and headed downstairs for day two of the trial. To my surprise, there were a lot less spectators than the previous day.

"They saw what they wanted to see and went home," Luis explained to me. We stood near the entrance to the room, drinking coffee. "A lot of this is just sensationalism. The thrill is gone, though some might come back for the sentencing."

I glanced over at the jury's table. "At least none of *them* left. I kind of expected it."

"Nah. They know better. There'd be serious consequences if they took off from something like this."

Apparently, though, none of the demonic jurors felt they had to do more than just be present. They proved just as negligent as yesterday. The suspect today was a demon named Kurtis.

"Kurt," he corrected Margo.

"Kurtis," she said, "can you tell us about your relationship with Anthony?"

"Relationship? We barely had one date. I'd hardly call it that."

A few people laughed at his joke. He'd chosen a lanky form and pale skin, with hair that kept falling into his face. If he was concerned about being accused of murder, he didn't show it. His chronic smile indicated how silly he thought all of this was, Margo most of all.

She glared at his impertinence. "What I mean, *Kurtis*, is how did you know Anthony?"

He opened his mouth, and I would have bet anything he was about to crack another joke. Just then, he happened to make eye contact with Luis, and the accused demon's face sobered a little bit.

As the story unfolded, we learned that Kurtis had once been Anthony's archdemon. This perked the jurors up a little bit. Archdemons, as the leaders and power players in our world, tended to be better at self-constraint. Luis, Noelle, and even Jerome were good examples of that. If archdemons did take on others, it was their peers—not underlings. If Kurtis had indeed destroyed Anthony, it would be a juicy scandal. An archdemon undergoing a five-hundred year flaying would be equally compelling.

"Nothing'll happen to him," murmured the demon sitting beside me, as though reading my mind. He was the one who was into peanut butter. "He's here because they wanted to make it look like they had a full group of suspects. You know, like they'd really researched all the possibilities. There isn't enough evidence against him."

I was surprised to hear something so astute from one of my colleagues. "That must be why he's so laissez-faire about all this."

"Yup." The demon's eyes studied Kurtis, then gave me a curious look. "What about Nutella? You into that maybe?"

When Anthony had worked for Kurtis, the two had apparently had a fair amount of tension between them. It wasn't entirely clear if Anthony had done something to warrant the antagonism or if it was just a personality conflict. Regardless, Kurtis had taken retaliatory measures against his unruly employee.

Margo was pretending to read her clipboard again. "So, let me get this straight. You burned him alive?"

Kurtis shrugged. "If you can call it that. I mean, it didn't do any permanent damage. And really, are we alive? Don't we just exist? Or, in his case now, not exist?"

"And you locked him in a box at the bottom of the ocean for a month."

"It was a roomy box."

"And you decapitated him."

"No."

Margo looked up from her clipboard, eyebrow raised. "I have several witnesses who say otherwise."

"I only partially decapitated him," Kurtis countered. "His head was still attached . . . technically."

Margo continued to go through a laundry list of assorted tortures Kurtis had inflicted on Anthony. Horrible or not, I had to admit the archdemon was pretty creative. Anthony had finally filed a complaint with higher authorities and gotten a transfer. He'd also gotten in very good with a high-ranking demoness. She'd made arrangements to ensure Kurtis was punished for his transgressions. No torture, though—well, at least not in the physical sense.

He'd been transferred to Belgium.

The mention of this dimmed Kurtis's humor a bit. The transfer was still a bitter point with him. It had happened four centuries ago, and he was no happier about his current locale than he'd been then. He'd apparently spent these last four hundred years being quite liberal in his slander and criticism of Anthony.

"And you're up for a possible transfer now, aren't you?" asked Margo.

"Yes," he replied.

"Hmm. Coincidental timing."

He snorted. "Hardly. Why would I destroy him now? You think I'd want to risk getting in trouble when my review comes along?"

"Or," said Noelle, suddenly speaking up, "maybe you wanted to make sure he wouldn't be able to influence the review committee."

Kurtis gave her a tight, mirthless smile. "That's your own wishful thinking, Noelle. You have no fucking clue who did this, and you'll take anyone you can find."

"I'll take whoever's guilty," she replied. She'd matched the steel in his voice but still wore her usual composure. "And I'll make sure they pay."

I left the proceedings that day with mixed feelings about Kurtis. With his history of violence and casual attitude about said violence, he did make a suspicious figure. On the other hand, I had to agree with him about the danger of taking out Anthony with the transfer hearing so close at hand.

Just like the day before, I was the only one to ask any real questions. I wanted to know when Kurtis and Anthony had last seen each other and if Kurtis had an alibi. He did, but again, I didn't doubt a demon could come up with any number of people to lie for him.

Post-trial parties held little appeal for me today, so instead, I decided to go straight to Seth's diner. The notion of just hanging out and doing something mundane like watching a movie had astonishing appeal. Besides, I was feeling guilty about my neglect.

When I stepped inside the elevator, I was surprised to see Noelle riding down as well. We stood there in that awkward silence elevator passengers often have, our eyes trained on the numbers as we descended. Daring a sidelong glance, I again admired her pretty features and remembered what Luis had said about her loving Anthony.

The words were out of my mouth before I could stop them. "I'm sorry about Anthony."

Her sea-colored eyes flicked from the numbers to me. Bitter amusement glinted in them. "You're the only one, I think."

I thought so too. "I . . . I know it's hard to lose someone you're close to."

"Close, huh? You've been talking to Luis. He might be the only other person who cares about this too." A small frown wrinkled her brow. "But I believe you. You do know what it's like. That's the thing with you lesser immortals . . . you're always around humans, getting caught up in their muddled emotions. Loving them. Losing them. Getting betrayed by them. You'd be better off staying detached from all that. Save yourselves a lot of pain."

I wanted to tell her that if she'd loved Anthony, then she wasn't a very good role model as far as emotional detachment went. Instead, I said something completely asinine.

"Well. I don't think you can really have happiness if you don't have pain too."

Something like a snort caught in her throat. Noelle's eyes swept me, and I felt as though she suddenly could see my life story without the benefit of a reading.

After several moments, she replied, "You must have a lot of happiness then."

I held back a glare and left the elevator when it opened, murmuring a polite good-bye as I stepped out.

I walked down to the diner and caught sight of Seth through the window. He sat at the same table, and so help me, that fucking waitress was there again. The door was propped open to let in the nice weather. I started to step through, hesitated, and then retreated. There was a small overhang around the side of the building, obscured from the rest of the street. I sidled over to it and shape-shifted into invisibility. Returning to the front door, I crossed the threshold, hidden from mortal eyes.

Beth was laughing when I approached. "Really?" she asked. "You get love letters?"

"Sure," he said. The abandoned laptop sat before him. Didn't he have deadlines or something? "Not sure I really deserve it . . . but they show up more than you'd think. I've actually gotten poetry too."

"Like dirty limericks?"

"No, thankfully. Got some haikus once, though."

She laughed again. "The more you tell me, the more I really want to read your books. I've got to go pick up one."

Seth shrugged. "No need. Give me your address, and I'll send you a couple."

"Oh, no. You don't have to . . ."

He waved her off. "They send me boxes of them. It's not a problem."

"Wow, thanks." She grinned. She had a cute smile for a shameless tramp. "That'd be great. Maybe . . . maybe I could get you coffee as a thank you. I mean, coffee not from here."

Seth didn't quite catch it at first, then I saw the surprise register on his face. "Ah," he said. The social ease and banter he'd just had abruptly shut down. "Well. I . . ." He hesitated, and suddenly, *suddenly*, I wondered if he was hesitating over whether to accept rather than choosing words to refuse her. After what seemed like an eternity, he shook his head. "No. I can't. Not . . . no. Not really. I'm, um, probably busy."

Her face fell a little. "I understand." A moment later, she mustered a smile. "Well . . . let me check on some tables, and then I'll be back."

She sauntered off across the restaurant, and I wished that dress wasn't quite so snug on her ass. Seth's eyes followed her, a bit regretful.

Suddenly, I didn't want to talk to him quite so much after all.

I left the diner, my emotions in a tangle. I discretely shifted back to a visible form and headed down the street, moving toward the hotel but not really sure I wanted to go back there either.

"He likes her," a voice suddenly said beside me.

Startled, I turned to find Kurtis walking along with me. He'd appeared out of nowhere. I didn't bother asking what he'd just seen. Demons could move around with their signatures masked, and I supposed it was time for his bribe.

"No, he doesn't," I said immediately.

Kurtis laughed, the same unconcerned laugh I'd heard in the courtroom. "Of course he does. She's hot."

"He loves *me*," I said.

"Love doesn't stop people from betraying each other."

It reminded me a bit of my conversation with Noelle. We passed near a bakery, and he beckoned me toward it.

"Come on," he said. "Let's talk. This place makes great éclairs."

Which is how, five minutes later, I found myself sitting at a table and eating a cinnamon roll the size of a car tire with another potential killer.

Kurtis didn't speak until he was halfway through his second éclair. "So. Where were we? Ah, yes. Your naive belief that love can keep a man from cheating on the one he loves." He fixed me with a knowing look. "Honestly, I never thought I'd hear that from a succubus. You of all people should know better."

He was right. I did know better. I couldn't even keep track of how many men I'd lured away from the women they loved. Affection and reason tended to get a little murky when the body and its hormones took over.

"Seth's different," I responded.

"Of course he isn't. He's a man. He likes women, and that woman wants him so bad, her panties get wet each time she refills his coffee."

"Doesn't matter. She's not his type."

"She's the female type. And she's pretty."

"She's a waitress. Seth wouldn't go for that."

"She's a waitress using her shitty job to put herself through college. You saying a geeky guy like him wouldn't respect that?"

Yes, Seth would indeed respect something like that. But I still didn't want to go along with any of this.

"He still wouldn't do it."

"Why? Because he's getting it somewhere else?" He gave me a pointed look.

I honestly shouldn't have been surprised if he knew everything about me. Still, I had to ask. "How do you know that?"

Kurtis licked chocolate icing off his fingers. "How do you think, little one? That guy's got a soul brighter than a five-hundred-watt bulb. If he was sleeping with you, it'd show. And if you were going to do it, you'd have already done it."

"He's above physical needs." It was quite possibly the stupidest thing I'd ever said, more so than the happiness and pain comment in the elevator.

"No one's above physical needs. Not even demons. Look at Noelle and her insane obsession with all this."

I tossed my hair back, putting on my best bland look. "Well, I don't care if Seth wants to sleep with that girl. Not like he'd leave me for her. Besides, we have an arrangement. He knows he can get sex on the side if he wants. I don't care."

Kurtis threw back his head and laughed. "The fuck you don't. I don't have to be an angel to know you're lying. It would kill you if he slept with someone."

"It wouldn't," I said, even though he was right.

"Have you noticed that their names rhyme? It's pretty cute."

"Look," I said angrily, "will you just leave my personal life alone and get on with whatever bribe you're here to offer me?"

"Actually, your personal life *is* why I'm here. And I'm here to bribe you too."

"Yeah? With what? Your compelling relationship advice?"

"Nah. You wouldn't listen to it. I'm here to give you what you really want."

"Yeah. Clyde said the same thing."

"Clyde's full of shit," he scoffed. "*I* can give you the real deal. You don't want to hurt your guy? I'll give you a night with him, consequence free."

I stared. The room seemed to stop moving.

"You can't do that."

"Of course I can."

"How?"

"You belong to Jerome, right? I'll get him to block you off from your power for a day."

I blinked. I'd never thought of that. Hell, in its complicated love for hierarchies and chains of command, had a weird organizational system. An archdemon's underlings were connected to him in such a way that their divine powers were "filtered" through him. It kept him in control of his subordinates and also gave him a sense of their whereabouts and well-being. It was also sort of like a string of Christmas lights. Take out an archdemon, and it'd cut off his lesser immortals from their powers until a new system was established. I'd never considered the notion of an archdemon willingly blocking someone out of the immortal chain.

The appealing fantasy quickly shattered for me. "Jerome would never do that. He doesn't approve of my relationship with Seth."

"Jerome owes me a favor."

"He does not." I had a hard time picturing my boss being indebted to anyone.

"He does." Kurtis held his hand out to me. "I swear, if

you vote for one of the other suspects, I'll make sure you have a night with your guy during which he'll suffer no damage to his soul."

I felt the slight crackle of a demon offering a bargain. They could lie and swear about the most extraordinary things . . . but they were bound to their deals.

I swallowed, a brief image of being naked with Seth flashing in my mind's eye.

"I can't," I said slowly. "I won't vote because of a bribe. How do I know you didn't do it?"

"Please. The evidence against me is ridiculous, and you know it. I could see it on your face at the trial."

"Then why are you worried? Why do you need to bribe me?"

"Because there are plenty of jurors who'd enjoy convicting me just for the fun of it. I need to make sure that won't happen."

Temptation, temptation. The story of my life.

"I . . . can't."

He shrugged. "If you say so. Keep an eye on your boyfriend and that waitress, and you'll see that I'm right about that. I bet he's a great *tipper*, and I bet if he starts getting it somewhere else regularly, he might find it isn't worth sticking around you. But, if you sleep with him sooner rather than later, you'll keep him from straying." He pushed his chair back and stood up. "Think on it. You vote for one of the others, and I'll make good on my promise."

His hand caught mine as he spoke, and a jolt shot through me. He'd sealed his vow.

I didn't know what to say; my mind was a blur. Kurtis recognized that and grinned. "See you around."

He walked out of the bakery, but I just sat there picking at my cinnamon roll, suddenly no longer hungry.

Chapter Seven

The third day of the trial brought out the last suspect, a demoness named Starla. She was a tiny little thing, all doe eyes and long golden hair. She was also a new demon, one who must have recently fallen. She had apparently been a lesser-ranking angel in her pre-Hell days because she was relatively weak now as far as power went. So weak, in fact, that there was absolutely no way she could have blown Anthony away.

However, as the questioning went on, it became clear she might have blown him in another way.

"You had a romantic relationship with Anthony?" Margo asked. She said "relationship" like it was dirty word. She probably hadn't had sex in centuries, and honestly, if there was anyone I'd ever met who needed to get laid, it was her.

Starla was fragile looking, but she *was* a demon, weak

or no. And even a weak demon was still a force to be reckoned with, particularly for an annoying lesser immortal like Margo.

"Yes," said Starla, her voice calm.

"So why'd you do it then? Jealousy? Lovers' quarrel?"

"I didn't do it."

"It's always the ones who are closest to the victim," continued Margo, glancing at us jurors. "This shouldn't be a surprise."

"I didn't do it," growled Starla.

"Were you afraid of losing him maybe? Sort of a 'If I can't have him, no one can' thing?"

"I didn't do it," the demoness repeated. "I *couldn't* have done it. You know that."

"You could have easily gotten someone else to," retorted Margo. "And while we'd like to find and chastise that person too, there's no doubt that you're the mastermind."

"Except that I'm not."

Margo brought out her idiotic clipboard again. "I understand that Noelle told you two to end your . . . relationship. She thought it was interfering with your work."

A flash of anger gleamed in Starla's eyes as she glanced briefly at her archdemoness. "It wasn't."

The imp shrugged. "So you say. But again, that would certainly lend credence to the 'If I can't have him . . .' theory, hmm? Someone like Anthony wouldn't have stayed lonely for long . . . there were certainly other ports he could have docked his ship in. But you? Who are you? Some minor, struggling little antisocial demon . . . so fresh from angelhood that you might as well still be wearing a halo. Not really worth anyone's attention unless it was someone who wanted to break you in. Anthony was your first, wasn't he?"

"That doesn't matter," said Starla tightly.

But apparently it did because it brought my fellow jurors to life. They showered her with questions, digging out as many personal details as they could. I could see Luis's ire growing, but it was Noelle who cut things off.

"We don't need to hear any more personal details," she snapped, sweeping the jury with those turquoise eyes. They radiated fury.

"I agree," said Luis. "If you guys can't ask anything useful, then don't say anything."

Unsurprisingly, the other jurors fell silent. I raised my hand. Starla regarded me warily.

"Did . . . do you have other friends? Aside from Anthony?"

She looked surprised by the question. "I have colleagues."

"Any that you're close to?"

"No."

Margo grinned broadly. "More proof as to why you'd have such a psychotic reaction to being separated from Anthony."

Starla glared at me as though I'd purposely just set her up. But I hadn't. Margo had called Starla antisocial earlier, and Starla herself admitted to having no close friends or colleagues. She could be lying, I supposed, but I didn't think so. The friendless thing only made her look more desperate; she wouldn't have purposely furthered that image by admitting to it. And if she *was* friendless, then I wondered who she could have gotten to kill Anthony. It was possible she could have made a business arrangement with someone. Maybe she had something to offer, but I doubted it.

Nonetheless, she found me afterward, just like Clyde and Anthony had.

"Wealth," she told me, standing with me in the hall by my room. "Money."

"Yeah," I said. "That's generally the definition of wealth."

She crossed her arms over her chest. "I'm offering you a great thing here. I mean, not like piles of gold or anything, but we're talking serious cash. Investments. Accounts in the Caymans. Stuff like that."

I shrugged. "I don't believe in bribes. And even if I did, I don't need the money. I've got my own stockpile. Besides, not like I couldn't find someone to give it to me if I wanted." It was exactly what Clyde had said.

I waited then for anger, for snippiness. What I didn't expect, however, was for her to suddenly start crying. I'd seen demons do a lot of things over the centuries. Torture. Destruction. Betrayal. Never, ever had I seen a demon cry. I didn't even know they could do it.

I started to reach for her in some sort of awkward attempt at comfort but thought better of it.

"Look," I said uneasily. "I'm sure there are other jurors who'll take the bribe."

She sniffed and shook her head, running a hand over her wet eyes. "No. Not from me. I don't have anything to give—not like Clyde and Kurtis. Everyone on the jury's stronger than me. There's nothing I can offer that they can't already get themselves."

"Well . . . I mean, I don't know. I guess you just have to wait for justice to run its course."

A harsh laugh cut off one of her sobs. "Justice? Here? There's no justice with this group. Even you can't be that naive."

I didn't answer. I knew she was right.

Starla exhaled heavily and leaned against the wall, tip-ping her head back. "For all I know, Noelle's giving bribes out for them to vote for *me*."

"Noelle wants to punish the person who did it," I pointed out.

"They're never going to find that out. There's both enough and not enough evidence on all three of us. No clear decision. In that case, she's going to just take it out on me. She *hates* me. Hates that Anthony . . ." She trailed off, and I was pretty sure she'd been on the verge of saying "love." Something else I didn't expect from a demon. ". . . that Anthony and I were involved. When she told him to end our relationship, he argued against it. He wanted a transfer, and she was going to try to block it; that's why he was so angry the day Clyde saw him. You can't imagine how jealous that made her—that Anthony would stand up for me. So, if she can't figure out who did it, she'll settle for seeing *me* punished. She'll do it out of spite."

"I'm sure she wouldn't . . ." But I wondered. Demons did stuff like that. And I'd seen Noelle's face when she talked about Anthony. His death had hurt her. When people get hurt, they tend to lash out to make themselves feel better. Torturing a romantic rival was just as good a way as any.

Like Noelle, Starla didn't need to use any powers to know what I was thinking. "You know," she told me. "You know she can do it. And you must know what it's like . . . being hated by other women."

A few moments of silence passed, then the demoness took a deep breath. She opened her mouth, swallowed, then said with great effort: "*Please*."

I stared. My mind couldn't handle any more demonic discoveries. "Please" wasn't in a demon's vocabulary. I was pretty sure they spontaneously combusted if that word crossed their lips. Maybe that was what had happened to Anthony.

"Please," she repeated, blue eyes wide. "Please help me with this. Maybe I can't offer you anything now . . . but someday I could do you a favor. Please. Just vote for one of the others."

Her pain made my own chest ache. "I want to . . . but I have to make sure . . . make sure I'm making the right choice . . ."

"It wasn't me," she said, eyes locked on mine. "I don't care what idiocy Margo was babbling about. That 'If I can't have him . . .' line is absurd. I l-loved Anthony. Why would I hurt him?"

I wanted to believe her. I wanted to believe in love and all the noble ideals it entailed. I shook my head.

"People do stupid things for love. Especially if they're afraid of losing the ones they love."

Starla stared at me for several more seconds, sighed, and then vanished.

Seth showed up later that evening, looking rather pleased with himself. I was lying on the bed, watching a reality dating show. The conversation with Starla had left me introspective.

"You get a lot of work done?" I asked.

"Tons."

He set the laptop on the desk and lay down beside me. His hand found mine, and he squeezed it contentedly.

We watched those poor, pathetic souls on TV for a while, but soon, I couldn't take it anymore. With great effort, I kept my voice as level as possible.

"Where'd you work today?"

Seth's eyes were on the screen where some girl ranted about how her boyfriend had slept with her mother. Most of her tirade was bleeped out.

"Hmm?" he asked. A moment later, he processed the question. "That diner again."

The fucking diner. Fantastic.

"Ah," I said. "You must like that place."

"They have good pumpkin pie."

And good company, I thought. Beth's cute face and jaunty ponytail flashed into my head. It was stupid. I had nothing to be insecure about. She was nothing in the grand scheme of things. Seth wasn't going to run off with her. Even if he did want to do something physical with her, it'd be nothing. Cheap, meaningless sex.

Suddenly, it was as though Kurtis was leaning over me with his laughing face.

It would kill you if he slept with someone else.

Gritting my teeth, I reached for the remote and turned the TV off. Seth glanced over at me in surprise. Shifting onto my knees, I crawled over and straddled him.

"What's this?" he asked, amusement in his voice.

"I'm tired of watching other people's love lives."

I pulled my shirt off over my head and tossed my hair back. Seth, still with a half-smile, watched me. His eyes drifted down to where a black velvet bra held my breasts. A cute little gold clasp unfastened in the front. I had better breasts than that whore waitress, of that I was certain. Better shape, better size. Grabbing his hands, I slowly slid them up my stomach, careful to avoid the breasts themselves. It was always a delicate balance, this pseudo-making out. Too much, and we'd be courting danger.

My skin tingled as those fingertips slid across it. I

brought his hands to the clasp, and he deftly unfastened it. Carefully, he peeled it away, and I wriggled it off my arms. His hands immediately withdrew, staying clear. Balance, balance. Always balance.

I slid off of him. Standing by the bed, I slowly and deliberately pushed my skirt down my legs. I wasn't wearing any stockings today, only a matching black velvet thong. It was my own creation. I'd searched high and low for one for a while. No luck, so I'd used my own resources. Shape-shifting was like a never-ending shopping trip.

My suitcase sat near the bed, and I rummaged through it, bending over as I did to give him a full view of my ass. Seth, I had long since discovered, wasn't a breast man or an ass man or anything like that. He was non-discriminatory. He appreciated it all.

Soon, I found what I wanted: a bottle of rosemary-scented oil that I'd brought along. Turning back to him, I poured some of the liquid on my hands, rubbing them until they were slick and shiny. I set the bottle down and brought my hands to my breasts, stroking them at an agonizingly slow pace—not unlike how Clyde had spread the life energy onto me. The memory made me shiver. The spicy scent of rosemary drifted around me as I leisurely rubbed the oil into my skin. My breasts took on the wet, gleaming look my hands had.

After several lifetimes of countless lovers, it always surprised me that I could turn myself on by doing this to myself. I think, however, it had less to do with my own skill and more with the act of being with Seth.

He still looked mildly amused, hands folded across his stomach as he watched me. I met his gaze full-on, knowing mine was smoky and full of sex. His was alert and interested, though I could read little beyond that.

When my breasts and stomach were finally oiled to my satisfaction, I moved one hand down, slipping it inside the front of the thong. A cry that wasn't faked left my lips. I was warm and slick between my thighs, hardly in need of any oil. My fingers stroked me slowly, then found their way into me. In and out I moved them, attempting to quench a desire for him that would never really be adequately fulfilled. My moans came soft and low as I got myself off, my mind ablaze with images of Seth's body moving against mine.

I didn't realize my eyes were closed until I had to open them. Still touching myself, I regarded him curiously.

"How do you want me to finish it?" I asked in a breathy voice. "Keep standing? Lay down?"

His eyes traveled down, watching my skilled hand. Sometimes he would touch himself when I did this; sometimes he'd wait until afterward. Since his hands were still folded, I assumed it would be the latter.

"Actually . . ." he began, hesitation in his words. The half-smile was gone. "There's, um, no need."

My hand froze, oblivious to the rest of my body's outrage.

"I . . . what?"

Sheepishly, he shrugged. "I mean, you're beautiful. Like always. Sexy. Really sexy. But, well . . . I'm not really into it tonight."

I stared, unable to speak. What kind of guy isn't into a succubus masturbating in front of him?

"You can finish for yourself, though, if you want," he added hastily, helpfully.

My brain started working again, and I pulled my hand out. "No . . ." I said slowly. "It's fine."

I shape-shifted away the velvet and oil. Jeans and a T-shirt took their place. Returning to the bed, I settled down beside Seth. This time, we didn't touch.

"I'm really sorry," he said. "I'm kind of . . . tired."

"It's fine," I repeated. I reached for the remote and turned the TV on again.

Neither of us brought the matter up again, but I was reeling. I'd just been rejected. This had never happened with us before. And what was up with the tired line? That was the lamest excuse in the book.

Beth, I thought. It had to be that goddamned waitress. But how, exactly? Had he fucked her in the diner's bathroom? I found that unlikely. Too unsanitary. Maybe she was just on his mind. Maybe that working girl image was what turned him on now, so much so that my seductive attempts were about as effective as a cold shower.

No, I thought. There was nothing wrong with me. I had no reason to feel insecure, not when it came to stuff like this. No way was he not attracted to me.

Seth turned his head to look at me. I must have had a troubled look on my face. He lightly brushed my cheek.

"I'm tired, Thetis. Really."

"It's fine," I said.

Chapter Eight

If Seth had any lingering feelings from last night, he didn't show it. He showered and packed up his bag like normal, called me Thetis, and regarded me with all the affection he normally did. I watched him as he moved toward the door.

"You going to that diner again?" I asked carefully.

He glanced up, face momentarily distracted. I could tell he was already getting sucked into the whirling plots of his stories.

"Hmm? Ah, no . . . they're closed on Sundays. Gonna go over to that coffee shop across the street."

"The one with the pig on the front? It looks horrible."

"Yeah. But just because it's not kosher . . ."

I groaned. "Oh my God. I really sleep with you?"

He grinned, one of the rare, genuine ones that flashed across his face like a sunrise breaking over the horizon.

"Yes. Happily."

He brushed a kiss over my mouth, then headed out. I stared at the door a few moments, felt a smile of my own cross my lips, and left shortly thereafter, suddenly feeling cheery about life again.

That cheeriness faded when I reached my destination for the day. The trial was over, the ballroom empty. No more court. Now it was time for the jury to deliberate.

Apparently, Hell had decided it couldn't spring to pay for another conference room in the hotel. The thirteen of us instead found ourselves crammed into one of the jurors' rooms. Admittedly, it was a nice room, but there wasn't enough space, and I chose to sit cross-legged on the floor. No one paid any attention to me, so I tried to make myself small as I listened to the conversation.

"I'm telling you, the internet is going to send more souls our way than the Inquisition and the Pill combined," one demon was saying. He had slicked-back brown hair and a weak chin.

Peanut Butter Guy shook his head. He looked remarkably alert today. "The internet's *taking* souls from us," he argued. "People don't have to sin in the real world anymore. They can do it virtually."

"Doesn't matter if they're actually doing it," said Weak Chin. "So long as they feel guilt from it. You don't think a married minister looking at gay porn isn't doing mental self-flagellation? Besides, the internet's a gateway sin. Experience it enough virtually, and eventually you crave the real thing."

"Let's not forget child predators," piped up a demoness who was idly flipping through channels. She had full lips painted glossy and bright with magenta lipstick. "You think they'd have as much access to thirteen-year-olds without the internet?"

"Oh, fuck," said Peanut Butter. "I love when Chris Hansen does those *Dateline* specials."

"Oh yeah," said Weak Chin excitedly. He appeared to have forgotten his earlier argument. "Did you see that one last week? With that guy they caught *again?*"

The entire room grew enthusiastic.

"That was fantastic! How could he let *Dateline* bust him twice? How stupid do you have to be?"

"Guys like that are keeping our coffers full."

"Yup, that and craigslist."

There was a pause, and then they all burst into laughter. I sighed.

Eventually, the rest of the jurors showed up. I straightened, figuring we'd get down to business now. Instead, the newcomers simply joined in on the internet conversation, which had now strayed into MySpace and stealing wireless internet.

After about a half hour of this, I took advantage of a momentary lull to ask, "Um . . . so, are we going to talk about the trial?"

Twelve sets of eyes turned to me. Silence.

I shifted uncomfortably. "I mean. Isn't that why we're here? To reach a decision?"

Weak Chin finally spoke. "Already reached mine. Clyde."

The demoness with magenta lips glared at him. "Starla."

"Kurtis."

"Starla."

They went around the room. Four, four, and four.

"What about you?" asked Magenta Lips.

"Um, well . . . I don't know. That's why I figured we'd be discussing it."

"Nothing to discuss," said another demon.

"How can you guys be so—" I stopped myself. "Oh. The bribes. That's why you're voting."

"Of course," chuckled Peanut Butter. "Why else?"

"I don't know . . . to get to the truth."

They all started laughing again. Even more than when craigslist had been mentioned.

"Darling, you've got a lot to learn."

"What do you expect? Putting a succubus on a jury."

"Well, yeah, but fuck. That was brilliant. Jerome's drinking mai tais somewhere while we have to put up with this shit."

"And a goddamned Marriott too."

I closed my eyes and took a deep breath. A moment later, I opened them.

"Okay," I said. "Even if you're voting by bribe, we still have to reach a unanimous decision."

They considered, and then, the whole room burst into noise. Arguments broke out as everyone tried to convince/ bully others into voting their way. It was dizzying. Most of them tried to do it by offering bribes of their own. There was more negotiating than in a game of Monopoly. Some, however, tried to do it by force. As I'd noted earlier, this wasn't the most powerful group of demons I'd ever seen, but they could compete with each other. As tempers rose, I felt power flare, filling the room like static before a storm.

I shrank back, briefly considered turning invisible, but knew it wouldn't matter with this group.

Finally, after a few more hours, our deliberation ended for the day. We dispersed, off to do our different things. No decision had been reached.

I left the room, nearly dizzy. Fuck. What had that all been about? We weren't going to reach a decision any time this millennium. I'd be stuck in Los Angeles forever. Seth would marry Beth and have ten kids. I'd have to move in furniture to the Marriott.

Speaking of Seth, I decided seeing him was exactly what I needed. That calm nature would help soothe my frazzled nerves and forget the day's insanity.

I'd reached the lobby when I felt someone walking with me.

"How'd it go?"

I glanced over at Kurtis' laughing face. I sighed. So much for forgetting the insanity.

"Not so well."

"Hmm. Not surprised. Bribes have been flying fast and furious. What's the split right now?"

"Four, four, and four."

"Really? I'm surprised it isn't even more split."

I stared. "How could it be more split than that?"

"Write-ins." He grinned. "What's your vote?"

"I don't have one."

His eyebrows rose in mock astonishment. "Really? Even with all the lovely things you've been offered?"

"I told you. I don't go for that."

"How are things with your guy?"

"Fine," I said automatically. "We have a great relationship."

"But not the kind where you wrap your bodies around each other and break out the handcuffs."

"Will you stop this?" I asked. "I already told you I'm not going for any of that. You're wasting your time."

"If your relationship's so great, then why isn't he here?"

"Because he's working."

"With Golden Girl."

"No," I declared loftily. "He's not even at that diner today."

"Why? Are they closed?"

"I have places to be," I snapped.

"Of course you do. Off to beg for his attention, right? Make him notice you with your stunning wit and charm, hoping desperately to keep him captivated while his eyes and thoughts stray to other women . . ."

In normal circumstances, I never would have walked out on a demon. But Kurtis was powerless to hurt me just now, so I picked up my pace and stormed out the front doors. I knew he could have easily reached me again, but fortunately, he didn't.

I crossed the street over to the coffee shop Seth had gone to and paused in front of the window. He sat there working, no cute waitresses in sight. I breathed a sigh of relief.

My insecurity embarrassed me. There was no reason I should let Kurtis' words get to me. I knew that. I trusted Seth. I trusted his love. Yet . . . the demon had been effective. Not surprising, of course. He was, well, a fucking demon. And Seth *had* refused my advances last night.

I stared at Seth, willing the queasy feeling in my chest to go away.

Hoping desperately to keep him captivated while his eyes and thoughts stray to other women . . .

Not tonight, Thetis.

I swallowed. And then . . . I did the craziest thing I'd done in a while. I slipped into the coffee shop, carefully avoiding his line of sight. Not that it would have mattered. He was so engrossed, like always, that a marching band could have come through without him noticing. I went straight to the bathroom, shut the door, and changed my shape.

Into Beth.

A barista gave me a startled look when I stepped out. I

think he'd seen me go in in my usual shape. But a few seconds later, he shook his head, apparently deciding he'd imagined it. That's how mortals were. They didn't expect the fantastic in their lives, so they tended to rationalize it when it happened.

Clad in blond, hourglass glory, I walked over to Seth's table.

"Hey," I said, hoping I had her voice right. I'd only heard her a couple of times.

There was a delay, as usual, then he looked up. "Hey," he said, clearly surprised. But he didn't look displeased. "What are you doing here?"

I shrugged. "Was walking by and saw you. I need some coffee . . . mind if I join you?"

He frowned. "I thought you didn't like coffee."

Fuck.

"Once in a while I do," I said evasively. "The only way I can get a real caffeine kick sometimes."

He nodded, thankfully not questioning it too much. After getting a cup of drip, I sat down across from him.

"So, how's progress today?" I asked.

"Slow," he admitted. "It happens sometimes."

A lapse of silence fell. I tried to think of something that idiotic fan girl would say.

"Slow for you is probably ten times faster than what I can write." Recycled material, but what could you do? Praying they hadn't had this conversation before, I asked, "How'd you get published in the first place?"

He smiled. "Slush pile."

"What's that?"

"It's where unimportant aspiring authors go when they're trying to get published. It often gets ignored. Or sorted by interns."

I frowned. "Then how did you get noticed?"

"Mmm . . . well, agents still go through it. They just take a while sometimes. Or sometimes you get a savvy intern."

"I thought only actors have agents."

"Everyone selling themselves has an agent."

"Is yours good?"

He nodded. "She's got me some great deals." He paused. "I'm not convinced she has a soul, though. The best ones never do."

"You know a lot of soulless people?" I asked glibly.

He flinched. "Um, yeah. Some."

Then, just like in the Robert Frost poem, two paths diverged in the woods. I could either make Beth sound completely idiotic and see if Seth would lose interest. Or, I could aim for compelling and captivating to see if he'd go for it.

I wasn't really good at idiotic.

"I dated a guy once who I'm pretty sure didn't have a soul." Beth's fictitious past rolled off my lips like it was my own. "He was a lawyer. I swear, I used to hear him mumble in his sleep at night. I think he was chanting Doors songs backwards."

"That's evidence of being soulless?"

"You seen Jim Morrison? That guy was so hot that there's no way he didn't have some deal with the devil."

Seth laughed genuinely, and I saw it. The interest in his eyes.

I pushed forward, chatty and funny, trying to do it in a way that was interesting but didn't sound like a Georgina clone. To my dismay, Seth forgot all about the laptop and displayed none of his usual reticence in conversation. He spoke to Beth as easily as if she were, well, me.

An hour or so later, I made my move.

"I know you've got a girlfriend," I said hesitantly. "And I know you couldn't do coffee the other day . . . but . . . I'd love to keep hanging out, and I'm really hungry. Do you think maybe you'd like to go grab some food? I'm starving, and I know a great place. And it'd be just as friends."

Seth's good humor faltered. "Well . . . I would . . . but, well, I've got to meet her later on. I don't have the time. I mean, but I would otherwise. It sounds fun."

This was true. Seth and I had made dinner plans. He had a legitimate excuse. But what if he didn't . . . ?

Stop this, Georgina, I told myself. *This trial's unhinging you. You're moving into psycho territory.*

"Okay. No problem," I said, smiling and open. I stood up. "Hey, I'll be right back."

I headed into the bathroom and pulled out my cell phone. I dialed Seth's number.

"Hey," he said when he answered.

"Hey," I returned, back to Georgina's voice.

"How's the jury thing going?"

"Ugh. It sucks," I grumbled. "Finally wrapped up for the day."

"Ah, cool."

"But, I've got some bad news. I got sucked into some dinner thing. I'm not going to be able to see you until a lot later."

A long pause.

"That's okay . . . I can fend for myself."

"I'm really sorry . . . I feel like I've been neglecting you."

"Nah, it's okay. Really."

"Cool. I'll catch you later."

We disconnected, and I walked back to the table, fully in Beth mode.

"Back," I said, returning to my chair.

Seth smiled. This time it was the bemused, pensive smile he got when he was thinking hard about something. Finally, I saw a decision snap into his eyes.

"So . . . hey. Maybe we can do dinner after all . . ."

Chapter Nine

The weirdness of technically being out on a date with my boyfriend and another woman wasn't lost on me. Nor was the fact that this sort of insane, paranoid behavior was typical of the kind of women you hear about on TV who drive themselves and their children into a lake.

"Georgina" never followed up with Seth on when "she" would be back later. This gave him no immediate reason to go home, and the night turned out to be a long one. The two of us ended up walking down the street to some cute little French café. It had outdoor seating, which was absolutely perfect for the balmy evening air. The tables were tiny and round, made of patina copper. Christmas lights, strung merrily along the roof's edge, twinkled down at us. Seeing them reminded me of my earlier metaphor about demonic power hierarchies. Kurtis only had to pull out one "light" in my string to give me a night with Seth, a night that could possibly stop insanity like *this* night from happening again. Pondering that brought the trial back to my mind. The thought of going back to the jury deliberation tomorrow made my brain hurt.

Beth's past still poured forth with ease, but then, I'd been making up identities my entire life. I also knew enough about Seth to adapt her perfectly to him. I could say exactly what he wanted to hear. Dinner flew by, the conversation fast and furious. Afterward, we wandered over to a beachside park and spent a long night continuing our conversation. A number of times, I had to remind myself to stay in character. Being with him and talking like this just felt so natural and so comfortable that it was hard to remember that he and *I* just weren't out on a normal date. He was with Beth. What was disturbing was that he treated "Beth" just as sweetly and familiarly as he would have treated me.

For all I knew, Seth might have stayed out all night, but I eventually made up some excuse about needing to go home and do homework. We didn't touch—no kissing or hugging—but Seth regarded me with genuine pleasure.

"This was really great," he said. "You're . . . very easy to talk to. Thanks for asking me out."

"Thanks for joining me," I replied. "It beat doing homework." I tilted my head curiously. "So, tell me again: How long are you in town?"

He shrugged. "Still not entirely sure. Another few days at least."

"Ah. Okay." I put on a look of demure shyness. "Well . . . I don't suppose . . . I don't suppose you'd want to maybe catch dinner again before you leave?"

He turned thoughtful, conflict in his eyes. "I don't know," he said. "I'd like to . . . but I mean, I don't know what my schedule's like." A palpably nervous pause followed. "Could . . . could I call you when I know for sure?"

Crap. No. He couldn't very well call Georgina's number.

"I lost my cell phone," I told him.

"Well . . . I'll probably be at the diner tomorrow. We could talk then."

Oh, yeah. Even better. The real Beth would be pretty surprised to hear about what a great night they'd had. Frantically, my mind whirled.

"A couple other friends have been coming in lately too, and my boss is getting annoyed that I keep talking to people during my shift. Might actually be better if you work somewhere else. I need to keep this job," I added, hoping I sounded like Pathetic Struggling Student Girl. "Why don't you just give me your number and I'll check in with you tomorrow?"

He scrawled it on a scrap of paper, and we walked off in separate directions. A few minutes later, I became invisible and caught up to him, following him back to the hotel. I let him go into the room first, waited several minutes, then walked inside in my usual form.

"Hey," I said, smiling. He was on the bed, watching some kind of improv comedy show. "You're still awake."

He smiled back. "Crazy night?"

I rolled my eyes and flounced onto the bed beside him. "You have no idea. What'd you do today?"

His eyes flicked back to the TV. "Wrote. Ate dinner."

Flirted shamelessly with another woman, I supplied.

"Same old, same old," I said instead. "Doesn't it ever get boring?"

He ran his fingers along my arm. "You're enough excitement for both of us."

I snuggled against him, and we watched TV in silence. When, after a little while, I made a few amorous suggestions, he again refused.

"No . . . it's not you. I'm just not up for it."

"You don't have to do anything," I teased. "*I* do all the work."

"I know, I know. It just doesn't . . . doesn't hold much appeal at the moment."

"Me naked and getting off doesn't hold much appeal?"

He held up his hands in innocence. "It's nothing personal, I swear. It's just well . . . it's not the same as sex, as that union, you know? Don't get me wrong . . . I like it, and I'm not saying I don't ever want to do it again. But . . . I mean, it's icing. You and me . . . our connection is what matters. We know the physical doesn't really enter into it." His hand found mine. "It's just enough to be with you."

I sighed and hoped he was right.

I didn't bother asking Seth where he was going to work the next morning. I kind of wanted to forget last night; it had been stupid of me. Nothing I should repeat. I hoped he'd take "Beth's" advice and just go somewhere else. If he planned on going back to the diner, I didn't want to think about it and the ensuing complications when they checked their stories against each other's.

Besides, I had other complications to occupy me. That fucking jury. Until this deliberation process started, I'd been pretty sure there could be no professional experience more painful than the time my bookstore boss made us attend a seminar entitled *How to Turn a Minimum Wage Job Into Maximum Fun*. I'd left that class wanting to drill a hole in my head to end the pain. Suddenly, though, I could have sat through that whole god-awful workshop again rather than face my "jury of peers" once more.

To my surprise, I was the last juror to arrive. I glanced at the time, wondering if I'd miscalculated and was late. Nope. I was a couple minutes early—which meant the others had arrived earlier still. Casual conversation sparkled around the room, but I saw a few sets of eyes turn toward me as I entered and sought out my corner from yesterday.

Once I was settled, the demoness with magenta lips who'd envied Jerome's brilliant proxy idea immediately started business. Everyone fell silent and paid attention. My apprehension grew.

"So," she said briskly, "let's get this over with, shall we? Who has thoughts to share on the case?"

My peanut butter friend spoke up right away. "Well, it seems pretty obvious to me. There's no way Kurtis could have done this. He wouldn't want to screw with his review, and besides, he doesn't live anywhere near here." I wanted to point out that a demon could transport from Belgium to L.A. in a heartbeat, but the others were nodding along eagerly, like his reasoning made perfect sense. "And anyway, it's been a long time. I think he's given up the grudge. I mean, Hell, if that whole thing he did to Anthony with the boars and cannibals wasn't enough revenge for him, I don't think obliteration would be much of an improvement."

The others laughed appreciatively.

"You're totally right," someone piped up. "He had nothing to do with this."

"Agreed," said another.

From around the room, more confirmations of Kurtis's innocence followed. After several minutes of this, Magenta Lips moved us on to the next stage. I could only stare, wide-eyed, astonished at this brilliant show of order.

"Right, then," she said. "What else do we think?"

The demon with the weak chin jumped in this time. "Well, Starla seems like the logical choice to me."

Starla honestly seemed like the least logical choice to me. Uneasily, I remembered her words about how she made an easy target. She had the least to offer in the way of bribes. I mustered the courage to protest her guilt but was cut off when the discussion took an even more bizarre turn.

"I agree," said a demon across the room. He put a lit cigarette to his lips, despite the little sign on the end table politely asking him not to smoke. "Of course, we all know she couldn't have actually done it herself. Which leaves only one explanation."

"Right," agreed Weak Chin. "Clyde."

"It *is* the only reasonable explanation," mused Magenta Lips. "Starla decides to kill Anthony, figures out the logistics, then gets Clyde to do it." Anthony had been incinerated. I didn't really know how much logistical planning that took.

"And we all know Clyde wanted to do it anyway," added Peanut Butter. "He probably didn't even need her provocation."

I looked from face to face, suddenly feeling terribly out of the loop. I felt like I was the understudy in a play. Everyone already had their lines down, and I was desperately unprepared.

Just as with Kurtis' acquittal, everyone in the room concurred with this theory. Immediately, twelve sets of eyes turned on me, their gazes smoldering—and not in a sexual way.

"What about you?" asked Weak Chin. "What do you think?"

"I . . ." I swallowed. "I think we don't entirely have enough proof to say for sure that Clyde and Starla worked together."

Peanut Butter scoffed. "Who needs proof? We have deductive reasoning."

"We need a unanimous vote," said the presiding de-moness warningly. "*We're* all in agreement. You're the only one who isn't."

The faces that I'd hitherto seen bored and playful were suddenly hard and cold. Menacing. They watched me with angry expressions, daring me to disagree.

Something had happened last night, clearly. While I'd been out being psycho stalker girlfriend, Kurtis had ap-parently done some serious lobbying to get the jury to agree with this theory. The quality of the bribes had to be off the charts. It was funny, though, that he hadn't come to *me*. Of course, considering the deal he'd already of-fered, he probably figured there was no greater reward he could give me. He was right. He also probably figured there was no point in swaying me because I wouldn't be able to stand against all these angry demons.

And for a moment, I thought he was right on that too. This group was scary as fuck. It would be so easy to agree with them, so easy to cast my vote for this unsubstanti-ated theory. I didn't want to have twelve servants of Hell hating me. I wanted to go home and end this insanity. I wanted to take Seth away from waitresses who might lead him into temptation.

And so, I think it was a surprise to everyone—including me—when the next words out of my mouth were, "I . . . don't think that explanation is right."

The following hours were horrible.

They yelled at me. They raged at me. They threatened me. None of them actually hurt me—the rules of this whole operation forbid it—but they came close. And sometimes, mental abuse can be worse than the physical kind anyway. I heard more creative options than Kurtis had come up with for Anthony.

I was almost in tears when salvation came in the form of Luis. He stuck his head in the room, having expected such a lazy jury to have recessed earlier. Seeing the demons gathered around me so threateningly, he arched an eyebrow and said, "Why don't we call it quits for the day?"

He escorted me downstairs, holding on to my arm. It was only when we walked into the bar that I realized I was shaking. We sat down, and he ordered me a vodka gimlet.

"You okay?" he asked, not unkindly.

I took a deep breath and told him what had happened. Little expression showed on his face.

"Clever," he finally said, once I finished the story.

"Clever?" I exclaimed, beckoning for a second drink since I'd inhaled the first in under two minutes. "That was fucking insane! Do you have any idea what they said to me? What they said they'd *do* to me?"

Luis shook his head, still looking unconcerned. "They're trying to scare you. And yeah, it's working, but you know they can't hurt you. You're protected under all the rules of this trial, and anyway, Jerome would string up any and all of them if they laid a hand on you. They're flies compared to him."

"It was horrible," I reiterated with a shudder. "I can't believe they all latched on to this idea. It's insane."

"Not really." Luis downed his own drink, bourbon and soda. "Kurtis has the most to offer, so his bribes would be the best. And this option also curries the most favor with Noelle. She hates Starla. Noelle would be happy to see her suffer. And Clyde was uppity when he got pissed off over the promotion thing. That had to have hurt her pride too. This way, he's taught a lesson about what happens when you talk back to your superiors."

I groaned. "So the jurors get their reward and earn brownie points with Noelle."

Luis nodded.

"What are the odds of the jurors changing their mind?"

"About as good as a snowball's chances in Hell."

I glared.

"Sorry," he said, looking chagrined.

I restrained myself with the second drink, instead stirring the ice around and around. "What can I do?" I asked bleakly. "I'm pretty sure Clyde and Starla didn't do this."

"You do the only things you can do. You either agree with the jury or stand against them."

I choked on a bitter laugh. "You think I can stand against them?"

"If anyone can, you can."

"Sure. That would be my 'annoying yet adorable sense of right and wrong,' right?"

He grinned. "It's what makes you so entertaining."

I turned back to my drink. "I can't stand against them. I'll go insane. And this thing will never end."

"Then cast your vote." I got the impression Luis's interest was now more in observing the moral snafu I was in, rather than seeing how the trial ended.

"Don't know if I can do that either."

He stood up and patted my shoulder. "Well then, darling. You're fucked. But if you survive all this, you can come work for me in Vegas anytime."

Luis left the bar, and I followed a few minutes later. As I did, I passed Kurtis. He smirked and started to join me.

"I don't want to talk to you," I snapped.

"I hear there was a little dissension in the jury." He chuckled. "But only a little."

I stopped and turned on him, forgetting for half a second I was squaring off against a demon more powerful than me physically and magically.

"I can't believe you did this! Arranged this. It's bad enough you wanted to bribe people, even if it made the wrong person suffer. But this? Now *two* people will suffer."

"I hear it's a pretty sound theory, though," he said glibly.

"It's horrible."

"We work for Hell, little one." When I didn't respond, he continued, "Besides, if it goes my way, I'll still make good on our deal. This is a win for you."

"I don't need your deal."

"Right. Because your boyfriend is proving true and stalwart against Blondie."

"He is."

Kurtis shook his head, still wearing that annoying smirk. "Georgina, Georgina. No wonder Luis likes you so much. You're adorable." He took a step toward me and lowered his voice. "I know about last night, and from what *I* saw, your guy didn't seem to do that good a job against your—I mean, *her*—charms."

"You followed me?" I cried. This got worse and worse. I bit back a stream of obscenities. "Well, it doesn't matter. He didn't try anything. He didn't offer anything."

"Well, it was only the first date," pointed out Kurtis.

"It wasn't a date."

He rolled his eyes. "Semantics. Okay, then. You think he could be so noble again? On the second da—whatever?"

"There isn't going to be a second da—whatever."

"Are you sure? Would he refuse?"

"Of cour—" I stopped because suddenly, I wasn't sure.

Kurtis laughed at my doubt and stepped away. "Go and see."

I watched him go. A thousand emotions rushed through me. Fear and frustration over the jury. Doubt and jealousy over Seth. Kurtis was a very good demon, I realized. And by good, I meant evil and despicable. Once again, he'd thrown me into the kind of state that's led mortals into temptation for millennia. My stress and anxiety from the jury debacle only intensified matters.

Which is why it shouldn't have been surprising when—despite my promises not to repeat last night—I called Seth and told him I'd be busy tonight. A half hour later, I found a lobby phone and called him as Beth, asking him for dinner again.

To my supreme dismay, he accepted.

Chapter Ten

I'd had pretty bad hand-eye coordination when I'd been a mortal, but centuries and centuries of practice will pretty much perfect almost any skill set.

"Whoa," said Seth, wide-eyed.

A Ping-Pong ball sailed from my hand and landed neatly into a glass filled with blue water. About twenty other glasses sat pressed together around the blue one, some with clear water and some with red. I eyed my target and launched another Ping-Pong ball. It too landed in the blue glass. It was the third time I'd hit my mark.

The guy running the game booth shook his head. "I don't see that very often."

Seth turned and grinned at me—or rather, he turned and grinned at Beth. We'd taken a cab to this small, beachside carnival and had spent most of our evening playing games and spinning around on rides that caused me only a little more nausea than jury deliberation had. After all that demonic bribery and intrigue, impersonating another woman in order to test my boyfriend seemed downright mundane.

"That was amazing," said Seth. "You play sports or something?"

"Now and then," I replied enigmatically.

"Here you go." The game attendant shook his head again and handed me a large, stuffed dragon. I handed it to Seth, who already held a unicorn and a bear.

"You sure you're okay with all that?" I asked him as we walked away.

"Hey, I'm not winning anything," he replied, shifting his hold on the animals. "You're doing all the work. I figure I should just help out the best I can."

I laughed. It was such a typical Seth thing to say. If his arms weren't full, I might have been in danger of reaching out and holding his hand.

"I can't keep those," I told him. "You want to take them home?"

"No," he said promptly. "Too much trouble." I wondered if he was contemplating the difficulty in fitting them in his luggage or the difficulty in explaining to his girlfriend how he'd acquired another woman's midway winnings.

Fluffy clouds of pale pink caught my eye, and I honed in on a cotton candy vendor. I bought a clump of it, and Seth and I sat on a nearby bench so that he could deposit his burden and eat the spun sugar with me.

"Good God," he said, putting a piece into his mouth. "I can feel myself getting diabetes already."

I didn't respond right away, instead luxuriating in the way the billowy sugar melted away to nothing on my tongue. "You look like you're in shape," I told him a few moments later. "I don't think you're doing any permanent damage."

"Not at the moment, no. But I can't make this a regular thing. I swim and jog, but considering how much time I just, well, sit around . . . yeah. Gotta watch this stuff." He tore off another piece. "But not right now."

I chuckled. "I hear you. I have to go to the gym every day and . . ." I paused. What trendy fitness activity were mortal women doing these days? ". . . and pay homage to the elliptical machine. Pain in the ass—no pun intended. I mean, I hate those people who can eat anything they want and never gain a pound."

He nodded. "Yeah, my girlfriend's like that—" He cut himself off and abruptly looked elsewhere.

"It's okay," I said. "You don't have to avoid talking about her. We're just friends, remember?" Several awkward moments passed. We weren't making out or anything, but no one in their right mind was oblivious enough to think this outing had no romantic overtones. "So? What about her? Is she in really good shape?"

"Um, yeah," he finally said. The dangerous topic had triggered some of his usual hesitancy. "Really slim."

"Cool," I said. "And she doesn't work out or anything? She must have good genes."

Seth choked on his cotton candy a little. "Yeah. Great genes."

"How long have you guys been dating?"

"A couple months."

"Is it serious?" He didn't reply. "Look," I said hastily, "if you don't want to talk about it, it's fine, really . . ."

"No, no." He sighed. "It's just . . . I'm sorry. This is just kind of weird for me. Us. You and me." He gestured toward the happy people mingling around the carnival attractions. "This. I just don't . . . I'm just not sure . . . I don't know."

"You feel guilty?" I asked.

He considered. "Yeah. A little. I mean, we're in town for her . . . thing, so it's not like I'm neglecting anything of my own by being here tonight. I got my writing in. She's busy. And, um, I like hanging out with you, but the whole thing is . . ."

". . . weird," I finished.

"Yeah."

"I understand. I know it's hard . . . men and women being friends always are. And I don't want to cause any trouble for you. We can go now if you want." I paused meaningfully before going in for the kill. "I mean, especially if you guys are having problems or anything . . . probably best if we don't . . ."

Seth stared off at the gray line of the Pacific. "Not problems. Just a few kinks here and there."

I waited for him to say more, but he didn't. So. Seth didn't think everything was perfect with us. No surprise there. *I* sure didn't. Hearing him acknowledge it—to a woman he hardly knew—yanked painfully at something inside my chest.

But, he didn't seem like he was going to elaborate on it, which was good. He also didn't seem like he was going to get up and leave, however, so he wasn't taking my—Beth's—offer to end tonight's awkwardness. I tried to think of what some ostensibly helpful and secretly lustful woman would say. God knows I'd played this role plenty of times in the past. Nothing like a helpful confidante to pave the way for seduction.

"Anything you want to talk about?" He glanced over at me, and I offered a small smile. "Want a woman's perspective?"

He provided a small smile of his own in return and shook his head. "It's more than that. The prob—kinks we have . . . well, they're just little cracks here and there in what's otherwise a . . ." The wheels of word choice spun in his head. ". . . a work of art."

"Little cracks can eventually destroy a work of art," I pointed out.

"Yeah," he said wistfully. "But for now, it's so beautiful." More silence fell, and at last, Seth straightened up from the slouch he'd fallen into. "You know, maybe we should go. I'm sorry . . . I don't mean to . . ."

Relief flooded through me. Seth was walking away from this situation.

"No, no, it's okay," I assured him, crumpling up the cotton candy paper. "It's getting late anyway."

We stood up, and Seth gathered my winnings again. Frowning, he glanced down at them and then let his eyes drift off to the people walking up and down the midway, watching and playing games. I followed his gaze and knew him well enough to immediately know what held his attention.

A woman—mid-thirties maybe—was walking through. She had two grade school children, a boy and a girl, walking with her while she pushed a stroller holding a toddler. The boy was pointing toward one of the games. I couldn't hear what he said, but he sounded excited. They passed near us, and I heard his mother's words clearly.

"No one *ever* wins those things," she told him. "It's a waste of money."

They kept going and then paused in the shadow of a crazily spinning ride, so she could kneel down and fuss with the toddler's bottle.

"Be right back," Seth told me.

A smile crept onto my face as I watched him stroll over, bearing the stuffed animals. They were too far away now for me to hear, but I watched him speak to the woman and present his offerings to the children. My heart fluttered, and my insides turned wispier than the cotton candy. Seth was amazing. There was no one else in the world like him. No one as sweet. No one as kind.

"Do you know," a voice suddenly said in my ear, "how easily the bolts in one of those cars could come loose? And at the speed they're going . . . wow. Yeah. It'd be pretty bad for anyone in the car—not to mention anyone it hit on the ground."

I turned jerkily and looked into the cold eyes of Magenta Lips from the jury. Weak Chin stood beside her. A slight shimmer to their appearance told me they were invisible to mortal eyes. Damn. For half a second, Seth's sweet nature had made me forget about my woes. Now, here they were, right in front of me.

"And did you also know," Weak Chin added, "how many people in a crowd like this are armed? Guns, knives. So easy for things to go awry if some would-be thief tries to steal from someone. Hell, there doesn't have to be a crime involved. A trivial fight breaks out, someone pulls a gun, some bystander in the crowd is in the wrong place at the wrong time . . ."

"And yet, even *that's* not as dangerous as the ride back," mused the demoness. "People still don't believe those statistics about flying being safer than driving, but it's amazing what can go wrong on the road. Drunk driver. Brake failure. Really, it's a wonder mortals live as long as they do."

"Fortunately," pointed out Weak Chin, "*we* aren't mortal, so we don't have to worry about anything like that."

He turned from me, and I followed his eyes to where Seth still stood talking to the family. "Poor bastards."

"Are you threatening me?" I asked in a small voice.

Magenta Lips' magenta lips turned up in a cruel smile. "Of course not, sweetie. You know the rules. We can't harm *you*. Wouldn't dream of it." But her eyes were on Seth now too.

"Look, if you guys think—"

"Oh, look at that," interrupted Weak Chin, glancing down at his watch. "We need to get back. Still got more deliberation in the morning, and I'm sure we'll all want a good night's sleep if it turns out to be as long as today's was."

"Well," said Magenta Lips crisply. "Let's hope it isn't."

They vanished. A minute later, Seth walked back over to me, smiling broadly. It was another of those full ones I loved so much, but I couldn't even appreciate it.

"Now *there* are some people who really value a good throwing arm." The smile faded as he peered at me. "Are you okay?"

No. No, I wasn't. I could barely focus on his face, and I felt cold all over, despite the warm weather. The two demons' words had ripped into me like shrapnel.

"I . . . yeah . . . ." I swallowed. "Just not feeling so great all of a sudden. Let's go back."

I didn't sleep well that night. "Not well" meaning "not at all." I tossed and turned and alternated between staring at the ceiling and at Seth. Apparently he'd gained no sugar high from the carnival food because he'd been fast asleep when I'd arrived back in my normal body. He slept heavily and peacefully throughout the night, a content look on his face. He didn't look like a guy who couldn't touch his succubus girlfriend or who had a death threat hanging over his head.

Surely . . . surely they wouldn't do it, I thought. They were bluffing. Trying to scare me. They *couldn't* do it.

Except . . . they could. As a juror and demonic "property," I was untouchable. But nobody in Hell's hierarchy would care what they did to Seth. He was a mortal, one who didn't play much of a role in anything that concerned them. No one would raise an eyebrow if he died under mysterious—or mundane—circumstances.

The thought that they would try to do this to me made me ill. And yet, I knew I had no reason to feel so wronged. I was a fucking succubus. I worked for Hell. Everyone who was part of this insane spectacle had given in to temptation and sold their souls out for greed, jealousy, or some other vice. There were no morals here. No sense of honor. No need for justice. No one cared about Seth. No one cared if Starla and Clyde were guilty or not.

Except, of course, me.

When morning came, I went to the deliberation room like someone sleepwalking. The others had already gathered, just like yesterday. When I entered, they all looked up, and the sight of those smirks and knowing looks made my stomach roil. I averted my eyes, looked straight ahead, and sat in my corner.

"All right then," said Magenta Lips. An image of her eyes on Seth last night flashed into my head. "Shall we wrap this up? Who's in favor of convicting Starla and Clyde?"

"Me," said Peanut Butter.

"Me," said Weak Chin.

Around the room they went. And just like yesterday, it all came down to me again. Twelve demons, eyes boring into me. Maybe it was my imagination, but I thought I could smell brimstone in the air. I hunkered back into my corner.

Just say the word, an angry voice in my head said. *Agree with them. End this. Go home. Keep Seth safe.*

Seth. Seth was what mattered here. Whatever happened to Starla and Clyde wouldn't kill them. It would hurt. Oh, yeah. It would definitely hurt. Like, five centuries' worth of hurt. But they'd survive. Not like Seth. Seth was mortal. One accident would kill him. And whereas both Starla and Clyde probably had a laundry list of *other* atrocities they deserved punishment for, Seth did not. Seth was good. Seth gave stuffed animals away to children. Seth came clean about his girlfriend with another woman he was attracted to. Seth did what was right.

Seth *always* did what was right.

The words hurt coming out when I spoke to the demons.

"I'm . . . not . . . convinced . . . yet . . ."

They'd been surprised yesterday to hear my dissension, but they were *really* surprised today. I don't think this many demons had been caught off guard since the Reformation.

The demon who'd lit a cigarette yesterday lunged for me. "Why, you little—"

Peanut Butter caught him. "Don't."

Another demon took up the cause. "But you heard her! She—"

"Yeah!" interrupted another. "Some succubus slut isn't going to keep me from being a lieutenant in Monaco—"

"Quiet," snapped Magenta Lips. Silence descended. Her eyes fell on me, and it was like frost spreading along my flesh. Her immortal signature swirled around me, cloying and fetid. Like greenhouse flowers starting to rot.

"She's not convinced yet." Her voice was very calm, very steady.

"I'll convince her," growled the restrained demon.

The demoness gestured slightly to Weak Chin. "Explain our logic again, please."

He did. There was an edge of annoyance to his words as he spoke, but otherwise he wound through the whole string of bullshit reasons that they'd contrived yesterday. When he finished, he looked at me expectantly.

Seth, Seth, my inner voice whispered. *What are you doing?*

I trembled as I started to speak. "I—that is—"

The demoness cut me off with a raised palm. "No, don't answer yet. Just think about what we said. Let's break for lunch, and meet back in half an hour."

I gaped. The others shared my surprise. Lunch? We'd been here for fifteen minutes. But this group, as impatient as they were for me to succumb, also welcomed the opportunity for a break. They scurried out or simply vanished. As they went, I expected someone to hold me back and issue a few threatening words, but none of them did.

I headed downstairs alone, uneasy and perplexed. I didn't feel hungry, but I hadn't eaten all day, so I figured I should at least have coffee and a doughnut. In the elevator, I found Clyde waiting for me.

"Don't talk to me," I said wearily.

His face was hard. "I've heard what's going on. They're setting us up. Starla and me."

"Yeah, I kind of know that," I snapped. "I've had to put up with twelve demons yelling at me over it for two days now."

"We didn't do it," he said fiercely.

"I know, I know. No one did it." God, I wanted to be

anywhere else. A warm beach or my bed would have been optimal, but honestly, I wasn't picky at this point.

"You can't let them convict us. It isn't fair." Fear and desperation hung in his voice, surprising me. He always seemed so tough, like a five-century disembowelment wouldn't faze him at all.

"Fair? Fair?"

We stepped out of the elevator. On the other side of the lobby, I saw Seth about to leave for the day. He'd paused to talk to the concierge and caught my eye. I held up a hand to tell him to hang on, and then I turned back to Clyde.

"I'll tell you what isn't fair," I said. "You see that guy over there? That's my boyfriend. He has nothing to do with any of this. He just came here to keep me company. But since I decided to take the high ground with your case, those bastards on the jury are threatening to kill him if I don't vote their way. *That's* not fair."

Clyde's face grew less angry. A sober, grim look took over. "They wouldn't do it."

"Wouldn't they? And anyway, even if they don't and I still manage to keep up with this nobility, I'm never going to sway them. This'll just keep going. Kurtis's bribes are too good. He offered me . . . well, something I've always wanted. And he apparently promised to make some other demon a lieutenant demon in Monaco. God only knows what else is on the table."

Clyde snorted. "He's lying then. Kurt's powerful, but he can't do that. You think he'd still be in Belgium if he could pull strings for a Monaco transfer?"

Great. Fake bribes. As if this thing wasn't bad enough.

"Well, even so," I argued, "that demon on the jury sure believed it. That's all that matters."

"So . . . you've given up."

"You act like you're shocked by that!" I exclaimed. "Why is it okay for everyone around here to have black souls, yet somehow *I'm* held up to a higher standard?"

He'd grown solemn again. "Because there's something in you that isn't gone yet. A glimmer of goodness."

"A glimmer of goodness?"

"Yes. And around here, that means some—"

That's when the chandelier fell without warning.

There was no shaking, no trembling. No sign that it was starting to slip. *Bam!* The same chandelier hanging over the lobby that I'd mocked for cheapness came crashing down and hit the hard floor in a spectacular explosion of glass. Shards of all sizes spread out in a glittering radius throughout the room. Apparently it wasn't plastic after all. It was like watching a production of *Phantom of the Opera*, except with better special effects.

We couldn't suffer any real injuries, but Clyde grabbed my arm instinctively and jerked me back. We stared at the mess, stunned. People were shouting. Somehow, inexplicably, no one had actually been directly under it. It was a miracle—ironic, considering most of the hotel's current guests. The spraying glass had done a fair amount of bodily damage, however, and almost everyone around the lobby had sustained some kind of cut.

Including Seth.

I broke out of Clyde's grasp and tore off across the room, circling around the wreckage. Seth still stood by the concierge's desk. He'd dropped his messenger bag and held a two-inch shard of glass in his hand. Blood coated one end of it, and I saw the complementary slash in his cheek.

"Oh my God," I gasped. "Are you okay?"

He grimaced. "I think so. Are there any more? It doesn't feel like it."

Tiny pieces of glass and a fine crystalline powder covered a lot of his clothing, but I saw no more stuck in his skin, fortunately. It was warm out, but undoubtedly out of habit from Seattle, he'd headed out today with a flannel shirt over his Lynda Carter T-Shirt. The long sleeves had protected him, as had the thick fabric.

I studied the cut on his face with dismay, resisting the urge to touch it.

"You should get that looked at." Clyde had walked up behind me.

Seth shook his head. "It's not going to need stitches or anything. Lots of people worse off than me here."

"You're so lucky that's all you got," I breathed, looking around the lobby at others who'd undoubtedly need medical attention. No one seemed to be dead or anything, just scratched up. This whole trip's increasing rate of awfulness was astounding, but Seth being hospitalized because of a falling chandelier would have defied belief. "I can't believe—"

I stopped. My eyes had fallen on four people standing directly opposite me. Four people who hadn't been injured at all. Four demons. Four jurors.

They watched me, malice in their eyes. Magenta-colored lips twitched into a knowing smile. Suddenly . . . suddenly I knew.

I turned back to Seth, my heart turning to lead as I squeezed his hand. Clyde, having noticed what I'd seen, looked at me with widened eyes.

"Georgina—"

I shook my head. "I'm sorry," I said, meaning it. "But glimmers of goodness really don't mean anything at all."

Chapter Eleven

Kurtis found me in my room later that day, after the jury had turned in its unanimous vote. He simply appeared out of nowhere. I was lying on my bed, staring at the ceiling while on TV, Oprah gave away a car to someone in need.

"I can't wait to go home," I told him nastily. "At least then I'll get some privacy. No one seems to respect it around here."

He leaned against the desk and tossed his messy hair out of his face. "That's why I brought you these." He reached into his pocket and produced a set of keys. He threw them over, and I caught them. The keychain's tag had an address on it.

"What are these?" I asked.

"Condo by the beach," he said. "I snagged it for you.

Figured you'd want someplace nicer than this for your big night tonight."

I closed my eyes and groaned. "No. I don't want it."

"You earned it. I keep my promises."

I remembered what Clyde had said about Monaco. "Not all of them. You promise things you can't deliver on."

He frowned. "No. I keep my promises. All of them."

I shook my head. "Whatever. It doesn't matter. I don't want your blood money."

"You might as well get something for selling out your principles," he said cheerfully. "Besides, you're never going to get this chance again. And you can save your crumbling romance at the same time."

"It's not crumbling. Seth told me—er, her, that he couldn't do anything that made him feel guilty about us. We don't need to have sex for me to keep him around." But oh, good God, did I *want* to have sex. It was hard to lie there and tell Kurtis I was throwing his gift back in his face.

"I don't believe it. If that waitress offered—if he was in a position where he really *could* do it with her—he'd do it. That is, he'd do it if he still wasn't getting any from you."

"He doesn't believe in cheap sex. Staying faithful to me is part of his morals, and unlike everyone else around here, there are still some people in the universe who hold to their beliefs and actually have a sense of right and wrong."

Kurtis straightened up. "Sweetheart, everyone sells themselves out in the end. Keep the keys. The reward's still yours, whether you waste it or not. But—be warned. The clock's ticking, Cinderella. Offer expires at midnight. Of course, then you'll be just in time to see the show."

Ack. There was going to be a public display back at the hotel of Clyde and Starla's first round of punishment. I had no idea what exactly that would be, but it was going to be horrible and disgusting. After that, they'd be sent off to somewhere in Hell for the remainder of the sentence. The spectacle tonight would satisfy the sadistic and sensationalist natures of those who had journeyed to the trial. The perfect encore. I had absolutely no interest in going.

Thinking of that horrific display—as well as Kurtis's smug condescension—suddenly made something inside me snap. It made me sick that he could do this, sick that he could bribe and flatter others into getting whatever he wanted. I jerked myself upright from my defeatist sprawl.

"You don't think he could do that? Resist? Well, here's a deal for you. What if I can prove you're wrong? What if I can prove that Seth really does hold to his standards in the face of temptation?"

He rolled his eyes. "Whatever."

"You see?" I said, attempting the same smugness he managed so well. "You *aren't* sure. You're not the great judge of human nature you claim to be."

Those laughing eyes suddenly hardened. It was never a good idea to mock a demon. "Careful, little succubus. You don't want to go down this road. Take your boon, fuck your guy, and leave it at that."

I lay back against the pillows. "Okay. I get it."

"Get what?"

"That you're all talk. You really don't know for sure that Seth would succumb."

"In the face of that woman half-naked and going after him? Yes, darling. He'd succumb."

"Then let's bet on it."

"What do you want?" he asked warily.

"The truth. I want the truth from you about whether you really killed Anthony."

He shook his head. "I've told you a hundred times I didn't."

"Yeah, and you promised Julius a house in Monaco." Kurtis blinked. "I don't believe anything you tell me. When I say I want the truth, I want *the truth*. You know what I'm talking about. I want to see inside you."

"What's that going to accomplish? Even if you found out I'd done it—and I didn't—it wouldn't hold as evidence."

"I know. But *I* just want to know, once and for all, the truth about just one thing in this whole tangled mess. Let me look inside. Just to be certain about *something*."

He stared, actually caught off guard. As I've noted before, to look inside another immortal was no small thing. It was traumatic, for both parties. Powerful. I honestly didn't know the full extent of what I was asking, but I liked the shock on his face, and honestly, after days of deceit, I just wanted something *real*.

"I'm not letting a succubus look inside me."

"Doesn't matter if the whole thing is a moot point."

He glowered. "What do I get if you're wrong about him?"

"What do you want?"

He considered, then a slow smile swept over his face. "I want you to fuck him."

"I—what?" My growing confidence promptly withered into confusion. I jingled the keys. "Isn't that what I'm already supposed to do?"

"No. I mean, fuck him after the gift expires. In all your power. Break that kindly naive notion you have of sparing his life and soul."

I felt the blood drain from my face. Sex with Seth? With no protective promise? No. No way could I do it. I'd promised myself that the instant this relationship started. I couldn't steal his energy for my own gain, couldn't shave off part of his life to feed my immortality. The thought made me queasy, and Kurtis could see that.

"Guess *you're* not so confident about him after all," he chuckled.

My heart hardened. I was angry about this trial, furious about what I'd been forced to do. And I was pissed as hell at Kurtis and his high-handed, arrogant attitude. Just once, I wanted to make some demon uncomfortable.

"It's a deal," I said.

"Really?"

I sat up. "Yup. Let's work out the details."

You couldn't ever make an open-ended or vague deal with a demon. Otherwise, they'd find any loophole possible to wiggle out of their end. So, Kurtis and I hashed out exactly what would be required to win the bet, what I'd have to do, and how each of us would have to pay up. By the time I was done, I felt like I'd done a pretty good job at covering all the contingencies. Probably not as good as if I'd had an imp present . . . but I felt certain it would suffice.

When we finished, Kurtis and I shook hands. Power crackled around us, sealing the deal. He vanished.

I climbed out of bed then and glanced at the clock to see how much longer I had succubus freedom.

It was time to go seduce my boyfriend.

The cold insanity of what I was going to do hit me a little while later. I was a total hypocrite. I'd made all these claims about the honesty and goodness between Seth and me, yet here I was about to entangle him up in a web of trickery which involved me deceiving him in order to test his fidelity—fidelity, by the way, which he wasn't even really forced to adhere to.

But I'd made my deal with Kurtis, and now I was in. So, I tried not to dwell on my guilt and instead attempted to focus in on how I would win this bet. After all, if I did, almost everything else would become irrelevant. Seth would prove faithful, I wouldn't have to sleep with him (how wrong did *that* sound?), and Kurtis would have to suck it up and do something he didn't want.

Still, I felt kind of bad blowing off Seth for the night. To make matters worse, I even did it a little coldly. I wasn't mean or anything, but I was definitely brusque with him in the hopes that my attitude would make him accept another Beth invitation.

It did. Of course, who could say? Maybe he still would have accepted if I'd been perfectly nice. Regardless, after "Georgina" took off for another party, "Beth" called Seth with an offer to come watch a movie we'd talked about at the carnival.

"Look," I said on the phone, "if it's too weird . . . I understand. I mean, I got what you were saying last night, and really . . . I don't want to cause trouble for you or anything. I mean you and your girlfriend probably already have plans, but I thought I'd check since my roommate actually just rented it . . ."

There was a long pause, and I could perfectly picture the look on Seth's face. "I don't have any plans . . ." More silence. I held my breath. "Okay. What's the address?"

I gave it to him, rented the movie, and got to the condo ten minutes before he did. That turned out to be a good thing because it took me about that long to recover from the shock of the place. Maybe Kurtis hadn't been bullshitting. When he delivered on his promises, he *deliv-*

ered. The condo had two floors and sat right on the edge of a stretch of gorgeous, private beach. Wood floors and leather furniture gave the place a swanky, sexy feel, and a fully stocked bar completed the image of a pimped-out bachelor pad—or in my case, bachelorette pad.

Of course, I realized the problem right as I let Seth inside. He stared around at the luxurious accommodations, at the six-figure sculptures and teak end tables.

"I thought you were short on money?" he asked in amazement.

"Er, I am," I replied. "This is my roommate's . . . place. Her family pays for it, and I rent a room from her." I didn't add that that room would technically have to be the bathroom since there was only one bedroom in the place. I had checked it out in my initial examination. The room had a round bed and mirrors on the ceiling. Honestly, Kurtis might have been trying too hard.

Seth looked a little skeptical, but I distracted him by asking about the cut on his face. Later, I found popcorn and tea in the fully stocked kitchen, and we settled down on one of the sleek black sofas to watch the movie. It was an independent film I'd seen several years ago and thought was amazing. I'd wanted him to see it for a while now; I never thought it'd be under these circumstances.

As we watched, I covertly maneuvered myself nearer and nearer to him. I used reaching for the popcorn as my excuse and pulled off the moves like a pro—because, well, I was a pro. Eyes on the screen, he didn't even realize what I'd done until the lights came up and we were sitting thigh to thigh and arm to arm. We weren't exactly groping, but we'd clearly moved past something platonic.

Seth noticed then, and he shifted himself away a little—but not too far away.

"What'd you think?" I asked.

He leaned his head back against the couch. Those long-lashed, amber-brown eyes stared off thoughtfully as he processed his opinions. In some ways, it wasn't hard playing Beth. Seth made both of us melt.

"Pretentious," he finally said. "But it had some good points."

"Pretentious?" I exclaimed.

We launched off into a critical analysis of the movie, very much like the ones we usually got into. I became so consumed that I didn't even notice the time passing until my eyes ran over the clock on the DVD player. Ten-twenty-seven.

The clock's ticking, Cinderella. Offer expires at midnight.

I hastily wrapped up the movie discussion, even conceding a few points to him. Moving on to the next stage, I brought us into personal matters.

"I'm really glad you could come over tonight," I told him, leaning against the couch in a way that made the space between us more intimate. "I was really afraid to call after last night . . . I mean, not that it was bad . . . but well . . ."

"Yeah, I know. But I'm glad you did call. Nothing else was going on."

Seth's eyes studied me in an appraising way. Then, as though realizing what he was doing, he averted them in a way common to him.

"You keep saying you've got a girlfriend," I teased, "but I'm starting to wonder if that's just a line to keep me away. You always seem to be free."

He flinched, undoubtedly reminded of the way I'd abandoned him tonight.

"Oh, she's real . . . mostly. She's just been really, um, busy."

"Is she, like, working tonight?"

His brow furrowed slightly. "She might very well be," he muttered in a dry tone.

"What's she do?" I asked innocently.

"Um . . . she's in . . . customer service . . ."

"Wow. I didn't know jobs like that ran so late."

"Well, it's a conference kind of thing . . ."

"Oh, yeah. That's right. So, she's, like, schmoozing. Like . . . working the room?"

"Something like that."

"Why aren't you with her? Seems like you could go to parties with her, even at a work function."

"I'm not much of a party type," he said. "Especially these parties."

I tilted my head and met his eyes with a knowing look. "Is that really the truth?"

"What do you mean?"

"I don't know. With the way you keep seeing me . . . and the way you talk. It just kind of sounds like you're avoiding her."

"Er, no, no," he said. "It's not that . . ."

"But you said you have kinks. Maybe you're avoiding her and don't realize you're avoiding her."

"No, I don't think so . . ."

"Oh? Well, then, what are these kinks? You guys have trouble talking to each other? Not much in common?"

"Nothing like that," he assured me. "We have lots in common."

I arched an eyebrow. "Sex?"

His mouth opened to form a protest, but he stumbled on it.

"Ah," I said sagely. "I see."

"No," he said firmly. "It's not what you think . . ."

I studied him—face and body—and made it very obvious that I was doing so. I nodded with appreciation, liking what I saw.

"Well," I finally said. "It must be on her end. Nothing wrong with you. And here I'd had this image of this slim, gorgeous model with great genes."

"She *is* gorgeous," said Seth. I was happy to see him come to my defense.

I frowned. "Then . . . wait. Do *you*, like, have problems . . ."

The faintest flush showed in Seth's cheeks. It was a rare phenomenon, one I would have found adorable under other conditions.

"No," he said. "No problems like that."

"Then . . . will she not . . . ?"

Again, he took too long to answer.

"Oh," I said.

Silence fell. I could hear the ticking of a shiny, silver-rimmed clock on the wall. Eleven-oh-seven.

At last, I spoke. "I don't want to be harsh here or overstep my limits . . . but well, she's an idiot."

He shook his head. "It's complicated."

"Is it? I mean, you say you guys have stuff in common. You're gorgeous. She allegedly is. You want to do it . . . I mean, if she's got some hang-up . . ."

"It's not that, not exactly."

I sighed. "Look, I won't lie. I like you. I *really* like you. But even if I wasn't interested in you like this, I'd still be telling you you're crazy. You shouldn't waste your life on someone like that, shouldn't waste your sex life . . ."

Again, he shook his head. "It's about more than sex."

I shifted closer and put my hand on his bare arm, trailing my fingers along his skin. He jumped but didn't stop me.

"When was the last time?" I asked.

"The last time what?"

"You know."

No answer.

"Seth," I said in exasperation, still touching him. "This is crazy. Do you hear yourself? You make it sound like you can go without sex for the rest of your life. Can you? Can you go without being kissed? Can you go without having someone's hands slide up your chest? Can you go without touching a woman? Can you go without throwing her down and peeling her clothes off? Can you go without being wrapped up with—*in*—another person? Having that union? That passion?"

Seth was staring at me like he had no clue who I was. That was reasonable since I was pretty sure I'd slipped out of Beth's personality and into my own. At the same time, I think my words and the lust in my voice had kindled something in him. I could see it in his face—a doubt over what he'd been trying so hard to believe all this time and a yearning for what he'd wanted.

That was all I needed to see. I made my move.

Pushing myself over him, so a leg draped over his lap, I kissed him. In the fraction of a second before our lips touched, I realized it was fully possible Kurtis had screwed with me this whole time and that I was about to suck away part of Seth's life.

But I didn't.

There was no rush of power, no flow of his thoughts or energy into me. It was just a kiss, an ordinary kiss like any two mortals might have. Well . . . except that it wasn't ordinary. Not for me at least. It was *Seth*. Me kissing Seth. And so help me, he was kissing me—Beth—back. His lips were as warm and soft as they'd been every other time we'd had our brief kisses, but this time we didn't pull back. It was . . . amazing. And that was when I learned that whatever shyness Seth might show in conversation did *not* translate to physical actions.

He returned the kiss with intensity, lips and tongue caressing my own, filled with an untamed energy that just barely managed to keep control. I pulled myself completely onto his lap, straddling him, and wrapped my arms around his neck. His own arms encircled my waist.

"How long?" I asked between kisses, my voice breathy. "How long since anyone's kissed you like this? Been on you like this?"

He didn't answer, but the hands on the small of my back caught the edge of my shirt and lifted it over my head. I'd dressed casual tonight—plain black T-shirt—but the bra underneath was red, and the hourglass figure made it look great.

I yanked his own shirt off and felt the heat in my own body increase as I took in the smooth, lightly tanned skin of his chest. I'd seen it many times, of course, but now— being able to kiss it and *really* touch it—I looked it in a totally different way. I leaned in and kissed him harder, pressing my breasts up to his chest. His hands were on my back again, but when they didn't unfasten my bra, I did the honors.

I saw his gaze travel from my face to my breasts, instinctual male desire filling his face. Pushing him over, I forced him to lie back as I crawled on top and continued straddling him. My hands found the edge of his jeans and unbuttoned them. Then, I took a hold of his hands and placed them on my stomach.

"Don't you want me?" I asked. "Don't you want to touch me?"

I didn't know who exactly I was speaking for any-more, Beth or Georgina, but it didn't matter. I'd forgotten the whole reason for this. All I knew was that we were going to do it. Seth and I were going to have sex. I had about forty-five minutes—forty-five precious, golden minutes—in which we could do anything we wanted with no consequences.

And what *I* wanted right now was for Seth to run his hands over me. He wasn't, though I could still see the longing all over him. And when I lay down on top of him and ground our hips together, I could *feel* the longing. I kissed him again, furiously, and then pulled my mouth back just a breath so that I could speak.

"We're going to do this . . . and it's going to be good. Very good. You . . . inside me. Good, so very—what?"

Seth suddenly struggled up, pushing me—not harshly—off of him. Once he was free, he stood up and backed away from the couch. He ran a hand over his eyes.

"Oh, God. I can't believe this is happening."

"It's happening," I told him, practically panting. "Come back—"

"No." He shook his head. "I can't."

"But you—you started to—"

"I know, I know," he groaned. He buttoned his pants. "I got caught up."

"You wanted me," I growled. "You still do." I stood up too and wriggled out of the jeans I wore, pulling my panties off in the process. Standing before him naked, I fixed him with a challenging glare. "Tell me you don't. Tell me you don't want to have sex with me."

Those serious brown eyes swept the length of me, of all my curves and smooth skin. The desire was still written all over him, but a hard glint in the depths of his eyes showed he was fighting it. The flesh was willing, but the spirit was weak—or rather, the spirit was strong.

"I'm sorry," he said, reaching for his shirt. "You're very beautiful. *Very* beautiful. And hanging out with you is fun. There's something about you—it's almost like— well." He shrugged the thought away, though I had a good feeling what it had been. "But I can't. I can't do this. I'm sorry. I shouldn't have come here tonight."

"But . . ." My lower lip trembled as I attempted confusion while still looking sexy. "She won't . . . she won't give you what you want . . ."

"I want *her*. I want to be with her."

"You can still have her," I argued. "And tonight you can have me. Then you can go back, and she'll never know. She probably wouldn't even mind."

"*I* would know," he said. He pulled the T-shirt on and smoothed it. "That's what matters."

"I don't . . . I don't understand . . . there are no strings attached . . ."

"I love her," he told me, moving toward the door. "I can't explain it any better than that. I'm sorry." He turned away. The door opened, then closed.

I stood there in the living room, naked, staring at where he'd last been. Kurtis materialized beside me.

"Well, well," he said, following my gaze to the door.

"Was I convincing enough?" I asked. Part of the conditions had been that I couldn't do a half-ass seduction job.

"Very," he said wryly. "So much so that I'm guessing there wasn't actually a lot of acting going on."

I tore my gaze from the door and looked at the demon. Clothing and my Georgina shape materialized onto me. "But he did it. He resisted and held to his beliefs."

Kurtis smiled. "Disappointed?"

I thought about it, thought how it had felt—however briefly—to have complete access to Seth. The possibility of actually having sex was tantalizing and bittersweet. Of course, if we'd done it, it wouldn't have really been *me* and Seth. It would have been him and . . . an illusion. That wasn't how I wanted sex to be with us.

"A little," I answered. "But not enough." I sighed. "This was stupid of me. Testing him like that. I never doubted him . . . not really. I don't know why I had to prove it."

"People do stupid things for love," he told me. I'd said the exact same thing to Starla. "They do stupider things when they're jealous."

"What are you, a shrink?"

"Just an observer of humankind."

I sighed again. "I wasted a once-in-a-lifetime chance tonight."

He cut me a look, and I noticed then how agitated he appeared. "Maybe not."

I glanced back. "What do you mean?"

"I told you, I always keep my promises." With a resigned sigh, he extended his hand. "Ready to look inside?"

Chapter Twelve

I jerked back, suddenly uncertain. This whole bet, just to satisfy my curiosity over whether or not Kurtis really had killed Anthony, had paled somewhat in my eyes. I'd proven he was wrong about Seth . . . but what did that really matter when compared to how stupid I'd been in the first place about Seth?

Kurtis' eyes widened. "What's this? Cold feet? After everything you went through?" He shook his head, amused. "What is it with you? Don't you accept any rewards?"

"I don't know . . . I'm just so . . . I shouldn't have done this tonight . . ."

"Oh, good grief," he groaned. He was playing lax and silly, but I could see how the idea of me looking inside scared him. "After I braced myself for this all night?" He made a big show of looking at the clock. "Well, decide fast because I don't want to miss the main event."

My anger kindled once more at being reminded of poor Starla and Clyde meeting a potentially undeserved fate. "Okay. Let's do this."

He attempted his cocky smile, but I could see the sweat on his neck and along his hair. His pupils were large. Wow. He was afraid. Really afraid. I wondered if I should be too. Closing his eyes, he held out his hand again. I grabbed hold of it and . . .

I was in.

I was in a place of white light, dizzying and blinding. It was filled with something—something I simply couldn't perceive. It was like a blind person staring at the color red. I could not comprehend what I was missing because it appealed to a sense I didn't have. In a flash, that surreal moment was over, and I stood on familiar territory, with sights and sounds I could comprehend.

I was on a battlefield at night, mud and bodies lit by a full moon and a star-clustered sky that had never seen city lights. Scraps of fighting still lingered around me, on the periphery of the battlefield. Groans of the dying filled the air. I looked around, disgusted.

Then I was in a city, an ancient city I didn't recognize, a city that had existed ages before my mortal life. I watched the town's life unfold, watched as the tyrant who ruled it trampled the citizens and abused them for their labor, denying them food and life when it was convenient. In the end, it didn't matter because a raiding army eventually came and destroyed the town, killing, raping, and enslaving its residents.

Scene after horrible scene flew past me in fast-forward.

It was like the proverbial life flashing before your eyes. Humanity suffered, and I watched it through Kurtis' eyes, felt his pain and frustration, until finally he couldn't take it anymore. Then the white screen was back, the whiteness that meant nothing to me and everything to him. He tore it asunder, and it was like tearing himself in half. Then, there was no more light, only blackness and a hole in his soul.

After that, Kurtis' demonic career unfolded before my eyes, and I watched him commit atrocity after atrocity—some worse than the ones he'd broken with Heaven over—simply because he didn't care anymore. I felt his pain, felt his emptiness, felt his apathy. The events blinked past me in seconds, an abridged version of a timeless life.

I saw his time with Anthony, saw the tortures that had been described in the courtroom. And as the present tumbled forward, I felt Kurtis' anger toward his former employee cool—and I felt his surprise when other demons hauled him off to the trial. I felt his frustration and fear, his desperate attempts to lobby and bribe for his innocence. His relief when Clyde and Starla took the fall.

And then, it was all over, and we were standing together in the condo.

Kurtis hadn't killed Anthony. He'd been telling the truth.

I broke contact and reeled from what I'd seen. I understood then why this wasn't done very often, even to prove a point. It was enough to live with the power of your own soul—or, in my case, of your leased soul—but to experience the emotion and intensity of another's was too much. The fact that I was a lesser immortal viewing a higher immortal made it that much more powerful.

I staggered backward and fell to my knees, arms

wrapped around me. Kurtis grabbed an exquisite blue glass bowl, veined in gold, and held it to me.

"You gonna be sick?"

It certainly felt that way. I leaned over, feeling the bile rise in my throat as I squeezed my eyes shut. The room spun. I carried a lot of pain with me, almost a millennium and a half's worth. But I knew then, knew without a doubt that it was nothing compared to the scope of what angels and demons went through. Even the shadow of what he felt was wreaking havoc with me.

Swallowing, I pushed the nausea down and looked back up at Kurtis. His long face was serious, his eyes infinite and knowing, even as he shuddered and tried to master his own reaction. The experience had been rough on him too. Rougher.

Looking away, I breathed a grateful sigh that the sensations were already fading, that horrible loss of an angel who'd turned his back on Heaven because he was angry at the way the powers-that-be let humanity suffer.

"I'm sorry," I gasped out.

"For what?" he asked, a sardonic smile on his lips. There was a tight set to his face that said even if he had a chipper persona, he would still feel the effects of me reading him for some time.

"I don't know." I could have been apologizing for anything. For making him open up. For what he'd given up in anger millennia ago. For what he'd had to do in the intervening time. For being accused of a crime he didn't commit.

Kurtis seemed to understand. He set the bowl down and helped me up, even though he was a bit unsteady himself. "Will you be all right?"

"I think so."

"Look at that," he told me. "Eleven-thirty. You have time to go back to your guy."

He was right. I had thirty minutes, thirty minutes in which to go back to Seth as myself and share a few precious moments with no treachery or subterfuge. Now that I knew Kurtis was innocent, the sting of his bribe had faded.

Suddenly, I frowned. The memories of looking in his head were disappearing rapidly, but while inside of him, I'd seen the events of the trial through his eyes. I'd seen him approaching other jurors, making his offers.

"Monaco," I exclaimed.

"What?"

"You didn't offer Monaco."

He tilted his head and studied me. "You might have gotten hit harder than I thought."

"No! When you offered people bribes, you didn't offer to transfer that guy to Monaco. Clyde said you didn't have the power."

"Of course not," snorted Kurtis. "You think I'd be in Belgium if I could arrange that?"

"Who did then? Who offered bribes to acquit you and convict Clyde and Starla? Someone else was working with you. But, I mean, not *with* you." I could say that with some conviction because I knew for sure now he'd had no ally that he'd been aware of.

Kurtis frowned, face lost in thought, then it cleared. "Noelle."

"She's powerful enough?"

"Oh, yeah. Absolutely. Makes sense too. There wasn't enough evidence to have a clear decision, so she pushed for a quick ending and got her cathartic revenge. Punished two people who were pissing her off in the process.

Very neat. Nice way to do it if you can't nail the right suspect."

It made sense. Starla and Luis had confirmed the same ideas. And yet . . . something wasn't making sense . . .

I blinked. "That's because the right suspect wasn't up there."

Kurtis' face registered mild surprise. "Oh?"

"It was Noelle. Noelle killed Anthony."

"Her own employee?" he scoffed. "Not likely. Especially since, as his supervisor, she could legally inflict any number of punishments." He grinned. "I of all people know the loopholes there. Besides, she had the hots for Anthony."

"So did Starla. A lot more than the hots, actually. Yet everyone thinks casting her as a murderer makes sense."

"Okay, you get points for that, but what else have you got, Sherlock? You can't just go accuse a major archdemon of murder." He made a face. "Unless it's one who's been sentenced to Belgium."

Scraps of conversation from the last few days began fitting together in my head. "Noelle was jealous of Anthony and Starla. He'd refused her advances, and it must have driven Noelle crazy that he preferred a new, weak demoness over her. She tried to split them up, right? Said it was interfering with his work. And that's when he lashed back. Starla told me how he wanted to transfer. Probably figured he could still date or whatever Starla without work problems. But Noelle said she was going to fight it—she didn't want to lose him. She loved him. And they had this huge, horrible blowout that made them both really mad. Clyde passed Anthony on his way out, and Anthony was furious. Then Clyde talked to Noelle, and she was livid too."

"So she kills Anthony over an argument?"

"No," I said. "Well, yes. More than that. The argument was the culmination of a lot of things. His rejection of her. The fact that she was likely going to lose him. Remember Margo's comment? 'If I can't have him . . .' That was Noelle's line of thinking."

Kurtis let out a low whistle. "That's quite a theory, little one. And a lot of circumstantial evidence."

"It's why she's been so angry over all this. It's not revenge. It's anger at herself for what she did—and fear to close this up fast and cover her own tracks. That's also why she didn't push to look inside any of you guys. She made it sound like she didn't want to violate you, but really, it was because she knew you'd all be proven innocent."

"Well, you've made some good leaps, I'll give you that." He pointed at the clock. Twenty minutes until midnight. "But there's nothing to be done for it, even if it's true. It's almost time. That group's in a frenzy by now, waiting for the torture. They're probably selling balloons and hot dogs. No one's going to listen."

I stared blankly at the window. "Luis would."

"*Maybe* he would." When I didn't answer, Kurtis laid an almost friendly hand on my shoulder. "Look, you really might be on to something, but it's too late. You're burning up time. At the very least, get in one kiss with your guy. Chase after this theory, and you blow any moment you have with him."

Kurtis was right. And I had already blown most of what time I could have had with Seth. I'd wasted it in the guise of another woman. But if I acted soon, I could have him now as me. I could have him, and Starla and Clyde would suffer. I'd noted before that they'd probably committed enough other crimes to deserve punishment, but it occurred to me that like Kurtis, they might have initially fallen from grace for more than just selfish reasons.

I looked up and met Kurtis' penetrating gaze. "Will you transport me back to the hotel?"

He was right about the spectacle. The ballroom-turned-conference-room was packed. The whole gang was there from the first day: imps, vampires, incubi, and demons. Kurtis and I pushed our way through the excited crowd. People slapped him on the back in congratulations as we passed. They made lewd comments to me.

Near the front of the room, a demon in black sharpened long, bladed instruments. Near him stood Starla and Clyde. The two "guilty" demons didn't move, though no visible bonds held them. They were frozen, trapped through some magical means. I averted my eyes from them.

"Help me," I told Kurtis. "Help me find Luis."

It was an impossible task. There were too many bodies mingling and moving. Luis was a big guy. I'd hoped I might find him simply by virtue of him being taller than others, but that seemed unlikely now.

Kurtis stopped walking. "He's not here."

I stopped too, nearly running into an annoyed vampire. "How do you know?"

"He's one of the strongest here, stronger even than Noelle. If he were in this room, we'd feel him, even above all this."

He was right, I realized. We fought our way back out. Once outside, Kurtis stood and looked around like a hound sniffing the wind. "Got him."

We found Luis sitting in the bar, stirring his bourbon

over ice. He appeared to be the only one of the demonic congregation who wasn't in the other room making balloon animals or getting face tattoos. Feeling us enter, he looked up in surprise.

"You have to help us," I said. Immediately, I sat down and spilled the whole story, laying out the evidence—circumstantial though it was—about why I believed Noelle was the killer.

Luis listened with an unreadable face. When I finished, he pretty much said the same thing Kurtis had. "There's no way to prove it."

"But it makes sense! Luis, they're five minutes away from punishing the wrong people."

"Georgina." Luis sighed. "Unfair things happen every day in the universe whether you live on Earth, in Heaven, or in Hell. If you're right, it's unfortunate, but well . . . that's that."

"I thought you wanted the truth," I accused.

"Then I have it. Your idea makes sense. Noelle did it."

"But it's not justice!"

"I didn't come for justice." He gave me a kind, sad smile. "I'm not the one with 'an annoying yet adorable sense of right and wrong.'"

"I don't believe that! You must still have *something*."

"Look, I'm not happy that Noelle could get away with this, but it's too late. And this isn't a Christmas special where I suddenly see the error of my ways. I'm a fucking demon. I spread evil in the world. I *am* evil."

I figured fighting that would just get me accused of more cheery good will. And honestly, I did believe Luis still had a sense of right and wrong . . . but if his life had been like Kurtis', he had good reason for apathy.

"If you call her out," I said finally. "You'll get accolades. Big promotion."

Luis' face registered surprise, then broke into a grin. "You're bribing me now?"

I looked between him and Kurtis. "I hear that's how it works around here."

Luis's smile faded. "There's no way of proving her guilt."

"Well," mused Kurtis. "There's one way . . ." He'd perked up at the mention of promotion. I think he hoped being in on Noelle's takedown could help his Belgium transfer.

He and Luis locked eyes, and something passed in those glances.

"No," said Luis. "She wouldn't agree."

"You're strong enough . . ."

Luis grimaced. "If I do that, and she's not guilty, *I'm* the one who gets flayed."

"She is guilty," I said, having no clue what they referred to, only that something big was on the line. "Luis, *please*."

The clock ticked. One minute until midnight.

Luis studied me for a long time. He exhaled and stood up.

"I can't believe I'm about to do this."

Kurtis gave him a friendly punch. "Don't worry. I've got your back."

"Really?"

"No."

Powerful presence or no, not many people noticed when Luis entered the ballroom. At least, not until he grabbed Noelle and slammed her against the wall.

Dead silence filled the room, except for Noelle's outraged cries as she fought against him. But he held her pinned with more than physical strength; she couldn't match his magical power.

"Are you out of your fucking mind? What the hell are you—?"

She quieted and blanched as he pressed his hand to her forehead. He paled as well, and I heard a collective gasp around the room. I realized then what he was doing. He was looking *in* her, just as Kurtis had allowed me. Only, Luis was doing it by force. It was a mental, spiritual rape of sorts.

I shuddered, remembering how it had been for me being the one to look inside. It had been a hundred times worse for Kurtis, and unlike Noelle, *he'd* consented. As she grew paler and paler, I could only imagine how it must feel for her to undergo that. No, scratch that. I couldn't even comprehend it.

The two demons broke apart in less than a minute. I wondered if that's how much time had elapsed when Kurtis and I had done it. I'd relived an eternity in my mind while it happened.

Luis and Noelle stood there, gasping, staring at each other. Both looked ready to pass out.

"Holy shit," exclaimed Luis. "You did do it."

Noelle frantically shook her head, black curls swaying, as she tried to hold on to the wall for support. "No, no." She looked desperately at the crowd. "He's lying! He's lying!"

Luis was visibly trying to recover himself. He grabbed nothing for support, but he had the look of someone who'd been gut-punched. "You want to let someone else look and prove me wrong?"

"No!" she cried. In power, she was second only to Luis here. None of the other gathered demons could actually force her as he had. She would have to allow it—unless an outside demon was summoned. "You can't prove anything, Luis. You're lying. You're—"

"I can prove it," he interrupted. "You showed me. I saw it inside you. I know where to go and—"

"No, don't. Don't."

He shrugged. "Your call. You tipped me off. I know how to get evidence now and prove it. I'm the one passing judgment. Make me go hunt down the proof, and your sentence will be . . . bad. Or, confess now, and your sentence will be . . . less bad."

A silent battle took place. I had no idea what evidence Luis had seen inside her, but her expression showed that she did not want it made public. Realizing she was fucked either way, Noelle finally nodded.

"All right. All right. Yes, I confess. I did it. I killed Anthony and set the others up. There. Are you happy? Are you fucking happy?"

Those gathered went crazy. They *loved* the new turn of events. It might have even been better than a flaying for them. As chaos broke out in the room, I heard Kurtis chuckling behind me.

"Sweet," he said. "I am *so* out of Belgium."

"What, for helping with this?" I asked.

"Yup. Well, that and I hear there's an archdemon opening in L.A."

Chapter Thirteen

Seth and I flew back to Seattle the next day. A lot of demons had wanted to talk to me, but I needed to get out of that hotel as soon as possible. In fact, I'd hightailed it out of the ballroom once Starla and Clyde had been freed. I hadn't stuck around because I had a feeling Noelle was simply going to be swapped into their place for the evening's entertainment.

Sitting beside Seth for the two-and-a-half-hour flight home brought all the *other* events of last night back to me. As we held hands and recounted the bizarre trial events, he in no way acted as though he'd faced temptation and won last night. I in no way acted as though I'd been the cause of that temptation and had subsequently lost the one chance we might have had for physical intimacy. The fact that my exploits had led to two demons' freedom was little comfort.

"She really killed him?" asked Seth in amazement.

"Yup."

"But she loved him . . . or something, right?"

"Yup."

"Then how could she have done that?"

I stared at his profile, at the cheekbones and brown eyes I loved. I thought about losing him, how I would feel if he chose another woman. I wouldn't be driven to kill him, of course, but . . . well, I could empathize with the pain.

"Because people do stupid things for love," I murmured sadly, thinking of my own sins.

He turned and met my eyes, compassion shining in them. "You okay?"

I hesitated, and for a brief moment, the instinct was there. I almost spilled everything I'd done in my silly Beth obsession. After all, Seth and I had recently had big discussions about honesty in relationships. He was a big believer in telling the truth, and I wanted to live up to his ideals. Yet, the words stuck in my throat.

"Fine," I said instead. "Just worn out . . . long week."

"Yeah," he said. "I hear you." His gaze turned inward, and I had a feeling he was thinking of the condo. He opened his mouth, like he too might say something, then closed it. I was pretty sure I knew what had been about to come out.

"So," I said carefully. "Where'd you go this morning?" He'd gotten in some writing before our plane left. "The pig café?"

He smiled faintly. "No. I went back to that diner . . ."

"Oh?"

"Yeah . . . weird thing. That waitress you saw . . . she was working, and I told her I was leaving and . . ."

My smile was frozen on my face as I attempted to play blasé. "And?"

Again, I had the feeling he was about to tell me about last night, and again, he held back. "I don't know. Just weird. She was acting really strange when I talked to her . . ."

Like, say, when he talked to her about events she had no clue about?

"What do you mean?" I asked.

He shook his head, letting it go. I wondered if he'd tried to apologize to her. He probably thought her obliviousness was feigned as retaliation. "I don't know. Like I said, she was just being weird."

He squeezed my hand, and we settled back into our seats. Both of us held our own secrets, our own guilt. Neither of us had the courage to bring them up. I wondered if that's how all couples were, hiding small, silent sins.

Nonetheless, I couldn't resist asking, "Weird, huh? Wait . . . didn't you say she reminded you of me? Are you saying *I'm* weird?"

Seth laughed. He brought my hand to his lips and kissed it. "Thetis, there are no adjectives for you. And the two of you are nothing alike."

"Really? I mean, you acted like we were twins or something."

"I did no such thing."

"You *did*," I teased. "It was like you couldn't tell us apart."

He sighed and rolled his eyes at my joking. "I told you, you're nothing alike. You don't act alike. You don't think alike. You don't talk alike."

"Or look alike," I added.

"Right," he agreed. After another squeeze of my hand, he released it and opened up his laptop.

Watching, I figured I should be glad he didn't suspect anything. I'd gotten away with my blunder, my test of his fidelity. I should feel glad. Except I didn't.

"People do stupid things for love," I muttered under my breath.

Seth glanced at me. "What'd you say?"

"Nothing."

Connect with Us

Visit us online at
KensingtonBooks.com
to read more from your favorite authors, see books
by series, view reading group guides, and more.

Join us on social media
for sneak peeks, chances to win books and prize packs,
and to share your thoughts with other readers.

facebook.com/kensingtonpublishing
twitter.com/kensingtonbooks

Tell us what you think!
To share your thoughts, submit a review,
or sign up for our eNewsletters, please visit:
KensingtonBooks.com/TellUs.